'This book is full of joy – and I devoured every page of it gladly' Milly Johnson

'Filled with nuggets of wisdom, compassion and humour, Cathy Kelly proves, yet again, that she knows everything there is to know about women' Patricia Scanlan

'Wise, warm, compassionate' Marian Keyes

'Packed with Cathy's usual magical warmth' Sheila O'Flanagan

'A lovely story of life and change' *Prima*

'Kelly manages to strike the perfect balance between romance and realism' *Irish Independent*

'An uplifting story of warm, larger than life characters. Comforting and feel good, the perfect treat read' *Good Housekeeping*

'Emotional, believable and smart, this is fiction at its best' *Heat Magazine*

Cathy Kelly is published around the world, with millions of books in print. A No.1 bestseller in the UK, Ireland and Australia, her trademark is warm and witty Irish storytelling about modern life, always with an uplifting message, a sense of community and strong female characters at the heart.

She lives with her family and their three dogs in County Wicklow, Ireland. She is also an Ambassador for UNICEF Ireland, raising funds and awareness for children orphaned by or living with HIV/AIDS.

Find out more at www.cathykelly.com or follow her on Twitter @cathykellybooks

The Year that Changed Everything

Cathy Kelly

ORION

An Orion paperback

First published in Great Britain in 2018
by Orion Books
This paperback edition published in 2018
by Orion Books,
an imprint of The Orion Publishing Group Ltd,
Carmelite House, 50 Victoria Embankment
London EC4Y 0DZ

An Hachette UK company

5 7 9 10 8 6

A CIP catalogue record for this book
is available from the British Library.

ISBN 978 1 4091 5373 3

Typeset by Input Data Services Ltd, Somerset

Printed in Great Britain by Clays Ltd, Elcograf S.p.A.

www.orionbooks.co.uk

For Mum, with huge love and lots of laughs.

PART ONE

The Birthday
The first Saturday in June

Callie

Outside the great sash windows, party lights snaked around the sycamores beside her bathroom, and even from two floors up, the pulse of party music could be heard.

The neighbours would hate it – the flash Reynolds family showing off again, Callie Reynolds thought with a grimace, standing ready in her dress and shoes, wishing fifty wasn't a birthday people felt that a person had to celebrate.

She'd have been happy with a small dinner, but no. Jason, who always wanted the biggest and best, had organised this highly expensive three-ring circus.

'You deserve it,' he'd told her earlier that day, as he'd proudly surveyed scurrying waiters and watched the party organiser ticking off cases of expensive wine. 'We've worked hard for this life.'

Callie had leaned into her handsome husband – everyone said they were a stunning couple – and murmured thank you.

Mentally, she was thinking: *but what if, after all the hard work, you find you don't really like this life after all?*

Still bathed in the party lights, Callie locked the door of her glamorous cream marble bathroom. Bending down, she reached under the sink right to the back of the bottom of the cupboard to find the small cosmetics bag stuffed behind the spare shower gels and old bottles of fake tan. It was an ancient bag, chosen on purpose because Poppy, her teenage daughter, was unlikely to rifle through it on one of her forays into Callie's cabinets in search of make-up.

Since Poppy had turned fourteen, she had grown tall, nearly

as tall as her mother, and was no longer even vaguely pleased with ordinary cosmetics, wanting instead to use her mother's wildly expensive Chantecaille stuff, which Callie herself felt guilty about using.

A full make-up bag of Chantecaille could keep a family of four fed for a month and still have enough left over for take-away pizza.

'I got you lovely MAC stuff,' Callie protested the last time she found that Poppy had whipped her foundation, primer and pressed powder and had broken the latter.

Poppy, who had her father's colouring and his utter self-belief, had flicked her long, dark hair out of her perfectly made-up eyes. 'Your stuff is nicer and I don't see why I can't share it,' she said with the entitled air that shocked Callie.

Where is my lovely, sweet daughter and what have you done with her? Callie wondered.

In the past six months since the radical conversion from Beloved Child into Daughter-From-Hell, Callie had tried everything in her maternal arsenal: withholding pocket money; loss of phone privileges; and the When I Was Your Age talk.

The When I Was Your Age talk had backfired the most.

'That was years ago, the seventies,' said Poppy dismissively, as if the seventies were on a par with the Jurassic period. 'This is like, now?'

Callie had ground her teeth. Poppy's generation had no clue what life had been like for Callie growing up, or for Poppy's father, Jason. Sometimes, when she thought of how having so little had given Jason and herself such drive and determination, Callie went with: *if you get too many things too young, Poppy, what values are you learning?*

The prepubescent Poppy, the one who loved animals, seals and sparkly nail varnish, might have teared up or let her bottom lip wobble at having upset her mum. The new, unimproved Poppy just rolled her eyes, went back to her phone and ignored her mother for the rest of the day, which was obviously what she was assiduously learning in school from the handful of other, equally privileged kids she was now palling around with.

Not having a clue how to handle this new, tempestuous child was partly to blame for Callie's need of the occasional Xanax.

Her oldest friend, Mary Butler, a real pal from her modelling days who'd lived in Canada for years and had three daughters older than Poppy, often said:

'I know it seems counter-intuitive, but making us want to kill them is a part of teenagers' growing up. It's how we let them fly the nest, because there comes a point where you think you might just smother them in their sleep when they've accused you of being passive-aggressive four times in one day and then demanded to know if you've handwashed their pink sweater.'

Mary was in her late fifties, older and wiser, no longer caught up in the hormonal maelstrom of perimenopause. Mary had three girls in college. She was not, Callie reflected, dealing with a daughter currently behaving like a particularly venal child from *Game of Thrones*.

From being around people like Mary, Callie had always assumed that when a person hit fifty, all knowledge flowed into them, automatically. But she was wrong. Because today, Callie Reynolds was fifty. *Fifty!* And she didn't seem to know anything more than she ever had.

All the books on menopause seemed to say her Inner Goddess would be along soon, bringing wisdom, new sex appeal and the glow of a new life, which was an Inner Goddess guarantee. Ha! That was a cosmic joke, for sure. Staring at herself in the mirror, Callie firmly believed that her blasted Inner Goddess had run off and had left the stand-in, Inner Crone, in her place.

Crone had dry skin, got irritable, cried at the drop of a hat and sometimes sweated so much in bed she wondered when Jason would start asking if he could sleep in the shallow end.

5

Crone snapped at her husband – not that he was around much these days, possibly because Crone was not experiencing the much-vaunted sexual surge but more of a sexual Saharan drought.

Plus, the anti-Inner Goddess wanted a daughter who appreciated what she had and didn't order stuff from the internet with Crone's credit card without asking.

Finally, Inner Crone missed her family and tended to cry when she thought of them. Which was the other reason Callie needed the odd Xanax.

It was ten years since she'd seen her mother, her brother or Aunt Phil. *Ten years.* They should have been at this party. But they weren't. Because of Jason, and the row and . . .

Feeling the panic rise, Callie unzipped the little bag and popped a pill out of its packet. She washed down the Xanax with some water and took a deep breath.

The Inner Goddess would probably suggest dealing with the family rift as well as talking to Jason about how they really needed to spend more time together as a couple. She'd advise a book on healing herbs and how to get through the tricky teenage years, and to take up meditation.

But Crone liked chemicals to block out the pain because it was easier.

Callie could hear music throbbing from the party two floors below and knew she had to hurry. Quickly, she took stock of herself in the mirror: golden blonde hair perfect, the charcoal silk shift dress with its modern Jackson Pollock-style pattern on the front caressed collarbones nearly as slender as those of the teenage models on which it had been photographed in the magazines.

At least collarbones never got fat, unlike waists.

She'd had her hair blow-dried but made her own face up. After those early years as a model, Callie knew what worked. She knew other people saw beauty – full lips, her face a perfect oval and eyes that someone had once described as huge misty grey orbs that dominated her face. She, who'd been the skinny little kid in school with the weirdly big mouth, now saw only flaws: the lines, the inevitable sag of her jawline, and a tiredness no multivitamin could shift.

'Like a Greek goddess with mysterious eyes, as if all the world's knowledge is upon those slender shoulders . . .' someone had once written about her.

Jason had teased her about it, but she knew that, secretly, he'd been pleased.

'Greek indeed,' he'd joked, 'when we both know you're pure Ballyglen.'

Callie had known he was pleased because normally he never mentioned their home town, having long since brushed its rural dust from his handmade shoes.

Their glamorous detached mansion in Dublin was a far cry from their council homes in Ballyglen, a small east coast town with no industry anymore, no jobs, and her family—

Stop thinking about the past!

She slicked on another sweep of lip gloss.

There had been little joking from her husband this week as the planner had consulted with Callie about the party. Jason, whose idea the blasted thing was, had been distant, on the phone a lot of the time hidden away in his study when he wasn't at work.

Callie, whose perimenopausal emotional barometer was set to 'high alert' anyway, sensed him moving away emotionally.

Worse, Poppy had gone into overdrive in teenage cattiness, a type of meanness that must register on some Teenage Richter Scale of Narkiness somewhere.

'Are you wearing *that*?' she had asked her mother earlier in the week, spying the shift dress on its hanger.

'Yes,' said Callie, summoning all her patience, waiting for what Poppy and her friends called 'the burn' – a caustic remark that hurt as much as raw flames.

7

'You wear that, it'll look like the eighties threw up on you,' said Poppy. 'Plus, the waist is in, you know, Mum.'

There it was – the burn.

Her friend Mary, who was as all-knowing as Google, had warned her that the teenage era was tough.

Remember when you were the most fabulous Mummy in the world, small people snuggled up to you on the couch and said you were beautiful? Mary emailed gently, when Poppy hit thirteen. *That's over. OVAH. You are now the thing Poppy tests her claws on, like a cat scratcher, only mobile. You've got to start reining her in, Callie, because it's Armageddon time and she will pick on you, not Jason. You are going to be the cat scratcher.*

Mary had been right so far.

Mild acne and raging hormones that made Poppy question Callie's every word both hit at the same time.

Armageddon, Callie thought, shell-shocked.

Poppy had fallen in with a different crowd at school, the gang with rich parents, the ultra-entitled gang who were always demanding money.

'Do you remember that Christmas she wanted Santa Claus to give her presents to poor children?' Callie asked Jason one morning.

'Yeah,' muttered Jason, scanning his iPad and barely listening.

'Where has that person gone?' Callie said earnestly.

Jason didn't answer, his attention already elsewhere. Jason thought that as long as the family had plenty of money, that was all that mattered. Growing up poor could do that to a person. Once, she'd been the same.

But now . . . now she was afraid her beloved Poppy was becoming someone else: someone who knew the cost of everything and, truly, the value of absolutely nothing. A child of the wealthy who had nothing with which to compare her life. No memories of jam sandwiches for dinner all week, no recall of not having proper school shoes.

In giving their daughter everything she ever wanted, Callie wondered if she and Jason had damaged her by making Poppy spoiled.

Not that Jason thought so: he thought Poppy hung the moon.

But Callie, though she adored her daughter, worried and she was determined to teach Poppy the right things again.

First, she had to get through tonight – this enormous, entirely unwanted fiftieth birthday party that Jason had insisted on throwing for her.

'People will expect it from us,' Jason had said. 'We've got an image to maintain, honey.'

Callie was sick of their damned image.

Sure, it seemed like Callie Reynolds had it all: the big house, the rich and glamorous businessman husband who never strayed, the looks of a former model, an interesting past, and a tall, beautiful daughter any mother would be proud of.

Yet it wasn't perfect. Nothing ever really was. Real life was not like the pretend world on some people's Instagram. Where was the Instagram that said 'My Not So Damn Perfect Life', with no happy-glow filters?

Jason had certainly pulled out all the stops, which meant a giant drinks party for two hundred people with the catering kitchen in the basement full of sous-chefs prepping for the plating of chocolate surprise bombes, tiny amandine biscuits shaped like stars, sashimi, sushi, cod and chips, Anjou pigeon (*watch out for shot*, warned the waiters and waitresses) and fat round pieces of beef that had been made into the most luxurious beef burgers ever. If any of the guests had an allergy, or even felt they might like to have an allergy on fashionable grounds, it would be catered for. There wasn't a bag of Peruvian black quinoa or a tin of organic matcha tea to be had within a ten-block radius, just in case.

Holding her stomach in, Callie slowly made her way into the party, knocked sideways by expensive perfumes and the noisy clatter of so many people drinking cocktails perfected by a mixologist.

'Fabulous party,' said someone, and a face Callie barely recognised from the newspaper air-kissed her. 'The house is divine.'

Callie beamed her photograph smile.

'Yes, it's lovely,' she said, poise in motion now that the Xanax had kicked in nicely and had chemically flattened her worries about Poppy and guilt over her family's absence at this party. 'Jason has such incredible ideas for the house.'

It was easier than saying that Jason was a nightmare when it came to the notion of improving everything he owned.

Everything had to be the best or most expensive. Like the recent renovation.

Thanks to endless months of building works on the mansion in the embassy belt, a huge basement had been dug for an extension which opened up to a three-storey conservatory complete with a walkway around the highest floor, at ground level, where tropical plants grew and solar panels in the giant glass panes made the whole thing work.

She didn't explain that her husband knew zilch about exotic plants.

He'd actually got the idea from an article in the *Financial Times*'s *How To Spend It* magazine about a billionaire who had a greenhouse in Manhattan where he grew all manner of exotic things.

'Cyrtochilum orchids,' he'd read out, admiring a photo of a yellow orchid with delicately ruffled petals.

His elocution and command of the Latin words were impressive for a man who'd grown up in a council estate not too far from Callie's own in a big county town, and whose knowledge of plants was confined to his mam's dahlias.

But Jason was a quick learner. He could now talk exotic

plants with the best of them. He expected Callie to do the same, as well as look just as beautiful all the time.

Unlike those husbands who died a little when their wives went to the shops wielding credit cards, Jason was always urging Callie to buy clothes.

'I want you looking good, sexy,' he'd say.

She could hardly complain, and yet lately she felt more like another *thing* in Jason's life. His wife, to add to the Ferrari and the yacht.

'Do enjoy yourself,' Callie said to the guest now and she moved as if something vital was happening somewhere and she must race off. It was her fiftieth birthday party, after all, and the hostess needed to be all over the place, a handy excuse when it came to conversing with some of the guests, who were clearly a rent-a-celeb crowd drummed up by the party planner.

Callie moved on through the beautiful grey reception room that soared up to a vast glass and steel structure which had guests admiring it all.

She could see her husband in the distance, surrounded by friends as if it was his fiftieth birthday party and not hers. But then Jason drew people to him with the magnetism of the handsome and charismatic. He was tall, even among the statuesque, Pilates- or barre-toned Amazons in heels who were flirting with him.

She had no idea how he'd grown so tall: his own father, now long dead, had been wizened, but then that was due to smoking untipped cigarettes for years and thinking pints of beer and greasy pub sausages and chips were nourishment. Jason was dark, with that Spanish/Irish combination of raven blue-black hair, blue eyes and skin that tanned when he so much as looked at the sun. Tonight, he was wearing a suit of such a dark navy that it appeared almost black. He looked like a movie star: an almost unreal presence among the rest of the guests.

'We were flying over Monument Valley and the pilot took

us really low. It was awesome. Nothing can do justice to that landscape, but flying over it comes pretty close,' he was saying, his voice at the same time husky – which was natural – and exquisitely modulated to sound posh Irish – which was *not* natural but the result of years of voice lessons.

His audience were more women than men. Jason was a rainmaker when it came to money and men loved that. Loved being close to someone who'd managed to buck recessions, the closing of tax loopholes, currency drops and world economic fluctuations to stay rich and grow richer. But tonight, it was a predominantly female crowd.

'There she is, my beautiful wife,' said Jason, spotting her and drawing her close. He was annoyed at her late arrival, she could tell from the glitter of his eyes. He was a stickler for punctuality, but he would never say a word. For the crowd, he kissed her lightly on the mouth.

The crowd purred and Jason smiled: he loved the limelight.

'Nice dress,' he whispered only for her and she felt the pressure of his fingers moving gently up the dress to caress the underside of her breast.

'I needed to look perfect for you, darling,' she said for the benefit of the audience, the knowledge that Jason approved of this dress, of how she looked, calming her along with the Xanax. When did she become this insecure? She hated it. Hated how her sex drive had plummeted and how intimacy had become a chore.

What if the Inner Crone drove her husband away?

He was a good man, despite his ferocious need for more: more money, more things, more prestige.

Now, his fingers traced a line along the skin of her exposed collarbone as if they were alone and the crowd of women all sighed a little at such romance.

'Where were you, Cal?' he muttered so nobody could hear. 'I thought I'd have to send out a search party. Someone keeps groping my backside.'

Callie grinned at the thought of her alpha-male husband complaining about being groped.

'Now I'm here, I'll keep your admirers in check,' she said, shooting a glance around at his harem and wondering who was drunk this early in the evening and feeling up the host. 'I was checking on Poppy.'

'Happy?'

'Oh, fine. I'd like to think she's miserable she's not down here, but she insists it's all wrinklies and she'd have no credibility if she came to it.'

'Made her point and now she has to stick to it,' Jason said with a hint of pride.

Poppy was in her room with four girls from school, and Brenda, who was the family housekeeper and Callie's closest confidante apart from Mary, was keeping an eye on them and feeding them.

'Daft kid, she'll be sorry one day, missing all this.' He gestured around the room and in the process, let go of his wife, which was her signal to mingle.

She didn't touch any of the cocktails, knowing that alcohol and Xanax were an unfortunate mix.

'Callie, it's a beautiful party and you are beautiful in that dress.'

The speaker was small, pretty, had short curling dark hair and, unlike most of the guests, was a real friend who'd known Callie for a long time.

'Evelyn, I'm so glad you could come!'

Evelyn was the first wife of Jason's long-time business partner, Rob.

She was a dear friend. They met twice a week at Pilates classes and giggled together over whether their pelvic floors had hit the basement yet. With Evelyn, Callie didn't have to pretend to be the super-rich, super-happy ex-model wife. She could merely be herself and discuss hot flushes, where this excess waist flab was coming from, and wonder where their sexual reawakening had got to. Before Mary had gone to Canada, the three of them had gone to Pilates together.

'You look lovely too, Ev. Red really suits you,' said Callie, admiring Evelyn's red jersey dress, which they'd shopped for together. She pulled her friend into a hug.

Rob and Jason had been thick as thieves ever since they'd got out of a big City firm and set up their own hedge fund brokerage. They weren't hedgies anymore, they told everyone. They did lots of things, mainly private property investment, which was very complex, the way Jason explained it.

'Oh, just a bit of this and a bit of that,' as Jason said expansively when anyone asked.

Callie didn't ask anymore.

Evelyn and Rob were now divorced. She'd finally thrown Rob out of the house when his sleeping around had got too much for her.

'I put up with so much for the kids, because I didn't want them to have divorced parents, but hey, he's never around anyway, always "working",' she'd said bitterly to Callie at the time. 'Which means screwing his newest girlfriend.'

Six years on, Evelyn and Callie were still friends and it had been a bone of contention between Jason and Callie when she insisted on inviting Evelyn to the party.

'Rob's coming with Anka,' Jason had said, jaw clenched. 'We don't want a scene.'

Anka was the girlfriend who'd stuck: the clichéd much younger, tall blonde with ski-jump Slavic cheekbones, a fragile beauty and no apparent issues with waist flab.

She was also very sweet, was now Rob's fiancée and the mother of his latest child.

'So? They meet all the time over the children. Evelyn doesn't blame Anka – she likes her. Anka's great with the children. And Evelyn's my friend,' Callie said, even though she rarely argued with Jason.

He got bored by arguments: he just ignored them and walked out of the room. Argument over – simple.

'You don't understand . . .' he began, actually engaging, for once, sounding on the verge of anger. 'Rob's coming. He's part of what pays for all this.'

With his hands spread, he gestured to the huge house around them, all decorated by an interior designer in paints more expensive than La Prairie face cream, filled with flowers and with staff to make sure Callie didn't have to lift a finger. 'Rob and Ev squabble with each other,' he went on. 'I hate it.'

Then he'd walked out.

'No sign of Rob or Anka,' said Evelyn now, looking around. She never said a word against her ex-husband's new partner. Rob had strayed. The fault was his and she tried to be nice to her replacement.

Callie felt huge pity for Evelyn. She didn't know how she'd cope if Jason was unfaithful to her. But then he never played around. She was damn sure of it. He was devoted to her, even if he wasn't the sort of husband who massaged her feet at night and said: 'how was your day?'

You couldn't have everything.

'If they're not here yet, they're not coming. I'm glad they're not,' said Callie now. 'Rob must be ill. He never misses any of Jason's parties but silver lining and all that, you can relax. Well, a bit,' she amended, looking round the house with its quota of done-up partygoers ready for a night out.

'Plenty of our well-dressed pack here,' sighed Evelyn, 'who all want to know am I seeing anyone else.'

She wasn't, as Callie knew.

The market for older women did not take into account maturity, wisdom or a sense of humour. The buyers were looking for firm flesh, thighs that had never seen cellulite and faces free from wrinkles. Sometimes Callie wanted to hit Rob for hurting her beloved friend so much.

'Is Poppy here?' Evelyn asked.

'Upstairs watching films with some friends,' said Callie, trying not to mind.

Evelyn did not have teenage girls. She had sons, who were kinder, it seemed.

'I'm going up there now to make sure everything's OK,' said Callie. 'I know Brenda keeps looking in, but I'm freaked out over thoughts of them drinking, after . . . you know.'

She'd already told Evelyn about the empty bottle of Beluga vodka she'd found under Poppy's bed last month, filched from the freezer. The row had been pyrotechnic.

She'd grounded Poppy for two weeks, but Jason, who was a fan of the 'chip off the old block' school of parenting, had only laughed and said: 'Kids are going to drink, Callie. At least it was good stuff.'

It wasn't that simple, Callie wanted to shriek. Genetics mattered. The age at which kids started to drink mattered. But Jason liked to think that being clever could get you past all that stuff. It had worked for him. But not for her brother, her drug-addict brother whom she hadn't seen for ten years. Poppy had those genes too.

Callie had hidden the anxiety and had another Xanax.

Jason refused to be serious about it all, which made her furious. After all, he'd grown up in the same area where she'd grown up, the not-so-lovely streets of Ballyglen's council estates where some people hadn't worked in years and where a hardened contingent considered drinking a full-time occupation.

She did not want that for Poppy. Binge drinking was the start of it. Expensive vodka or cheap beer: it didn't matter. All the same path, a path to risky choices that could affect her life.

Eventually, Callie managed to leave the room, and went through the corridor the hired-in catering staff were using to access the specially designed catering kitchen. She slipped up the stairs and came out in the back hall, then into the actual family kitchen. There she found Brenda, who'd looked after the house for them for twenty years.

Poppy was in the kitchen with Brenda and another girl from school, Zara, and they were busily loading up two trays with pizzas, soft drinks, and tiny desserts from the caterers.

Poppy had her mother's mysterious eyes, and was wearing a vest top, leggings and a pink shirt from Callie's own wardrobe. The time upstairs had given the girls a chance to pile on the make-up at drag-queen levels, so that Poppy was now caked in cosmetics that made her look far older than fourteen. Callie bit her tongue.

'Hello, girls,' she said brightly and she went over to her daughter, about to pop a kiss on Poppy's forehead until she remembered, again, that it wasn't cool to kiss your daughter when one of her friends was present.

'Hi, Mum,' said Poppy, in a voice that said *don't touch*.

'Hello, Zara,' Callie said to the other girl, doing her impersonation of a totally happy and cool mother. She was really good at the old impersonations these days. 'This all looks completely yummy.'

'Hi, Callie,' said Zara, 'thanks. It's totally delish.'

Callie remembered her mother's friends and how she'd always called them Mrs: Mrs this or Mrs that. Nowadays all her daughter's friends called her Callie and called Jason 'Jase', which he found wildly amusing.

'Nice pizzas,' Callie said now. She had to stop thinking about how things used to be when she was growing up. Was this another offshoot of being fifty – thinking about the past all the time? 'Your home-made ones?' she asked Brenda.

'Course,' said Brenda, finishing arranging the tray.

'How's it going downstairs at Help the Aged?' said Poppy to her mother.

'Great,' said Callie. 'We're not that old, you know.'

'Says you, Ms Fifty!' taunted Poppy. 'If I was fifty, I wouldn't let people know and have a party.'

Callie grinned and she and Brenda exchanged another glance. Brenda knew quite well that Callie hadn't really wanted this party. Mind you, Brenda wasn't too keen either. She didn't like the sort of parties Jason gave. Someone would undoubtedly set up shop in one of the loos and do lines of coke, which both Callie and Brenda disapproved of.

Brenda opened the door for Poppy and let the two teenagers go up to Poppy's huge bedroom where three other girls were waiting.

'Is she all right?' asked Callie.

'Behind the sniping, she's in brilliant form,' said Brenda. 'Stop worrying about her. You're a good mother, enough already. D'ya want a cup of tea or do you have to go back down to party central and schmooze?'

'I'd love one,' said Callie, sitting down on one of the kitchen stools. 'It's full of people I don't know and you know how hopeless I am with names. I'm calling everyone "darling" out of desperation. I honestly have no idea what Jason said to that party planner, but for every four people I know, there are another twenty-five I've never seen in my life. And they're not just people Jason's trying to impress – they're supposed to be there for me. "An aspirational guest list", as the planner said,' Callie finished.

'You should have put your foot down about going away for a nice weekend instead,' Brenda pointed out. Brenda had very firm views on how everything should be done and on how Callie should deal with Jason.

Brenda and Jason had a love/hate relationship. They were like scorpions in a brandy glass – circling, each with their stinging tail arched. Jason knew the house would not run like clockwork without Brenda and he knew that his wife both loved and would be lost without her. However, Brenda did not do deference and Jason liked deference from the people he paid.

He pretended to laugh when Brenda called him 'the master'

18

out of mischief, but secretly, both she and Callie knew it drove him mad.

'The party will be over eventually.' Callie looked at the kitchen clock. 'Only another few hours to go. By then the stragglers will be so drunk, nobody will notice that I've gone to bed.'

Brenda laughed. 'You hungry? Bet you haven't eaten. I've got some more of the caterers' desserts in the fridge. Tiny chocolate things that look as if fairies made them and elves decorated them. Hold on.'

One of the waitresses appeared.

'Mrs Reynolds, there are some . . . er, people at the door for your husband.'

Brenda and Callie exchanged confused glances. Anyone with an invitation to the party would just come in, having cleared the very heavy security on the gate. Anyone without an invitation would have been sent packing.

'I'll go,' said Brenda.

'Er . . .' The young waitress shuffled a bit. 'They asked specifically for Mr Reynolds, but we can't find him so they asked for you next,' she said, eyes on the floor.

'It's the staff of Tiffany's,' joked Brenda. 'Go with her,' she told the waitress, 'in case she needs help carrying the loot or if it's Aerosmith come to do a special birthday gig and she faints.'

Callie laughed out loud.

They were waiting in the hall, not Aerosmith, but about seven men and one woman, some in police uniforms and some in plain clothes. Callie's hand flew to her throat.

Ma. Aunt Phil, Freddie, she thought.

She'd walked out of her old life a long time ago. Twenty-five years since she'd left Ballyglen. Ten years since she'd seen her mother, Pat, her aunt, Phil, or her brother, Freddie. Ten years since the huge argument. What might have happened to them?

'Mrs Reynolds?' said a man of her own age; tall, lean, with glasses and an intelligent face.

'Yes,' she replied, feeling weak.

'Detective Superintendent John Hughes of the Garda Bureau of Fraud Investigation. We're here to speak to your husband and we have a warrant to search your house.'

He handed Callie a piece of paper but she didn't take it.

She stared at him, not understanding.

'This . . . this is my party,' she stammered, looking around at the waitress, now rapidly disappearing.

Callie saw the hall filled with flowers and giant lit candles, all perfect scene-setting for the modern art that hung on the walls.

Relief returned. Not her family.

'It's my fiftieth birthday party. My husband is a business-man, Jason Reynolds. You obviously have the wrong house.'

She waited for the detective to say something about it being a mistake, but he gestured to the piece of paper.

'It's not the wrong house,' he said and there was something about his voice that made Callie feel more frightened than weak.

She looked at the piece of paper for an address and saw it all printed perfectly before her: their address, Jason's name. She'd never seen a search warrant before and it looked so ordinary: ordinary and dangerous. She felt her legs shake the way they'd shaken when she first stood in front of a camera, before she'd learned to handle her nerves and the anxiety.

'Where is your husband?'

'Downstairs,' said Callie. 'We're having a party . . .'

'The guests need to go,' said the detective.

'What?' asked Callie. She knew she sounded stupid but her brain, normally sharp, had hit slow-motion. 'No, really,' she said again in desperation, 'there must be some mistake, you are in the wrong house, you can't be talking about my husband.'

'Jason Reynolds,' said the policeman. 'That's your husband's name?'

'Yes.'

'And you are Claire Reynolds?'

Callie nodded. Nobody called her Claire anymore, not since she had turned into Callie years ago, when she'd sloughed off her past and turned into someone totally different.

'We need to locate your husband.'

'Why?'

The detective looked at her slowly and she thought she could see pity in his eyes. 'To help us with our enquiries,' he said smoothly, which she felt was not the whole truth. His men began to move, some downstairs.

'Does your husband have an office here?' asked another man.

The unreality of it all began to sink in. The police were here to search her house. To talk to her husband. They must have got it wrong, but it was still happening, like a movie when the wrong people were targeted.

Shock made her want to sit down, but she had to stay strong. Poppy was upstairs with her girlfriends, Brenda was in the kitchen making tea and there were two hundred people downstairs drinking cocktails and nibbling blackened cod, tiny exquisite burgers, sashimi.

A door opened and Brenda marched through. Callie felt a sigh of relief. Brenda would sort it out. Tell the police that Jason Reynolds could not be the person they were looking for.

'What is it?' she said, looking at Callie then looking at the policemen who were leaving the hall speedily.

'You are?'

'Brenda Lyons, Mrs Reynolds' friend and housekeeper.' She put an arm around Callie. 'And you?'

'Detective Superintendent John Hughes, GBFI, Garda Bureau of Fraud Investigation.' He handed out a card to Callie.

'Right,' said Brenda with a sigh.

Callie didn't have time to think why Brenda wasn't in the slightest bit surprised.

'There are five teenage girls upstairs,' Brenda said.

'I'll go up,' said the female officer in uniform.

'I think I need to come, as does Mrs Reynolds. We can't upset the girls. But first . . .' Brenda looked back at the detective superintendent. 'What's the plan?' she said as if they were discussing something quite normal instead of a team of police detectives coming into Callie's house late at night at her actual fiftieth birthday party.

Callie stared at her old friend in horror.

'We are here to arrest Jason Reynolds and search the house,' said the officer calmly and this time Callie felt her knees go totally and everything went hazy and then blank.

When she woke up, she was sitting on one of the squashy chairs in the kitchen.

'Lucky they caught you,' said Brenda, waving a glass of brandy in front of Callie's nose.

'Was that a dream, did that really happen?' said Callie.

'No dream,' said Brenda bitterly. 'All true. At this exact moment, there are police officers getting everyone out of your house, carefully taking every computer and every bit of paper with them and searching the whole place.'

'Oh God,' said Callie. 'No,' she said, pushing the brandy away. 'You know I don't like spirits.'

'I know you don't like spirits, but drink this because you are going to need it.'

Brenda held the brandy glass up to Callie's mouth and made her drink it, like Callie used to make Poppy drink things out of a beaker cup when Poppy was a baby.

Her baby.

'Where's Poppy?' she said in alarm.

'It's fine for the moment, I got one of the waitresses to go up there and the female Garda is there too. I've told her there's something strange going on but the police are here to fix it and you're sorting it out and will be up in a minute. The men are not going near her room until you are ready to be there and supervise, but to be honest I'd say get out of here pronto, both of you. We need to get you and Poppy somewhere safe before the story hits the media.' Brenda appeared to be thinking about it. 'I don't even know if you can bring your clothes or what,' she added in a very matter-of-fact tone. 'They're not the Criminal Assets Bureau, so they can't impound it all or anything, but when the Fraud Squad come, they're going to be looking at every asset in terms of legal redress.'

'What story? This is a mistake, surely? Jason will sue.'

Brenda patted her hand tenderly.

'Callie, the Fraud Squad don't make mistakes.'

'But us? Jason's a businessman.'

'Drink,' was all Brenda would say.

Callie shuddered as she finished the rest of the brandy. She hated all strong spirits.

'What do we do now?' she said, making herself come back into the world again.

Everything still felt very unreal. She wanted another Xanax, a whole one, and to go to bed and find out this was all a dream.

'You prepare yourself for the next shock,' said Brenda, patting her hand again.

'I'm not preparing for any shocks until I have Jason beside me and I find out what the hell is going on,' said Callie, as the alcohol hit her system, putting fire in the hold. 'The embarrassment,' she went on.

The people at the party knew all the gossip columnists in the country. Everyone would be writing about this. Jason would go mental. 'Where is Jason? I hope he's trying to turn the police away.'

Brenda perched on the edge of the armchair.

'That's what you needed the brandy for,' she said.

Callie stared up at her.

'They can't find Jason.'

'What?'

'I really hate to be the one to tell you, lovie, but he's done a runner.'

Callie felt the world shift around her.

The words were slow coming out: 'He can't have gone. Why would he go?'

The look Brenda gave her was pitying and Callie flinched under it.

'The most likely excuse is that he's run because he's guilty of whatever they are accusing him of,' Brenda said. 'Which is why you and Poppy need to get out of here now with whatever you can. I don't know what Jason was doing, but the game is up, Callie, and you need to be out of it.'

'What do you mean, *what he was doing*?' said Callie fiercely.

'For heaven's sake, Callie, you must have figured it out by now. I always had my suspicions. Nobody else was making money during the recession except your husband. Nobody else bounced back so quickly. Did you not find that weird?'

'No!'

'Come on,' said Brenda. 'You're a clever woman. I thought you knew his business wasn't entirely kosher. We can talk about this another time, but now, we need to get those girls home, get you and Poppy out of the house and . . .' Brenda stopped for a minute. 'Could we take the Range Rover? It might be confiscated. Whose name is it in? Probably the company's, so you can't take it. Right, we need taxis to get the girls home or, better still, I'll ring their parents.'

Callie watched, mute, as Brenda thought out loud, running through the various permutations and combinations of keeping her daughter out of this crisis.

'I am not running,' began Callie. 'I am going to stay here and wait until Jason comes back from wherever he is and fixes it all—'

'Fixes it? This won't be fixed. Tomorrow morning, every newspaper in the country is going to be at your door wanting to know all about it,' said Brenda harshly. 'Wake up, Callie. I am your friend and I am telling you it's all over. You have to get out. Now. For your sake and for Poppy's.'

Poppy.

'More brandy,' said Callie, Brenda's words beginning to penetrate. 'I need another one.'

'Not a good idea—' began Brenda.

'I don't care,' hissed Callie. 'I need something.'

Brenda watched silently as Callie half filled the brandy glass and downed it, wincing as it burned.

Callie stood up and looked around her kitchen, the cosy kitchen that she'd insisted on decorating herself. The rest of the house was where Jason had supervised the interior décor, places that were fit for proving to people how rich, successful and gracious the Reynolds family were. It was nothing like the home she'd grown up in, a small terraced council house in Ballyglen, where the whole Sheridan family of four, and her aunt, had lived.

Callie felt an ache deep in her heart.

I wish my family were here. I wish my mother was here.

Sam

Early on the morning of her fortieth birthday, Sam Kennedy was woken up by the phone, and not by her beloved Baby Bean pressing a foot or an elbow into her bladder, which had been the case for the past few months.

She struggled out of her cosy cocoon of duvet, disentangling herself from Ted's long warm leg which was comfortably entwined with her own, and answered.

'Happy birthday, Samantha!' said her mother.

'Who's phoning at this hour on a Saturday?' groaned Ted, pulling his pillow over his sleek dark head, and then, remembering what day it was, pulling it off. 'Happy fortieth birthday, honey,' he said, putting an arm around his wife's very pregnant body and kissing her gently on the shoulder through the curtain of her long tangle of dark hair. 'Love you.' He leaned down and kissed her bump, covered with an unsexy floral nightie. 'Love you, Bean.'

Sam never stopped loving the gesture: Ted bending from his great height to kiss her and her belly with complete adoration. He was six foot two to Sam's five foot three and their wedding photos had made her realise how incongruous they might have looked together had Sam not been addicted to very high heels. With a four-inch heel, her pocket Venus body in a simple lace dress had looked just right beside her long, lean husband. Up close, her head fitted perfectly against his broad chest and if he sometimes whirled her round with her feet off the floor, nobody noticed.

'Love you, too,' Sam murmured now.

'Samantha, are you still there?' Her mother's voice sounded irritated at having been made to wait.

'Yes, and thank you for calling, Mother,' Sam said into the phone, not mentioning that pregnant women longed for their Saturday morning lie-in.

'You sound odd. I hope you're not getting maudlin about your age,' her mother went on in the cool tones that commanded respect in St Margaret's School for Girls, where she'd reigned as headmistress for thirty years. 'Age is merely a number.'

Six-thirty on a Saturday is merely a number, too, thought Sam but didn't say it.

Instead, she mildly pointed out: 'I was asleep.'

'Right. I trust you're well and have a good day planned,' said her mother with the same formality she probably used to address the school's board of governors. 'Again, happy birthday. Here's your father. Goodbye.'

With that unmaternal sign-off, the phone was handed over.

'Happy birthday, lovie. Sorry for the early call but . . .'

'I get it, Dad,' said Sam, warmly. 'Early morning swim? The garden?'

Her parents lived close to Dublin Bay, where hardy souls swam in all weathers, Sam's mother among them.

'The former,' her father said. They'd communicated this way for years: Sam would speak and he'd answer in the 'yes/no/absolutely' code that was hardly Enigma-machine-quality but worked for them.

Her dad, Liam, was as mild, chatty and forbearing as her mother, Jean, was cool, uncommunicative and distant. It was one of the great mysteries of Sam's life as to how the two of them had ever married. That they'd stayed married, she put down to the social mores of the times and some concept both parents had about staying together for their daughters.

Nobody talked about the ice-cold rows between her parents when she'd been growing up, and now, this part of life appeared to have been airbrushed out of family history. It was like the fridge magnet said: *If anyone asks, pretend we come from a nice, normal family.*

Only she and Joanne, her younger sister, talked about the past now.

Their parents' marriage of opposites had made Sam determined to be nothing like her mother and to marry a man she adored, rather than one she merely tolerated.

She'd succeeded. Nestling closer to her beloved Ted in bed, she thought that, yet again, being with him should feature in the number one slot on her daily gratitude list.

'How are you feeling and how's the little baba?' her father asked.

'Wriggling,' said Sam, putting a hand automatically on her hugely swollen belly and smiling, another automatic move. She'd been smiling since she'd found out that she was pregnant, which was astonishing because, after three failed IVF cycles in her early thirties, she'd assumed that babies were out of the question.

Ted had been smiling pretty much non-stop too, a giant grin that brought out that dimple in his otherwise acutely masculine face, a dimple Sam really hoped their baby would inherit.

After many painful years of longing, they'd finally somehow come to terms with the fact that they were going to be child-free people, and that a dog/cat/hamster was the answer – or so everyone said.

They would deal with the grief, they would not let it part them. They would do their best to move on.

'Let's be happy with each other,' they'd agreed.

So they'd got two dogs, Ted began the marathon running that had been put on hold during years of planned babymaking schedules (the fertility-drug years) and Sam filled her weekends with botanical watercolours and the odd yoga class, so she could learn again to love the body she'd felt had betrayed her.

And then suddenly, the previously infertile Sam had become pregnant.

Incredibly, miraculously pregnant with no help from anyone apart from Ted.

'Last dash of the ovaries,' said her GP. 'Evolution is incredible. If you haven't given birth by a certain age, your body can launch into action.'

'Wow,' Sam had said, which was almost all she'd said since she'd gone to the GP to discuss her strange tiredness and morning nausea, thinking there must be a medical reason other than the obvious.

On the phone, Dad said it was a good sign the baby was a week late.

'All first babies are late and the later they are, the smarter they are. I can't remember what site I read it on, but it's true.' Liam spent hours consulting the internet every day on pregnancy issues. 'I was going to drop round later with your birthday present,' he added.

'I'd love that. We'll be here. Ted's going to walk the dogs, but I plan to tidy the kitchen cupboards.'

'Ah, love, not on your birthday,' begged her father. 'Watch old movies and drink hot chocolate. That's the right sort of plan. Do you have marshmallows? I'll bring some.'

'Just like old times,' said Sam, smiling into the phone.

When her father had hung up, Ted nuzzled into her.

'Happy birthday, sexy pregnant lady,' he said, sliding up her nightie to stroke her bare belly.

Baby Bean wriggled and they both gasped to feel Sam's small guest poke an elbow up.

'Incredible,' said Ted, marvelling.

'I know,' agreed Sam, stroking her belly gently. 'Incredible.'

Ted swung out of bed.

'I'll let the dogs out and bring you tea. Camomile and apple? Earl Grey?'

Sam considered it. 'Earl Grey. Any more camomile and I'll turn into a camomile lawn.'

She used to love her morning coffee but had given it up as

soon as she'd learned she was pregnant – not that a certain amount of caffeine was necessarily bad in pregnancy. But Sam had spent too long wishing and praying for this child to do anything but turn her body into a temple until he or she was born. This was the legacy of every failed pregnancy test: a fear of doing something, anything, to hurt her baby.

She snuggled back down into the bed and talked nonsense to Baby Bean. She did that a lot now – running commentaries, telling the baby what she was doing and how she couldn't wait to do it all with Baby Bean.

'Grandpa will be over later with a present for me, baba. It's my birthday today! You're my best birthday present, though.'

Ted returned with a cup of Earl Grey tea for her. Sam took a sip. She'd never been able to touch it pre-pregnancy, but now she wasn't drinking coffee and the idea of milk in tea made her want to gag, Earl Grey, black, no lemon, was perfect.

He got back into bed with her and gently stroked her shoulder.

'Sleep?' he asked.

'Bean is undecided about whether to be a footballer or a gymnast,' Sam sighed. 'Lots of moving and kicking. I don't know what that means. Oh, but Dad says that late babies are smarter.'

'Aren't you clever,' crooned Ted to her bump.

He'd been amazing all through her pregnancy: kind no matter how ratty she'd got and perfectly happy to sit on the side of the bath rubbing her back as she soaked in the water. No matter how enormous she'd become – and boy, she was enormous now – he'd still told her every day how gorgeous she was.

'Now that your dad's got that new bit of information, there's still time to start that blog about baby advice,' Ted suggested.

Sam loved this game. She started first.

'Number one, people need to know that babies who are carried low can be boys/girls/llamas.'

'Or that fish is good and bad for you, simultaneously,' added Ted.

They laughed.

By now, forty-one weeks into her first pregnancy, Sam and Ted had come to the conclusion that everyone on the planet believed themselves to be an expert in babies.

And that they all had advice they wanted to impart – whether Sam or Ted wanted to listen or not.

'Don't eat fish – mercury kills babies.'

'Eat fish – it's good for their brains.'

'One glass of wine occasionally relaxes you. I'm sure the World Health Organisation said that. Or was it my sister . . .?'

'Your baby will be born with Foetal Alcohol Syndrome if you so much as smell alcohol from more than a distance of four feet. I saw it on the Discovery Channel.'

'Natural births are the best for mother and baby. Who wants drugs in their poor baby's system?'

'Ask for the drugs early on, like, really early on. If you don't get them in time, you'll scream and the pain . . .'

'You're carrying low – definitely a girl.'

'You're carrying low – a boy, for sure!'

'Go back to sleep, Sam. You need to rest,' Ted said. But Sam felt wide awake now. She knew she'd never get back to sleep for even a few minutes.

'Dogs still out the back?'

'Yes. Four magpies in the garden – did you not hear the orgy of barking? The neighbours will love us for dragging them out of their hangovers at this early hour on a Saturday.'

Four magpies, Sam thought, hauling herself out of the bed to hit the bathroom for her first of many trips of the day. Was she having a boy? Three magpies meant you were having a girl, four meant a boy. If she saw five magpies, Sam wondered if a silver baby would slither out.

From all the painful birth stories she'd been told, she hoped slithering out was part of it all.

They'd asked not to be told the sex of the baby. 'It's not long until we'll know and it's life's biggest secret,' she said to Ted. 'Let's wait.'

'I thought life's biggest secret was whether there is life on another planet,' said Ted, deadpan. 'OK, you win. No asking the radiographer if they can see a willy or not.'

The spare bedroom was turned into a nursery decorated in a riot of yellows and white and Ted, whose father had a lathe, had slaved over a handmade cot.

She wriggled her feet into her slippers after the bathroom. It was a long time since she'd been able to see her feet, much less bend down to pull on shoes.

'You try and snooze,' she said, kissing Ted on the head as he rearranged the pillows.

She went into their tiny kitchen to make toast with honey – she could eat it for the Olympics. Also ice cream. Gallons of it.

Being pregnant had made her ravenous. Nobody had mentioned that, although she'd been told of women who'd licked coal or consumed Marmite by the bucket.

She had no idea how she was going to get the baby weight off, but from the size of her rear end, which was admittedly hard to see in their wardrobe mirror, Sam was pretty sure it wasn't all baby.

When she'd confided this to Joanne, her sister had laughed and said, 'It'll come off: sleep deprivation does that to you.'

'I hope you're joking,' said Sam, because she knew how shattered Joanne had been when she'd had three children one after the other.

'I am not joking, not remotely.'

Joanne smiled with the Mona-Lisa-like smile which implied that, for once, the younger sister knew something the older one didn't.

Sam looked through the back window to see if Dixie and Horace, the two small, bitsa-everything rescue dogs on whom she and Ted lavished their affection, had finished their morning run around the garden where they barked at birds, gave worms the evil eye and peed liberally in order to remind all other creatures that this was their territory.

But the dogs were busy and, knowing their lap of investigation could take some time, and because her lower back ached strangely, Sam sat down on a kitchen chair.

She hoped the dogs would be fine with the baby. They'd been playing crying baby noises whenever they fed them, as per internet advice, so the dogs would associate the baby with the loveliness of dinner, which was one of the highlights of Dixie and Horace's day. Their Pavlov's bell way of getting the dogs ready for the new arrival.

'Do you think it will work?' Sam had asked anxiously.

'Course. The worst crime they'll commit is to try to slobber kisses on the baby or clamber onto your lap for breastfeeding,' Ted teased. 'They'll adjust.'

He'd been raised with dogs and was relaxed around them. In contrast, Sam's mother had an allergy, or so she said, and no animal had ever graced Sam's childhood home.

On the hard kitchen chair, Sam moved to try to find a comfortable position.

The ache was getting weirdly lower and deeper. Was this a sign that the baby was moving into the birth canal? she wondered.

Some women said pregnancy made them feel at one with their body: Sam, who had spent years having her hormones artificially manipulated in order to stimulate a pregnancy that never came, no longer felt as if she had a clue what was going on with hers. Which worried her, although she hadn't breathed a word of this to anyone. The baby fear, that something would go wrong to stop her having this child because her body had failed before, was too ridiculous to voice out loud.

And there was another fear, one that loomed bigger each day: in all those years of trying to get pregnant, she'd barely allowed herself to imagine becoming an actual parent.

Now she wondered how on earth she could be a proper mother. Because she had no experience of how a warm, kind, motherly figure behaved.

'Happy birthday, Sam!'

Ted appeared in his T-shirt and boxers, his body marathon-lean and tanned from sunny evenings spent in the garden sanding and painting the crib.

He'd been in a vintage Rolling Stones T-shirt and jeans at the college party where they'd met, a night when Ted said he was walking her home to keep her safe.

'I can keep myself safe, thank you very much,' snapped Sam. Ted had grinned and walked her home anyway.

'You were like an angry pixie, those eyes flashing at me, and I just couldn't keep away,' he'd said later, when they were inseparable, Sam's prickly defences long since lowered.

'Honey.' He leaned down and kissed her. 'I couldn't sleep and it's not fair that you're up alone on your birthday.' With a flourish, he put a small box on the table in front of her and stood back proudly. 'It's a really small gift,' he explained. 'Tiny so I can get you a proper something when the baby is born or you can enjoy going out shopping with me, because forty is a special birthday. You should have diamonds and—'

Sam opened the box, gasped suddenly and stared at the interior blankly.

Ted squinted at her. 'You don't like? They're gold-plated earrings. The gold will rub off, it always does, and I can return them if you'd like, but I know you like purple stones and—'

'Ted!'

'You really hate them?' Ted picked up the box and looked at the contents critically. 'I thought you'd hate it more if I spent money buying any proper jewellery without you—'

'My waters have just broken,' hissed Sam, as she felt the surge of liquid move from a trickle to a flood. 'I love the present, Ted, but we need to go to the hospital. I can't have the baby on the kitchen floor – it's not clean enough with the dogs, and the baby will get kennel cough or dog flu or something . . .'

'Your waters have broken?' repeated Ted, not sounding like someone with a PhD in data analytics.

He sat down beside her, then immediately got up again as if someone had switched his brain off and then back on, and all the circuits were recalibrating.

'Right. OK. Will I time your contractions or . . .?'

Her reliable, steadfast husband stared at her as if all rational thought had been sucked out of him and he wanted her to tell him what to do.

'Get me to the hospital,' she whispered.

Stopping only to ring the doorbell next door so they could tell their neighbour, Cynthia, that Operation Baby was ON and would she go in and take the dogs, as agreed, Ted helped Sam into the car.

Despite several strong buzzes on her doorbell, Cynthia didn't appear.

'She's in the shower,' said Shazz, Cynthia's twenty-three-year-old daughter, coming out onto the shared driveway still in her skimpy denim cut-offs and a leather-look bra worn with a net top, her short pale pink hair fluffed up into a halo round her head. Definitely just in from the night before.

'Good luck, Sam, it'll be fine,' said Shazz, draping her beautiful fake-tanned self over the car door and flattening Sam with the scents of fags, booze, club and not-been-to-bedness.

'How do you know it'll be fine?' demanded Sam, her politeness filter entirely knocked out by the knowledge that Baby Bean wanted out and there were no medical professionals around to help.

'I've seen it on the soaps,' said Shazz thoughtfully. 'It'll work out. Babies are, er . . . you know – natural.'

'The soaps aren't real!' Sam yelled. 'And it's scary. Imagine giving birth right now. Big baby.' She lowered her voice and pointed downwards. 'Small exit.'

'Yeuch.' Shazz took a step back, thinking about it. 'That's going to mess it all up down there, right? In the lady garden palace.' She shuddered.

For a brief moment, Sam thought about her own lady garden palace and getting the baby out of it. She'd watched lots of Discovery TV birthing shows and right now, she was scared.

Ted got into the car.

'Hospital bag!' Sam reminded him.

He got the bag.

Looking right and left like a racing driver, Ted whizzed through every red light on the way to the maternity hospital. Beside him, Sam panted and screeched with a combination of nerves and pain.

Another wave hit her. This was not what she'd anticipated, not this searing pain that felt as if it would rip her in two. Plus, she might kill Ted before they got to the hospital. He kept going over speed bumps too fast.

That was the problem, she decided grimly as the pain receded. She was having a baby with an idiot. An idiot who loved his computer, thought the sun shone out of the Tipperary hurling team's collective backsides and had no idea what women had to go through in life. Any of it.

Women understood pain. Or women *were* pain . . .? Something like that. She'd read it on Pinterest.

Another pain bloomed inside her.

'Drive faster!' she hissed.

Ted broke all the speed limits and, at last, they slid to a halt in front of the Rotunda Hospital in the ambulance bay.

As she was put into a wheelchair at the hospital door, she was half sobbing. 'My waters broke an hour ago and the baby's coming,' she said.

A nurse shooed Ted off to park properly because he wasn't allowed to abandon the car in the ambulance bay.

'I am going to have this baby here and now!' went on Sam,

watching with dismay as her husband left. She loved him. She'd been so horrible to him . . . he couldn't go—

'You probably won't give birth this quickly with your first,' soothed the nurse. 'Let's see how you're doing.'

'No, it's a week overdue, it's coming very soon, I can feel it,' said Sam, who was not feeling remotely soothed.

'Everyone thinks that, but it's a first baby and they take time.'

'No, I do know,' said Sam wildly. 'I'm giving birth now, here and now! Get me into the delivery room!'

'All right, pet, let's check out how dilated you are.'

Somehow, assisted by two nurses, and a midwife with an even more soothing voice, Sam got onto a bed.

'It's coming!' she shrieked as another pain hit her.

'It's not,' said the midwife calmly as she emerged from between Sam's legs. 'You're only three centimetres dilated.'

'Three!'

Three centimetres would not let a Barbie doll emerge. Barbie's insanely perky bosoms would get stuck.

'Yes, only three. I'm sorry, Sam,' said the midwife with the awareness of a professional who'd delivered enough babies to know that smugness in delivery rooms did not help anyone.

Three was nothing, Sam knew. *Nothing.* How could she be in this pain with no sign of a child appearing? What was next? Red-hot pokers of pain?

Ted came back from parking the car as another contraction ripped through Sam.

'Darling,' he said, taking her hand.

'Don't darling me!' she yelled, fear coming out as rage. 'If you ever think you are coming near me again with that . . . that *thing,* you have another thing coming!'

'But . . . but . . . we want this baby,' muttered Ted, who had read all the baby books with mentions of fury bouncing off the walls in the delivery suite. But not his Sam, surely?

After this long journey of IVF, he was going to help, hold Sam's hand, man the phone.

Not get screamed at.

'Relax, dear,' whispered the midwife to Ted. 'They all say things like that. In fact, that's mild. No sex forever or having their bits chopped off is what some partners hear in these rooms, but afterwards, it's OK, you wait and see.'

'It's her birthday,' Ted said, desperately trying to shift the conversation on from parts of his anatomy he did not want to discuss with strange women. 'She's forty.'

'We know, she's an elderly primigravida.'

'I am not elderly!' said Sam, who had nothing wrong with her hearing even if it felt as if a giant wriggling emu with a bowling ball for a head was trying to emerge from her body, *sideways*. This could not be normal. There must be something wrong.

'Not old, just old to have your first one,' soothed the midwife. 'Once you're thirty-five or older, they call you elderly.'

'I'm forty today,' Sam said, tearfully. 'That's not elderly. Life begins at forty: everyone says it.'

'Happy birthday!' said the midwife, who was thirty-nine and hoped so too.

Four hours later, two more centimetres dilated and after a lot of screaming at Ted, interspersed with sobbing and saying sorry because she loved him, Sam thought she might just be going mad with pain. Nobody told her it would be like this or that it would take this long.

When people said 'I was in labour for sixteen hours', she'd thought it was exaggeration, not reality. Like saying 'I didn't sleep a wink last night', or 'I lost all that weight without doing anything'.

A whopping big baby-birthing fib.

But in this case, it seemed as if it was true.

Doing his best to be helpful, Ted extracted Sam's birth plan from the hospital bag.

The birth plan was full of ideas for the perfect birth and

involved soft music – they'd done a track list and it was on both of their phones – no drugs in case they affected the baby and, if possible, Ted to cut the cord.

The birth plan was a paean to glorious natural childbirth.

The woman in the prenatal class had praised their approach, telling them how it was better for Baby to be shoved, drug-free, into the world.

So Ted innocently handed the sheaf of paper to Sam, who sent it flying as another contraction hit her.

'Jesus, the pain!' she roared.

'Breathe,' said Ted, watching as the birth plan scattered all over the floor.

'I can't,' gasped Sam as she felt as if her insides were being torn apart. 'I must have been mad with all that breathing crap. Screw breathing. Where's the anaesthetist?'

'The one on call is in theatre with an emergency Caesarean,' said the midwife.

Sam stopped grabbing the bed bars long enough to grab Ted.

'Find him,' she hissed, in a voice uncannily like that of the little girl from *The Exorcist*, 'and bring him to me.'

'I can't,' said Ted, shocked at seeing his wife behaving like someone possessed.

'Dr Lennox will be along soon.'

'I need him now.'

'Dr Lennox is a she.'

'Does she have kids?' growled Sam.

'Yes.'

'Then beg her, she knows what this is like.'

'She had twins first time.'

'I don't care if she gave birth to two fully grown hippos without medical intervention, I need her and her bag of drugs. Please.'

'But your birth plan,' went on Ted, thinking that perhaps it was his job to make Sam stick with the plan she'd wanted for so long. 'You know we don't want drugs for this delivery and I have your music ready to go—'

He ignored the warning looks on the faces of the midwife and nurses, who had seen all of this played out many times before.

'Babies don't read the birth plan,' began the younger nurse, who was used to shattered husbands, men who came in all gung-ho and went home bruised and traumatised wrecks. 'You never really know how a delivery is going to progress.'

Sam launched into Ted: 'If *you* are having this baby, *you* can do it without drugs, but *I* am having it, *I* am trying to pass a bowling ball from an orifice that has never had a bowling ball emerge from it before, and I want everything! ALL the drugs! Everything in the hospital.'

There was nothing close for Sam to throw but Ted ducked just in case.

This was nothing like the Sam he knew and loved.

Two more hours elapsed with just pain and the anticipation of it in Sam's landscape.

'I love you,' Ted kept saying.

'I know,' she said when she wasn't in actual pain.

She was tearful and sweaty, and in her saner moments, wondered how people appeared in celebrity magazines at the hospital door a day after giving birth, all groomed and perfect.

She had seen herself in the bathroom mirror when she'd been trying the 'keep walking and let gravity help' method. She was puce in the face, sweating, and her hair was a greaseball. A month left alone in Sephora with a crack team of beauticians would not make her look good ever again.

'I keep thinking the baby's going to come, but it doesn't,' she said weepily to Ted, who was half hugging her, half holding her up. 'I know they say long first labours are normal, but this can't be normal? They're not telling us something.'

She began to cry again.

'We don't know what normal is here,' Ted said manfully. He

was being ultra-careful in case he upset the balance between possessed wife and crying wife, the latter being upsetting but easier to handle.

The young nurse arrived back in the room to check the foetal heart rate and Sam's cervix.

'You're fully dilated!' she said, peeping up from between Sam's legs.

'You see, nobody knows when a baby wants to make an entrance.'

'My baby's coming?' said Sam, almost shocked.

'Your baby is coming,' smiled the nurse.

Within minutes, it was all action and still no anaesthetist.

Ted was, to his delight, up the head end of the bed because he wasn't sure he could cope with seeing the baby emerging from the birth canal, no matter how much he and Sam had discussed how this was important for both of them.

Instead, he remembered his friend Lorcan, who'd said: 'It does something to you, mate, seeing her producing a baby out of *down there*. Can take a while to get over it, uh, sexually.'

Sam screamed, pushed, and nearly ripped a hole in Ted's hand as she pushed their baby into the world.

'Push,' said the midwife at the right times.

Sam pushed, feeling every tendon straining, every bit of her body ripping.

Despite the noise of machines and other women giving birth, screaming too, there were moments when she felt suspended in time – lost between pain, joy and anxiety and, above all, that wild primal desire to birth her baby safely.

Women had been doing it since the beginning of time; she had to do this. Couldn't fail.

Now, now, now, please let it be now . . .

And then, the last push—

The baby let out a little bleat and Ted began to cry.

'A little girl,' said the midwife with pride and Sam began to cry too, tears of joy and exhaustion.

'Good breath sounds, pinking up,' said the paediatrician, swooping in.

When she was finally put in Sam's arms, Baby Bean – seven pounds exactly and scoring a perfect Apgar score – was the most infinitely precious creature her parents had ever seen.

Almost afraid to touch this little person, astonished that she had grown this child inside her body, Sam gazed at the tiny fingers with awe. The baby's little nails were translucent, her fingers tiny but perfect. Even with some of the film of childbirth over her, she was exquisite.

Her lovely eyelids were so delicate, like petals draped over blue eyes that stared up at Sam as if she could see her perfectly.

'She's ours,' said Sam, staring at her baby.

'She's beautiful,' said Ted, and Sam looked up to see his eyes brimming with tears and the trails of more tears down his face. 'Just beautiful. I never thought this would happen,' he said, choking the words out, 'and look at her: perfect and ours and we get to bring her home, bring her up. We are a family . . .'

At that moment, something strange happened to Sam.

Something that made her feel fiercely protective, deeply in love and terrified all at the same time.

This tiny little being was hers to take care of.

She would kill for her baby.

'Mummy loves you with all her heart and will injure anyone who tries to hurt you,' she murmured into the baby's fragile skull with its covering of downy dark hair.

Suddenly, she understood all those nature programmes where lonely leopard mothers risked taking down bigger animals all for their cubs, where birds flew across dangerous deserts to sip water at deadly waterholes surrounded by predators so they could regurgitate the water later to keep their tiny baby birds alive.

She would rip out the throat of anything, anyone, who hurt her baby. Anyone.

And then, the great love and the great sense of protectiveness were overwhelmed by another, fearful thought. The one that had been stalking her.

All her life, she had been in charge. The woman people went to when they wanted a task accomplished and fast.

Suddenly she didn't feel any of those things. Not organised, not competent.

She had a tiny baby in her arms. In a couple of days, maybe even *the next day*, she and Ted were going to bring this tiny creature home.

Sam had simply no idea how to do this. No mental template from her own childhood.

How could *she* now become a proper mother with no background to help her with what was supposed to be the most natural thing in the world?

On her fortieth birthday, cradling her new baby, Sam made a wish.

Please let me learn how to be a good mother. Please.

Ginger

Ginger Reilly danced with her head on Stephen's shoulder and tried to ignore the wire-like bite of her control tights into her waist. She was impervious to such things, she told herself, inhaling the scent of Stephen's spicy cologne and resting her face against his dinner jacket, not caring that it was hired and had probably been to more weddings than the band currently murdering 'Unchained Melody'.

She wasn't, for once, wondering if she looked hideously enormous, despite today's bridesmaid's dress – peach taffeta on a woman who wore head-to-toe black at all times – being a bit too Scarlett O'Hara to disguise Ginger's substantial bosom and curvy hips. Sometimes, Ginger stood outside rooms and wondered how to walk in as thinly as possible, or else how to walk in so that nobody noticed a larger girl daring to exist in a skinny-girl world.

But none of that mattered today: what mattered was that she was dancing with a man who'd just asked her to go out with him. A good-looking, tall man who'd chatted her up, admired her and had asked her – unpushed by relatives, even though he was Liza's cousin – out onto the dance floor five times.

'People will talk,' Ginger joked weakly the second time Stephen took her hand for a slow dance. She'd even looked around to see if Liza, the bride and her best friend, had manoeuvred this second dance so that Ginger wouldn't have to be her normal wallflower self. A wallflower who did a remarkable impression of a woman having a fabulous time, because *nobody* was going to pity Ginger Reilly, but still, in the deepest, most hidden part of her brain, a wallflower.

'Let them talk,' Stephen had said, looking down. He was really tall and clearly a sporty guy, with big shoulders and a slightly too-thick neck. But he had wonderful dark hair, matching dark eyes and a smile just for her. How had she never met him before?

For the first time in her life, Ginger did not mind a man looking down into the Grand Canyon of her cleavage. In work, she wore polo necks or crew necks to cover up and had a smart retort to anyone who eyed her 42EE chest with leering interest.

In work, she was sassy Ginger who nipped all smart remarks in the bud.

But today, clad in a dress that had *buxom wench* written all over it, she found she liked Stephen openly admiring her cleavage. He'd also admired her hair, the auburn tangle of curls that had meant that when her eldest brother called her Ginger as a child, the nickname had stuck.

Her hair, wrapped up into a sheeny coil at the back of her head by the bridal party's hairdresser that morning, was her most beautiful feature, Liza often pointed out.

'Wish I had hair like that,' said Liza, who'd got bum-length extensions onto her platinum hair, which she'd had tonged into long curls that trailed down her fake-tanned back for the wedding.

Ginger's father, Michael, said his only daughter's best features were her kindness, her sense of humour, a warm face and eyes like her mother's: huge, trusting amber eyes with eyelashes longer than any giraffe's. Michael had brought up his two sons and Ginger all on his own when his wife had been killed in a road accident on the way back from visiting relatives in her home town of Ballyglen. Ginger's hair was like her mother's too, her father said.

'What about next week?' Stephen was asking as they danced. 'We could see a film. What do you like?'

Ginger, who quite often went to the cinema as it was something you could do alone, had seen all the films she wanted to. But pleasing a man, Liza insisted, meant kowtowing to him without him knowing. As she'd had at least fifteen steady boyfriends, from the age of fourteen onwards, Ginger – current boyfriend total to date: nil – felt that Liza must know what she was talking about.

'What do *you* like?' Ginger asked, quashing the feeling that she was letting down the sisterhood by not answering honestly. But she had to give it a try. The initial kowtowing clearly was only *part* of the process. When you knew someone, then you could be honest with them.

She envisioned her and Stephen when they were happily in love, perhaps on holiday in a cold country because Ginger didn't do beachwear. 'I lied that first night about films I like,' she'd say and he'd laugh. 'I know, silly. It made me fall in love with you faster.'

Stephen led her off the dance floor as the band finished up, and he began talking about the new *Fast and Furious* spin-off movie he'd take her to see.

Ginger, who had two brothers after all, and had been forced to sit through most of the original series, already knew the entire plot. She did not mention this but instead said: 'That sounds wonderful.'

And it would be: a date with something other than the remote control.

Ginger Reilly, thirty years old today, and a spinster of this parish, as her Great-Aunt Grace might say jokingly, had only ever been on one other date in her whole life. He'd been a guy from college who'd eventually asked her out to the pub. He'd then proceeded to tell her about how much he fancied her college mate. End of date.

'You're curvy, not fat, and you're a late bloomer,' Mick, her eldest brother, had said, kindly, as she'd sobbed to him that it was because she was fat, wasn't it? 'Your time will come, sis.'

And it had.

Being thirty, Ginger decided, was going to make all the difference.

She had more confidence, more experience of life, more . . . more *something*, she was sure of it.

Working for Caraval Media had sharpened her up, helped transform her into the tough cookie with the smart mouth who made gangs of people from work think she was the funniest thing ever. More money, thanks to her agony-aunt column in an online teenage girl mag, meant she could afford cool, well-fitting black clothes. She was getting places.

Except with the opposite sex.

Her sex life was a wasteland. Always had been.

To Paula in work, she pretended she had lovers on speed dial. Telling Paula was the gossip equivalent of WhatsApping the whole planet.

Therefore in Caraval Media, Ginger Reilly was seen as one of those large, sassy girls who had men falling at her feet so fast, she had to kick them out of the way to leave the house in the morning.

With Liza, her friend since they were four, Ginger dropped the facade and fell into the relationship they'd had forever: a size eighteen woman who would not stand in front of the mirror naked and who had never, ever had a proper date with a man, never mind actual sex.

Liza knew Ginger's secrets, knew she dressed to hide herself, knew she longed for real love.

And then tonight had come . . . and with it came Stephen, sexy, kind and liking the version of Ginger in the poufy dress she'd worn purely to please her best friend.

As the wedding band shuffled off and the hotel staff brought in sandwiches and pretty wedding-themed cupcakes for the latecomers who would arrive for the after-party with the DJ, Stephen led Ginger out onto the hotel terrace and leaned her against the wall in a dark corner.

'You look so beautiful in that dress,' he murmured.

His hands were touching her bare shoulders and he kissed her briefly on the lips, so she tasted the heavy red wine they'd both been drinking.

As bridesmaid, Ginger had merely had a glass of champagne early on during the toasts. She knew she must be on call all day, ready with anti-shine powder and perfume. But Liza was happy now and Charlene, the other bridesmaid, who was as thin and beautiful as Liza herself, had been sitting beside Liza for ages, giggling and chatting, so Ginger had allowed herself a half-glass of wine with Stephen. Now she felt the wine and sheer passion warming her up, not to mention Stephen's large body pressed against hers.

'You're so gorgeous, Ginge,' he said.

Normally, anyone who called her Ginge got their head verbally ripped off, but she could allow beautiful Stephen the luxury.

Then his mouth moved in a fiery line down her neck and it felt so wonderful that she didn't care what he called her. This was passion. This was what other people had had. Why had she waited so long? Why hadn't she joined an online dating site or even tried out something as openly sexual as Tinder and put herself out there instead of hoping for someone to ask her out? Why not be what she'd pretended to be for so long? A sexually modern woman who enjoyed the glory of her own body and the pleasure sex could bring.

Stephen progressed down towards her breasts and Ginger felt herself surge with sensuality. This was wonderful.

She cradled his large head against her and, despite having read hundreds of erotic historical fiction novels where sex by chapter three was a given, sheer lack of experience in the real world meant she wondered what to do with her arms.

She could only reach his head, so she began raining kisses on it. He nuzzled the curve of her breasts, rising like Venus out of the foam of the dress, and Ginger felt a burning heat inside her. Ginger had had orgasms before – on her own – so she knew what that burning heat meant: the slow rise of passion as her body awakened. Imagine a real man touching her where she'd only touched herself.

But this was so different from being in her own bed, this was real. As she felt his hands start to slide up under her flouncy dress, Ginger froze. Not from fear of sex, no. From fear of what Stephen would find if he kept exploring: the hated control tights, and even though she was wearing her nicest knickers – coral lace Victoria's Secret hi-thighs – the first thing he'd feel was the sausage-like encasement of her lower body and the fat spilling out over the top of the tights.

It would ruin everything. No blog or book she'd ever read had said that men's groins went as hard as lead pipes at the feel of ample curves spilling over control tights.

'No,' she said, shoving his hand away, attempting to sound sophisticated instead of panicked. 'Not here.'

'But you're so beautiful, darling Ginge,' coaxed Stephen.

'I mean . . .' Ginger paused. 'We need privacy.'

Privacy for her to first get the bloody tights off and let the Victoria's Secret hi-thighs work their magic, and privacy so that her first ever sexual encounter could be in an actual bed instead of against a wall outside a ballroom.

Despite both her fierce desire for this man and her fierce desire to offload the millstone of her virginity, she wanted this to be right.

Sure, she wrote an online column where she told teenage girls about the perils of letting some guy have sex with them and then slut-shame them via social media.

But they were young and she was thirty.

It was time.

This was real, not a one-night stand. She would not seem easy if she told him she had a room in the hotel. And as for her millstone and what he'd think when he found out she was a virgin – the studly guys in the historical fiction novels loved virgins. Unsullied women were the ultimate prize, which did offend Ginger's feminist hackles, but hey, that was historical stuff. Pre-condom, pre-pill. Modern virginity was absolutely not a prize men should use to keep women in check.

'Whaddya mean, privacy?' said Stephen, his hand no longer able to burrow as Ginger kept pushing it away.

'I mean, not here, darling. We need privacy,' purred Ginger, astonished at her own daring. 'Somewhere we can be alone.' She'd called him darling, she'd purred like a sex kitten to a real man and she was implying that serious action would take place in a room.

But the control tights, which were possibly now cutting off the circulation to the bottom half of her body, would ruin all plans of serious action. One feel of them and Stephen would bolt.

'I think I'll wear Spanx,' Liza had decided early on, even though she was as slender as a twig, and Ginger – who knew all about control garments and owned a panoply of them – wondered where Liza would find Spanx small enough to fit her.

As Ginger herself knew that wearing the all-encompassing hold-it-in garments was like being wrapped in bulletproof cling film, she had gone with control tights and the prettiest minimiser bra she could find, a bra that was fighting a losing battle.

Nothing had ever minimised her breasts and nothing ever would, not since they'd appeared like downy pillows on her chest almost overnight when she was thirteen and boys had stopped asking tomboyish Ginger to play footie and had started staring at her breasts instead.

Bridesmaid dresses with tight waists, billowing skirts and fitted bodices were not designed for buxom women with body issues.

Still, Stephen didn't seem to mind.

'Oh sugar, come on,' he murmured, nuzzling her neck again.

'Give me a moment, babe,' she said in what she hoped was a sultry, come-hither voice. 'I'll be back. And then . . .' She channelled someone sexy and said: 'I actually have a room in the hotel.'

Stephen's face lit up.

'I'll wait, Ginge,' he said.

She grabbed her handbag from the table inside and half ran to the small, discreet loo the wedding venue manager had told the female members of the bridal party about to save the bride schlepping up to the bridal suite every time she needed a moment to herself.

In the stall, Ginger sighed and thought again, this was the best day ever. Better than the day she'd got into college to study journalism, better than the day she'd got her first job, better than all that. Today, she'd found someone special and that mattered more than anything.

She hauled up her voluminous skirts but stilled when she heard some people come in.

She must pretend not to be taking tights off because that might be an 'about to have sex' sign, she thought, registering what they were talking about.

Just idle mutterings, women's room stuff.

'You don't need more blusher.'

'The base is good, though, isn't it? Glowy.'

The voices belonged to Liza and Charlene, and Ginger relaxed as the conversation meandered on. It was now well after ten and the wedding party was going strong.

Ginger would never admit it to Liza, but she was not a big fan of Charlene's. She'd entirely taken over the organising of the hen do, which they'd all attended the previous weekend. As chief bridesmaid, Ginger had set up dinner in an elegant restaurant in Dublin because Liza said she wanted 'something classy'. Despite this, Charlene had quietly booked a club for afters and a neon pink stretch limo to take them all there.

Liza had loved it, which was the most important thing – but

Ginger had felt out of place the entire evening. She'd felt she'd failed her friend. Liza must have wanted a wild night and not a sedate dinner. And what a wild night it had been, with all sorts of mad dancing, plus members of the bridal party attempting to pole dance and doing shots.

Charlene had called her a boring old cow for not joining in.

Determinedly, Ginger pushed it all out of her mind. Tonight was going to be *her* night.

She heard perfume spraying and she began wriggling again with her tights, which were as hard to get off as they had been to get into. She was nearly there, and once she was, she'd come out of the stall to ask Liza all about Stephen.

She leaned against the stall again and sighed with happiness.

For the first time in years, she felt as if she liked her body. He liked it, loved it. She would stick on some more perfume too . . .

'Oh, and really, what is Ginger like? Talk about desperation,' Charlene said.

Ginger smothered a gasp. The bitch. Charlene must fancy Stephen herself.

Well, turns out he isn't interested in twiglets but likes curvy babes instead, she thought with a satisfied grin.

She waited for Liza to stand up for her.

'I know,' sighed Liza.

Not a warm-hearted '*I know*'. More of a resigned tone. The way you spoke of a relative who went off the rails at parties and let the side down.

Ginger breathed out shakily.

'I love Ginger, but she's her own worst enemy. Won't exercise, won't diet. I've spent years trying to help her, Charlene. *Years*. You and I both know it takes effort to stay thin, but she won't and then she whines that she can't get a guy.'

Whines? In the stall, Ginger was shocked. Did she whine about not having a man to share her life?

'Sometimes I think of doing a friendship edit and getting

Ginger out of my life because she totally wrecks my head,' Liza went on. 'I hate seeing her so huge, hate watching her eat all sorts of crap and then be surprised when she gets fat. That bridesmaid's dress is a size eighteen, you know. Eighteen! If a girl in the salon was that size, she'd die! Or diet.'

'Totally,' agreed Charlene.

'She's the friend I've known the longest but I've totally moved on. You do, right?'

'Totally.'

'But ugh.' Liza's distaste was audible. 'I really didn't think she was going to slobber over poor Stephen like that. He has a lovely girlfriend, you know: fabulous skin, amazing clothes, runs half-marathons. But she's away for a work trip and I don't know how Ginger latched onto him.'

'Have you seen the way she's pushing her boobs up at him? It's embarrassing to watch,' Charlene said.

'Have I seen it?' Liza groaned. '*Everybody* can see it.'

Disbelieving, Ginger listened as *her best and oldest friend* spoke.

'I know she's desperate for a date, but really.'

'What I don't understand,' said Charlene, enjoying sticking the knife in now that it was clear Liza was amenable to it, 'is why she's your chief bridesmaid?'

Ginger felt as if the whole world had slowed.

'Ma said I had to. I've known her since I was four. Ma said Ginger was my oldest friend. But let's face it, it was fine when we were four, not anymore. Not now it's so obvious she doesn't fit into my life. She's hardly a friend like you, hon,' said Liza, and Ginger knew, from years of standing beside her best friend in bathrooms and watching Liza apply make-up in mirrors, that Liza was now putting on lipstick.

She always stretched her lips to get it into the furthest corners of her mouth and she was speaking in what Ginger thought of as her lipstick voice.

She'd heard that voice countless times: in school bathrooms

when Liza had been upset and Ginger had been the one to comfort her; after their big exams when Liza had done badly and Ginger, who could have gone and whooped it up with her pals from higher level English, had stayed and taken care of her.

'Honestly, Ma, I said. I've taken her under my wing my whole life! But Ma said I had to, what with Ginger having no mother.'

'But . . .' Charlene's voice was almost a whisper as she said it and, alone in the stall, Ginger felt herself tense because she knew just what word Charlene was going to use, '. . . she's fat. The photos! You don't need a fat bridesmaid! Liza, you're too gorgeous to need a fugly.'

A fugly – a fat and ugly friend, Ginger knew.

Liza laughed, happy at being called gorgeous, not saying that looks weren't important – all the things she said to Ginger when Ginger stared at herself in mirrors and hated what she saw.

Clearly, that was what she said to Ginger – not what she felt.

Charlene was on a roll now.

'At the fittings for the dresses, did you see the way she kept trying to hide in the dressing room?'

Stand up for me, Liza, whispered Ginger in her lonely bathroom prison.

'She's always been like that. Buys her clothes from catalogues,' Liza said dismissively, as if she understood what it was like to go into a shop and search in vain for something modern and in her size when there was always one saleslady who looked at her as if she were an alien beamed down onto Planet Thin. 'Some people just want to be fat, they hide behind it, comfort-eat and whine that they can't get thin.' She paused. 'You finished?'

'Yup,' said Charlene.

The door slammed and they were gone.

*

When she was sure she was alone, Ginger came out of her hiding place. In the mirror, she was the same Ginger as she had always been: big and curved in her dreadful pink ship of a dress. She had worn this dress for Liza, even though she had hated it. Knowing she was the biggest woman in the bridal party had sliced through her today, especially beside Liza and Charlene, who were slender in columns of cream silk and blush silk respectively rather than in enormous ballgowns.

'The sort of thing Charlene's wearing won't suit you, Ginger,' Liza had said that day in the bridal shop, standing back to assess her friend's outfit.

'Whatever you want,' Ginger had said valiantly, even though she was sure something a bit more fitted would be better than this dress with its acres of fabric and boob-enhancing qualities. But if Liza wanted her wearing this, Ginger would wear it. That's what friends did.

Friends.

She'd thought Liza was her friend.

But Liza thought she didn't want to be thin, that she hid behind her body when, really, she wanted to be seen in spite of it. For people to see the tenderness of her heart; to see that a larger physical body could as easily hide a fragile soul as a thin one.

That the outside and the inside were so terribly, terribly different.

Today, on her thirtieth birthday, it turned out that her best friend only thought of her in terms of her body weight.

Thought she was fat. That horrible word. As if being fat was the worst crime in the world.

You could be anything you wanted in this world, but you couldn't be fat. No matter what else you achieved, that wiped out the achievement or whatever was on the inside.

To add to the pain, Liza wanted to edit her friends list and Ginger hadn't made the cut.

Just like that.

Time, friendship – none of it mattered except for her weight.

Ginger wanted to cry, could feel the traitorous tears rearing up, but she wasn't going to, not now. She would not rush around, red-faced and blubbering.

Blubber and blubbering: that was her.

Oh yes, she could insult herself just as easily as Liza and Charlene did.

Ginger did self-hatred on an industrial scale.

Only she'd never expected Liza to do it too. Not after twenty-six years of friendship.

She closed her eyes and thought. Getting out of here would need a plan and she needed to be out of this hotel or she would break down completely.

She had her tiny bridesmaidy handbag: there was nothing else in the reception room. If she could sneak upstairs to her bedroom, she could speedily change into her ordinary clothes and leave. She wasn't going to talk to anyone, not explain anything. She knew she could get upstairs via the back staircase.

Summoning up the courage from somewhere in her bruised heart, she left the women's room.

To distract herself, Ginger thought of all the tough things she'd had to do in her life.

Exist in a world where she had no mother and everyone else did. Smile and pretend it didn't hurt when the girls in her class made Mother's Day cards and she couldn't. She'd made one for Great-Aunt Grace, who was not precisely motherly but who loved Ginger fiercely in her own eccentric way.

She'd braved college, scared of leaving people like Liza – what an irony – to swim in waters she was sure would be full of sleek sharks. Yet it was there that she'd found her tribe: people who liked knowledge, books, seeking things out.

Her first job: where that first, terrifying day someone had called her a 'fine big lump of a girl who'd keep a man warm at night'. Ginger hadn't run crying or screamed harassment. No, she'd begun developing her tough-girl persona.

'You can dream, old-timer,' she'd said, dredging up a wide smile, as if he hadn't hurt her to her marrow.

She'd done all that. She could do this, too.

Then she rounded a corner and reached the bit of the lobby where she needed to slip into the corridor to the back stairs.

Despite being almost hidden by a selection of giant palms, she could see the after-party guests arriving. She recognised some of Liza's outer circle, people Liza didn't really hang around with, so they wouldn't have been considered good enough to ask to the wedding but were still perfect for the after-party.

If they saw her, they would look at her dress and smile, or worse, say: 'Oh, you look lovely, Ginger.' Which was a lie, Ginger thought. A complete lie. She obviously looked terrible and everyone thought it but nobody had said it to her face.

And then she stilled. Over to one side of the lobby stood James, Liza's new husband, along with Liza, Charlene and Stephen, the man that Ginger had really thought she was going to take upstairs to her room. The man who'd asked her for a date, when he *had* a girlfriend.

He still looked handsome but also strangely conniving at the same time, and how had she not noticed that his eyes were so close together?

She was overcome with a desire to slap him, but Ginger, who had never used physical violence in her life, wanted to hit Liza even more.

Liza had betrayed her totally.

Ginger wanted to scream: *When were you going to edit me out of your life, Liza?*

The four beautiful people were laughing. Probably about her.

Stupid, sad old Ginger – fancying a man who would only want to grope her because she'd pushed herself on him.

Rage, which had been absent when she was in the toilet cubicle reeling from shock, asserted itself.

With fierce determination, she walked right up to the quartet and stood in front of them, not caring that the tears she'd tried so hard to suppress had begun to roll down her face.

'I heard you,' she said, staring at Liza, ignoring everyone else. 'I heard you in the bathroom, I was in one of the stalls. I can't believe you'd talk about me like that. I'm your oldest friend. How could you say all those things?'

Liza looked discomfited, which was something Ginger had rarely seen before.

'Well,' blustered Liza, faced with this new, angry Ginger. 'Nobody said you can't snog Stephen. Might be good for you. Get you over the drought . . .'

'What drought?' Charlene was eager to know.

'The permanent bloody drought,' said James, who looked bored. 'Let's not ruin our day, Liza,' he said to his new wife. 'Ginger, go and do the wild thing with Stephen. Get it out of your system. You need a fuck. Virginity's only for the really religious. At your age, it's embarrassing. You just need a kick-start.'

Ginger felt the words like a fist to her solar plexus.

'You've never had sex?' gasped Charlene, fascinated. 'Like, ever?'

'You told James about me,' said Ginger quietly to Liza. 'My secret.'

'We're married, now,' Liza said defensively. 'I tell him everything.'

'Liza was only trying to help,' interrupted James. 'I told Stephen because he's a decent guy and he's been around the block, you know, could give you what you want.'

He slapped Stephen on the back.

'*What I want?* Meaningless sex to get rid of my embarrassing virginity with a man who has a girlfriend? How could you?'

'Listen, Ginge,' said Stephen, wading in. 'We would have had fun, babes, we could still have some fun – don't be so heavy.'

It was the wrong word to use.

Ginger stared at him.

Heavy.

So the wrong word: a fat, heavy, pitiful virgin on her thirtieth birthday who thought she'd finally found somebody special.

Instead she was part of some cruel fix-up where everyone would laugh about her afterwards.

Satisfied that Ginger had at last had a man, Liza could happily unfriend her and the twenty-six years of knowing each other would cease to exist.

How had she ever thought Liza was her friend?

Her brothers, Mick and Declan, hated Liza, always had.

Great-Aunt Grace, her father's aunt, and her only female relative, had agreed.

'A little madam – take care of yourself around her,' she'd warned. Grace was wise. Utterly eccentric, but wise.

They were all devastatingly correct and it had taken this for her to see it: this public humiliation.

Ginger swivelled and walked towards the corridor where the back stairs lay.

Nobody called after her, nobody said 'please come back'.

Liza, who could have hurried after her in the high but comfortable shoes Ginger had helped her choose, did none of those things.

They let Ginger go alone and she kept walking, ramrod straight, not once looking back.

At the small staircase, she went up to her floor, sweating as she hurried.

Finally, she was in her hotel bedroom – had it really only been a few hours before that she'd been here getting ready, so happy for her friend? Why hadn't she come up here to take off her damn tights?

Then she wouldn't have heard those horrible words.

But she'd had to hear them, Ginger thought sadly.

Fate had wanted her to. *The truth shall set you free*, she thought, remembering her Gloria Steinem from college, but wow, it was utterly devastating. She would need a lot more time for it to merely piss her off.

She began to laugh, and then the laugh turned to tears as she thought that, really, there couldn't be anyone having as bad a birthday in the whole city as her. And then she closed her eyes, and let the tears fall.

I wish that next year, everything in my life could be totally different.

PART TWO

One Month Earlier

Callie

Callie Reynolds sat in the cosmetic surgeon's chair and winced.

This was going to hurt, no doubt about it.

'I think you need a little more filler . . .' Frederica, the cosmetic surgeon pointed, '. . . just there. A little lift.'

Callie held the small mirror up to her face and knew why she never had enlarging mirrors in her bathroom. Up this close in the heavily magnified dermatologist's mirror, she looked about seventy and her skin was as pitted as Pompeii on Day Two of the disaster. And as for the increasing growth of fine facial hairs . . .

If it kept up this way, she'd look like a baby chicken by the time she was sixty.

Once, sixty had seemed old, but not now. She would be fifty in a month.

Fifty. She'd never thought she'd care and yet, now that it was around the corner, she found that she did. Worse, she kept thinking of her family and all the bridges she'd burned.

Was that why people hated the big birthdays? Not the age but the retrospection?

'I don't want to look *done*,' she said again to Frederica, who was the best in Dublin.

'Nobody who comes to me looks *done*,' said Frederica indignantly and then they both grinned. They'd often had this conversation. Just across the hall was a dermatologist who specialised in turning out people who looked expensively retouched from a distance of fifty yards when viewed even by people who were legally blind. They came out of her office with big lips, puffy cheeks and glassily smooth foreheads that couldn't move a muscle even at the onset of an earthquake.

'Sorry,' apologised Callie. 'I'm just anxious, Frederica. I feel old, irritable and anxious.'

'Hormones,' said Frederica firmly. 'Have you seen anyone for HRT yet?'

'No. It's like admitting I need it. Being on the verge of menopause makes me feel so . . .' She searched for the word. 'Ancient. Dried up. Unfeminine.' There, she'd said it.

'We all fight ageing the best we can, Callie. You could be mourning the lack of fertility. And for the moods with peri-menopause, you need help. If you needed insulin, you'd take it. I've given you the name of the best gynaecologist I know, please see her.'

'I know,' muttered Callie. 'I didn't know it was going to be like this. I thought I'd sink into elegant fiftyhood and, instead, I just feel like a dried-out prune on the inside, with no sex drive. I've no energy and zero interest in the party my poor husband is planning.'

'That's sweet of him.' Frederica went to the fridge where she kept her magical ampoules and filled up a syringe.

'Yes, he's very good,' agreed Callie, even though she knew that Jason was driven to have the party for them, the fabulous Reynolds family, rather than as a love letter to her.

Jason, bless him, loved to show off.

She got ready for the pain as the doctor flicked on her special light, put on her glasses and looked closely at her.

'So, where are you having this fabulous fiftieth birthday party?'
'At home.'

It would all look amazing, though, she thought, almost tearfully. Jason would stop at nothing to make sure it would be sensational. He loved her. He wanted to show off both her and their fabulous house.

So why didn't she feel more excited about it all? What the heck was wrong with her?

Afterwards, Callie snuck out the back entrance to the surgeon's rooms wearing her sunglasses. She walked coolly and elegantly to her car, like the former model she was. Not that she'd been a Chanel favourite or anything like it. No, she'd modelled in Ireland in the eighties when she'd been the muse for an Irish designer who'd never made it on the international stage but had been an utter genius. Simon had been kind, clever, gay, and the AIDS plague had taken him from the world too soon.

Simon had made her name and he'd understood her, intuitively recognised her anxieties and that just because she looked like Grace Kelly didn't mean she came from the same social strata.

'Beauty, darling, is your ticket out of here,' he used to say when he was draping fabric on her in his small fourth-floor studio from which the spires of Dublin could be seen. 'Ignore the bitches with the money who might mock your accent – I was hardly born with a silver spoon in my mouth.'

Callie had jerked in astonishment and got a pin stuck into her by mistake for her trouble.

'Sorry, just don't move. Elocution lessons. Changes the grubby tin spoon into a silver one.'

Simon had been the one to get her to change her name, from Claire to Callie.

'Sounds better, different,' he'd said. 'You've got to stand out. Callie's the shortened version of Calliope, tell people that.'

'Callie-what? They'll know I'm lying.'

Simon had fixed her with a knowing look: 'Everybody lies, sweetpea. Didn't you know?'

She'd had the elocution lessons. Had read books, had gone to galleries and museums, read the papers earnestly.

She could now move in the higher echelons of the rich with ease, but the thing that had transformed her from being a working-class girl with notions had been her relationship with Ricky.

Wild, beautiful and often emotionally lost, he was a posh boy from her home town who had a guitar, big dreams and sat writing songs all day. At night, he prowled the pubs and clubs, hating himself for not being successful yet, worrying that his parents had been right and he should have gone into medicine, like his father. Poor Ricky, he'd always been searching for something and he found it in Callie, with her wise eyes and her tender soul.

They fell into each other's arms and in love. Somewhere along the way, Ricky had found fame. Then, almost inevitably, he'd found drugs, and Callie had been left behind.

One of his band's most famous songs was 'Calliope', an ode to her, and she never listened to it when it came on the radio. She'd switch channels, pushing down all the emotions the music conjured up. Of another time, another her. When she still saw her family, her darling Ma and Aunt Phil, and even poor Freddie, who'd tried rehab twice but still couldn't escape the power of drugs.

At home, Callie drove the Range Rover into the underground garage and made her way round Jason's Ferrari. Bright red.

'The ultimate mid-life crisis,' he'd joked as it had been delivered, and Callie had thought 'yes, indeedy' but said nothing.

As long as buying a penis-shaped car was the worst of Jason's crises, then she didn't mind. Big boy toys she could handle.

In the house, she heard the hum of the vacuum.

Brenda was there. Great. With Brenda, she didn't have to pretend.

Without worrying if she was red-faced, Callie walked through the basement, past the wine cave, then up to the kitchen, which was the cosiest part of the house. It was all rich creams, wooden countertops and scarlet gingham cushions, like the American fantasy kitchens in magazines she used to read when they had no money.

'You look like a pincushion,' teased Brenda, when she turned off the vacuum.

'It keeps your eyes off the rest of the wrinkles and my furry face,' deadpanned Callie.

'If you have wrinkles and fur, I'm turning into an ancient kiwi fruit,' said Brenda, reaching into her pocket for her cigarettes.

Brenda was half-Irish, half-Brazilian, and five years older than Callie. To her disgust, she had fair Irish skin instead of the honeyed Brazilian variety like her dad, but she still loved to sit in the sun and smoked forty a day, neither of which were skin or healthcare tips recommended by Dr Frederica.

'Give up the fags, then,' teased Callie.

'That is an old, old song, baby,' was Brenda's reply and she went to the back door, opened it, pulled out her cigarettes with the ease of practice, and lit up. 'If himself comes in and complains, tell him to eff off,' she added.

Jason, an ex-smoker, was notoriously anti-smoking in anyone else.

'But Jason's in work,' said Callie, putting a cup under the boiling water tap to make herself some tea.

He was gone every morning at half six and only the direst emergencies got him back before six p.m.

'No.' Brenda sucked on her cigarette like her life depended on it. 'He's here. Came back half an hour ago and is in the study roaring into the phone.'

'What?'

'Yeah, must be some big crisis. I made him coffee. Don't think he even noticed me.'

Callie took her tea and wandered towards the study. From outside the door, she could indeed hear her husband shouting into the phone. Not his posh voice, the rounded vowels were gone: he was husky-voiced, enraged and spoke like the man from Ballyglen who'd been brought up the hard way.

'Just make it fucking work! What do you think I pay you for, you little shit!'

Callie shivered, the anxiety rushing through her again. The rage in his voice wasn't good.

There was obviously something wrong.

She'd love to ask, but Jason never talked about work.

Annoyingly, when she said anything, he'd snap, 'just business stuff', and stalk off into the study, dismissing her, which she hated.

But this shouting – this was new. Something was up? Was it Jason himself?

It was a niggle in the back of her mind, a shiver of awareness that something in their relationship had shifted. If his irritation was just business, fine. Yet in some deep part of herself that Callie didn't want to look too closely into, she wondered could her husband – faithful always – be straying?

Brenda, who was so cynical she should have run for election, would probably say she wasn't in the least surprised.

And Evelyn . . . Telling Evelyn would mean admitting that, after years of watching Evelyn get over Rob, finally Callie was in the same boat.

The next day, she and Evelyn went to Pilates, and afterwards, Callie was ready: 'Coffee?'

'Definitely,' said Evelyn.

They walked down the road to a chichi little café that served every coffee known to woman as well as a wonderful variety of paleo/gluten-free/dairy-free snacks. God forbid that any woman in her lululemon gear ordered a plain old bun.

'We are about to undo all the good work we did,' Evelyn said cheerfully, looking at the menu once they'd found a table and ordered coffees.

'Yeah,' said Callie absently.

Ev, who had known her for a very long time, said: 'What's up?'

Callie rested her elbows on the table.

'It's Jason, isn't it?'

'I, oh – I don't know. I might be imagining it,' blurted out Callie.

'Tell me.'

68

'You're the only person I can tell. He's so distant lately, he's out a lot and—'

'You're wondering what that means,' Evelyn finished for her.

'Yes.' Callie couldn't help it, she nibbled her thumb, working her way at a tough bit of skin.

'Go on.'

'I hoped that maybe it was a hassle with work and things he needed to do at weekends and late-night dinners and—'

The coffee arrived and Callie put off finger-nibbling for the relief of stirring a quarter spoon of sugar into hers.

'And?' pushed Evelyn.

'I feel something's wrong. I have nothing to go on, Ev, but it *feels* wrong . . .'

Evelyn fiddled with her coffee spoon for a moment. Displacement activity.

'You think he's got a girlfriend, right?'

Callie looked down and hoped she wouldn't start crying, not now, with half the Pilates class close by.

'First, I don't know anything, Callie, and if I did, I'd tell you. I wished I'd trusted my instincts from the start. It was always like that with Rob when he was seeing someone new. He'd become totally involved with her and there would be lots of' – Evelyn put her fingers in the air to make quote marks – '*dinners with clients* and *last-minute meetings*.' When I found out the first time, there had been a weekend trip away because someone they were working with had tickets to the opera in Milan and they needed to cement the relationship. Rob. Opera. As if!' She rolled her eyes.

Callie drank some of her coffee as she listened but it tasted bitter.

She had consoled Evelyn plenty after she and Rob had broken up, but there was a difference between listening to your dear friend talk about betrayal and facing it yourself.

'I knew for years that Rob was a serial cheater – not that we ever discussed it, how stupid was that? – but the real Rob would eventually come back to me and the kids. We'd have a glorious few months before it would all start again.'

'Why *didn't* you discuss it?' said Callie and then thought *pot, kettle, black*. Why hadn't she confronted Jason? Because she didn't want to hear what he had to say. Hearing him say the words and imagining it going on were two very different things to deal with.

Evelyn sighed. 'I didn't want to, that's why. I was stupid and needy. I wanted to be with Rob because I loved him. I told myself that we had kids together and a history . . . Eventually, I ran out of space in my head for all the lies. One Friday afternoon, when we were all supposed to be going to a pizza restaurant that night, he rang to say he'd had to fly to London suddenly and he'd be away till Sunday.'

Evelyn stared into the distance, remembering.

'I just flipped. I yelled at him that I was sick of his girl-friends and all the lying. He blustered, told me I was wrong and I hung up. Gave him time. Time to choose. Time to get on the plane and come back home. To us.'

Callie reached over and grabbed her friend's hand. She knew what had happened.

Rob hadn't come home. He'd stayed away.

'Rob was an idiot, Evelyn, you know that.'

'Yes, but I have to pretend it was all mutual to the kids be-cause you can't punish them,' Evelyn said with the fluidity of someone who had told herself this often enough. 'Although I'd say the poor counsellor I saw is now deaf from all my screech-ing. But I didn't screech at home with the boys. I went off-site. That's important – keep your nervous breakdown out of the house.'

Evelyn laughed without humour.

'Tell me about it,' she went on. 'Gut instinct?'

Callie sipped a bit of her coffee.

'My gut says something's up and what else can it be? It's hard to put my finger on it, but Jason has been working late a lot and he's stressed. His picture is under the words "emotionally absent" in the dictionary.'

She realised she felt relieved to be saying this out loud.

'He's been away for a few weekends and he never used to work weekends, never.'

They both considered this.

Callie backtracked a bit.

'Of course, you know how he loves going out and how he and Rob liked to have a dinner together once a month with us,' she said, feeling suddenly guilty because once upon a time it had been Evelyn and Rob at those dinners and now it was Rob and the much younger Anka.

'It's OK, you can say it,' said Evelyn. 'I'm over Rob, it's fine. I know you guys go out because he'll phone and mention it, and I go out into the garden and pour salt on the slugs eating my plants. Great for inner rage.'

They both laughed.

'Callie, I honestly don't think that Jason has been cheating on you. I think I'd know.'

'How would you?' said Callie, desperate for consolation.

'Rob and I talk all the time, mainly about the kids but he goes on about work and I think there's something hassling them with the office right now. I honestly think that's it and trust me, I would tell you if I thought Jason was seeing someone.'

She was quiet for a moment as if considering how to put this. 'Rob's a good liar but I'd pick up on it if he was hiding something about Jason. And he's always admired you. He talks about you, Jason and Poppy like you're a perfect family.' Evelyn smiled wryly. 'I think he fancied you a million years ago. I used to feel jealous of you in the early days.'

'No,' said Callie stunned.

'I did actually,' said Ev, 'sorry. It's really stupid, but you're so beautiful and had such an exotic background—'

'What? Ballyglen and a council house?' said Callie, laughing with relief and disbelief combined.

'You hid that very well, honey,' said Evelyn. 'I felt totally intimidated until I met you and got to know you – obviously.'

'Got to know what a fake I was behind all that mysterious facade,' said Callie, smiling genuinely for the first time since they'd left the Pilates class.

'Rob always tells me about the nights out you four have together.'

'Ouch.' Callie grimaced. 'That is thoughtless in a whole new dimension. Apart from that first time I had to meet Anka and I told you so, I never discuss the dinners in case it hurts you, and besides, you know I'd far rather be out with you.'

'You're a kind friend who worries about my feelings, but he's an ex-husband, Callie,' said Evelyn. 'Thoughtless is pretty much what he does. He thinks it's quite reasonable to say to me that he and Anka are going to the Seychelles for a week when I'm worrying about how the windows are rotting and need re-placing. Then, he starts telling me about the villa with private butler and I can truly see how women kill their ex-husbands and bury them under the patio.'

'He left you enough money in the settlement, didn't he?' said Callie, astonished at the revelation about rotting windows and the implication that this could be a problem. Rob was rich. How were Evelyn and his children living in a house that needed work they weren't able to afford? She'd never asked this before. Finances were so personal. But then, Evelyn had never told her that Rob discussed dinners with Anka, Callie and Jason before, either.

'He gave me more or less enough money,' Evelyn agreed, 'although he hid a lot of it.'

Callie was stunned. She'd just assumed Rob had been decent to Evelyn: Jason had implied as much.

'I felt ashamed. I just couldn't tell you,' admitted Evelyn. 'And I mean, you're married to Jason, Rob's friend and partner, how could I possibly say, *I think my husband is hiding shedloads of money from me. Funny, right?* So my lawyer did a little bit of forensic accountancy work in order to track down the money, but there comes a point when you have to stop. Besides, Rob was all over it and said to my lawyer, "Let's do a deal for a lump sum rather than alimony." It's OK, we're happy with that, he provides for the kids pretty well. I have locked-in college funds for them. But the house is old and the maintenance is a nightmare.'

Callie inhaled sharply. Evelyn had gone so far as to make sure her sons had their college money sorted – she must really not trust Rob.

'I'm stunned, Ev,' she said.

In her mind, she was thinking about Jason and the possibility of him trying to hide money from her in a divorce.

This must have been written all over her face.

'Jason adores you,' Evelyn said instantly. 'I truly believe that. Just don't do what I did – ignore your fears. If you're really worried, say something. I let Rob carry on with other women for years and he began to think it was normal: having women flirt with him, sleeping with them.'

'That's not what marriage is supposed to be about,' Callie said quietly. 'It's supposed to be forsaking all others.'

Evelyn shrugged. 'Rob was always a bit of a player, Callie, but I honestly don't think Jason is. He adores you.'

'I know,' said Callie, relief in her heart. It must be just business upsetting her husband. The alternative was horrible. What would she do if the lens of his admiration was turned away from her? How could she cope with that?

And yet, did she want to start a conversation with her husband about the possibility that he was cheating on her? She had nothing to go on, nothing. Perhaps Evelyn was right and it was just work. Rob would know and he appeared to tell Ev everything.

And all marriages went through ups and downs. It couldn't all be a bed of roses. Even roses had thorns.

Sam

Mamma Mia!

I look like I've eaten a basketball.

I look pregnant – at last!!

Sam stood sideways in the mirror of her bedroom – not something she had ever spent much time doing before she got pregnant because she was tall and annoyingly slim, as her little sis, Joanne, liked to say – and examined the bump protruding from her body.

She hadn't thought she was showing too much for the first six months, but now she'd hit the eight-month mark it was a whole other story. She, the woman who couldn't conceive, looked hugely pregnant and it had happened almost overnight.

Showing was one of the secret pregnancy words. *Carrying* was another. Joanne had explained it to her and this blissfully arcane pregnancy language had come in handy during the early months.

'You're carrying to the front,' the woman in the corner shop had said out of the blue when she was fifteen weeks. 'Definitely a boy.'

Sam had nearly dropped the milk and the emergency chocolate biscuits she'd gone into QuikShop for in the first place.

'Do I look pregnant?' she asked the woman eagerly, as she put her stuff on the small counter.

'Ah, love, when you're my age, I can almost spot the pregnancies five minutes after they've had sex.'

'Oh, right.'

'Any other kids?'

74

'Er, no, this is my first,' said Sam, then waited for the Sage of QuikShop to sigh and mutter about women leaving it too late to have babies because they were obsessed with their careers.

Half the planet appeared to think nearly forty was old to get pregnant.

But the woman on the QuikShop counter had said no such thing. 'Good plan to wait till you have a decent job, love,' she said shrewdly. 'Fellas don't tend to hang around. Better to have a job so when he legs it, you've got a few quid coming in.'

'There is that,' agreed Sam with a grin, thinking that Ted better not have any plan to leg it or she would nail his kneecaps to the floor. They'd waited so long for this miracle.

In front of the mirror now, Sam twisted a bit and combed her fingers through her dark hair – long, glossy, blow-dried straight in Speed Salon twice a week and fixed by herself today. Day two of the salon-dried hair used to last perfectly.

But not now the baby was kicking like a soccer superstar and Sam tossed and turned in bed at night, so her dark hair went from a sleek long bob to Little Orphan Annie fright wig over-night. Now, every morning, she had to drag herself out of bed half an hour earlier to wash her hair and get the straightening irons out.

And she was so tired. Growing a human being was so much more tiring than she had imagined possible. How had the human race survived this long?

As for the breastfeeding lark . . . she was terrified of it. Other mothers-to-be might decide easily to bottle-feed but Sam had the weight of years of trying for a baby behind her. Breast, as every advert reminded her, was best, and she was scared of messing that up too.

She asked her sister for an opinion.

'I breastfed for six months with all three girls, but that was just me. There's enough pressure on women to get everything right. Do what feels right to you,' said Joanne firmly.

Sam couldn't explain that the person pressurising her to get everything right was herself.

Their mother, who could certainly spell the word maternal – possibly in Ancient Greek as well – had never worried about such a thing. She'd gone back to work as soon as she possibly could.

Ted stirred in the bed and Sam looked up from the mirror.

In sleep, he looked even more handsome: a cross between a Southern-talkin' Matthew McConaughey and that guy who did the aftershave ads for Dolce and had an eight-pack. Once, Sam would have been tempted to sinuously insert herself into bed with her husband and indulge in some hot, speedy sex.

Ha! Who was that woman and where had she gone?

Instead of any sex-related activities, she wriggled into insanely expensive black maternity leggings. Who knew that a roundy bit added on in the belly department could increase the price of leggings by 250 per cent?

She added wedge boots and a floaty charcoal shirt that swung around her body. Businesslike and pregnant: result. Her face was still slim, with its firm chin, almond-shaped dark eyes like her father's, and a mouth that allowed her to wear power red lipsticks when she wore power business suits.

It was nearly seven. She was running late. Sam liked to be in the office by eight.

Ted moaned a little and rolled over, happily.

Sam grinned evilly and contemplated kicking him. It was his baby too. He was not getting fat, sweaty and up four times a night to pee. His hair didn't look like he'd been electrocuted in the night.

Strange women in QuikShop who had never before spoken to him did not suddenly strike up conversations with him. Pregnancy had not turned him into a commercial property.

No, his friends thumped him triumphantly on the back as if Sam being pregnant was a sign of wild virility and a willy fit for a porn movie.

'Dat's my boy!'

'Whadda man!'

Sam wished she'd gone in for baseball in school so she'd have a bat with which to whack them all over the head.

Sam looked at her reflection in the mirror. She could handle being a mother. Women had been doing it for years, after all. She *had* to stop worrying – that would be bad for the baby.

For most of her working life, Sam had worked in banking, where she got to use her master's in economics. She'd worked in a major bank for the past ten years until finally, worn out by fertility treatment and office politics, she'd decided to restructure her life.

She did a part-time philanthropic course and, over a year, decided that she'd like to work in the charity sector.

Ted backed her totally, as did her father.

'You've got to follow your heart, love,' said Ted as they talked about it endlessly and what it might mean for them financially.

'Yes, but what about the money? Following my heart won't pay the mortgage, will it?'

He held her close and kissed her on her temple, which was somehow one of the most comforting gestures she'd ever felt. 'We'll manage. We can take in lodgers. I vote for good-looking young women from cold countries who can't cope with Dublin's wild heat and have to strip off as soon as they get home from work.'

'No, young *men* from cold countries,' said Sam, snuggling closer. 'Ones who do extreme gym time and are spectacularly handsome but have no idea of how gorgeous they are, and spend all their time having showers and walking round afterwards with towels hanging off their hips, showing off . . . what's that bit of muscle just below the abs, the deep V if someone works out a lot?'

'Maybe no lodgers, then . . .?'

Sam laughed, delighted with her teasing. 'Deal. But really, money . . .?'

'We'll manage. If you hate charity work, you can always prostrate yourself on the altar of big banking again. You are eminently employable. Plus, you have the iPhone footage of your boss at the Christmas party three years ago, right?' he joked.

Sam laughed again. She loved this man. 'Blackmail my boss if I hate charity work? Me likee. Now that's a working plan.'

They had savings and a financial portfolio that Sam managed herself. Their only big spending over the past few years had been fertility treatments and Sam would never allow herself to see it as wasted money. Trying for a beloved child had been their dream: to belittle the money spent on it would be to belittle that lovely, but failed, dream.

Sam's search for a new life led to her discreetly checking out which charities were hiring.

Then she heard about Cineáltas. A forty-five-year-old charity set up to help sufferers with dementia, Cineáltas meant kindness in the Irish language and had been established by Edward Beveldon, a wealthy Anglo-Irish man whose beloved wife, Maud, had been ravaged by the disease. Edward had long gone and his son, Maurice, now past seventy, ran the charity himself.

By all accounts, Maurice's father had been a fabulous man – able to persuade rich people to put vast sums into the charity. But under Maurice's aegis, the organisation had fallen apart. Until the hugely successful but highly reclusive businessman, Andrew Doyle, had come along.

Joanne had pushed her to apply for the top job.

'I'm a newbie at this. Presumably he's hiring more than a chief executive,' Sam said.

'Sure he is, but you should aim high,' Joanne said. 'Go for the big job. Get your power red lipstick out and go in all guns blazing.'

In her interview, Sam had found herself almost talking herself out of a job.

'What I want to know,' she said, facing down Andrew, who was the entire interview panel, 'is why you don't try to merge Cineáltas with the Alzheimer's Society of Ireland. That makes more sense.'

Andrew gave her the cool look she had already read about in many business magazines, a look that was supposed to send executives scurrying away with fear.

'It's because I want to set up an entirely new sort of charity,' he said. 'I want to focus on serious corporate fundraising for research as well as offering the sort of support that my parents got in the final days. I want to link up with research teams all over the world so we can make a difference worldwide.'

'That's a big challenge, but I'm ready for a challenge now,' said Sam thoughtfully, speaking as she would to an equal, a fact which she subsequently decided had secured her the job.

'I liked you,' said Andrew later when he offered her the job. 'You were straight up, didn't talk any bullshit. I like that in a person.'

Sam had heard those words before. Various bosses over the years had said they liked her straightforwardness and then it would turn out that they hadn't liked her straightforwardness. In men, yes. In women – no, no, no.

Men who were straightforward were strong and leadership material. Women were just bitches.

But Andrew bucked the trend. It transpired that he genuinely liked her ideas and her directness.

She'd only been in the job two months when she learned she was pregnant, and had instantly rung Andrew to tell him.

'You're not fired – it's not legal, anyway,' he said, in the blunt way she was becoming accustomed to. It made a lot of sense to her that Andrew was not married.

'I know the law, Andrew,' she said patiently. 'But I have waited a long time for this baby and I don't want to sully my pregnancy or my work here with stress or any question that I've

79

conned you by coming in and immediately getting pregnant.'

'You were the best person for the job,' he said simply. 'We'll work it out, you're good at this. You'll need a deputy for when you're off. Organise it. Bye.'

Which was as good as a balloon-filled *Congratulations On Getting Pregnant!* baby shower from anyone else.

Since then, she'd been doing her very best to turn around the rather archaic ship that was Cineáltas and transform it into something entirely new.

There was so much Sam wanted to do, because the more she worked there, the more she saw the potential for greatness: fundraising in the corporate world to put dementia on an emotional par with searching for a cure for cancer.

'Because people of all ages get cancer,' she'd said to Ted earnestly. 'They put their hands in their pockets to pay for research for cancer, but dementia . . . it's something that happens in the distance. People don't like to think about it. They might think about their parents maybe or their grandparents getting it. They honestly don't think about themselves getting it. To use marketing-speak, which sounds hideous in this context, it's not "sexy". But imagine if research we'd helped to fund finally managed to do something to reverse dementia, a philanthropic cure – that would be spectacular.'

She only had a few days left of work before her maternity leave kicked in. She'd found a wonderful man, a former Red Cross guy called Dave, to take over when she was off, but she still had so much work to do before she left.

The offices of Cineáltas were deserted at eight when she got there, so she flicked on the lights, went into her office and surveyed her perfectly tidy desk.

Sam's mother had taught her the value of neatness in the office.

'I hate mess,' her mother used to say.

When Sam had been a teenager and had, unhappily and inevitably, been a pupil in the school of which her mother was headmistress, she had been into the head's office many times, never in trouble, though. She knew better than that.

'I expect the absolute best from you, Samantha,' her mother liked to say, an uncoded warning.

'Should we get that chiselled on a piece of stone for her gift?' Joanne joked one Christmas.

'No point,' Sam had replied. 'Mother would fail to see the irony and hang it up in her office.'

'No, at home,' Joanne said gleefully. 'It could be the family motto.'

On those trips into her mother's office, everything had been just so. No photos of her family because her mother did not believe in displaying personal photographs.

'Family pictures in an office are unprofessional,' she'd say and briefly mention a time when women were second-class citizens in the field of work and how no chance should be given to naysayers to accuse them of sentimentality.

Sam reflected now, as she looked at her perfect desk, that she owed her sense of organisation to her mother.

Today, she was interviewing for a digital marketing manager.

By quarter to nine, Rosalind, the grey-haired ladylike assistant she shared with Andrew, was in.

'Can I make you a cup of tea? One must mind baby,' Rosalind said.

'One of my herbal ones, perhaps,' Sam said, grimacing at the thought of more herbal tea.

'Shall I bring you some biscuits?'

'That would be lovely, Rosalind, thank you.'

Sam was grateful that at least her assistant was not one of the many who felt that they alone knew all the information about babies – from feeding them when they were in the womb to feeding them when they were out of the womb. If Sam got one more email from someone recommending a book about baby food/sleep/toilet training/good schools to apply to, she'd scream.

Biscuits and herbal tea arrived and Sam prepared herself for the first interview.

By the third one, she was wondering had the recruitment agency had a bit of a breakdown. All of these people were spectacularly qualified as digital marketing managers, but she didn't see a hint of charitable nature in any of them.

Not that you had to want to live in an organically grown yurt on the side of a windswept hill and wear hair shirts to work in a charity, but it helped if you had a desire to make the world a better place.

The charity was paying a reasonable salary, but possibly people could get more in other sectors, so this would have to be a job for somebody who wanted to give something back. That was certainly why Sam had done it.

That and the desire to step off the treadmill of all those years in the higher echelons of banking, where life was something to be measured out in hours and slivers of weekends.

No wonder, she sometimes thought darkly, it had taken leaving her old job to get pregnant. Mother Nature had clearly decided that anyone who worked quite as hard as she did would not have the energy or the heart to conceive a baby. She knew plenty of female executives who were wishing they could work part-time because the exhaustion of parenting, work and housework was draining them as successfully as vampires did in horror movies.

'The slow disintegration of the "doing it all" generation,' one banking friend had called it. 'Which won't end until guys have the babies.'

'The last candidate is waiting,' announced Rosalind formally.

'Thank you,' said Sam.

'Shall I tell him you have been a bit delayed, and you could possibly lie down for a minute?' Rosalind pinked up at this blurring of professional lines. 'You do look a little peaky.'

'No, I'm fine, but could I have . . .' Blast it, she needed some sugar and caffeine, despite her plans to have no coffee at all during her pregnancy. 'A small coffee, if you wouldn't mind: just half a spoon with a little bit of milk and half a sugar.'

'Of course,' said Rosalind, who had never married nor had children and thus had not been brainwashed by the litany of things pregnant women should or shouldn't do.

The coffee helped enormously and felt like a double espresso to her out-of-caffeine-touch system, and so too did the next candidate. He was young, younger than the others, and full of energy. His CV was impressive, his ideas amazing and even more, he mentioned the elephant in the room.

'I know this isn't the most well paid job in the world,' he said. 'I mean, I could get better money somewhere else, but at this point in my life that's not what I'm looking for.'

Sam sighed somewhere deep inside herself.

His name was Gareth and he was saving for a deposit on a house. 'I know this isn't the job where I'm going to become rich, but something is calling out to me in the charity sector.'

He had a round face, a thatch of blond hair and an engaging smile.

Sam felt that tingle inside her, the tingle that her sister was always talking about: trust your instincts, Joanne used to say; it was how they had both fallen in love. Sam had fallen for Ted instinctively. Joanne certainly hadn't got the motto from their mother, Jean, who did more of a 'what would the parents/board of governors/neighbours think' sort of thing.

'I'll tell you what,' said Sam now, smiling at Gareth, 'you're a wonderful candidate. I think a second interview would be a very good plan.'

'Really?' said Gareth. 'Oh wow, that's just amazing, I can't believe it, I think I'll phone my mum.'

Sam hoped he wasn't making this adorableness up, because he was just perfect.

At that precise moment, she realised that if she had heard

good news she wouldn't have wanted to phone her mum, she'd have phoned Ted, Joanne or her dad. What if the same thing happened with her and this beloved baby? What if she was a hopeless mother and turned into a clone of her own mother: cold and unmaternal? Sam shivered: *please no, anything but that*.

But instead of letting any of that doubt show on her face, she beamed a confident smile at Gareth. Fake it till you make it, that was her motto.

At half seven on a bright summer's morning the next day, Sam and Ted sat in the consultant's waiting room along with lots of other pregnant women and their partners.

Despite the early hour, Sam's dad had texted at six: *Good luck to you both. Phone me when you're out, love Dad.*

From her mother, who knew about the last-minute scan in case the baby was breech as Sam's own doctor now suspected, there had been no communication.

From Ted's mother, Vera, who had three grandchildren already and operated on a lovely non-hassle mother-in-law style of relationship, there had been a speedy phone call the night before.

'I'm saying a novena,' she'd told Sam.

Vera had a novena or a special prayer for everything. 'I know you don't believe in that sort of thing, lovie, but I'm doing it. Father McIntyre has said a Mass for you. I've another cardigan knitted, too. Cream this time with a hint of yellow.'

Sam had teared up.

'Vera, you're so good.'

She got so weepy these days and now, with the scan, she felt extra teary. She was an old mother: things went wrong. She was half expecting billboards out every time she appeared near the hospital – *Elderly mother en route. Should geriatrics have babies? Public debate later.*

Who knew what this scan would bring.

But Vera kept repeating the magic words: 'Don't worry.

You'll be fine, Sam. You're strong and healthy. You'll be fine.'

To keep her mind off potential problems, she thought about a daft conversation she and Joanne had had about hair, of all things. Sam said she'd have to get up extra early when she went back to work after Baby Bean was born in order to get her hair blow-dried.

'You are *so* not going to do that,' said Joanne, when she heard about that plan. 'Getting up earlier than is absolutely required will be a nightmare and you are going to be in severe sleep deprivation.'

'But you know I can't do my own hair and I can't go into work looking like I've been plugged in,' said Sam. 'You have normal hair – I have insane hair. I have spent my whole life battling it.'

'You'll stop caring when you have a baby,' said Joanne, and added ominously: 'Babies change everything.'

'Of course, the baby is going to change a huge amount, but you know I'm still going to be me and Ted is going to be Ted. We're going to have a normal life.'

'Yeah, right,' said Joanne, straight-faced. 'You're going to be the only woman on the planet whose life is not utterly changed by the birth of a baby,' and she'd laughed.

Joanne was brilliant at rolling with whatever plan came along. Sam had been really good at crisis management when she'd worked in the bank, but baby crises . . .? They were an unknown.

Sam breathed deeply. She had to stop with this negative self-talk. She was going to be able to handle it fine. She and Ted were clever, intelligent people and babies were a normal part of life.

It was going to be fine.

This wisdom was going to be the one bonus to being an older mother.

Finally, the scan was over and when a relieved Sam had emptied her bladder, sitting on the loo till she thought she'd welded herself to it, she and Ted waited again to see her obstetrician.

Dr Laurence looked the way she always did at first: glasses on, eyes focused on notes as if she was about to diagnose something dreadful.

'Yes,' said the doctor finally. 'Baby's doing well. Might have been in the breech position but has shifted back. I know you're worried about your age.'

Sam nodded.

Ted squeezed her hand.

'We've gone through so much fertility-wise over the past few years and it makes me terribly nervous to hear about the risks, even though I do need to know them.'

'But you and your baby are going to be fine from the looks of this scan,' said the obstetrician. 'Baby's progressing well, in the correct percentile growth-wise, all good.'

'Yes,' said Ted, squeezing her hand, again. 'Fine. That's wonderful news, thank you.'

As they walked out of the clinic, they both sent joyful text messages: to Sam's father, to her sister Joanne, to Ted's mother. They spread the news wherever it needed to go. Seconds later the phone rang.

'Darling Sam!' said Joanne. 'I'm so thrilled! I was worried, I know it's crazy – I mean, when you have to have extra scans, you worry.'

'I am patenting worry,' said Sam. 'But it's all perfect. Oh, got to go, Dad's phoning.'

'My dearest Sam, I am so pleased for you and Ted,' said her father, audible in every part of his voice.

Sam could hear Ted on his phone talking to his mother and she could hear Vera's voice excitedly saying, '. . . the relief! Did you find out whether it's a boy or a girl, because really I'd love to know what colour to knit the cardigans. I'm doing creams, whites and yellows, but it would be lovely to know either way . . .'

Sam grinned. Vera was not a woman for delayed gratification.

'We didn't, Ma,' said Ted.

It was a full ten minutes before they were able to progress any further and they went into a little tea shop to have tea for Sam and a strong coffee for Ted.

They held hands and smiled at each other, not needing to say anything but just happy it was working out. Miracles did happen. The phone buzzed and Sam at first thought of ignoring it. It was only half eight in the morning, she thought, looking at the number and seeing Andrew, her boss's name on the small screen.

'Surely he can wait?' Ted said mildly.

'I suppose,' said Sam. 'I just want to cherish this moment,' and then normality kicked in. 'No,' she said, 'I'll answer.' Everything was rushing through her head, the wonderful news of the scan and the sense that perhaps, just perhaps, she and Ted would have this glorious Baby Bean. Then her conscience took over – after all, she was going to be on a certain amount of maternity leave after she'd had the baby, and when she had taken the job in the first place, she hadn't been pregnant. Employers were rarely delirious with staff who got pregnant soon into a new job. Even though Andrew had been very accommodating about it, he needn't have and . . .

She picked up the phone.

'Hello, Andrew, how are you?' she said cheerfully.

'Sam, I need you in the office immediately,' he said.

'What's wrong?' said Sam, slipping instantly into work mode.

'You know the south-east part of the organisation? The bit we thought had been closed off? Well, it transpires it had a special bank account with a credit card nobody knew about and, finally, the last remaining volunteer from some speck on the map called Ballyglen phoned Rosalind this morning to say she was sorry about the money and she'd pay it all back—'

'Pay all what back?'

'The fifty-five thousand euros of donations she'd been si-phoning off over the years.'

'*Fifty-five thousand euros?* How many years?'

'Twenty. It's every charity's nightmare. Sam, I'm sorry, I know you're just about to go on leave, but I need someone with your experience to co-ordinate this. I know you're doing a very thorough handover with Dave, but he doesn't have your experience – and we'll need a media strategy if it gets out.'

It'll get out, thought Sam, grimly. Bad news always did.

'I'll be there as soon as I can.'

She hung up, thinking. One of the earliest problems she'd encountered with the charity was that it was run in such an archaic fashion. As someone who had come from the banking industry, Sam had been horrified at first to see the logistical set-up for their many, many accounts.

Once Sam's careful banking strictures were in place, every account was tied up and any back-door money heading off to Ballyglen would have stopped.

The volunteer would have sat with increasing credit card company demands.

She explained it all to Ted and they made their way to the car park, still holding hands.

As she drove into the office, she felt a hint of worry that had nothing to do with missing funds. This sort of scenario – her mother racing off because of some crisis at school – had been part and parcel of her home life. What if Sam was going to be that sort of mother too? One called too strongly by her job and not enough by her child?

Perhaps that's why she'd found it so hard to get pregnant – divine intervention.

What if the lure of her job made her just like her mother?

Ginger

Ginger sat on the train and watched the girl opposite eat a chocolate bar: blithely, unselfconsciously. Ginger longed for both a taste of the chocolate and the ability to eat four hundred calories of pure sugar for breakfast without anyone so much as blinking.

But then, the girl was a skinny little thing in skinny-little-thing jeans with those baby deer legs that looked as if they couldn't hold a real human up.

Skinny girls could eat four thousand calories of chocolate and say things like 'I just burn it off, I don't know how!' and giggle, and people – OK, men – gazed at them longingly as if the ability to desire chocolate meant they were good in bed.

People – OK, also men – never thought that about girls like Ginger. Although to be fair, Ginger never ate chocolate or anything else on the train. She didn't eat in public. Ever. So nobody got the chance to wonder if she was fabulous in bed from the way she sensually ate a Twix.

Big, curvy women eating chocolate in public could get looked at with the faint scorn that said: *no wonder you're fat*.

She forced herself to look back at her phone and clicked into her daily affirmations for dieting.

Today's, which she had read over her low-sugar muesli, the one that tasted least like ground-up packing boxes, said: *Imagine yourself as a better you. A happier, more contented you. This all will come if you just believe and let go. What you imagine, you draw towards yourself.*

Ginger closed her eyes and tried to imagine a happier, more contented her.

Her life would be different. Entirely different. She would be thin. Really thin, in fact. People would say things like: 'Ginger, darling, you have lost so much weight – you look amazing, but don't get too thin . . .'

And Ginger would shrug so that her bronzed collarbones would be visible and everyone would sigh enviously at her exquisite bone structure, and she'd say: 'I drink lots of water, and really, I forget to eat half the time because I'm so busy with Jacques/Dex/Logan . . .' and said hot boyfriend would smoulder from across the room and people would die with envy . . .

The train stopped with a jolt.

Her stop.

She hoisted her handbag across her chest, pulled her extra bag from between her knees, and made her way out of the carriage into the throng of people wielding coffee and newspapers. Getting off packed buses, trams or trains was a particular hell for larger women, and every time she did it, Ginger tried to engage nobody's eye so as not to invite the censure she would see there.

As she quickened her pace along Hinde Street on her way to Caraval Media, she knew she was transforming herself into the Ginger office version: 2.0.

With her old school friends, people like Liza, she fitted into another slot: that of helpful friend, a person whose shoulder you could cry on.

At home with her family, she was the Ginger who took care of everyone.

But in work, Ginger was a different person. In fact, she was pretty sure that the people she knew from her non-work life wouldn't recognise her. Here, she sloughed off the cloak of the girl who'd been plump forever.

Here, she was the reinvented Ginger.

On the fifth floor, Ginger went over to her cubicle and saw a message on her desk from Paula, who sat at the next desk.

Alice Jeter called – wants 2 c u.

'Lo,' said Paula, poking her head round the cubicle. 'What are you going up to the tenth floor for, anyway?'

'Research for some online thing,' said Ginger, managing to sound bored.

'Oh, yeah, I forgot. Snoresville,' said Paula, instantly uninterested.

Ginger took her things – several big folders that looked very important – and beetled out to the lifts.

She was amazed at how remarkably good she'd become at lying over the past six months. Six months like no other in her life.

It was like being a spy in a novel, living a double life and telling nobody. Six months previously, Ginger had been an ordinary staff member of the *Dublin Clarion*, a small local paper which had just been bought up by the giant Caraval Media group, who'd never seen a bit of media they didn't want to buy, Monopolies Commission excepting.

People liked reading actual newspapers for local news, unlike so many other types of news, so the *Clarion* was a good buy in a struggling industry hit by the internet downloading of news. Ginger was a general reporter, but by the unspoken edict of male-dominated journalism, she got to do all the stories where female empathy was required. She loved it, but she often wondered if it was what she was truly destined to do. Then the paper moved into the giant Caraval Media Towers and she got the company-wide email about the agony aunt required for *Teen Now*, a magazine that was going totally electronic – from paper to e-format.

Ginger, who had been considered an old head on young shoulders since she'd been very young, felt that thrill of excitement that told her *this* could be the job of her dreams.

We need someone who has empathy, some qualifications for this role and is able to turn out copy quickly. Apply to the above email, said the ad.

Well, Ginger could turn out articles at high speed, as anyone who had ever seen her write that two-page emergency advertorial on a peanut company could testify.

'You made peanuts sound sexy, interesting almost,' said the chief sub in astonishment when she emailed him the required 1000 words.

'Just doin' my job, boss,' said Ginger, tipping an imaginary hat at him, although it had been a nightmare to write. Peanuts were not sexy or interesting, unless you were a monkey.

That was the Ginger she was in work – funny, sassy and someone who took no crap from anyone.

She applied in secret to *Teen Now* and, also secretly, had two interviews on the tenth floor, which was one of the executive floors and was decorated far more beautifully than her floor, which was a warren of desks and had a scratchy blue carpet that gave off enough static electric to power the national grid.

Ginger had done her homework. She read past online editions of *Teen Now*, which was aimed at a fourteen- to sixteen-year-old age group but probably read by twelve- to fourteen-year-olds, before they moved on to *Cosmo* and how to do more than make out with boyfriends.

She had realised quickly that the previous agony aunt had veered towards the lightweight.

All in all, she had never dealt with any serious questions. 'The previous agony aunt,' she said at her interview, 'what was her background?'

'Why do you ask?' said Alice, who'd just been made boss of the e-magazine department, staring hard at Ginger. Alice Jeter was exquisite: slim, dark-eyed, hair a sheet of fashionable silvery pink.

'I just wondered because she seems to have kept to light topics and there's nothing meaty or serious there. What did she do if she got any real, in-depth questions? I mean, how does she handle those. I can't find any of them.'

'That's because I'm pretty sure she made up most of the questions, so making up the answers wasn't that difficult,' said Alice wryly.

'She made them up?' said Ginger, astonished.

'Yup. She was a college kid, had never worked in journalism before and had no clue that you have to keep it real. She taught us all something, though: never hire the daughter of someone in management. Which is why she is out looking for another job and we're looking for another agony aunt who can deal with online threads about self-esteem, slut shaming, sexting, body image. Do you want to try your hand at it?'

'I'd love to', said Ginger, flattening down the fear.

'OK. Good.' Alice's eyes travelled up and down Ginger. 'We're going to use a pseudonym. We all like "Girlfriend" as the column name until we get the right person. If you don't work out, we need continuity for the readers until we do get the right person. Probably best if you do this on your own time and we'll pay you freelance rates. Four columns to see if you can do it, OK?'

Ginger bit her lip. She thought she knew exactly why her name and picture would not be on the column – a photo of an overweight woman was hardly seen as aspirational to a readership of young girls who watched models' vlogs and worshipped skinny singers and actresses.

'I understand,' she said evenly. She would not be upset by this: she would stand tall and be herself. Her brain was what they were going to pay her for.

Her brain.

That first week, when she emailed over her column, she felt as shaky as she had done as a brand new reporter.

A succinct email had come back from Alice an hour later. 'I like this. It's good. You've got empathy and don't shy away from the tough ones. Keep going.'

Three columns later, Alice said they wanted to put her under contract for a year.

As Alice had suggested, Ginger hadn't discussed her new role with anyone. The girls who read e-*Teen Now* were looking for big-sister sort of advice from someone who was cool and trendy, like one of the modern vloggers who could throw on a pair of skinny jeans, flat shoes and a funky little T-shirt and tell them how to get over that guy or how to stand up for themselves. But Ginger didn't look like that person.

She wasn't aspirational, a thought which hurt, but she needed to pay the mortgage.

So she put on her big-girl panties, and took the implied insult.

She could have fought and said it was time that bigger role models were used and where better than in a young woman's magazine? But that would have been the office Ginger 2.0 speaking. The real Ginger, the private one who felt her weight meant she was judged cruelly, could not have faced it.

Writing the column was a joy. Her alter ego, Girlfriend, was sassy and truthful. Girlfriend had no time for boyfriends or girlfriends who wanted to belittle their dates or friends who weren't supportive. There were shades of grey in her column because life was all shades of grey.

With each week, the letters got more serious, as the audience could see that the woman behind the Girlfriend column had changed.

Girls wrote in about eating disorders and hating their bodies; about whether they should sleep with that guy who really wanted them to but they didn't want to go that far, and if they didn't, he'd dump them. They wrote in about having sent semi-naked pictures of themselves to guys on their phones. They wrote in about being gay or bisexual and worrying about who to tell.

Ginger learned the hard way how to deal with these letters; she learned to explain the rules of the law, but she learned that the law didn't protect the girls who found themselves at the mercy of the modern world.

Instead she went up to Alice on the tenth floor and said, 'I'd like to do some feature articles.'

'On what?'

'This week about some guy who wants you to send him topless pictures of yourself. Because that's what's happening to thirteen- and fourteen-year-olds.'

'OK,' said Alice, who never appeared shocked no matter what Ginger came up with. 'Write it under the Girlfriend pseudonym.'

'Absolutely,' said Ginger. 'That's what you pay me for.'

'I like you, you remind me of . . .' began Alice and Ginger thought that perhaps she had been about to say '. . . me when I was younger', but Alice didn't finish it because her phone rang and she nodded at Ginger to go.

All the way down in the lift, Ginger thought of how Alice was skinny and all gym-toned. There was no way she'd ever *looked* like Ginger.

No way *she*'d ever bought clothes from a catalogue, no way she had ever slid into a room sort of sideways, hoping that was the thinnest way possible to enter a space. No.

Alice's strength was real and Ginger's was a cloak she put on every morning she entered the Caraval Media building. Still, she thought, taking a deep breath as the lift slid to a smooth halt on the fifth floor, the cloak was working so far.

If work was busy, her private life was busier.

Twenty-six years after they'd bonded in the classroom with lots of crying four-year-olds, her best friend, Liza, was getting married and Ginger was asked to be chief bridesmaid.

However, Liza's desire to get married quickly, because she didn't do delayed gratification, meant the day had to be planned in just three months. A wedding planner had managed to swing a marvellous deal on a beautiful hotel because of a wedding that had been cancelled. Ginger had promised to help plan all the other details.

A fan of internet 'magical weddings', Liza first decided she wanted white horses with crimped manes faked up to look like unicorns – 'impossible', the wedding planner had sighed and had launched into a long and complex story of brides who had gone down this road before. The horn/headdress creations had frightened every horse bar a nearly blind one and had been a health and safety danger on many grounds.

Once the unicorns were nixed, Liza was fiercely determined to be even more creative. This would be a fairy-tale marriage because she had waited until she was nearly thirty – thirty! – to be married and it had to be the most special ever.

Ginger forgave her the comment about being nearly thirty. Ginger was the same age and Ginger had never even dated anyone. Liza just wasn't thinking when she'd said it, she convinced herself.

'Let's have a serious planning night where we fill in all the extras,' Ginger suggested.

Liza was delighted, but the wedding planner couldn't make it.

So in the end, it was just Liza, Ginger and Charlene, the other bridesmaid and a friend of Liza's from beauty college, who congregated in Liza and James's rented flat.

The flat didn't have the homey touches of her own place, but then, they couldn't paint any walls and do their own thing.

Liza positioned herself on a leather couch once they'd organised the snacks they had brought.

Charlene had brought wine and sushi.

Ginger had brought wine and chocolates. She felt stupid now, looking at the big box of Dairy Milk, untouched on Liza's coffee table, while the two other women wielded chopsticks and discussed how helpful sushi was for dieting.

'A thought occurred to me last night,' said Liza. 'Swans. What do you both think?'

'Swans, right.' Ginger wrote it down in her notebook doubtfully.

Swans were beautiful wild birds and were definitely not to be used as part of a ceremony. She could explain it all to Liza later, she thought, and absently reached over and picked up the unopened chocolate box.

Her fingers froze mid-cellophane-rip as she realised Liza and Charlene were staring at her, not a hint of muffin top between them.

'You skinny girls can eat all the sushi you want, but us big girls like chocolate!' she said valiantly, and the other two laughed.

'Ginger, you're so funny,' said Liza. 'I told you she was brilliant, didn't I?' she added to Charlene.

Because there was nothing she could do at this point, Ginger had beamed at the other two girls and opened the chocolates rapidly as if she could not possibly exist without oxygen, water and Dairy Milk.

'Chocolate and nuts, yummy,' she said, picking up two and putting them in her mouth.

'You're fabulous,' squealed Charlene, who didn't appear to have much else to say other than *fabulous*, Ginger thought, with a hint of sourness despite the chocolate melting in her mouth.

No, she thought, *stop being an absolute bitch*. Just because Charlene and Liza's apparent closeness meant she appeared to have taken over Ginger's position as Liza's best friend, there was no need to take it out on the poor girl.

'Right,' she said. 'What next?'

'Butterflies,' said Liza. 'I've been thinking that butterflies would be lovely as soon as we arrive at the hotel.'

'Right,' said Ginger in relief, scrawling a big line through swans on her notebook. 'So, no swans then?'

Butterflies had to be easier to organise, but where did they go afterwards, poor things? She wondered how to nix this idea.

'No,' said Liza, 'swans *and* butterflies. I mean it's got to be magical and special.'

'I'm just a bit nervous about the swans, Liza,' Ginger said, because she felt this was slightly getting away from them with all the wildlife.

'Oh for goodness' sake, Ginger,' snapped Charlene, 'it's got to be possible to organise swans and butterflies. People do it all the time. I've seen it in the magazines. It's going to be a very special wedding.'

Liza beamed at Charlene and Ginger felt that horrible pang of jealousy again. It had been the same the day Liza had gone off to choose her wedding dress. She wasn't sure how Liza had ended up picking a day when *she* couldn't go, but Charlene had been happy to step into the breach, and from all accounts, it had been a glorious day of trekking around beautiful shops trying on fabulous bridal gowns without Ginger.

As the only way Ginger felt she was ever going to get into a wedding shop to look at bridal gowns was with a friend, she felt her chances were gone.

'Next, we have to discuss the bridesmaids' dresses,' Liza went on, looking meaningfully at Ginger. 'Charlene and I have been speaking about this and we don't want you to get upset.'

Ginger blinked.

'Why would I get upset?' she stammered.

'Because, you know . . .'

Liza looked at Ginger, who felt every inch of her size eighteen at that exact moment. Nervously she stuffed another chocolate into her mouth and took a big gulp of wine, not a good combination.

'Er . . . OK, what were you thinking of?' said Ginger, feeling the colour begin to come up from her chest into her neck.

Soon it would hit her face and she'd be bright orange. She used to go that particularly unappealing shade during sports in school.

Liza warmed to her theme: 'I was thinking that we should

perhaps go for a similar colour for you and Charlene but a different shape. Charlene loves elegant streamlined dresses, quite like my own actually,' she said. 'So I'm thinking violet or a sort of blush pink or . . .'

'Or crimson,' said Charlene.

Ginger, who had never hated anyone in her life, felt a tinge of loathing.

Crimson would be absolutely beautiful for someone with Charlene's colouring and shape. But for a woman who went orange when she flushed, a woman with rippling auburn curls, crimson was the very worst colour in the book.

'I'm not really much of a fan of crimson,' she said.

'Oh.' Both Liza and Charlene stared at her as if she'd just mentioned clubbing baby seals.

'It doesn't suit my hair colouring,' said Ginger.

'I love the idea of crimson,' said Liza mournfully.

The Ginger who had let Liza Hannon walk all over her for twenty-six years resurfaced.

'But, of course, if that's what you want,' said Ginger, abandoning all hope of looking beautiful in an elegant bridesmaid's gown. She was going to look like a giant cherry. Red all over and round.

'Well, we'll see,' said Liza. 'Let's pick a date to go shopping.'

In order to keep her cheerful, us-fat-girls-LOVE-chocolate thing going, Ginger had to eat half the box, even though it made her feel ashamed. Comfort eating always did. That was why she could never lose weight: when her heart was heavy, she numbed it with chocolate or biscuits or ice cream. Hating herself for being fat meant she could keep all other feelings at bay.

And for a while, food filled all the dark, sad holes inside her.

Liza and Charlene were still talking about swans, butterflies and how crimson bridesmaids' dresses could suit redheads if they made the effort.

Liza's mother had always been on a diet. Maybe Charlene's

had too. Was that the trick, Ginger wondered: to have a mother who showed you how to do dieting and things like make-up and clothes?

Dad was brilliant, but he didn't know any of that stuff.

'I'm sorry your ma isn't here to help you with this,' he'd say mournfully, and Ginger would change the subject at speed. Under no circumstances did she want to talk about her mother. The lack of her hurt too much. Some pain needed to be buried deep. The deeper the better.

When she was growing up, he dressed her in the same sort of stuff as her brothers. For years, the three siblings all had the same short haircuts until Ginger was about six and Liza, who'd been her bestest friend for two years, said, 'Why do you have boy's hair?'

Ginger had gone home crying to her dad. He'd felt so bad, he always said when he remembered the story now.

'I said, "Right, long girly hair, let's do that. Grace has been nagging me about it, but I said kids get nits in school. Still, we can't have my girl looking like a boy." And oh, Ginger my love, when it grew, it was stunning, but the tangles! I wasn't used to combing out tangles, but we did it. And now look at you,' he liked to say, pride in every word. *'Your hair is your crowning glory.'*

In misery, Ginger ate another chocolate, swallowing it down like sawdust. Her crowning glory would look horrendous on top of a crimson gown.

She'd had such plans for this wedding: she'd be part of Liza's life in a way that she wasn't anymore, not really. Liza hung out with people from work and Ginger was always so busy. This wedding and her being chief bridesmaid would bring the closeness back.

But it wasn't looking that way at all.

Callie

Callie sat in the back of the limo with Jason on the way home and felt herself relax into the buttery soft leather seat. It had been a wonderful dinner after all. A Saturday night, an elegant restaurant with soft lighting, a jazz pianist in the corner and a busy, happy crowd of diners, enjoying fine dining.

Rob was on form, telling stories, being charming and funny, and Jason – Jason had been his charismatic self.

Everyone, from the sommelier to the waiters, loved him. Her husband treated everyone well – he was not one of those people who talked down to waiters and looked over people's shoulders to see if another more important personage was in his eyeline.

They'd been celebrating some tricky business deal in Bulgaria and both men were on a high. Vintage champagne had been ordered and as she'd watched Rob dickering over the wine list, laughing that they needed the most expensive vintage, Callie had felt a blast of anger that he'd tried to hide money from her dear friend in the divorce.

It was a sliver of gritty harshness piercing this lovely atmosphere. Did you ever truly know anyone else? Rob always appeared so honest: it was part of his charm, part of why so many people wanted to invest with the business.

Jason noticed the look on her face.

Leaning so that he was close to her neck, he had put one arm round her waist and with the other, he adjusted the platinum and sapphire necklace he'd bought her several years ago, and which worked so wonderfully with the silver lace dress she wore. His large fingers caressed her collarbone delicately.

'OK, honey? You looked like you might reach over the flowers to stab Rob there for a moment.'

She hauled her anger back in. 'It's nothing,' she lied. 'Tell you later?'

He nodded.

Now, in the back of the car, she allowed herself to lean against him, smelling his cologne and feeling the warmth of his body as he put an arm around her. She wanted to ask him about Rob, find out if he thought his best pal might really have hidden money from Evelyn in the divorce. But Jason was obviously so happy with the whole evening and she didn't want to ruin the closeness between them.

'Great evening,' he said, loosening his tie and popping his collar button. 'You looked amazing, babes. Did you see those guys at the table to our right? They kept looking over at me and Rob: full of naked, undisguised envy.' His hand slid under the bodice of the silvery dress and he cupped her breast with longing.

'Not in the car!' she said, although the feeling of his warm hand on her flesh gave her a shiver of desire.

Wonderful, she thought with pleasure. It seemed that Old Crone was off duty tonight. Maybe her menopausal flesh hadn't withered and died.

Jason's hand kept stroking. 'The driver's paid not to notice or watch.'

'If I want an audience, I'll try being a porn star,' joked Callie. 'Honey, let's wait till we get home.'

Reluctantly, he pulled his hand out, but not before squeezing her nipple.

'Jason!'

'You look so hot tonight,' he murmured. 'Rob and I are lucky guys. Talking of which, what was up with you and Rob? You looked so angry with him. Don't tell me – Evelyn was spinning more anti-Rob propaganda?'

Just like that, she felt her sexual urges vanish. Callie was so annoyed, she slid across the leather seat away from him.

'Anti-Rob propaganda?' she said. 'He tried to hide assets from her when they were getting divorced. They have three sons, were together since school, Jason. That's not how you treat someone you respect.'

'He didn't hide anything,' said Jason, jaw tightening. He stared straight ahead, not looking at her, which was what he did when he was angry. 'Don't swallow everything you hear, Callie. You're so bloody naïve sometimes.'

'*I'm* naïve?'

'Yeah, very naïve. Rob was good to Evelyn. He's a rich man, he didn't want to give her everything he'd worked his butt off for. So what? Does that make him the bad guy?'

'They were together since they were teenagers!' went on Callie. 'Fine, he didn't want to pony up every penny he ever had, but please don't tell me that he treated Evelyn with respect when they were married. He screwed everything that moved, Jason: you knew that, even if you never told me. So he owed her decency and some honesty when they were divorcing.'

'She got a good deal,' said Jason.

'Why did she need to get forensic accountants onto it then?'

'It was a misunderstanding. Rob didn't want to go through all that. He was good and fair to her in the end. Hell, he was just upset it was over. He loved her, despite the women, you must know that. Rob just needed a bit of variety. He'd have stayed with Evelyn forever if she hadn't pushed him out.'

Callie said nothing. Was that really what Jason thought? That it would have been better for Evelyn to turn a blind eye to her husband's philandering and then they'd still have been together?

The car pulled up outside their house and the driver silently got out and opened Callie's door.

'Thank you,' she said, feeling ashamed that this was the first time she'd spoken to the man. Once, she'd have talked to every cab driver.

'You're better than nobody and nobody's better than you, Claire' – that had been her mother's mantra.

Now she'd turned into one of those people who said nothing to the man who'd driven her home, and she'd let her husband feel her up in the back of the car, treating the driver like he was nobody, just hired help to be ignored. What sort of awful cow was she turning into?

Thoughts of her mother made her think of the row – again. Her birthday was looming and some of the most important people in her life wouldn't be there.

That horrible scene from ten years ago was burned into her brain like a cattle brand. Jason and her mother had never got on, but when her mother had come for a rare trip to Dublin, Jason had had a few drinks at dinner at home – he would not bring his unworldly mother-in-law out to a posh restaurant – and unwisely, Pat Sheridan had sparked it all off by wondering why they needed such a big house, so much money. Would he never be satisfied? His own mother, long since widowed, missed him. His brother had long left Ireland, whereabouts unknown. Pat had not bitten her tongue on the matter.

'She has nobody else, Jason. You need to visit her.'

Jason, an expensive cigar in his hand, had stared at her with a cold gaze.

'Nobody tells me I need to do anything, Pat,' he said harshly.

Callie could tell he was getting angry: that small muscle in his jaw was twitching He was furious. Why couldn't the people she loved get on?

But her mother was angry too.

'You're with me now, Jason,' she said harshly. 'You can cut the posh accent.'

The row had been pyrotechnic. Jason had yelled that he'd got out of his past and she was just jealous. He began to boast about the plans he had for a villa in a private estate in Portugal and how dare she think she knew what was enough. *He* would decide that.

'You're nothing but a jumped-up control freak who manages to fool people,' her mother had said when Jason was mid-boast. 'You don't fool me, you never have. You control my Claire. I can see it even if she can't. You've cut her off from her old friends and you try to cut her off from us—'

Jason had interrupted. 'What's wrong with cutting her off from drug addicts?' he had spat back, eyes enraged. 'Your precious son Freddie is nothing but a heroin addict who still tries to pal around with Callie's ex, another damned junkie, even if he thinks he's Mr Big Rock Star.'

'Freddie's clean, he's getting help,' hissed her mother, all sense gone now.

'How many times has Callie paid for him to go into rehab with my money?' Jason's voice was icy. 'Twice? Is the third time a charm, Pat?'

'How dare you?' said Callie's mother, beginning to cry. 'You have no idea what it's like, what I go through, and God help him, he tries his best.'

'We got out of the backwater of Ballyglen for a reason,' Jason went on. 'Because it would drag us down. Like the people. If you keep that druggie son of yours at home, then forget about coming to my house ever again—'

'Jason, no!' said Callie, distraught.

Her husband's hand had shot out and held her back. 'No, Callie. We've moved on and up in the world. Your mother and Freddie want to stay in the gutter. They're not welcome here. I won't have Poppy exposed to a junkie and the sort of viciousness your mother likes to dish out.'

'Please, no, Jason.' Callie was crying now, desperate to fix it all. 'Ma, we'll get Freddie help, we will and—'

'Not with one cent I've earned, you won't,' warned Jason fiercely.

He'd stormed out of the room, throwing a Waterford crystal goblet onto the marble floor, where it had shattered into hundreds of tiny shards.

Callie ran after him to get him to reconsider.

'That woman is never coming into this house again,' he'd told her when she'd found him in his study, smoking one of his precious cigars. He was still shaking with rage.

'It's crazy,' she said. 'We're not living in the Middle Ages. You can't banish my mother. Yes, Freddie is not welcome here while he's still using, and he knows that, but my mother—'

'Nobody speaks to me like that in my own house, *nobody*! To say that to *me*! To say I'm jumped-up . . .'

'Jason, lovie, Ma had a couple of drinks. You know she's not used to wine—'

'She's not used to good wine,' he said harshly. 'Only thing she likes is that rotgut they serve in the bar round the corner from her house. Fucking lush.'

'My mother is not a lush!' said Callie furiously. 'She rarely drinks.'

'And she never has a cigarette out of her hand,' Jason went on, oblivious to the cigar he was holding. Jason had managed to convince himself that a few Dunhills every day and the odd Cohiba were not smoking.

'She just lights one from the old one, sucking the life out of it. Well, she is not coming here again to contaminate our daughter. I won't have anyone who doesn't respect me in this house. We're finished with that life in Ballyglen and your bitch of a mother is not setting foot in here again! That's final!'

'Jason! She's my mother.'

He'd been so filled with rage, he was almost frightening. 'You choose, then, Callie,' he'd sneered. 'Her – or me and Poppy, because you can't have both.'

God help her, she'd chosen Jason and Poppy.

She hated herself for being helpless in the face of his control.

'Please apologise to him, Ma,' she'd begged the next day,

when her mother packed up early and rang for a taxi.

'I won't apologise for speaking the truth,' her mother said. 'What's he done to you, love? You used to be your own person and now you're like a tame creature he keeps on a lead.'

Callie had flushed. She could see the truth in it, but she'd experienced the world before Jason, the world of Ricky and the drug-infested life he loved. There was no security in that. And Callie craved security. She never wanted to go back to eating jam sandwiches again.

When she and Jason had bumped into each other in Dublin, just after she'd broken up with Ricky, she'd been drawn to his calm control. Here was a man who was charismatic, handsome, and far removed from the world of addiction. They had Ballyglen in common, knew each other already. He was perfect. He adored her, cherished her, made her feel safe.

She could barely look at her mother: she loved Jason. She couldn't turn her back on that, not even for her family. They didn't understand. Sure, Jason could be possessive, but he loved her, that was why.

'Claire, pet.' Her mother took Callie's face in her hands, hands worn from hard work and no time for hand creams. 'He's not good for you or little Poppy. This world' – and she'd looked around the hall of the house, glamorous, elegant, as far removed from their small Ballyglen home as the North Pole was from the Amazon – 'this world is just fakery. Jason likes nice things and you're one of them. You're so beautiful on the inside, pet, but he only sees the outside. You don't work anymore, you have so few friends, you have so little for all that you seem to have so much. He's made a museum for his nice things and you're one of them.'

'I'm not, Ma, and he's not done that,' protested Callie. 'He adores me, can't you see?'

'He adores the wrong parts of you, Claire: the bits people see, not the bits that are inside you, the parts that make you you.'

'You're wrong.'

Her mother shook her head.

'I love you, pet, but I won't be coming here again. You and Poppy can come to me anytime. We'll be there for you. I know he'll show his true colours one day and we'll be waiting for you then.'

That conversation seemed a lifetime ago now.

Brenda, who'd stayed over to babysit Poppy, was in the kitchen.

'Good night?' she asked, then she saw Callie's anxious face.

Callie sank into an armchair.

'My mother never wanted me to marry Jason,' Callie sighed, staring into the distance. 'She said he was a fly-by-night merchant and I was on the rebound.'

Wisely, Brenda said nothing.

'But the row . . . how can we come back from that?' Callie went on.

'Jason caused it by showing off his toys,' said Brenda. 'Your mother just responded. He's an evil genius when it comes to pushing people's buttons.'

'He pays your wages,' Callie snapped back.

'Doesn't mean I have to like him or not see what he is underneath the charm. Tea is made,' Brenda said.

'He's my husband, you know he's a good person,' Callie said instinctively. 'No, I don't want tea,' she added. She didn't want to argue with Brenda too. It seemed to be her night for arguing.

She went silently upstairs and checked on Poppy, who was asleep, looking fourteen again out of her make-up. Watching her daughter sleeping peacefully, Callie's mind was racing.

Rob's behaviour upset her. Jason's reaction to it upset her even more.

What if Jason was cheating on her and he was already working out how to hide his money so she got just enough?

She went into her dressing room and slipped off the silver

dress, leaving on her underwear and pulling on a dressing gown before heading into the bathroom. In front of the mirror, she began taking off her make-up and as she worked, all she could see was crêping skin and wrinkles, places where her face had once been youthful and where now, all the dermatological work in the world couldn't hide the passage of time.

She didn't think she looked her age. Models could age beautifully. But hey, who was she kidding?

Her husband could easily be screwing a twenty- or thirty-something like Anka. He might be working all the details out now. Evelyn might think Jason would never look at another woman, but that could all be bullshit. He might be on the phone to *her* right now in his study, whispering that he'd tell his wife soon, that they'd be together . . .

'What's really bugging you, Callie?'

Jason stood in the bathroom, shirt open, tie off, cuffs undone.

He still had a tan from their last holiday: he only had to look at the sun to go dark. And he was toned. He and Rob were always at gyms when they were away.

They'd completed one triathlon together. Sworn off them altogether because it was too hard to combine all their travelling with the training, but still, they worked out.

She could see his defined abdominal muscles, the strength in his pectorals. With the blue eyes startlingly pale against his tanned face, he looked every bit as handsome as when she'd first fallen in love with him.

'You,' she said, blinking back tears and wishing she didn't feel so emotional all the time.

Damn this perimenopause.

'What about me?' His face softened and he moved to take her in his arms.

'I don't want to be like Evelyn. I don't want to be discarded with you figuring out how to appease me, how much money to give to me so you can get on with your new life—'

'What gave you that idea?' he demanded. 'I'm going

nowhere. There is nobody else. Why did you even think that? Hey, I was proud of you this evening because those idiots at the table nearby were staring at you and I was thinking "she's my wife, guys – hands off!" Why would I leave?'

With his arms around her, Callie allowed herself to sink into her husband's embrace. She leaned her head against him, letting all the pent-up worry flood out of her.

'I love you, only you. And Poppy, our own Teenager From Hell!' he joked. 'I adore you both, you never have to doubt me. Don't you believe me?'

'Yes,' she sniffled. 'But you've been so preoccupied lately, busy, not talking, and I thought—'

'You're one crazy woman,' he said, and swooped her up in his arms. 'I don't care if you're not finished with the creams and the serums, honey, you're coming with me. Now. To bed. To have wild sex.'

'I'm getting old,' wailed Callie.

'We're getting older,' corrected Jason, negotiating the bed-room door with his foot. 'So what? You're still as beautiful today as you were when I met you.'

He laid her on the bed, pulled off his shirt and trousers until he was down to his boxers.

'Let's get you out of those wet clothes and into a nice warm bed,' he said.

Callie laughed.

'They're not wet,' she said.

'Work with me here,' he said, unclasping her nude bra and letting her small breasts spill out into his hands. 'Definitely wet,' he murmured, leaning down to suck her nipples. 'And these . . .'

His hands found her panties, a wisp of lace. He reached past the lace to touch her and she arched her back.

She felt ready for him: soft and ready, unlike so often lately when she'd felt as if lovemaking was akin to having her desert body invaded.

But tonight, now, she felt sexual and loved. Desirable.

The next morning, Callie practically danced down the stairs to the kitchen. Her body ached pleasurably, the tiredness of lovemaking she hadn't felt for a long time.

So, she thought, looking at herself in the mirror as she shrugged into a sweatshirt and sweatpants, *you're not twenty anymore.*

Who gave a damn?

You're a modern, intelligent woman with a man who loves you and get over yourself with your neuroses and your fears of your husband cheating.

No man who was cheating on his wife could make love to her twice in one night when they'd been together for over twenty years.

Beat that, you smug young things, Callie thought.

Mug of coffee in hand, she wandered into the newly completed conservatory, where Jason sat at one end of a huge Norwegian table, the Sunday papers spread out in front of him.

'Hi, honey,' she said, leaning over Jason and giving him a lingering kiss on the mouth.

He didn't kiss her back.

'Your ex is all over the news again,' he said.

Callie sighed. She hadn't had enough boyfriends to wonder which one – and only one of them had become one of the most famous men in the world. Damned Ricky.

She'd dated him for three wonderful years, but by the time she turned twenty-one, Ricky was an addict. Callie had ended it, terrified by the ferocity of his addiction. Ricky had gone to London, made it big there and then vanished totally from her life.

It was years since she'd seen him and yet thanks to Tanner being one of the world's biggest rock bands, who seemed to have an endless supply of hits, Ricky and the band were often in the papers.

Nothing could be more guaranteed to make Jason furious with jealousy than newspaper coverage of Ricky.

Callie was used to it. The trick, she'd learned, was to deal with Jason's fierce jealousy by pretending utter indifference, even dislike.

'I guess I should be pleased that you get jealous over my old boyfriends,' she said, determined to tease him out of his misery. Last night had been wonderful: he'd made her feel loved and she'd understood that things were tricky in work right now, which was why he'd been distant.

She was not going to let Ricky ruin it.

When Jason had gone into the office, Callie took a quick look at the papers.

There was a piece on Ricky, who was recording a new album. People were still talking about his amazing and enlightening talk at Davos about climate change. Jason would have given his right arm, left leg *and* the Ferrari to be asked to speak at Davos, but it was never going to happen. Callie knew that. But Ricky, her first ever boyfriend, first lover, and one of the most famous men in the world, had been asked and had been a huge success.

Jason had hated that – it meant he couldn't say that Ricky was just a moron with a guitar. Morons with guitars did not get invited to the prestigious Swiss think tank where world leaders gathered every year.

And he particularly hated it when Callie was mentioned in these articles, as she sometimes was because of the song 'Calliope', which had been the breakout song for Ricky's band – the song that had transformed them from a small band into a band who could fill Madison Square Gardens.

But Ricky had been long gone from her life when she met Jason and back *then*, it had thrilled Jason to be going out with the famous rock star's ex-girlfriend.

Callie picked up the paper and put it in the recycling.

The past needed to stay in the past. Except, it kept pinging into her consciousness. Her party was very soon.

She tried not to think about it because of the people who wouldn't be there: her mother, her brother, her aunt and uncle-in-law. All her relatives, the people that Jason had basically banished from her life ten years before.

Fiftieth birthdays were a time for family, but if she got in touch with her mother now it would look like she was only doing it for appearances' sake.

How did you come back from that sort of family row? You couldn't – that was the answer. Instead, you had to be passionately grateful for all you had.

Sam

Posy shoved a multicoloured fluffy dog at her Uncle Ted and said, 'This puppy has a broken tummy. Fix him.'

'Yes, oh Empress Posy,' said Ted, as Posy poked the stuffed puppy in a way that would guarantee a broken tummy or, at least, severe gastric discomfort. 'Exactly what sort of puppy is this?'

'A zebra shetta puppy,' Posy said. 'You're silly not to know.'

'Yup, silly me.'

Sitting in an armchair, watching, Sam thought happily of how Sunday dinner at Joanne's was always fun. Fun because Joanne's three little girls were a delight.

They adored Ted and pulled him down onto the ground so they could get him to be the vet for a line-up of teddies who would all have injuries.

'He's going to be a great dad,' Joanne said as she somehow managed to shut the oven door with her bum while carrying the roast and shoving some children's toys out of the way with her foot. Sam marvelled at her sister's ability to multitask. Joanne could cook, mind kids, talk and not get the slightest bit fazed by any of this.

Sam was good at multitasking when she was at work, but at home, she liked a different, more laid-back sort of vibe. But this was motherhood, she knew: she had to watch and learn because that was very important.

'What are we eating today?' she said.

'Roast lamb stuffed with rosemary and garlic,' said Joanne, her voice slightly questioning. 'Sound good?'

'If she winces and asks for fish paste,' said Ted as he wrapped up another teddy, a bright pink one this time with the bandage made out of toilet roll, 'say no. No matter how much she begs. Gives her heartburn.'

'I have not had fish paste for ages, in my defence,' said Sam.

The door banged and the sound of Patrick, Jo's husband, ushering in Sam's father could be heard.

'Liam, how are you, and Jean – we weren't expecting you to make it, but gosh, er, you look lovely.' Patrick was using his most respectful voice.

Joanne and Sam exchanged a glance.

'*Mother,*' they mouthed at each other.

Jean swooped into the room. Her greying hair, cut short, was curled the way she did it with heated rollers, her limited make-up was perfect and she wore a silky cream knitted suit with a single loop of discreet beads round her neck.

Sam looked at her mother and wondered if she had ever seen her dressed down. Sam loved dressing down: taking off her work clothes when she used to work in the bank and slipping into comfortable stretchy leggings and fluffy socks with one of Ted's sweatshirts on. Then, she'd curl up on the couch with the dogs, relax and watch delicious junk on the TV.

She had never seen her mother in such a state of undress – even her mother's nightwear was a collection of quasi-Victorian nightgowns. No comfy pyjamas in that house.

Joanne recovered first. 'Mother, delighted you could come. I thought you were busy.'

'I'm never too busy to see you all,' said their mother and, yet again, Sam and Joanne exchanged a glance.

Their mother had always been too busy to see them. Their father had raised them. But that ship had sailed a long time ago.

Sam managed a brittle smile and knelt with difficulty down on the floor, where her youngest niece was playing with trains.

There was something about her mother these days that was bothering her and she just couldn't put her finger on what it was; just something there in the background that was niggling away.

'It's ridiculous,' she had said to Ted a few weeks before, after her mother had sent her a terse email hoping she was feeling well with her pregnancy. 'Whose mother *emails* about their pregnancy? That's fine if you live in a different country or you're on the space station, but if you live in the same country, *not that many miles away*, you'd phone, and then you'd come over, like a normal mother would.'

She was aware that her voice was rising with each breath.

'Honey, don't get your blood pressure up. It's bad for the baby,' Ted said.

Sam had groaned. 'That's the best excuse ever,' she said. 'You can stop me getting irritated with my mother by reminding me it's bad for the baby.'

'You haven't got annoyed over your mother for years,' he said, 'so it's a little weird, but hey, hormones! Just remember to take the annoyance down a notch or, I promise you, I will buy one of those little blood pressure machines.'

Sam hadn't answered the email. If her mother wanted to behave like a robo-mum, she was not going to go along with it. Step away from the crazy!

Posy wanted all the toy train-track joined together. Ted and Sam had bought it for her when it was clear that Posy liked what were officially termed 'boys' games'. Joanne was entirely laid-back about it all: 'If she wants to play with boys' stuff, fine. Why are there girls' toys and boys' toys? Why not just toys? I was never into Barbie myself.'

'No guns, though,' Patrick said.

'Definitely,' agreed Joanne. 'But a crossbow when she's old enough, so she can be cool, like Katniss . . .? And I think karate or tae kwon do lessons when they're older. Girls need to feel empowered.'

'So nice to see you aren't using gender-stereotypical toys for the children,' said a cool voice.

Sam felt that tightening in her guts again. Her mother felt that non-gender-stereotypical toys were useful in that they might convince a girl to do higher level science and maths and go off to prove themselves in male-dominated worlds.

She didn't seem to realise that a three-year-old wanting to play with trains was just a three-year-old wanting to play with trains. No, everything had to have a superior purpose down the line.

'Isn't this great, Posy,' said Sam, trying not to grit her teeth in case the ensuing rictus grin frightened her niece.

There was something therapeutic about making a curved track, she'd found from previous visits. Finally, after what seemed like an interminable amount of time, with Jean exchanging idle chit-chat with Joanne while Sam studiously ignored it all and played with Posy, it was time to eat.

The calm of track-making vanished over dinner.

'I sent you an email enquiring about the pregnancy,' said her mother, looking at Sam over the top of her bifocals, precisely the way an irritated headmistress would look at a misbehaving student. For a moment, Sam felt just like a misbehaving student, preferably one from St Trinian's.

'I get so many emails, I just never got round to answering it, Mother, but I had been talking to Dad. I was telling him things were going really well. Phone calls are easier – you can only imagine the number of emails I get from work.'

'Yes,' said her mother. 'Talking of work, your father told me about this scandal of the missing money and some volunteer person who has been helping themselves with a credit card over the years. Goodness, what a mess that appears to have been. It's . . . how shall we say . . .' Jean seemed to be considering the correct Oxford Dictionary definition of a mess, '. . . tricky to extract oneself from that sort of scandal. You don't want your career blighted.'

Sam glared at her father, who mouthed *sorry*. What on earth had made him divulge this bit of information?

'Have you sorted it out yet?' her mother went on, excellent in the role of High Inquisitor.

'We're trying to get to the bottom of it but it's complicated,' said Sam, which was an understatement. 'It's an older lady who didn't mean any harm.'

'You shouldn't make excuses for people,' her mother interrupted. 'We all make our choices in life.'

Sam stared down at her plate, rage surging up inside her.

Her inner voice was screaming: *And your choice was to have children and then never be there for them! Where's the apology for that? And you're still doing it!*

'Wasn't that a fabulous match yesterday,' said Patrick, determined to break the impasse.

'Yes,' said Ted, picking up instantly. 'Some great tries.'

'Oh fabulous, fabulous match,' said her father and the three men talked loudly as if they might somehow banish the frostiness by discussing tackles and points and really why was there not special eye surgery for referees because they kept missing fouls.

Posy wanted to clamber onto Sam's lap and she let her.

'Hello, baba, what's wrong?'

'Not a baba, I'm three,' said Posy crossly.

'Three, I thought you were seven,' said her Aunt Sam, hugging her and feeling the comfort of having this little scrap of beauty sitting on her lap.

Luckily Sam's parents didn't stay long and with a final hug from her father and a whispered, 'I'm sorry I mentioned the problem in work, Sam,' they were gone.

'Please tell me when she's invited for dinner again, will you,' said Sam, sinking down into an armchair and then wondering why because she knew she wouldn't be able to get out of it without help.

'Don't you like Granny?' said Isabelle, standing in front of Sam, little hands on her tiny little girl hips. 'I like Granny. She's in charge of a school. I'm going to be in charge of the world when I grow up.'

'You're in charge already,' sighed her father. 'She is, you know,' he said to Sam and Ted, 'totally in charge.'

'That's because I'm the oldest,' said Isabelle, staring smugly at her sisters. 'I'm the oldest so what I say goes.'

As the tidying progressed, a mild scuffle broke out over who was really in charge, but a roar from Joanne settled them all down.

'No TV all week if you fight. Shouting hurts Auntie Sam's baby's ears.'

'Ooohh.'

Three little girls arrived to stand in front of Sam and looked at her belly curiously, as if wanting to see evidence of the baby's ears, a diagram of possible ear damage or even a real, live baby they could dress up in doll's clothes.

'You can touch if you like,' said Sam.

Pixie patted the bump, but Posy laid her head on Sam's belly.

'I am your cousin,' she whispered. 'I will take care of you, but stay away from my trains 'cos they are mine, right?'

The grown-ups laughed and eventually, bored, the three girls went off to various parts of the room to play.

'I'm sorry,' said Sam, 'I know I should be doing something to help but I just can't – I have to sit here, I just feel like a, a . . .'

'A whale?' supplied her sister.

'Yeah, a whale. Exactly. It's really weird, this growing a person inside you.'

'How does a baby get inside you?' said Isabelle, arriving back at speed.

'We want to know.' Pixie and Isabelle were both staring at her now, fascinated.

Busy playing with her trains, Posy explained: 'The mummy eats a seed from the daddy and the mummy has to be careful not to poo out the seed until the seed is a baby.'

Isabelle giggled.

'Is that it?' said Pixie. 'I don't want to eat one of those seeds because I don't want a baby. Babies cry all the time, like Posy.'

'I don't cry.'

Suddenly there was a full-scale riot going on, complete with screaming. Posy, who had clearly been having ninja training from somewhere, began hair pulling.

'I'd cancel the karate lessons,' remarked Ted. 'No need for them.'

'Mummy, she pulled my hair,' screamed Isabelle.

'You were mean to me,' shouted Posy, and to prove that she was indeed the youngest and most injured, she let forth a few blood-curdling roars that made her father pick her up. Her mother went to comfort the other two girls.

'You stay there,' said Ted to his wife, putting a kiss on her forehead as Patrick and Joanne defused the row. 'I'll finish the tidying up. It's only fair.'

'OK,' said Sam, content now to just sit there.

The rioters were eventually calmed by their parents with threats of timeouts. Joanne and Patrick made it look so easy, Sam thought.

She just hoped she'd be able to calm her own child half as well. Ted would be brilliant at it but, for a moment, she had a glimmer of anxiety: what if she was hopeless at that type of thing? What if she hadn't a maternal bone in her body and should have stuck to dogs?

After all, her mother had swanned into the lunch, spoken little to the children and had had the gall to think that an email was an acceptable form of contact to find out how her pregnant daughter was.

What, Sam thought again – the thought that was circling endlessly in her brain – if she was just like her mother?

Cold, unyielding, unable to form a bond with her child?
What then?

PART THREE

The Birthday

Callie

It was nearly eleven o'clock on the night of her birthday and, in her bare feet, Callie stepped delicately around the plastic bags and piles of books in Brenda's tiny spare room and tried to work out which suitcase contained her make-up remover and night cream.

She needed to get this faceful of make-up off. To brush her teeth. To scrub the day from herself.

Her skin itched with the desire to be clean. Then, she wanted to fall into the single bed covered with a simple white duvet and sleep. Forever. Like Sleeping Beauty, except there would be no prince kissing her awake.

No prince at all.

No husband.

Nothing but an aching emptiness in her heart. She couldn't cry – not because crying would make her make-up slide down her face, but because if she started to cry, she wasn't sure how she'd manage to stop.

How long ago had it been since she sat in the chair in the hairdressing salon, drinking coffee and thinking about the party?

Years ago: that's what it felt like.

Feeling like an addict desperate for the fix of her special remover oil and some rich face cream, she pulled and pushed the cases, wrenching them open and then shoving them to one side when they weren't the right one. The packing had been so haphazard. Callie had just watched Brenda do it, too numb to help.

There was barely any space in the tiny spare room for all the suitcases, so Callie tried to stack them on top of each other as she searched. She had slowly managed to half pack one at home before Brenda had taken over, ripped things from the wardrobe and stuffed it all into the old cases at speed. Not the Mandarina Duck leather suitcases, she'd said, and Callie, who'd sat slumped on the floor of her and Jason's dressing room, still in her charcoal party dress but with her Manolos off, had seen a look exchanged between Brenda and the female police officer watching them.

Nothing was said but Callie understood because Brenda had explained it to her brusquely in a brief moment alone: it might be better if she took nothing valuable. Nothing that might be the proceeds of a crime which was being investigated.

'What do they think Jason's done?'

'Not sure,' whispered Brenda. 'Something dodgy.'

'That's ridiculous,' said Callie.

'So where is the lord and master, then?' asked Brenda. 'The Fraud Squad come when there's fraud. Did you ring the lawyer?'

Callie had rung Jason's personal lawyer many times but there was no answer.

'Probably done a runner too,' Brenda had snarled and begun packing.

'I can't get my husband's lawyer on the phone,' Callie had said to the female police officer in the dressing room. 'I don't know anything about any of this . . .' she added helplessly.

Despite her shock, Callie could sense the other woman's disbelief and the words not spoken.

We're here with a search warrant, Mrs Reynolds. How could you not know you were in trouble, Mrs Reynolds? How could anyone be that stupid?

Brenda had bypassed the wardrobes with the expensive evening dresses, designer suits, handbags worth the price of a small car and shoes lined up with exquisite care, but had swept out the lingerie drawer.

'No resale value in this,' she'd said calmly, stuffing it all into a squashy case. She'd taken the ordinary clothes: jeans, plain trousers, sweaters, the expensive little camisoles Callie loved, cardigans, her old leather jacket, the everyday things Callie wore around the house like her yoga pants, and a couple of very plain black dresses and matching shoes.

Court shoes they used to be called, Callie had thought blankly. To be worn in court?

She'd felt the nausea rise up but, somehow, it backed down into the pit of her stomach. Brenda had told her to get her creams and potions, but the only thing Callie's shaking hand had reached for was the old make-up case under the sink with her Xanax in it. She'd stashed it in her handbag, unable to do anything else. It was a big handbag, expensive, but old. Worth money in a resale shop? Was this how she was to pack? Only take what would not be worth anything?

Brenda scooped up books, phone chargers, photos, the pile of Callie's vitamins, her face creams, all the personal bits and bobs on her dresser.

The Loewe, Bottega Veneta and Dior handbags sat in her wardrobe in their dust bags, polished and perfect.

All the while, she tried to empty her mind, because if she allowed herself to think, it would allow her to remember that Jason was gone, leaving her with this.

As Brenda swept back into the bedroom, Poppy sat on her parents' bed, pretty face reddened with crying, watching the TV with the headphones as if she could somehow block out what was happening.

Brenda had already dispatched Poppy's friends and had packed up everything Poppy owned at high speed. A motley selection of bags sat ready and waiting.

Poppy wouldn't look at her mother since she and Brenda had come in to break the news.

'What have you done?' she'd screamed at Callie, mascara cascading down her face as if she was auditioning for a horror movie, while Brenda was ushering her confused friends out and Callie and Poppy were left alone.

'*Nothing*,' protested Callie.

'You must have! Where's Daddy? He can fix it. You can't,' Poppy screamed and then cried again, until her face was transformed horribly with make-up, but she wouldn't let Callie help her take it off.

'Get away from me!' she'd hissed.

'Please, darling . . .' Callie had begged, trying to hold her daughter, to comfort her, but Poppy screamed some more, until Brenda had marched in and slapped her on the cheek.

At that, Poppy had collapsed against Brenda, sobbing in her arms, while Callie had stood to one side, devastated. How could she fix this when she didn't know what to fix?

The police had let Callie and Poppy go – with their limited belongings, no computers, no papers – in Brenda's car with a pal of Brenda's coming with another car to haul the suitcases.

From the safe, with two police officers watching, Callie had taken her passport and Poppy's, but had been told she was not to leave the country. Jason's passport was gone, as was the wodge of cash he always kept in there. Callie had said nothing about this being missing. The safe was quite empty, apart from their passports and her jewellery in the leather cases.

'Can you tell me what's going on?' she'd said as they left to the police detective in plain clothes, the one who'd spoken to her first.

'This is a criminal investigation into your husband, Jason Reynolds, and we are searching this premises.'

'Crime? What sort of crime?' Callie could barely ask but she had to.

'Large-scale fraud,' he said bluntly.

'But who could he defraud?' asked Callie, bewildered.

'Investors in his property business, abroad and here.'

Some of the investors were people they knew. The policeman had to be wrong.

Jason wouldn't commit fraud. He was honest. He was no white-collar criminal.

But he was gone, wasn't he? Wasn't that proof of something?

'We will need to talk to you over the next few days,' the detective had said.

'We can't get one now, but she'll have a lawyer present,' said Brenda.

'Good plan,' he said evenly.

'She doesn't know anything about any of this, you know,' Brenda said, 'but then I guess you know that.'

The policeman said nothing.

Callie stood mutely as Brenda asked one final question: 'Are the bank accounts frozen?'

'Yes.'

Brenda had played the radio in her car on the way to her home, and she'd shoved in a Carol King CD when the news came on.

'I hate this music,' said a voice, the old Poppy resurfacing for a moment from the back of the small car where she sat surrounded by black plastic bags and cases.

'I love it,' said Brenda cheerfully, then whispered to Callie: 'I can't turn on the radio in case of a news report.'

'Is it on the news already?' Callie was stricken.

Brenda shrugged as she turned a corner, driving them away from the glamour of their part of the city to the bohemian style of her own. 'Who knows. It won't take long for some smart-arse to connect the dots and find you at my place, though. You need a bolt-hole or else you'll be facing the press.'

Callie didn't answer. Where was Jason? What had happened to make him run?

At Brenda's, the three of them hauled in the bags and cases, then Brenda brought Poppy up to the office-cum-box-room at the front of the house. From downstairs, Callie could hear them.

'If we push the desk against the wall, you can turn the sofa into a bed,' Brenda had said.

From Poppy, there was nothing: no anger at the size of this room which was the size of her en suite bathroom at home.

'I don't have Netflix, I'm afraid, but there's reasonable Wi-Fi and there's Sky on the TV downstairs.'

Then, there was sobbing and Callie imagined Brenda holding Poppy in her arms and murmuring comforting things.

Callie should be doing this, but Poppy hadn't even so much as glanced in her mother's direction since they'd left the house. Refused to hug her. It was as if she blamed Callie for everything. And why not? Callie thought. Callie had not stopped this happening.

'You OK in here? I've got camomile tea downstairs,' Brenda said to her, appearing at the door to the spare room, which was marginally larger than the study.

'That would be lovely,' said Callie, stopping her search. 'I can't find my creams or stuff. I want to . . .'

'Yeah, take the face off.'

Brenda shoved things around and found a small suitcase. 'In here. I brought as much as I could. Even got the retinol cream. Dermalogica will go out of business if you stop buying. Plus,' her eyes twinkled, 'I got some of your jewellery.'

'You did what?'

'Hey, you'll need every penny,' Brenda said. 'I doubt if Jason ever paid anything but cash up front for anything in his life. No trail of receipts.' She opened the case and handed a black leather case to Callie. 'Here. The pearls, the gold Cartier tank watch, some diamonds. The big stuff is in the safe, but fuck it, you need some collateral, things to sell at some point.'

'It's going to be sorted out, Brenda,' said Callie fiercely. 'I won't need to sell anything. Jason will fix it. This is all a—'

'Mistake? Yeah, right,' said Brenda, her voice as caustic as acid. 'If it's a mistake, why isn't he here fixing it now? Because this is no mistake, Callie. You and Poppy are on your own. You've got me, and Evelyn too, I imagine, because she's decent to the bone, and Mary Butler in Canada, but that's it. So get used to it and start thinking clever. Tomorrow, we'll find out if you can take stuff from the house – you need a lawyer for when they talk to you. But right now, we've got enough.'

Alone again, Callie wiped off her face, tears mingling with the cream. She felt strangely numb. There was a dreamlike quality to this whole evening. Like a bad movie that had somehow stuck in her brain to be replayed in her REM sleep. Yet she didn't want to think too much about it because if she did, she would come back to the inevitable: if Jason was a fraud, how had she not known?

When she'd rubbed on moisturiser, pulled on sweatpants and a T-shirt and tied her hair back with a band, she stood outside Poppy's room and knocked, but there was no reply. She might bring up a cup of hot chocolate to her daughter and try again in a few minutes.

'I'm sorry, Brenda,' she began when she reached the kitchen.

'No, *I* am. I'm giving you the tough-love treatment right now and it's probably too much.'

Everything that had happened was too much, Callie thought, but no point in saying that.

Brenda sat at the small table in the kitchen, her three cats in three different cat beds. There was a scent of tobacco in the air, a small Japanese teapot and two little cups on the table, along with an opened wine bottle and two glasses. Soft jazz music played in the background.

'Seriously,' said Callie, 'thank you for everything. I'm still a bit shell-shocked. Maybe sleep will sort me out.'

There was silence. Neither of them believed a good night's sleep would do much, but still, it was something you said, Callie thought. Sleep. Hot tea with sugar. Kindness. None of which could take away the fact that Jason had run off, leaving her with this trail of disaster.

'Is Poppy coming down?'

Brenda shook her head.

'She blames me,' said Callie, pouring herself some tea and trying not to let her hands shake too much.

Joe, the marmalade cat, uncurled from his bed and began to weave around Callie's bare ankles.

'You're the only one who's left to blame,' Brenda said, shrugging. 'Shitface went off and left you both, so there's nobody else to pin it all on.'

'I wish you wouldn't call him that,' Callie said automatically. 'We don't know what's happening.'

'He left when the police were at the door – that's what happened. You and Poppy would have been on the street tonight if I wasn't there. Your bank accounts have been frozen. You couldn't have rented a hotel room with credit cards attached to frozen accounts. So yes, I think Shitface about sums it up.'

Callie was too shocked to be angry, but clearly Brenda was channelling enough anger for both of them. She abandoned the camomile tea and poured herself some wine.

'What do I live on if our bank accounts are frozen?'

Brenda shrugged. 'They want Jason. He'll be on an arrest warrant now and they have to track him down. Freezing the accounts is what they do.'

'But what about Poppy and me?'

'I'd love to ask fucking Jason that,' said Brenda.

'I still don't believe it,' said Callie staunchly. She finished her glass of wine, went to the sink and rinsed it out. 'He wouldn't do this to us!'

Brenda closed her eyes. 'He has, Cal. He has. I am so sorry for both of you.'

'But why?' Callie knew she was about to cry and she didn't want a tear-stained face, not when she had to go into Poppy's room. 'He loves us.'

'People are complicated, Cal. He loved the lifestyle, didn't want to give it up when the economy tanked. Went over to the dark side? Who knows.'

'But us? What about us?' Callie said.

'I don't have an answer.'

Callie finally said it out loud: 'How did I not know? You seemed to know.'

'Jason adored you and he protected you,' Brenda said finally. 'I'm wiser, I saw between the cracks. I've had my suspicions for the past couple of years, but what could I say to you? "Do you think the business is no longer legitimate?"'

Callie shuddered. She wouldn't have believed it, and if she'd talked to Jason, he'd have fired Brenda.

There was silence. Brenda lit a cigarette and Callie got to her feet.

'You have hot chocolate anywhere?'

Brenda opened the correct cupboard, and Callie made speedy hot chocolate in the microwave.

She couldn't talk anymore. Didn't want to hear anything else that could hurt. To imagine that her husband would just abandon her and Poppy to the police was too hard to bear because it meant she'd been wrong about him all along. That he hadn't been a safe harbour.

And if he wasn't, what sort of idiot did that make her? Because she should have known.

Upstairs, Callie knocked on Poppy's door. There was no answer. She pushed in past the suitcases and found her daughter curled up on the sofa bed with her headphones on and tears dried on her face.

Callie put the mug of hot chocolate on the floor, sat down on the sofa bed and Poppy allowed herself to be pulled into her mother's embrace.

'Mum, what's going to happen?' sobbed Poppy.

Callie held her tight, relieved that Poppy had let her guard down finally. 'I don't know, honey, but I know Daddy's going to fix it. He loves us, loves you so much, like I love you. It's going to be fine. You wait and see.'

'Promise?' said Poppy, hiccuping because she'd cried so much.

Callie hesitated a beat. She couldn't say that she really had no idea if things would be fine. She was terrified things would be the opposite, but Poppy was just a kid. She had to be handled gently, not hurt with a lightning bolt of harsh reality. 'Promise,' she agreed, scared she wasn't telling the truth.

She found her daughter's make-up remover and gently cleaned away the layers of make-up until, once again, Poppy's fresh fourteen-year-old face was revealed. Sorting through the bags, she found pyjamas and the small cuddly toys that Poppy still kept on her bed. Callie arranged them carefully, then pulled the covers back.

'I'll fix your pillows, sweetheart,' she said softly, 'and then have your hot chocolate.'

Like a small child, Poppy dutifully got into bed, held on to her favourite soft toy, a much-loved and grimy bunny with a once-pink velvet ribbon round his neck, and hugged him.

Callie leaned down and, taking Poppy's face in both hands, kissed her daughter on the forehead. 'I love you,' she said. 'It will be fine.'

Was she lying? she wondered as she left the room, turning off the light.

In the spare bedroom, Callie took out a Xanax and swallowed it with some water. She needed to be able to sleep, and if she didn't have some help, she'd just lie there thinking, imagining the worst.

Although the worst had already happened, hadn't it?

Sam

Sam watched Ted hold their baby daughter cradled close to him and she could hear him crooning, almost purring at her.

'What do you think of India as a name?' he'd said that first night in the hospital when they both sat there blinking, astonished, watching the baby sleep for what felt like a few blessed minutes. Sleeping did not appear to be something that babies did.

In fact now, after a night and a morning in the hospital listening to the roars and the screams of what felt like every child in Ireland, Sam decided that sleeping like a baby was a concept that had been badly misnamed: babies did not appear to sleep at all.

They dozed, then woke at the slightest noise to shriek at the top of their tiny lungs. And wow, the noise that came from those lungs.

'We'd always planned to visit India,' went on Ted. 'It's such a beautiful name . . .'

'India, I like it,' said Sam truthfully, although she knew her mind was still hazy: giving birth to India – yes, *India* – she'd been so fearful that something was going wrong. She still hadn't recovered from that fear. And as for the pain. Wow.

In no way could childbirth be compared to breaking eleven bones in the body. A mere eleven? More like twenty-two, she decided. Yet perhaps such a miracle needed pain because it *was* a miracle: she had produced this living being from her body. The enormity of it was staggering.

'Yes, India, it's the perfect name,' Sam had said, 'because it's totally unknowable. The great mystery of the glorious, beautiful subcontinent we are not going to be able to visit for quite a while now,' and Ted had laughed with her as they stared down at their tiny baby daughter. Unknowable summed up the whole baby experience pretty well.

She loved looking down into the small bassinet attached to her bed and staring at the tiny baby, their baby. India seemed so fragile, as if her skin was only a filament thin and anything could break her. When Sam had been lying down earlier and a nurse had put India on her chest to try to get her to breastfeed, the nurse had been called away suddenly and in that precious moment Sam had gloried in the sense of her tiny baby lying on her, this tiny form on her breastbone, skin to skin, heartbeats melding. Despite the crazy noise all around her, Sam felt calmer than she had since India had been born.

This she could do: this lying with India on top of her, like mothers since time immemorial. It felt peaceful and natural.

She loved the feeling of her darling daughter; loved the glorious softness of that baby skin, the scent of a tiny baby, the beauty of those big eyes.

'You know everything, don't you, darling?' she crooned as India looked up at her wisely.

Sam wanted time to stand still so that this moment of perfection could be hers forever.

Then, the nurse had returned for the breastfeeding session. There was a lactation expert, Zendaya, but she was sick, the nurse said, looking tired and harried.

Instantly, Sam's anxiety spiked. From thinking she knew how to be a mother, she descended into thinking she had no idea whatsoever. What had happened to her? It was like she'd morphed from a woman utterly at peace into a bundle of nerves in an instant.

The nurse manoeuvred one then the other nipple into India's deeply uninterested little mouth.

India made little mewling noises like a kitten but refused to drink.

'Oh India, it's all my fault,' murmured Sam, feeling tearful.

'Zendaya would kill me if she knew,' said the nurse, 'but let's make up a bottle until we have more time. We're so short-staffed today. You should express some milk if you can for her next feed. She'll get it next time.'

Sam nodded. She'd failed at the first hurdle.

As India gulped the milk from the bottle, Sam swallowed back feelings of hopelessness. She knew nothing. All the nurses and the other women on their second and third babies knew it all. But not her.

The nurses whizzed in and out of the ward, whisking back the curtains on her cubicle, checking her and the baby, handling India with ease.

Apart from that time when India had lain on her, Sam still wasn't sure how to hold her daughter. Her arms ached from desperately trying to protect India's fragile head. Why had nobody told her babies' heads looked so fragile? She could recall how the bones had not fused totally in the baby's skull, which meant she could be hurt so easily.

How had nature let such a thing happen? How could so many animal babies be born and be able to run immediately, while baby humans were so delicate that their tiny skulls were a risk to themselves?

She said this to Ted.

'It's because humans have such big brains,' he said. 'Human babies wouldn't be able to pass through the pelvic canal if their skulls were fused.'

Sam stared at him.

'You knew that?' she said, looking at India in anxiety. 'I didn't. When does it fix? It must be so dangerous . . .'

She felt overpowered with anxiety until one of the nurses calmed her down and told her it was normal.

'Babies are hardy little things, you know,' she said.

'No,' whispered Sam, 'they're not.'

She whispered all the time now. Ted did too. Even now, he was murmuring incredibly quietly to Sam because they were both afraid that the slightest noise would wake India up.

They had both read that it was important to make lots of noise so the baby got used to it, but neither of them could bear to do it. Sleeping, India felt manageable.

Awake, Sam was terrified of what needed to be done. The initial joy she'd felt at her baby's birth was overcome with the fear of her own inadequacies as a mother.

Why was the baby crying? Were her nappies OK? Surely this colour of baby poo wasn't right?

There was an enormous gap between the concept of reading something in a baby manual and then trying to put it into practice.

A head poked itself round her cubicle curtains and in marched her sister, Joanne, beaming and holding her arms out: 'Show me her! I can't wait to see her. She's been out in the world since late yesterday and I can't wait to see her. The hospital visiting rules are murderously cruel.'

'Shush,' said Sam automatically.

Ted looked proud, but Sam stared at India in her little crib beside the bed as if waiting for her tiny blue-veined eyelids to open.

'Ohh . . .'

Sam turned to watch Joanne staring at India and start to cry.

'She's beautiful. I'm so happy for you both.'

Jo launched herself at Sam and hugged her tightly, making Sam's breasts – engorged with milk – ache.

'Thank you, hon, but whisper,' said Sam. 'She'll wake up.'

'I hope she does.'

Joanne stood and peered into the crib again. 'Your auntie wants to hug you, little baba,' she said in an entirely non-whispering voice. 'People, I have told you, you need to start doing the hoovering when the baby is in the house. There is no point doing this tiptoeing around, because if you don't make a noise so the baby can sleep, trust me, you'll never make another noise again. The baby will only be able to sleep when there is complete quiet, so you'll never be able to get on and bring her in the car or to a restaurant, or do any normal stuff.'

'A restaurant, are you mad?' Sam stared at her sister. 'I'm wondering how we are going to get her home from the hospital in the car and you're talking about restaurants.'

Joanne laughed. India stirred. 'Oh look at her,' she said and reached in to expertly pick the baby up. 'She's so beautiful. Yes, you are,' she said, nuzzling India's downy little head.

As if sensing she was in the hands of an expert, India made a little whimper and settled in closely. 'Auntie Jo brought you lots of nice gifts and things for your mummy so she doesn't go nuts,' murmured Joanne.

'What sort of things did you bring me so I wouldn't go nuts?' asked Sam, trying to hide her anxiety. 'Because unless it's a very big baby instruction booklet, I can't imagine what it could possibly be.'

'I brought in a couple of new comfy T-shirts,' Jo said, putting a bag down on the bed, 'and in the car I have some shopping, because that's what you need when you have a baby: big, non-pregnancy things to wear and food for when you get out of hospital. Later today? Tomorrow morning?'

'The morning,' said Sam. 'You're a sweetheart, that sounds brilliant.'

Ted looked stricken. 'I never thought to do shopping,' he said. 'I wasn't thinking.'

'Of course you weren't thinking,' said Joanne gently. 'You've just become a father. It's very hard to think and fall desperately in love at the same time. No, I popped into the supermarket and got a load of pre-cooked meals so you'll be fed. I'll drop it off at yours on the way home, all ready for tomorrow. And chocolate too!'

'But I'm breastfeeding,' said Sam anxiously. 'I have to eat only really healthy stuff.'

'There's good stuff in there: pasta salads, spinach,' said Joanne. 'Not too much, though, babies don't like too much spinach in their milk.'

'Was there a study done?' Sam asked.

'No,' her sister said placidly, 'it was more of an on-the-ground field study sort of thing. Isabelle hated when I'd eaten spinach. I was so lacking in iron when I had her, but I tried to take in as much of it as I could bear, and Lord, the state of the poor child's nappies.'

Sam managed a grin. She felt safe having her sister around. Joanne knew stuff. For years, it had been Sam who had known things: all sorts of stuff about politics and finance and what garages to go to get the car fixed where the mechanic didn't talk to you like you were a complete idiot because you possessed female chromosomes.

But now Joanne was the one who knew it all.

'You all right?' asked Joanne, taking in Sam's suspiciously red eyes.

'Fine,' lied Sam. 'Tired.'

She would not give into her fears: she could do this.

Ted had gone home and the ward was on full noise alert when the social worker came round.

Unlike the lovely nurses on the ward, this woman did not look full of the milk of human kindness. She looked as if she'd found no human kindness anywhere, thank you very much, and she had long since given up looking for it.

She looked at Sam as if she found her lacking.

Sam tried to tell herself that this woman's job was tough: that she saw the worst in life and might have just come from some horrific case. But four minutes in the woman's company made her feel that if Ellen, the social worker, was suddenly turned into the Dalai Lama, she'd still be this cranky.

She had a questionnaire to be filled out, she explained, and went through it all, talking about the importance of registering the child's birth—

'India,' interrupted Sam.

Ellen glared at her.

'Have you ever suffered from any depressive incidents?' demanded Ellen, changing tack instantly.

'No,' said Sam.

'Any previous pregnancy problems?'

'No,' lied Sam. She did not plan to discuss her infertility pain with this woman. Her nerves felt stretched enough as it was.

'Fine.'

Job done, Ellen gave Sam some leaflets, took her questionnaire and marched off.

Sam didn't know why, but she felt shaken. She reached out and touched India's tiny hand with the softest touch.

'Love you, India,' she whispered.

Ginger

In her lonely hotel room, Ginger stripped off the hideous bridesmaid's dress at high speed and pulled on the clothes she'd packed for the morning after, normal clothes. A big sloppy jumper in a charcoal colour, extra-stretch black leggings, long boots and a scarf round her neck that looped over her boobs and sort of hid them. Her camouflage.

The kind of clothes she wore as her casual wear. For work, she had long black jackets that flowed around her and looked businessy. She brightened it all up with geometric jewellery. Nothing feminine, ever.

Next, she stuffed everything into her tiny little suitcase, except for the dress, which she left on the bed, crumpled.

The words she'd heard in the toilet stall ran through her brain like ticker tape in the stock exchange:

'I love Ginger, but she's her own worst enemy. Won't exercise, won't diet. I've spent years trying to help her, Charlene. Years. You and I both know it takes effort to stay thin, but she won't and then she whines that she can't get a guy.'

Worse were the comments about how she'd pushed herself at Stephen:

'Have you seen the way she's pushing her boobs up at him? It's embarrassing to watch.'

And then the finale, James saying he'd told Liza's cousin that Ginger was a virgin and that he could *'give you what you want'*.

Ginger shuddered at the horror of it all.

She left the key on the vanity table and made it down

the back stairs within ten minutes. Her room was pre-paid. Nobody at the front desk seemed to notice her go out onto the street where there was no problem picking up a taxi. It was still early: no mad rush after the pubs had closed.

She got into the back, still panting slightly from all the rushing, and gave her address. The taxi driver repeated the address slowly, speaking English as one who had only recently learned it.

'Yes, that's it, thank you,' said Ginger.

She was so glad this lovely driver wasn't a natural English speaker because that meant there would be no conversation, no 'where are you going at this hour of the night with a suitcase?' or 'what do you think about the government, life, the universe?' – the sort of conversations she had all her life.

It wasn't just taxi drivers, it was people in shops, people on the train, and just about everyone because people talked to Ginger.

'It's your face, pet,' her father said. 'You've got that lovely warm, open face and people feel they need to talk to you, to share their secrets.'

Most of the time, Ginger wished they wouldn't share their secrets because she got quite enough of that, thank you very much. Tonight, she was spectacularly grateful for a non-chatty taxi driver so she could sit numbly in the back of the cab and watch the people racing around town having fun. People who were going places, doing all the usual things that people did on a Saturday, except for people who had just had their life ripped out from under them by someone they thought was a friend.

On their birthday, too.

'I can't believe she's getting married on the day of your thirtieth,' Great-Aunt Grace had said.

Grace was a spiky, funny woman, but one who would walk through fire for her Ginger. Her home had been where Ginger and her two brothers went when their father was working late.

Grace regularly sat with them as they laboured through home-work, although she said she wasn't responsible for teaching them any religion.

'All hocus-pocus,' she maintained. She liked both science and shocking people by saying to them, if God was so good, she'd like a new car, thank you very much.

She liked to brush Ginger's hair and tell her how proud her mother would be of her. Ginger had no memory of her mother, although her father sometimes said they looked alike. Same hair, same eyes, same open face.

'Your mother wasn't as beautiful,' Grace liked to say, which Ginger knew to be a lie. In the old photographs, her mother was slender as a twig.

How could you not be beautiful if you were slim?

Grace never talked about Ginger's mother anymore. Ginger had asked her not to and Grace, sorrowfully, had said fine.

'You'll have to face it one day, my pet.'

No, thought Ginger, *I won't. It's gone. It hurts, but it's gone now.*

As the taxi sped through the city night, Ginger stared blankly out of the car window.

It was well after ten forty-five at night now, and the stars glittered in the clear summer sky. They were so beautiful, like jewels thrown across a canvas. It was a cloudless night and she thought of the pagan festival of Lughnasa which ran through-out the whole month of August, a time of festivals to praise the god Lugh and ask his benevolence for the harvest.

Was life easier then? she wondered. Possibly not. No medi-cine, no modern music, no cake. But then, rounded women were much fancied. They were considered very hot in some periods of history because curviness was a sign of wealth. It was the other way now, Ginger thought sadly.

The taxi rumbled along closer to her apartment and she got nearer home where absolutely nothing awaited her but the guinea pigs – who were not, it had to be said, great cuddlers because of their desire to belt off and explore – and the frantic remains of her rushing out of the house that morning. There was nobody waiting to hug her and ask her how her day had been. Nobody to kiss or massage her neck. And never would be.

Had she whined to Liza? she wondered. She couldn't remember Liza ever offering diet or exercise advice.

As Ginger sat in the taxi on the night of her thirtieth birthday and felt as if her heart would break, it seemed to her that she was the only person who'd ever had her heart broken in that particular way.

When the taxi pulled up outside Ginger's house, she felt strangely immobilised in the back seat. She didn't want to move – moving would mean going into the house and confronting the mess. Not the mess in her house, but the mess her life seemed to be in.

'We are here, yes?' said the taxi driver and finally Ginger stirred into action.

'Yes, thank you,' she said. Typically Ginger, she left a big tip, even though she couldn't afford big tips. The mortgage on the tiny 1920s terrace house along the canal would not be paid for zillions of years, but Ginger always tipped people, smiled at people, put money in charity boxes rattled under her nose. She was the person who crossed the road to give money or a cup of takeaway tea and a kind word to a homeless person hoping for some human contact.

'Thank you, have good night,' said the taxi driver, as she pulled her small suitcase out and went to her door.

Ginger's home was her nest – part of a beautiful row, Hamilton Terrace had been built in the 1920s and was elegant yet rather tiny, as if people had decided they wanted attractive houses but size had not been a factor. They were two-storey and when she'd bought the house, it had been modernised in the sense that the whole downstairs had been turned into one airy open-plan space.

Unfortunately, the recession had hit the owners and the open-plan part was the only modernisation done. She'd bought it four years ago and thanks to some amazing work from her brothers Mick and Declan, and her father's help with creating the best kitchen ever for his beloved Ginger, the tiny house was now a very different place.

Downstairs was pretty and eclectic with huge white bookcases and white walls apart from one midnight-blue gallery wall where she hung photographs and pictures. The room had an old-fashioned fireplace where a real fire blazed in the grate in the winter. A small dining room table that doubled as her desk overlooked a postage-stamp back garden with which she had done absolutely nothing.

She dumped her suitcase on the floor and looked at the gallery wall. There was her life laid out – that's what she hadn't been looking forward to seeing. There was her and Dad, Mick and Declan, photos of them all with Aunt Grace.

There were ones of some of the family dogs over the years: herself and Dad watching the boys playing football, both boys with skinny legs appearing from the bottom of football shorts. In posed shots, Ginger was in the middle: plump, red-haired, beaming with joy and pride at her big brothers' accomplishments. There were pictures of Mick's wedding to Zoe, a wonderful event just a couple of years ago where Ginger had been a bridesmaid and had worn an elegant olive green dress. She looked at the picture now: herself in the long slithering dress, the pretty little fake fur bolero in a matching olive green over her shoulders, and thought how much she loved Zoe and Mick. Then, there were all the older pictures of Liza and Ginger at kids' birthday parties in silly hats with balloon animals, and later ones of discos and parties, arms around each other.

Now Ginger knew it was all fake.

'I hate you, bloody pictures,' she said to the wall. She began taking the ones with herself and Liza off the wall, wriggling them from the hooks angrily, leaving only the pictures of herself and her family.

This was her lovely wall of happy memories and now a big chunk of it was ruined.

She gathered up all the frames, brought them into the kitchen, opened the bin and threw them in. Then she took a carton of orange juice from the fridge and poured it into a wine glass. That would be her night-night drink: not the cheap Prosecco Liza and James had been giving out at the wedding.

Turning off the lights, she climbed the stairs. If the downstairs of her house was all eclectic and unusual, upstairs was a shrine to creams and whites. The floorboards had been too far gone to do anything with them, so Declan had sanded them and she, Mick, Declan and her father had painted them many times until now they were all a glossy white covered with rag rugs. The walls were a beautiful off-white hue with pretty old-fashioned pictures. Everything had a faintly Swedish, Gustavian look to it, which she'd achieved thanks to darling Leo from college, who'd started out in journalism like herself and then realised that it wasn't really for him.

Leo now worked in an interior design company and was gloriously successful, but it had been a joy, he'd insisted, to help Ginger out. He'd been the one to find the exquisite old 1930s dressing table and helped Ginger strip it down and repaint it cream. He had had the idea of turning her ordinary bed into a four-poster thanks to poles her carpenter father had hand-carved. Painted cream and with muslins attached, the bed was a joy.

'You see it's very simple,' Leo had said, wielding his staple gun as he stood on the stepladder and attacked the plain crossbeams in a cavalier way that would have had her father turning pale. 'I think a few lights up here, what do you think, darling? White muslin, white lights: romance central.'

'Can we have the lights twinkling, like stars?' Ginger had asked.

'Of course! I wish we'd been able to get one of those bulb dressing table mirrors, but the proper ones aren't cheap and the cheap ones look hideous.'

Ginger shut the door of her beautiful bower and turned down the lights. She was home, alone as ever. After what had to be one of the most horrible, horrible evenings of her life. Dad and the boys had begged her to leave the wedding early so they could celebrate her birthday, but she'd been firm.

'No,' she said, 'tomorrow is fine. We can celebrate my birthday tomorrow.'

Tomorrow was going to be a family meal in the gorgeous old Reilly house in the countryside, with all the people she loved who would *instantly* divine if she was suffering.

She wasn't sure if she could face them all, not after today.

Callie

Callie woke early the next morning to a faint scratching noise that she couldn't quite identify.

'Jason,' she said, 'what's that?' and then she became aware that there was nobody in the bed with her. She opened her eyes and sat up. Reality crashed in. She wasn't in her and Jason's bed: she was in the small guest bedroom of Brenda's house, alone, and surrounded by suitcases that Brenda had plundered from her house, suitcases stuffed full of the only things she'd been allowed to take with her.

The horror of it all sank in again as if the whole catastrophe that was last night was happening once more.

Still the noise went on, accompanied by a faint mewing: the cats, that was it.

Callie got out of bed, feeling every joint in her body ache. It was as if she had been on a huge mountain hike the day before and every part of her was sore. Maybe this was her body's reaction to the intense stress.

She opened the door and Brenda's marmalade cat, Joe, crashed fatly in. Instantly, he wound himself around her ankles and began purring. Despite everything, Callie smiled. She loved the feel of his fur against her bare ankles, the sensation that this beautiful animal was happy to see her. In the midst of the chaos, it was a moment of simple, momentary happiness. She picked him up and crooned to him, and all the while Joe purred with a deep rich purr like something motorised.

'Aren't you wonderful,' she said, burying her head in his fur.

'Yes,' he seemed to be saying, 'I *am* wonderful and I'm allowing you to pet me and I might even allow you to give me some breakfast.'

He was like a baby, Callie decided.

'Will you come with me to the bathroom before I get you breakfast?' she said.

Joe didn't reply, so she took that for a yes.

She popped the cat on the bed, riffled around in her many suitcases and found a pair of jeans and a sweatshirt, shoving her feet into old tennis shoes, then she picked Joe up and went into the bathroom. Brenda's own bedroom had a tiny en suite, so Poppy and Callie shared this little bathroom with its old bath and what had to be the original black and white tiles from the 1930s above the sink. There were ferns growing healthily, art deco prints on the walls advertising various French liqueurs, and towels with retro trim. Minimalist it was not, and Callie loved it.

Joe followed her in and waited slightly impatiently while Callie performed a high-speed toilette. She ran a facecloth over her face and brushed her teeth quickly, thinking of how usually she'd spend ages with her electric toothbrush and rub special moisturiser into her skin. Right now those things felt like such a waste of time. She pulled her unbrushed hair back into a ponytail and tied it up with a band she found on a windowsill. This would do.

She looked tired and drawn in the mirror, and without her base and undereye concealer, her face was blotchy, with deep shadows under her eyes.

Who would be looking at her? she thought wryly.

There was no noise from either Poppy's or Brenda's bedroom, so she crept downstairs quietly, although the stairs creaked the way stairs in old houses always do. It made Callie think of her home in Ballyglen, the old house where she had grown up. Callie had been brilliant at holding onto the banisters and swinging herself over the creaky steps if she wanted to sneak downstairs in the middle of the night – or sneak upstairs, for that matter.

In the kitchen, the other two cats blinked at her.

'We need to go out, we need breakfast. Where have you been, slave?' they seemed to be saying.

'Am I going to have your voices in my head forever?' Callie asked them and the cats stared at her serenely. 'Right. You don't care as long as you get out and get food, am I correct?' she asked.

Callie let them out into the garden, boiled the kettle and poked around in the fridge for the cat food. Soon Joe and the white and grey fluffy cat were back and eating contentedly while the black cat sat on the windowsill and looked disdainfully down on her bowl as if food was for peasants.

'On a diet, darling?' said Callie, and the black cat sniffed and looked away. 'Fine, you can have it later.'

She made herself a cup of filtered coffee, knowing she couldn't possibly face breakfast, and finally sat at the kitchen table, keying her phone into Brenda's Wi-Fi. She couldn't put it off any longer. She clicked onto the news sites and it didn't take long to find the story in all its gory glory. There were no names mentioned, but it was a front-page story on several of the news sites – police had uncovered a multimillion-euro property fraud scheme and last night had raided two Dublin houses. No arrests had been made but the search for the people behind the scheme was ongoing.

So Rob hadn't been found either, Callie thought as she read. At least none of the reports mentioned them by name, but that wouldn't last long, would it? Brenda didn't seem to think so. Brenda thought the TV cameras would be on to them at any minute, and then where would she and Poppy go? How could they hide this out? They wouldn't have any money, nothing—

Suddenly, she thought of the jewellery Brenda had taken out of the house and felt both guilty and passionately grateful to Brenda at the same time. It was wrong to take something that perhaps had been bought with fraudulent money, but she and Poppy would need something to live on until this was all sorted out.

And it would be sorted out. Of course. Her Jason wouldn't do this. She could not have lived with and loved this man for so many years and not known this about him. It simply wasn't possible. She *knew* him, loved him. She'd have known.

Brenda was wrong – it was all a mistake.

She took her coffee into the garden where Brenda hadn't done much except make sure the old apple trees her mother had planted hadn't died. The grass was a tiny patch, neatly cut if a bit mossy. Jason would have gone mad had he seen it. He liked the grass in their garden to look like a lawn from a lawnmower commercial.

There was a scratchy old wooden bench outside the door and Callie sat down, looking at the houses behind. It was a long time since she'd lived in a house where there were neighbours able to look in on you. The mansion she'd left had neighbours, but you wouldn't know it.

It was only half seven but Callie decided she'd text Evelyn. Perhaps the police had called around to her too?

Hi Evelyn, she texted, *sorry to bother you so early but I don't know if you heard what's happened with Rob and Jason? I know it's got to be all an awful mistake. Could you phone me back? Callie*

She put the phone down, not sure what would happen, if Evelyn would get back to her. But instantly the phone began to ring. Callie grasped it up.

'Evelyn?' she said.

'Oh, Callie, love,' said Evelyn's familiar voice, 'you poor, poor darling. I was afraid this would happen one day.'

'Afraid what would happen?' said Callie.

'That they'd get caught.'

'Doing what?' whispered Callie.

'Doing whatever it was that they were doing, because it couldn't be legitimate.'

There was a long pause. Callie watched the black cat meander past and then leap onto the trunk of one of the old apple trees and speed up in a vain attempt to catch a bird.

'Honey,' said Evelyn, her voice soft, 'I always suspected and surely you must have too?'

Callie said nothing for a moment. This was not the conversation she wanted. She wanted Evelyn to tell her that people in finance sometimes made vast sums of money and governments wanted to know why. That it was going to be fine.

That Jason was a good man, a good husband. Just because Rob had been a bastard to Evelyn didn't mean Jason was the same.

'Where are you?' Evelyn asked.

'We're here with Brenda,' she said in a high, stilted voice she didn't recognise as her own.

'Great,' Evelyn replied. 'Brenda will know what to do.'

Callie realised that her hands were shaking. She'd spilled her coffee on her jeans and had barely noticed.

'Callie, I know you don't want to have this conversation, but whatever they were doing, they've been caught. You're the one left behind. They've left the country.'

'What?' Callie knew she'd spoken so loudly that even Poppy, who could sleep the teenage sleep of the dead, must have heard her. 'How do you know? Have you heard from Rob?'

'He phoned the kids last night to talk to them,' Evelyn said. 'The babysitter was there, I was still in the taxi coming home from your party. Apparently he said that he, Anka and the baby were going away for a little while and not to worry, everything was going to be OK, and not to listen to anything that was in the papers. He said it was going to be fine.'

'Anka went too?' said Callie, disbelieving.

'Yes. He and Jason obviously knew something was up and they got out quickly. Nobody better than Rob for making a quick getaway,' she added with a hint of bitterness.

'Did he say that Jason was going too?' Callie was distraught.

No way would Jason leave her and Poppy to face this mess alone, no way.

'He told the boys they were flying out last night. Said something about a trip on your boat and not to worry.'

The damn boat. The *Maribou Princess*. Jason had organised some sort of insane timeshare on a luxury yacht. Callie had only been once: she'd felt seasick the whole time. But Jason adored it. If Rob and Anka were going to the *Maribou Princess*, Jason was going too. It was his baby.

'So Rob brought Anka and the baby, and it looks as if Jason went too.' Evelyn's voice was gentle.

'Jason left us behind,' said Callie mechanically. 'Poppy and me.'

'I'll come right over now . . .' began Evelyn, but Callie had stopped listening.

She'd had a flu once that had made her feel incredibly light-headed, so light-headed she could barely think straight, and she had perfect recall of that now: the feeling that nothing was what it appeared to be.

'He must have known what would happen,' she said suddenly. 'Last night, probably shortly after you left, the police made everyone leave the party, searched my house and I had to leave with just some of my stuff. Our bank accounts are frozen and Brenda said we better not take much, just in case. They're probably still there, searching. I'm wearing old jeans, an ancient sweatshirt and I have about fifty euros in my purse. I was told I shouldn't leave the country and my husband is gone. There's been not a word from him. His mobile phone is out of service – I've phoned about thirty times! It's like he has disappeared off the face of the earth and . . .' She paused. This was worst of all. *'He left us, while Rob took Anka.'*

'I'm really sorry,' said Evelyn, 'really sorry, Callie.'

'This is actually happening, isn't it?' said Callie and started to cry. 'I just don't believe he could do this to us.'

'I would never have believed he could have done that to you either,' said Evelyn sadly. 'Jason loves you, he loves Poppy.'

'*Loves* us?' questioned Callie angrily. 'Are you sure you don't mean *loved* us, because whatever is going on, he could have stuck around and we could have got through it together. But he's gone. And bloody Rob brought Anka and the baby, while Jason just left me and Poppy here to suffer on our own.'

She looked up and realised that Brenda was standing in the kitchen and had overheard every word.

'I've got to go, Evelyn,' Callie said. 'Thank you. I'll keep in touch.' She looked at Brenda.

'Hold on. Don't hang up yet. Tell her you'll probably need a different phone,' said Brenda, in the same matter-of-fact tone she was using all the time now, 'because people will get that phone number from somewhere so you'll need to get rid of it.'

Last night Callie would have protested, but this morning she just nodded. Brenda had become the person who understood this new world, the person Callie could rely on.

'Ev, I'll text you my new number when I get it, and don't give it to anyone.'

'Fine,' said Evelyn. 'I'm here for you, for you and Poppy, but I don't know what I can do.'

'Be grateful you got a lump sum,' said Callie bitterly. 'Seeing as how Jason, Rob and Anka all got magically out of it because they knew what was coming, you're going to need it, Ev.'

She hung up and looked at Brenda.

'Have you seen the news?' Brenda said.

Callie nodded. 'He left us behind, Brenda.'

'I heard,' she said, going to the kettle. 'I made a few calls last night. We have a lawyer you can talk to. Today, preferably. He'll want money up front.'

'Ha!' Callie said shakily. 'Does he take frozen plastic?'

'Unlikely,' Brenda said. 'You'll need money.'

Callie looked down at her hands and realised they were shaking. She had to sit down or she would collapse. Taking a chair at the table, she said: 'Last night, I was thinking that it was wrong to have taken the jewellery if it truly was part of some awful white-collar fraud. I don't steal – I've never stolen anything in my life – but right now I don't care. I need to take care of Poppy, we need somewhere to live and we need some money to live on.'

'That's what I was thinking,' said Brenda. 'Real-world scenario versus pink fluffy unicorn world.'

Callie laid her forehead wearily on the table and spoke: 'Brenda, if Jason's been ripping people off for years, I've been living on stolen money. I am a – what do you call it?'

'Accessory to the fact,' said Brenda. 'You've been watching too many TV detective shows. You were the nice person caught up in all of this with Shitface and his pal, Other Shitface. Not an accessory to anything.'

'That's almost worse, though.' Callie raised her head. 'I was too stupid to see what was going on. How could I not have known? That's what I keep asking myself – why didn't I see what was obviously under my nose?'

Sam

At least, thought Sam, cleaning up another nappy, the black faeces that had frightened the hell out of her had stopped. It was meconium, the nurses had explained to her in hospital when she'd stared aghast at the black liquid coming out of her exquisite little baby's bottom. 'This can't be normal,' she'd cried, fearing there was something wrong with India.

'It's perfectly normal,' said the nurse talking to her, an old hand at explaining this sort of thing to new, terrified mothers. 'Meconium is the early excreta and nothing to worry about, although it looks a little bit frightening. Soon the baby's stools should be a more normal colour.'

Sam wanted this confirmed once more. In fact, she'd really have liked a notebook where she could write all this down and then have it typed up in triplicate and stuck around the house, because she needed to know that whatever her baby was doing was normal.

Plus she was beyond irritated with Ted, who seemed more upset at the scent of India's tiny nappies – why was he so upset about that? How dare he get upset about it when she was the one in the hospital dealing with the impossible task of taking care of their tiny child, of worrying full-time.

The next difficult step in taking care of the baby was the feeding, or latching on as the nurses called it. 'Latching on' was such an innocuous phrase, sort of like hanging a picture frame onto a wall. At no point did the words latching on imply getting a small, bewildered, hungry and increasingly cross baby to attach itself to a nipple that was already painful and then making said baby suck.

That first day, when the lactation nurse had been off and India had had a bottle, had made Sam terrified she'd mess up breastfeeding again. The more terrified she was, the more India sensed it, cried and refused to feed. Sam's breasts ached. India wailed with misery and Sam's breasts ached even more at her child's cries.

'How is this so hard?' Sam had said tearfully twenty minutes after her fifth attempt at feeding, when India had just cried harder, pitiful little wails that broke Sam's heart. The inner voice screamed at her: *bad mother!*

'It can take a while,' said the lactation nurse. 'Not everyone finds it easy at first, but keep trying, you'll do it.'

They gave India a little bit of milk that Sam had laboriously expressed earlier from a machine that sounded like it was pumping oil from eight thousand feet beneath the earth.

'I know you are going to manage this when you go home tomorrow,' said the lactation nurse, beaming with encouragement, and she left Sam with a sheaf of papers about the right way to do it.

Finally, India slept in her little bassinet, Ted was gone and the ward was mercifully quiet because all the visitors had been sent home by the ringing of a bell.

There was snoring in some corners where exhausted women tried to sleep. There were little murmuring baby noises, the odd small whimper, and sometimes, full-blown baby wailing. And all the while, Sam looked at beautiful India with that precious little face, the fluffed-up dark hair. She looked so like Ted with those huge eyes and all Sam could think was that she had failed her baby because she hadn't been able to feed her.

The woman next door, Larissa, who was on her third child, had juggled her baby onto enormous bosoms and the baby had grappled on like a mountaineer grabbing a crampon expertly.

'It's very easy,' said Larissa, in a relaxed tone that Sam envied from the bottom of her heart. 'I don't know what you need all them bits of paper for. Come here, I'll show you,' she said, when Sam had been lying in bed on the verge of tears, still failing to get India to latch on.

'No, no, I'll try later,' Sam had said.

The nurse passed by again and, seeing Sam's devastated face, said: 'It can be a little stressful if you have people beside you who are doing it so easily, and remember, Larissa has had two more babies. She's used to this now, it's all new to you and it's new to India.'

'But it's new to Larissa's baby too and he seems to know how,' said Sam tremulously. 'India doesn't know how and that's all my fault, because if I knew, then India would know and I would be able to transfer that information to her and . . .'

'She's not a computer,' the nurse said kindly. 'Now get a bit of rest and it will look easier the next time.'

The next time was two o'clock in the morning and Sam did not feel as if it was any easier. She was zombified with tiredness, woken from an uneasy sleep and desperately trying to get India's tiny little mouth to attach onto her nipple. Another nurse tried to help her, holding Sam's breast and squashing it up into India's mouth, trying to squeeze milk out and get India to suck. But it was no good.

'Why am I such a failure at this?' said Sam, giving up and bursting into tears.

'You're not a failure at all,' said the nurse. 'I'll get the pump.'

The breast pump, nicknamed Daisy by Larissa next door, made enough noise to wake the dead, but miraculously none of the other women or babies on the ward stirred. It hurt, too. Sam had thought that the whole breastfeeding business was such an earth-mother thing to do that it wouldn't feel uncomfortable in the slightest, and yet letting the pump remove the milk from painfully engorged breasts was agony.

'You might have a touch of mastitis there,' said the nurse kindly.

'Mastitis?' said Sam, 'I thought cows got that?'

'We're mammals too,' the nurse said wryly.

When she'd expressed enough milk via Daisy, she managed to feed little India from a bottle and at least there was the pleasure of watching her baby drink her milk even if it hadn't come straight from the breast. Where were all her visions of perfect motherhood now?

She'd thought of the ideas she'd had of lying on her hospital bed and her darling baby snuggled up beside her attached to a breast, happy and serene like an Old Masters painting of motherhood. It was nothing like that. It was messy and sore and she felt she was doing everything wrong. What was gloriously joyful about that? The only perfect thing was India herself, who was the most exquisitely beautiful creature to have emerged into the world. Despite years of yearning for this very time, Sam's primary emotion was fear.

The next morning, both mama and baby were ready to go. No breastfeeding had been managed.

Instead of feeling like the serene madonna Sam had imagined she would be, she felt on the edge of an enormous panic attack.

'Have you fixed the car seat properly?' she snapped at Ted.

'Yes.'

'Really?'

'The guy came out of the shop when we bought it and made sure I knew how, plus Patrick came over this morning and helped me, OK?'

'Fine.' Sam sat uncomfortably on the edge of the hospital bed, and knew she sounded like a bitch, not Earth Mother supreme, but everything was suddenly so complicated. She didn't know what to do, and it was scaring her. Apparently fear emerged as wild irritation and bitchiness. But she couldn't help it. Today, somewhat less than two and a half days since India had been born, they were leaving the hospital.

Sam didn't want to go. Only her long, painful labour had meant she'd been kept in a second night. Today was going-home day, come what may. But she needed this place, despite the noise and screaming babies and no sleep. At least it was safe.

Here, there were people who knew how to handle babies. The fear that resided in Sam was enveloping her.

'Did Patrick say Joanne was going to be there?' she asked Ted again.

Joanne had promised to be at Ted and Sam's when they got home from hospital. And Ted's mum, Vera, was going to be there too. Both women understood what to do.

'I thought you'd want a bit of time on your own,' Joanne had said when Sam asked if some of the family could be there when she and Ted brought India home.

'It's a celebration!' Sam had said, injecting excitement into her voice.

It was insurance.

Without people around, people who knew about babies, she might cry. Or worse, she'd kill Ted.

He appeared to expect her to know everything now.

He looked to her as the baby guru.

'Is this all right, the way I'm holding her?' he'd asked anxiously in the hospital and Sam had stared at him in annoyance. He knew as much as she did. And he'd had more sleep. Bizarrely, instead of this momentous event bonding them, the birth of their baby made Sam feel that every woman-clouting-stupid-man-over-head-with-rolling-pin cliché was entirely true. She wished she had her own rolling pin around, just in case.

India cried when Sam shakily woke her from sleep. Despite how tiny she looked, she could make a lot of noise.

'Our little yeller,' said Ted affectionately, touching his daughter's downy head with a large, gentle hand.

How could Ted find India's screaming to be endearing? Sam

found it frightening because she couldn't decode the yells. Was it normal for a tiny baby to scream when she was woken up?

All her working life, she'd asked questions and studied to learn how to do her job better. But there was no MBA in being a mother, no book of diagrams and handy hints. It was on-the-job learning. In work, Sam had never minded this. She was enthusiastic and eager. But here, with India, she was such a novice.

She felt entirely out of her comfort zone, terrified of that fact, and even more terrified that this great abyss of knowledge would harm her precious baby.

This was no bank division to be run; no charity to oversee. This was a human life she was responsible for and she was singularly unprepared for it. The thought was terrifying.

She'd asked the nurses so many questions, trying to get some sort of procedural baseline for what was normal.

'All babies are different,' said one of the older nurses happily, a woman who had two children of her own and had worked in the maternity hospital for twenty years.

She was an expert and this was her best answer?

'But it's daunting, isn't it – trying to work out what your baby wants . . .?' Sam went on in desperation.

'Ah, Sam, you have maturity on your side. You'll work it out: mothers do. Now, some of the very young girls who come here to have babies, they're so young, they're almost babies themselves: eighteen- and nineteen-year-olds who haven't the first clue about looking after themselves, never mind a baby. A few years makes all the difference. Of course, they have the energy. You want to make sure you have a good diet and take care of yourself too, because when you're that little bit older, your age means it can be a bit tougher in terms of lack of sleep and general energy levels. Research shows that the ideal time to have a baby is—'

'Yeah, twenty-five,' said Sam drily, who had heard this many times.

At twenty-five, she'd been trying not to get pregnant.

At forty, she was apparently too lacking in energy to take care of a baby.

Nobody had mentioned the fear that came with facing this exquisite little human being who would be in her sole care soon.

The fear that was overwhelming her.

Ginger

Ginger woke late and her head felt as if she had a hangover, even though all she'd had to drink the previous day was half a glass of champagne and a glass of red wine. It was an emotional hangover, she thought miserably, lying in her bed, the beautiful bed that nobody was ever going to share with her.

She should have been staying in the hotel and going down to breakfast with all her friends, happy in the aftermath of the wonderful wedding of her best friend Liza. And possibly – how had she even *thought* this was possible? – she might have been there holding hands with Stephen, finally part of a couple.

Instead, she was in her lonely bed and her only accompaniment in the tiny house was the sound of her guinea pigs rattling around in their duplex.

Perhaps, if reincarnation was really where it was at, she could come back as the small pet of a lonely woman. Miss Nibbles and Squelch were treated like princesses, adored. She'd quite like a cat, too, but knew that Miss Nibbles and Squelch would then need a mini-defibrillator as cat/guinea pig relationships were rarely good ones. But a cat could sit on her lap, purr, help in a way that the guinea pigs – whom she had not been able to house-train – could not.

Ginger reached over to her cluttered bedside table to pick up her phone, wondering would Liza have texted her with any sort of apology.

Over the twenty-six years of their friendship, they'd fallen out before, but they'd been only small things. Apart from that horrible time after their final school state exams when Ginger got such fabulous results and Liza was shocked to have only scraped by.

Or recently, that time Ginger had had a big work event – the relaunch of the digital paper – and hadn't been able to go out with Liza on the spur of the moment to comfort her because she'd broken up, briefly, with James.

Liza hadn't spoken to her for an entire week.

It was always Liza that did the falling out, Ginger reflected now. That should have been a warning sign. Really, how dumb was she? Clever at books, an idiot at humans.

But there were no texts from Liza.

Instead there was a raft of happy birthday messages from her crew in work sent the day before, some with bits added on late last night:

Hope you're having a marvellous time! Happy Thirtieth!

Catch yourself a hot man. That was from Paula, who felt that a hot man was the main requirement for happiness in life.

Don't go too wild. Busy week in work next week!!! and a few exclamations marks from Brian, her boss. Given that Brian was a curmudgeonly sort of guy, that was almost a hug, a kiss and a birthday cake with sparkles from him.

Ginger smiled.

We'll have cake on Monday! was the text from Deirdre, one of the researchers with whom Ginger was friends. *Big gooey chocolatey with cream in the middle!!*

Wow, reflected Ginger.

Was that the sum of her parts to her friends? Either into cake or men?

Or was that just Deirdre and Paula?

She'd have to stop everyone assuming she was a cake- and man-obsessed woman. Besides, how could she be madly into sex when she'd never had any?

She imagined the email to her own agony column.

Dear Girlfriend, my pals all talk about sex all the time – I have not had sex. Ever. And I am thirty! Is this normal, because there is nobody else I can ask without being humiliated?

Normal is a setting on the dryer, Girlfriend would reply. *You can be into what you want to be into, and if anyone asks, tell them all you are a Christian woman and you are waiting for marriage before you give the precious gift of your virginity to anyone.*

Ginger lay back on the bed and started to laugh. Maybe that's what she might tell everyone in future. She was a truly Christian woman who didn't believe in sex before marriage or dating before marriage or even having a boyfriend before marriage.

Yes, it was the perfect excuse.

Or else she could become Amish. Or did they have arranged marriages? Still, a husband . . .

But how would she cope with no TV? No Starbucks hot chocolate. No lipstick.

OK, maybe not.

Finally, she dragged herself out of bed and went into the living room to where Miss Nibbles and Squelch were scooting around in their duplex. They were genuinely delighted to see her, pushing their little pink guinea pig noses at the tiny bars of their cool perspex and cage home.

'Come on, my little babas,' she crooned, taking them out for a little meander. They were sweethearts and liked to sit on her and snuffle her instead of running off like the clappers, which was what they'd done before she'd socialised them enough to enjoy being held. Miss Nibbles was apricot-coloured and Squelch was a misty grey. They were affectionate, although once at the vet's Miss Nibbles had managed to bite both the vet and Ginger in a one-off fit of temper.

'I don't know what I'd do without you both,' she said. 'Otherwise I'd be talking to myself, and isn't that the first sign of madness? Can I take you both to my birthday family lunch as my guests? I will pretend I don't want dates ever: just you two.'

*

The house Ginger had grown up in was out in the country, although the city was encroaching now with several housing estates coming closer and closer. Her mother had come from a small town much further down the coast called Ballyglen, but there was no family left there anymore and Ginger could barely recall ever having been there.

Her father still went, though: to visit their mother's grave. Declan and Mick did too, but not Ginger.

'I don't believe in that visiting grave stuff,' she'd told Aunt Grace. 'You can remember people without seeing where they're buried,' which was a handy way of saying she had nothing to remember because her mother had died when she was so young. And it was easier not to remember, anyhow.

For all Ginger's life, the Reilly family home had been a true country farmhouse, although nobody had farmed the land for a long time, but still a kitchen garden sat to the back of the house and, behind that, a large meadow around which, on summer days, the young Reillys used to gallop and play games. To the right of the house was a large barn converted into a work shed which had once housed just a kitchen-renovating business. Then, about fifteen years ago, Michael Reilly got his hands on a wonderful old table with incredible decorative legs.

Ginger could remember his absolute delight as she was wearily studying and he'd come in brandishing an exquisitely carved leg with delight.

'Look,' he said, 'I had this amazing idea, Ginger, darling! I could turn this into a wizard's chair! Imagine these posts coming up the back with roundels on the top. I could carve a beautiful back around them and then the other posts could be the armrests and – don't worry,' he added, mistaking Ginger's surprised expression for one of disbelief. 'You know I'll still be doing the kitchens.' Putting in kitchens was his main job, the job that had kept them all going since Mum had died.

'But this . . .' His face lit up as he looked at the old table leg.

'Dad, whatever makes you happy,' said Ginger.

And he was off to his workshop, singing, delighted.

Now he still did the odd kitchen, but his heart was in those special commissions where he made beautiful, one-off furniture, working away for hours in his big shed, music on in the background.

In the true style of the shoemaker, while Michael Reilly had been fixing everyone else's kitchens and bedrooms, his own home had been left to itself in later years.

The house itself was a bit higgledy-piggledy but there was a lovely wooden porch her father had made. And in June, the climbing roses were clambering all over it with amazing old floribunda blooms clustering around it.

Seeing all the cars parked in front of the house as she drove up made Ginger realise that everyone else had arrived before her. Taking a deep breath, she used her key and went in. The scents of her childhood home assailed her. Beeswax polish because her father thought it was the best thing for wood; wet dog as the family's old sheepdog, Ronni, could never resist a roll in the river every day; and just . . . *home*. It was here that Ginger felt safest and most loved.

Yet she'd wanted to be a journalist, wanted to get out into the big world all those years ago because she had done so well at school and she'd wanted to write.

Moving into the city when she'd got her first job had made so much sense and she'd thought a whole new life awaited her, a life away from being the chubby girl in St Anne's secondary school, always the third wheel in every party. And yet only some of that wondrous new life had happened. She had her beautiful little house, even though the mortgage was murderous, and she had her tiny little car, old banger that it was.

The job was going well and she was making more money because of the Girlfriend column. Professionally, everything was good. Personally, everything was dreadful.

She caught sight of herself in the hall mirror and knew she'd done a good job hiding the ravages of a face ruined from crying the night before. Her hair was washed, rippling like copper. She'd worn a coral top and a turquoise necklace that made her look bright and sparkly. Just because things had gone so hideously wrong yesterday, she was not going to ruin this party for the people who loved her.

In other words, she was going to fake it.

'Hello, everyone,' she said, striding into the big open-plan kitchen sitting area to find her father and her sister-in-law Zoe busy in the kitchen and her brothers Mick and Declan standing up with a glass of beer each, shooting the breeze, while Margaret, her soon-to-be sister-in-law, sat on the couch and knitted.

Margaret looked like an advert for kitesurfing – tall, leggy, tanned – yet she was a mad crafter, always knitting, always had needles and a ball of wool attached.

'Easier than meditation,' she kept saying to Ginger, encouraging her to get into it.

'It's the birthday girl,' said Dad, delightedly putting down his wooden spoon and racing over to grab his daughter and twirl her around. Mick joined in, and then Ronni, clearly recently dried from the pungent wet dog scent of him, jumped up on his back paws and tried to help.

It was beautiful to be home, Ginger thought, and she almost let herself go, almost let the tears fall, because now that she was here and in the warmth and the comfort of their love she could tell them and . . .

'Did you have a great day yesterday?' said her father, going back to the saucepan. 'Sorry, I can't let this burn. It's a special sauce I'm making for your birthday. I know you love the old hollandaise and it's a nightmare.'

This reality check made Ginger convinced she couldn't tell them all about the day before and how betrayed she'd felt.

'It was great,' she lied, feigning happy exhaustion. 'Just

brilliant. I'm so tired though. We were all up late – it was a fabulous day.'

'Do you have pictures?' said Zoe eagerly. 'I bet Liza looked amazing.'

'Goodness, you know I didn't really take that many pictures of the afters. I took a few early on, but not that many later,' said Ginger, deadpan. 'But you know, loads of other people will have and I'm sure they'll be up on Facebook later. Yes, Liza was beautiful and, yes, her dress was fabulous.'

'And yours?' said Zoe anxiously, knowing how worried her sister-in-law had been about the whole bridesmaid as battle-ship in full Scarlett O'Hara dress.

'Perfect. The colour was really nice after all,' said Ginger.

Another lie. She would go to hell, or whatever sort of hell there was for people who lied through their teeth and were good at it. Although there had been many times when she'd been in this very house and she'd lied about things: *yes, school was grand*; *yes, the disco was fun*.

All those things that came back to not fitting in and feeling like the fat girl. Nothing changed, did it?

'Where's Aunt Grace and Esmerelda?' she asked. 'They're not here?'

'Grace has got the flu,' said her dad. 'She's hoarse and she can't talk, which means there is no point to her existence.'

Everyone giggled. Grace was a fabulous talker.

'But she wants you over soon because she's got a special present for you.'

It *was* handy that Aunt Grace wasn't here, because Grace had gimlet eyes and could search out a secret faster than a bird could pick a worm off a lawn. Grace was the one who'd scrutinised Ginger when she was a teenager and said things about not believing in standing at gravesides.

Ginger was aware that Mick was watching her now. He was a bit like Grace – very perceptive.

'All right, sis?' he said, leaning over and squeezing her shoulders.

'Yes,' she said, trying to channel exhausted-thirty-year-old vibes. 'Just weary.'

'Sit down there,' interrupted their father. 'Birthday lunch is about to begin.'

It was a delicious lunch full of all the food that Ginger loved, food her father knew she loved. There was asparagus with lots of butter dripping over it to start, followed by salmon with that complicated hollandaise sauce that her father had taken years to master. There were mashed potatoes because they were Ginger's favourite and salad that Ginger noticed her two sisters-in-law ate loads of. Slim people always ate salad. She liked salad, but when faced with a plate of mashed potato and a plate of salad, the mashed potato always won. And afterwards, there was a huge chocolate cake.

'Professionally made,' said Dad proudly as he brought it to the table with two candles, a big 3 and a big 0, lit up on it.

'Call the fire brigade!' shrieked Mick, and Ginger slapped him affectionately.

They sang 'Happy Birthday' to her and Ginger thought she really might cry then because they loved her so much. She wanted to unburden herself, but she knew it would break their hearts. She'd keep this in if it killed her.

After dinner, Ginger didn't want to sit at the table and reminisce. She couldn't cope with that, so she said: 'Now you've done all the work, Dad, I'm going to do some tidying up.'

'It's your birthday,' Declan said. 'You should sit down.'

'Oh yes,' she teased, 'and you are going to do the tidying up? You were the worst tidier-upper when we were growing up.'

'He was,' said Mick.

'Nearly as bad as you, Mick,' Ginger added and they all laughed.

Ginger headed to the sink. It was a comfort being a little

bit away from them all in the kitchen, the same old kitchen she had grown up with, the same old cupboards as when they had been kids. The shoemaker's children were never shod, she thought wryly, thinking of all the kitchens her father had put in though he had never quite got round to redoing his own. The units were sturdy and workmanlike, but there was nothing glamorous or fabulous about them.

Mick began to help her. 'Move out of the way there,' he said. 'You're useless at loading the dishwasher.'

'Go for it,' she said and moved over to the sink to start scrubbing away on the saucepans.

They chatted a little about this and that, work, politics, and she winkled some information out of Mick about their father having coffee with a newcomer to the village.

'Very nice woman,' Mick whispered. 'Just moved into the area, six months in anyway. Dad was putting in a kitchen for her and somehow they hit it off.'

'I'm not deaf – I can hear you,' said their father's voice from the dining table.

'Most people his age are going deaf, his hearing is getting better,' grumbled Mick. 'Come on outside, I'll tell you about her. You never know, we might marry him off yet.'

They went out the back door into the garden which their father had kept very beautifully because apparently gardening had been something their mother was into.

Outside, Mick eyeballed her. 'You haven't told us much about yesterday,' he said. 'So how was it?' Mick always knew when there was something wrong.

'It was fine,' Ginger said lightly. 'Normal wedding carry-on: photos, champagne, people fighting over bouquets. I thought there'd be a murder over who got it because Liza has some friends who are very keen to get married, you know, the usual . . .'

But her eyes brimmed over and the tears began to fall. A person could only embroider so much.

'Ah Ginger, tell me, love,' he said and he pulled her into his arms.

Feeling held and loved, it all came out, but she was too ashamed to tell her brother the bit about her virginity or even how she'd almost brought a man up to her room. However, she told him how Liza had tried to set her up for a pity date with her cousin.

'I'll kill her,' Mick said grimly, after hearing all the vicious things Liza had said.

'No,' Ginger answered gloomily, 'killing her is not a good plan. If you were in jail I'd never see you. I just have to live with it. It's all true.'

'It's not true! Don't believe a word of it! You have to get away from Liza, I never trusted that bitch,' Mick said.

'What bitch,' said Zoe, walking out, and somehow shame overcame Ginger in front of her lovely, confident sister-in-law.

Zoe was everything Ginger aspired to be but somehow never managed: slim, pretty, sure of herself . . . She would never let anyone make a fool of her.

More shame and the pain flooded out of her. Ginger started to cry and thought she would never stop.

'I don't want Dad to know about any of this,' she said frantically, wiping her face futilely, knowing she was probably all red and blotchy, the way redheads cried. 'He's so happy and he had a coffee with someone new and he made the lovely lunch and everything . . .'

'No, it's fine, don't worry,' said Zoe. 'Come on, we'll go around the front of the house. Mick, let us in the side door and get my handbag, will you? It has my make-up kit in it and we'll fix your face up, Ginger. Nobody is going to know, right. We can be having a girl talk and I'm showing off my new make-up.'

'I think something should be done,' said Mick, glowering in the background. 'That little cow; she deserves to pay.'

'No,' said Ginger, taking a deep breath. 'I have to handle this my own way.'

*

The Tuesday morning after Liza's wedding, Ginger arrived into work convinced that devastation was written all over her face.

She was scared somebody would ask her how it had been, had she had fun – something utterly simple – and she would collapse into a heap of heartbreak on the floor and let it all out.

The humiliation, the pain, the betrayal.

To add to it all, she'd overeaten all day Monday, a day she'd booked off in case she was exhausted from the whole wedding and birthday dinner weekend. She'd felt the shame of it as she'd put three ice cream cartons, four pizza boxes and many, many empty biscuit wrappers into the recycling. But instead of being stopped at the office door and interrogated about precisely how much fun she had had as chief bridesmaid at her best friend's wedding – she hiccuped with pain every time the words came into her head – all she felt was an undercurrent of high anxiety in the whole office. People were scurrying around like rats.

There was no group lounging around the coffee machine, nobody hanging over anybody else's mini-desk divider shooting the breeze.

Feeling the anxiety whizzing around like an electrical current, Ginger hurried over to her desk, her best black jacket on plus her most slimming trousers, which had felt woefully tight on her waist that morning.

'Hi,' she said, peeping down to look at Paula, who sat beside her and who watched all goings-on in the open-plan office more than she looked at her computer.

'Email,' hissed Paula. 'Sit down, shut up and read it. And don't talk to me afterwards: we might be being watched.'

Ginger sat, dumped her bag and checked her emails. It all made sense to her then.

Due to a company-wide mail first thing that morning, the entire staff in Caraval Media Towers were clearly scared out of their minds. A super communications guru beloved of their ultimate boss, the scary Edward Von Bismarck, was coming in to take over and 'reorganise all the structures at Caraval Media to take us firmly into the twenty-first century'.

Mr Guru was a guy called Zac Tyson, 'brilliant at management, formerly of Harvard Business School and the man who entirely reordered the company's vast US media holdings', who was going to 'shake things up to give all of us a better future in communications . . .' gushed the in-house email sent to everyone and their lawyer.

'Shit,' said Ginger in a whisper to Paula.

'Shit cubed,' Paula whispered back.

Brian, who was Ginger and Paula's immediate boss and editor of the *Gazette*, the group's recently acquired free-sheet newspaper, stuck his head out of his tiny glass-fronted office and yelled: 'Tuesday morning meeting, everyone.'

'We don't have Tuesday morning meetings,' Paula said.

'Guess we do now,' Ginger replied, taking her phone, tablet and notebook with her.

The team was ten people – three reporters, one photographer, two subeditors, Deirdre who did everything, two sales guys and Brian, who shut the door when they were all in.

His first words were not encouraging.

'We're all for the high jump.'

'This is a pep talk, then?' said Ginger and everyone laughed nervously.

Brian ignored her. 'We used to call them time-management people in our day,' he went on gloomily. He said everything gloomily. As far as Brian was concerned, the world was a sad, miserable place and he faced it with an equally sad, miserable face, ready for the slings and arrows to take him down at any moment.

'They come in, spend ages writing things down and secretly watch your every move,' he went on. 'They say things like ". . . don't mind me, go on and do your work, I'm just here to help fine-tune the place . . ." and then three weeks later, you're fired.'

'Oh.' Ginger and Paula shuddered simultaneously.

Ginger didn't have a full-time job, she was on contract, like pretty much everyone else in Caraval Media. There were no full-time jobs anymore, expect for the top execs and they got paid buckets, if the urban myths coming out of the pub when everyone was four pints in were to be believed.

'We have to prove ourselves,' Brian said. 'Friday's edition has to be the best yet. We need plenty of advertising money as that's all these guys are interested in. Money.'

Ginger tuned out and imagined herself with everything going fabulously with her career, with her own wonderful column in the *Sunday News*, Caraval Media's flagship newspaper. It would be clever without being patronising and read by everyone. She'd write witty, marvellous and incisive columns which would make people love and admire her. She'd be on news panels and in magazines, much in demand on the radio, and Liza would look at her and feel consumed with guilt over how badly she'd treated her so-called best friend.

'Ginger, have you finished that advertorial article on the industrial estate yet?' snapped Brian and woke her from her reverie.

Advertorials were advertising articles written as actual stories and surrounded by adverts. People who were not wise to this carry-on thought they were faintly boring articles. People who had to write them thought they were the spawn of the devil in word form.

'Oh, er . . . yes, nearly . . . nearly finished,' said Ginger, standing up. 'I'll go now?'

'Yes,' barked Brian.

Scurrying out of the office to her computer, Ginger could hear Brian barking at everyone. She sat and logged on.

It was, she thought as she looked at what she had written so far, very difficult to write a thrilling advertorial on an industrial estate, particularly one with several unthrilling tool shops, a big garage dedicated to tyre repair, and a meat wholesaler business, the boss of whom had looked her up and down with a frankly lecherous grin. She'd had to spend the entire interview shuffling her chair away from his because he kept leaning closer, putting a hand on her arm to make a point, edging his fingers breastward. He wouldn't do that to a male reporter, she thought grimly. Or to someone like Paula, who could banish men with a single sharp glance. Ginger had no such tools in her arsenal.

How was she ever going to become fabulously successful if the extent of her writing was industrial estates, peanuts and pervy meat wholesalers?

Her only breakout area was her online agony-aunt blogs and nobody knew about them.

She couldn't tell anyone, either, because she had been so personal in her writings.

At the start, she hadn't thought about that when she answered questions from desperate people seeking help. She'd taken stories from her own life to illustrate them. But now – now how could she let people know that she, Ginger, was the face behind Girlfriend? Girlfriend understood pain, loneliness and the sensation of being alone on Friday nights knowing everyone else was having a fabulous time. Girlfriend knew what it was like not looking like a Victoria's Secret runway model or, indeed, a plus-sized catalogue model.

Girlfriend knew the pain of feeling different, of no Valentine's cards, families who wondered if you were ever going to settle down, the pain of being invisible.

Girlfriend talked to her cats – she'd given her online alter ego cats because to say she had two guinea pigs, Squelch and Miss Nibbles, would have given the game away entirely.

Readers had asked several times if Girlfriend would vlog, but Ginger couldn't do that.

And if people knew who Girlfriend really was, they'd laugh at her, surely.

Ginger gave herself a mental slap. What sort of agony aunt was she when she couldn't even sort herself out?

She tapped away at the information about the industrial estate, nearly at her magic thousand words deadline. But despite her determination to be brave in the face of firing, her mind kept running off to the time-management person.

Newcomers arriving in Caraval Towers to be interviewed were always fascinated by the organised chaos: photographers meandering across newsroom floors having delivered fabulous pictures, while frantic reporters listened to digitally taped interviews, looked up information online, tried to jam it all into a coherent piece that wasn't too short, wasn't too long and wasn't weak beside the piece in *The Predator*, the year-old online newspaper that was creating havoc in journalistic circles for ripping into their circulation figures.

Someone was always shouting, the bank of TVs on the wall were always on too loud because the subeditors at the windows couldn't hear them otherwise, and a mild fight was always breaking out in the news department, full of people like thoroughbred racehorses on speed: fiery, high-spirited and argumentative.

What if the management guru was let in on the secret that she wrote the online column? It would become common knowledge and people would know all her secrets . . .

'Psst.'

Ginger looked quickly up from her computer to see Paula peering over it. Ginger jumped.

'You gave me a fright,' she said. 'Brian is watching us. He's waiting for this blasted article.'

'Oh, he's gone out,' said Paula. 'Probably off to the pub to have a pint to drown his sorrows. If anyone comes in to see who is working the hardest, Brian will be the first to go as he never does anything. Just shouts at the rest of us.'

She perched on the edge of Ginger's desk.

'Listen, gossip central: I've been messaging around and I've got some amazing answers to who this Zac dude is. I don't care what he does, but he's in his thirties and wait till you see his pics! Or his pecs!'

Paula smirked at her own joke.

'What about Keith?' said Ginger, feeling a moment of protectiveness for Paula's existing boyfriend.

'Oh.' Paula waved him away with a flick of a wrist. 'Keith isn't serious, I mean, he doesn't really know what he wants to do with his life. Imagine if me and Zac hit it off . . . older men like bright young things like me.' Paula was staring into space. 'Go on, look him up,' she said.

Ginger typed his name into her computer and a picture of an extremely attractive guy came up. Zac was richly tanned in a way that spoke of a lot of time spent outdoors. Dark hair coaxed into a short, controlled cut fell over eyes so shockingly blue both she and Paula peered closer to see if he was wearing coloured contacts. He was indeed fabulous.

As Ginger scrolled through the shots at speed, Paula sighed, 'Man candy, ten out of ten. Actually, eleven out of ten.'

'Absolutely,' Ginger agreed. 'He's drop-dead gorgeous.'

'I know,' said Paula. 'Imagine all that testosterone walking around Caraval. I hope he comes here first, because if they get their hands on him in the *Sunday News*, they'll never let him go. That ho Carla Mattheson will get her gel nails into him and forget it, he'll be another notch on her ornately carved bedpost.'

'You can't call another woman a ho,' said Ginger, shocked. 'It's unsisterly.'

Paula fixed her with a knowing stare. 'You haven't met her, babes. Her arms are so long, she can smile at your face while she's stabbing you in the back. Watch out for her.'

Callie

Brenda's friend, a brilliant lawyer named Fiona McParland, had got a lot of people out of a lot of sticky situations.

'I'd like to think I'm not in a sticky situation,' Callie said as they drove there.

'I hope you're not in a sticky situation either,' said Brenda, 'but it all depends on what Shithead has put in your name.'

'I wish you wouldn't keep calling him that,' said Callie, 'and how can he have put something in my name. I mean I have to agree to that, right?'

'Don't be naïve,' Brenda pleaded. 'He could have used your name. You've got to look after yourself and Poppy now. It's that simple. You've got to find out has Jason tied you up in any of it by forging signatures, do you own any part of the house, because who knows? How do you go about unfreezing the bank accounts, how do you get any money of your own. Can you take anything out of the house – all that sort of stuff. And if you can't unfreeze a bank account, you'll have to get social welfare, and that's going to be fun – not. So the other way around it is to go to the courts and ask them to unfreeze some of the money and I'd say you'd not have a hope in hell of that happening.'

'You're a little ray of sunshine,' said Callie.

'Sorry. Too real?'

Callie managed to laugh. It was late in the afternoon and she'd had some of Brenda's cheap wine instead of lunch. She'd also taken a Xanax: the days of the half a Xanax and no alcohol were now over. Callie was relying on the little pills quite a lot.

They helped her at least push the pain to the back of her mind and she could be calmer and think straight. The only problem was that she didn't have an awful lot of them left. Her own doctor had given her a one-off prescription months ago, but she could no longer afford to pay the sixty-five euros to see him.

'How's Poppy?' asked Brenda.

'I left her lying on the bed on the Wi-Fi looking at her phone.'

'You need to keep her off social media,' Brenda said. 'They are saying some pretty vicious things.'

'Oh, like what?'

'Like Jason Reynolds defrauded friends and charities, and that he's on the run from Interpol.'

'He's not on the run from Interpol,' Callie said and then she thought about it because she didn't really know if he was or not. She guessed she'd find that out.

Fiona McParland's office was big, airy and it had a huge table at one end of it. Fiona's desk was covered with files and her assistant brought tea and coffee in to them in takeaway cups.

Criminal law was a whole different arena, Callie thought, noting that there were no copies of the broadsheets lying around, nor glossy magazines.

Fiona, glamorous in a dark suit, sat at one end of the table and gestured for Callie to sit beside her.

'OK,' she said, 'let's go over exactly what happened.'

Callie went through everything the night of the raid and what she had done since.

'And there has been no contact from your husband since?'

'No,' Callie said. 'I've rung him but the number is now disconnected.' Saying it out loud made her sound so pathetic.

'Right,' said Fiona, 'we need to see what this detective superintendent has to say and we can figure out our strategy from there.'

'I don't want a strategy,' said Callie. 'I haven't done anything wrong.'

'But you are going to need money to live on,' said Fiona, 'and these white-collar-crime cases take a very long time to come to fruition. You could be looking at years of trying to survive.'

'But the house,' said Callie. 'There's a law about it belonging to husband and wife together, right?'

Again, Fiona faced her straight on.

'The house should belong to both you and your husband, but it's highly likely that it's in the company's name and tied to the fraud. That is not uncommon in fraud cases. You should own half of it, but you possibly don't. You may own absolutely nothing.'

Callie stared at her new lawyer, the one she wasn't sure she was going to be able to pay unless she sold something taken from her old home, something she felt sure she wasn't entitled to take. 'Nothing,' she repeated.

'If your husband doesn't come back with a bag of money and a very plausible story, what are you going to live on? Until they can bring him to trial, this is all up in the air and it will take a lot to unfreeze those bank accounts with him still on the run. Unless he comes back, you're looking at years waiting for something to resolve this for you. Do you have any property you brought to the marriage? Any savings?'

'No,' breathed Callie. She'd never been good with money and since she'd been with Jason, he'd paid the bills. She'd stopped modelling when she met him and had never gone back. She'd thought she was safe. 'Right,' she said, 'Brenda said you were good for cutting the legalese.'

'Yes,' said Fiona, 'that's me. I deal with people who are on the edge, Mrs Reynolds, so there's no point in sugarcoating it. I'm not doing my job properly if I do. The bottom line is that you could sue your husband in a civil court, but if he doesn't have anything to give you because it's all been taken in the criminal case, you don't really have a leg to stand on. There's no point suing someone for money when it's all gone.'

*

'Good luck with getting any money out of a court,' Brenda said grimly as they walked down the back steps of Fiona McParland's building. 'I've heard of people trying to unfreeze assets before and if the assets are the proceeds of any sort of crime, you have no hope. You have no assets and you're perceived as a wealthy woman, a member of the glitterati, who watched her husband rob people blind. That's how it will look. The media will turn it into a witch hunt. *You* will be everything that is wrong with the world, you with your beauty and your nice clothes. Your only hope is to get away. Hide.'

Brenda stepped over a used condom.

'Romantic spot,' she said drily.

She began walking quickly away from the courts' complex where so many of the criminal lawyers had their offices.

'At least they won't find anything with my name on it,' Callie said, desperate to find something cheerful to cling to. 'We can manage for a bit,' she added, thinking of the jewellery, although they'd have to sell some of that to pay Fiona's fee. *The diamond earrings and the tennis bracelet*, she thought.

She couldn't subject her daughter to the hideous publicity Brenda had described if she tried to get the money from out of Jason's estate. Poppy was a kid, nothing more. This would break her.

'I should have watched Jason more, Cal, for your and Poppy's sake,' said Brenda as she drove home.

For the first time since it had all happened, Brenda looked like she might cry.

'I can't imagine a life without him, you know,' said Callie, staring out the window.

'Even now?' Brenda reached around for a tissue.

'When I'm with Jason, I feel so loved, so secure . . .' began Callie and then she wondered if it was the Xanax speaking.

Negotiating a tricky junction, Brenda didn't look at her.

'I'm going to say it now, love,' she began. 'Jason is not a

fucking mirror. You don't have to look at him to see your re-flection. You have to be your own mirror and like what you see without anyone else's help.'

'We've been married so long, it's not easy. How do I do that?' said Callie

'I don't know. But he's in it all for himself. Not for you, not even for Poppy, poor kid. She'll learn that the hard way.'

'He adores Poppy,' protested Callie.

Brenda looked at Callie: a pitying look, the way people looked at commercials of abandoned dogs in dog homes. Callie flinched from it.

'He adores himself, first and foremost.'

'He'll phone, it'll be fine,' said Callie, urgently, as if saying it made it true, as if they hadn't spent hours with a lawyer where it was very much not fine.

The other woman held a hand up.

'Stick on a CD. Better if we don't talk till we get home.'

As soon as they turned into Brenda's road, they saw them: a great crowd of people standing outside the gate of Brenda's tiny house. There were news photographers, people with TV cameras, sound booms, all talking, idling and yet watching all at the same time. Journalists. People who wanted to write about the big financial case of the week, people who wanted to write about the only person left to answer any questions about the big property investment scheme which had been the subject of the most outrageous fraud.

Brenda's road was one-way only so there was no backing out. Callie could feel her heartbeat race and the pain in her chest increase. There was nothing for it, short of abandoning the car in the middle of the road and getting out and running, they would have to drive past. Callie grabbed her sunglasses and stuck them on as they passed the house, but it was no good. They were waiting for her, guys leaning forward with cameras, snapping almost dangerously as they drove by – anything to get a picture. It was horrendous, so frightening. How had they found out where she was?

'What the hell are we going to do now?' Callie had never seen anything like this, even in the early years with Ricky and Tanner when the band were on the up.

'Let me think about it,' said Brenda, easing the car through the path of photographers towards the garage, where at least they'd be secure.

If she ran the gamut of the press now, maybe they'd leave her alone.

'I'm going in the front door,' Callie said. 'It might stop them.'

'You sure—' began Brenda, but Callie cut her off.

'I'm sure – you get inside and check that Poppy is OK.'

Callie stared up into the sky as if looking for something magical to come and fix it all.

But there was no fixing this. She and Poppy had to leave Brenda's house – that was the only option, she had to go somewhere else. Somewhere they couldn't find her.

Somewhere like home. As she pushed past the reporters and photographers, all shoving tiny recorders or cameras in her face, she barely breathed and said nothing.

Nothing she could say would help. Only Jason could fix this and he had run away.

Home, her real home, suddenly felt the like only place she could run to.

Sam

Ted kept leaving the radio on in the kitchen and it was driving Sam insane.

Joanne had claimed that babies raised in total silence would only be able to sleep in total silence, so she insisted that vacuum cleaners, hairdryers and street noises were vital in making sure the mother didn't go insane.

'Joanne's so good at this stuff,' Ted said the night before, while India slept upstairs and he roamed the internet looking for more information on this baby-living-in-noisy-households theory.

Sam gritted her teeth and kept folding small baby things. Ten more minutes and she was off up to bed. She was awake only due to sheer willpower and it was dying by the moment. With luck, crossed fingers and prayers, India would sleep till one, when Ted would feed her a bottle of breast-pump milk.

Once India woke, Sam woke anyway and she couldn't help herself listening to the sounds of Ted picking her up, talking loving nonsense to his daughter and asking the dogs to be quiet.

Sam felt as if she had two moods these days – irritation towards Ted, which he was aware of but said nothing about, and fear around India.

Sometimes her hand shook as she measured out the formula for the bottles. She was combining bottles with her own pumped milk because she had never managed to get India to drink from her breasts and she didn't seem to be producing enough milk. One more thing to feel guilty about. When her hands shook, she tried to still them: what if somebody saw them and said she was a bad mother and took India away from her?

Most of the time, she knew this was crazy, but still, there were fragments of every day when she felt so strongly that she knew nothing. Someone would be able to tell. She'd be exposed as a bad mother and her baby would be taken from her.

There were times when she sat with India on the couch, the dogs gathered fascinated at her feet, and there was peace. India would sleep and Sam would examine the tiny little face with pure love: that button nose, her eyelashes resting on her cheeks, the softness of her skin. But those moments of calm seemed like oases in a long day of worrying.

She was lying on their bed watching afternoon TV one day while India slept and Ted was making them both sandwiches when she heard a faint ring of the doorbell. The dogs barked and Sam hoped India wouldn't wake up.

'Where are my special girls?' she could hear her father ask Ted and she smiled weakly, thinking how wonderful it would be to throw herself into her father's arms and sob: 'I don't know what I'm doing.'

All of which might have been a possibility if he was on his own, but then she heard her mother's voice.

'Ted, hello.'

She could hear the voices in the hall and all thoughts of sobbing in her father's arms vanished.

Not with her mother anywhere near.

Her mother had never admitted to any sort of failure in her life. Failure was not one of the words in her vocabulary.

She could say things like, 'Goodness, you're not going out dressed like that? It makes you look cheap.'

Sam had long since got over her mother's unfortunate way of explaining things to her.

'I think,' said Joanne diplomatically, 'that what Mother was trying to say was that she feels uncomfortable with us leaving the premises wearing short skirts or tight jeans.'

'Who died and made you a saint,' Sam used to snap.

But over the years she'd come to accept that her mother was different from lots of other mums. It didn't have to be a self-fulfilling prophecy, she reminded herself. Joanne was nothing like their mother had been as a parent.

'It was the way she was brought up, Sam,' Jo would say. 'Just get over it.'

Sam had done her very best to get over it.

In fact, up to ten months ago, she would have said that she was entirely over her mother. She had no mummy issues whatsoever. She was a cool, calm woman who understood that people were different and reacted differently in certain situations, and yet now . . . now that she was the mother of a small baby and was not sure what she was doing half the time, it was different. Now that she was exhausted and failing at breastfeeding, *now*, she did not want to see her mother.

Her mother seemed to stand for all her fears and insecurities. Her mother had made her this way.

She stayed upstairs for a few moments, not wanting to endure Jean's supercilious glance as she looked around the small house and found baby clothes draped over every radiator and the clothes horse laden with little vests, cushions askew on the couch and the dog bones – proper bones from the butcher's given to the dogs to keep them calm because they weren't getting the love and affection they were used to – all over the place, smelling like hell. Sam was not ready for her mother to stare coldly at any of that.

She wanted to stay in bed and pretend to be asleep until her mother left.

But this would not be an option. Her mother had only visited once before to see her new granddaughter.

So she plastered a fake smile on her face, went downstairs

and wished she could pull in her stomach, the doughy stomach that had strangely not gone away with the birth of her baby. Many weeks had passed and she still felt as if she was carrying something inside her. Darling India may have emerged but a big load of splodgy-spongy stomach was left, so that Sam was still wearing her maternity clothes.

'I thought you said I'd burn it all off breastfeeding,' she'd said to her sister on the phone, trying to sound like her old, amusing self. She was so scared of Joanne realising something was wrong with her. She'd never been this insanely anxious before. It must be sleep deprivation.

'You will,' Joanne said. 'Anyway, you don't have time to be worrying about your belly – it will go. Come on, sis, bellies aren't important in the grand scheme of things.'

'Ah, Sam love.' Her father was upon her as she got to the bottom step and he hugged her tightly and then, aware in a way her mother was not that she had mastitis, because in a rather tired phone call she'd let it slip, he pulled back. 'Sorry, love,' he said uncomfortably, 'I didn't mean to hurt you.'

'The savoy cabbage leaves are not working,' muttered Sam, knowing she sounded a little nuts and not able to help it. Her father did not want to know.

She couldn't quite believe that modern women with distended painful breasts were urged to stuff cabbage leaves down the front of their nursing bras.

Ted had gone on a big mission looking for savoy cabbage leaves, but there were none in the corner shop, none in the local supermarket and he'd finally tracked down one measly, dead-looking cabbage in the vegetable shop four streets over. It was now all used up.

'Your father said you needed this: savoy cabbage,' said her mother, coming up behind them, smiling and holding out a beautifully wrapped little gift, along with a plastic grocery bag containing said cabbage. 'You're not having a dinner party,

Samantha? It's probably a bit too early, you know, entertainment is quite difficult with small children and—'

'No, I am not entertaining,' said Sam, doing her best and somehow failing to hold her temper in. 'I have—'

She couldn't bring herself to say the word *mastitis* in her mother's presence, in the same way she hadn't been able to say things like periods or tampons or menstrual cramps. Sam had taught Jo all about those things, but nobody taught Sam. Dear Mrs Maguire next door had helped her, she thought bitterly. Not her mother. Never her mother.

Blind anger at this state of affairs suddenly ricocheted into Sam's mind and she felt furious.

'A present, too?' she said frostily, taking the gift and ignoring the cabbage.

'A little dress. I thought it would be sweet. In the photos you send your father, the baby is always in these Babygro things and I thought it would be nice to have some proper clothes,' said her mother.

Ted, sensing danger, whisked the present away.

'Jean, you are so kind,' he said. 'Why don't you all sit down in the living room and I'll make us a cup of tea. I'm sure India will be awake soon.'

'Can't wait to see her,' said Sam's dad. 'If it wasn't for the fact that I know you'd kill me, I'd go up and wake her.'

'Please don't,' said Ted, laughing. 'Her schedule is all over the place.'

'Totally,' groaned Sam, forgetting for a moment that she was so angry with her mother. 'I read this book where it said that you needed to establish a routine and we were trying to have a night-time schedule. But then it turns out that if you want a night-time schedule, you have to have a daytime one too. We apparently have no schedule at all and are exhausted.'

Her mother moved some clothes off a dining table chair and sat down neatly and precisely. She was dressed as if for playing golf, in a colourful sweater, little blouse and casual perfectly creased chinos. Pearls glinted at her collar and her hair had obviously been done beautifully in the hairdresser's the day before.

Sam knew what she herself looked like stuffed into her pregnancy jeans, wearing a T-shirt that had baby sick on it. She was wearing no make-up, hadn't washed her hair for at least three days, and the only co-ordinated parts of her were the bags under her eyes, which were soon going to be joining the hollows under her cheeks. She sank down into an armchair, determined not to sit beside her mother.

'You look worn out, love,' said her father.

'A maternity nurse would be a brilliant idea,' ventured Jean.

Sam held it together to speak civilly.

'We can't afford a maternity nurse. I wish we could, but we can't. We just have to manage like everybody else does, which is messily.' What she'd liked to have said was: 'if you were like a normal mother, you'd be around here all the time helping us, folding the endless baby clothes, doing something,' but she didn't, because what was the point?

Her mother looked distinctly uneasy when they trooped quietly into India's little nursery. All the paraphernalia of a baby made it clear that this was a much-adored child. Ted and Sam had worked so hard on making the nursery beautiful, and even though their initial colour scheme had been the careful whites and yellows of would-be parents who didn't know what sex their baby was going to be, they had since branched out. The room now burst with colour – turquoises and purples, beautiful pinks and glorious sea-blues, sap greens, all coming from the flowers, giraffes, elephants and rabbits that Ted had pasted onto the walls. It was like a living zoo.

India was asleep in her crib, lying on her back, thumb close to her rosebud mouth.

'Isn't she adorable,' Sam's father sighed. 'You said she smiled yesterday?'

'Absolutely,' said Ted, 'and no, it wasn't wind.'

Both men laughed quietly, but Jean was merely staring into the cot.

'That's a sturdy piece of furniture,' she remarked. 'You could have had your old cot, Samantha, and saved some money.'

Sam blinked in astonishment. Her mother had looked at India and this was all she could say: save money and use an old cot?

The rage bubbled up in her.

It was not her fault she was hopeless at motherhood.

Sam knew nothing about how to be a mother. Simply nothing.

And the reason for that was in the room. Genetics.

Her father had passed along all his wonderful parenting genes to Joanne while Sam had been left with her mother's faulty genes, the ones that would have decimated evolution had they been widespread in the population.

Sam turned and slightly rudely made sweeping-out hand gestures to her parents. A smile still nailed to her face, she whispered: 'Let's go. She needs her sleep.'

'Fine.'

Downstairs, Jean perched on a chair and the dogs, who knew her of old, kept away.

'When are you thinking of going back to work, Samantha?' she asked.

Sam, her father and Ted all gasped.

'Not yet,' said Ted hurriedly.

'Well, you want to hold on to that job. Your replacement must be handling the credit card crisis rather well – nothing in the newspapers. Mind you, they're all full of that dreadful property investment man who's conned so many people out of millions. Police reports say the wife isn't involved, but honestly, how stupid could she be. Of course she knew.'

Sam had barely registered the story on the news: the outside world had so little impact on her life, but she wanted to argue that nobody ever knew the real side of any story. From the outside, their childhood had looked perfect, after all.

'Tea?' said Ted, desperately.

'No thank you. I have a lot to do,' said her mother, not really lowering her voice. 'Do enjoy the savoy cabbage,' she said, and with a frosty smile, she headed for the door.

'I'll drop over tomorrow,' Sam's father said, hugging her. 'I'll text first and you can tell me what would be good. You could have a sleep and I'll be on baby duty.'

Sam leaned against her father, feeling his warmth and strength.

'Thank you,' she whispered. 'Thank you.'

'Lie down, Sam,' Ted said when they were gone.

Mutely, she did just that. But she couldn't rest, couldn't concentrate on the TV show.

Thoughts of her first period earlier meant she found herself remembering that very time. Not that she'd known much about periods, mind you. Her mother's version of the mother-daughter talk was to give her a booklet on menstruation when Sam hit twelve and leave Sam to it.

'You might find this useful,' her mother had said with a hint of distaste as if the female body and its menstrual carry-on was not suitable for any conversation.

When the thirteen-year-old Sam had found blood in her knickers, she'd been at home, scared and with only Dad and Joanne there. She wouldn't, couldn't, ask her father what do to. So she'd stuffed toilet roll into her knickers and had braved her next-door neighbour's house, where a lovely woman with grown-up kids and grandkids lived.

All her fears had come out in a flood of tears.

Mrs Maguire had provided clean knickers, sanitary towels and made it all seem entirely normal. A hot-water bottle on her belly, and a seat curled up by the fire with the family's cat had helped too.

'Don't tell my mother,' Sam had begged. 'Please.'

'But where does she think you are?'

'She's not home. She's working late.'

'This is important, she'd come if you phoned her,' said Mrs Maguire, somewhat doubtfully.

Sam thought of her friends' mothers who had jobs and how they somehow made their children come first in spite of it all. Her mother was not of that tribe.

'She wouldn't, Mrs Maguire,' said Sam. 'She's busy.'

And Mrs Maguire had wondered again about her coldly polite neighbour who looked after other people's daughters but had not managed to teach her own child that real mothers would walk through fire for their daughters, job or no job.

Ginger

Ginger parked the car on Great-Aunt Grace's drive, got out, admired the lawn which did not have a single daisy on it, and then rang the doorbell.

As usual, nobody replied. Being increasingly deaf, Grace tended to have the TV volume turned up to an eardrum-splitting level which only other deaf people could stand.

'I don't know how the dogs stick it,' Mick said whenever he visited.

'They're deaf too,' said Declan. 'Or they are now.'

Grace had been the major female figure in Ginger's life as a child and she had been wonderful, even if she had never been blessed with children herself.

When it came to picking up the Reilly kids from school or helping them with homework, Grace, recently widowed, had been there.

Ginger gave one more blast on the doorbell because she never wanted to startle Grace by turning up unannounced.

Cloud and Pepperpot, two overweight cockapoos, did not arrive at the door barking madly and when Ginger pushed open the letter box and yelled again, no furry friends leapt up to sniff hello.

She could hear loud TV blaring from the living room and reckoned it was the QVC jewellery show, Grace's favourite.

Ginger got her house keys out of her bag and opened the door, feeling, as she always did, the fear that dear Grace would be laid out on the parquet flooring of the kitchen having had a heart attack.

Although, really, Ginger thought, as she shoved the door open and found herself standing in what was the only entirely clear area in the whole house, if her great-aunt was lying on the floor, it would be from being concussed by a falling box.

Grace was a hoarder. Not a common-or-garden person with a closet stuffed with too many pairs of shoes or handbags or sweatpants. No. Grace was a hoarder of epic proportions with added shopping-channel-aholism. When the fruits of her late-night shopping arrived, she got the postman or the delivery man to shove the box into the closest available space. Consequently, the entire downstairs was like the Argos warehouse with boxes everywhere, many of which were unopened.

Ginger worried desperately about her great-aunt, but nobody else seemed to: 'She's happy,' Ginger's dad said.

'Ah, she likes a bit of shopping,' said Declan.

'Bit of shopping? It's like a warehouse in there,' protested Ginger. 'Besides, the house could be falling around her with rot and she wouldn't know.'

'That house is in perfect condition, worth a fortune: three thousand square metres, gas heating and a conservatory, and not a speck of damp. Grace won't let it rot and neither will I – I check on her, you know,' Ginger's father always said, upset at the thought that he would let his beloved aunt wither away in her home. She had helped him rear his children and he owed her forever for that. 'And she has Esmerelda.'

'Who is just as bad when it comes to shopping,' sighed Ginger.

Grace's husband, Arthur, had died over thirty years ago, when she was fifty-five. For years, Grace had steadfastly helped raise the Reilly children, gone out to see films and to restaurants, and generally socialised. But a bad fall at the age of eighty had made her more housebound, which was when she'd discovered internet and telly shopping and a whole new world opened up.

Because Grace Devaney never saw a fake gold pendant with

matching earrings and bracelet that she didn't like.

Now boxes, opened and unopened, covered the whole house and Ginger worried that emergency services wouldn't be able to reach her great-aunt if she were ever ill.

'Aunt Grace!' yelled Ginger now.

Finally, someone answered.

'Helloooo?' said a voice and Esmerelda appeared at the top of the stairs. 'I upstairs hoovering, I no hear you,' said Esmerelda, who was a statuesque Romanian lady of incalculable age with jet-black hair and lively make-up, which featured much blue today. Esmerelda cooked, vacuumed between the boxes and, sadly, spurred Grace on in the purchase of electric fly swatters, non-slip wellington boots, sink plugs for travel in Africa and useful kitchen implements neither of them would ever use.

'I just dropped in to say hello,' said Ginger, smiling warmly. 'How are you?'

'No good, the arthritis. But we order new vitamins. They coming soon. Good for dogs too,' said Esmerelda, pleased. She looked Ginger up and down. 'There is new drug we see on telly – make the fat stick to it and not to you. Grace get it for you, no problem. You want?'

'I'm good for now.'

Ginger was used to Esmerelda's constant efforts to make her thin, and strangely, unlike if anyone else had suggested such a thing, it didn't upset her. Esmerelda herself was built like a tank. She merely wanted Ginger thin enough to catch a man and then she could do what she wanted.

'You no want, it your funeral.' Esmerelda shrugged. 'You never get married.'

'I don't want to get married,' lied Ginger.

'You marry girl if you want,' Esmerelda pointed out. 'All is good. Man, woman, love. Who cares if you the gay. All love.'

'Ah no, I'm fine,' said Ginger. Neither men nor women were interested in her, but there was no point explaining this to Esmerelda. Ginger retreated to the source of the noise.

As soon as she opened the living room door, two furry creatures threw themselves at her.

'Hello, pooches,' said Ginger, hunkering down to pet the dogs.

'Ginger, my dear, how lovely of you to visit,' said Grace, like the Queen welcoming someone to Buckingham Palace instead of into a large room filled with Leaning Towers of Pisa of books and old newspapers with pages left opened because Grace wanted to reread them.

Grace herself was a stately woman with bouffant white hair and she wore a fair amount of her shopping-channel jewellery over a fuchsia chiffon blouse ('on special offer with a pair of slacks!') and an old cardigan that looked as if Ginger herself – who had no craft abilities whatsoever – had knitted it out of porridge.

'Give me a kiss, dear,' said Grace.

Ginger kissed her aunt, inhaling that familiar scent of Mitsouko. Beside them, a few boxes wobbled.

Ginger had to say something. It was a death trap, a death trap made up of clever kitchen implements and jewellery that Grace and Esmerelda would need four more necks each to ever wear.

Ginger rearranged the boxes.

'You know I worry,' she began.

'Oh, stop, please,' said Grace, but not unkindly. 'Worrying never gets you anywhere. If I had done nothing but worry all those years ago, would I have survived without Arthur? No, I would not. I made a life for myself and I lived it to the full and that's what you should do too, Ginger, and stop worrying about other people.'

Grace was into her stride now.

'I'll be fine. Myself and Esmerelda and the doggies are perfectly fine here. We have one of those things for putting out fires in the kitchen, you know,' she added, delighted with herself. 'I got it out of a catalogue from the weekend newspaper.'

'There are too many things out of catalogues,' said Ginger. 'With this many boxes lying around, the place is a fire hazard. I bet you can't find the fire extinguisher for a start, and the ambulance people would never be able to get to you if something happened.'

'You got to me,' said Grace, ever the debating expert.

'I know,' said Ginger, 'but that's because I know the pathway.'

Grace laughed. 'It's a bit like Indiana Jones in that lovely film,' she said. 'I did always like that Harrison Ford man. Very attractive. Still, how are you, seriously?'

She looked at her great-niece with those piercing blue eyes that hadn't dimmed a bit ever since Ginger had known her. Grace might hoard like a maniac, but there was absolutely nothing wrong with her mental faculties.

'Has Esmerelda been trying to tell you you should get a man again or go on a diet?'

Ginger laughed.

'You know, she's the only person who doesn't upset you if they say that type of thing,' said Grace, 'and she only does it because she cares for you. But nobody has the right to tell you how to live your life, darling. Have a man, don't have a man—'

'She suggested "woman" this time,' interrupted Ginger, grinning.

'Oh, lovely,' said Grace delightedly. 'We could be thoroughly modern and you could have the wedding here. Is that it, because don't think you can't tell me because I'm old-fashioned. Rita up the road nearly had a heart attack when she heard her grandson was gay, silly old fossil. She's a total hypochondriac and doesn't have an open-minded bone in her body. I mean, who cares who anyone goes to bed with. It's nobody else's business—'

'I'm not gay.'

'It was just a thought,' said Grace. 'You could both wear white dress suits. I have just the necklaces . . .' She sighed at the beauty of it all. 'You're quite sure?' she asked beadily. 'Because

I could go down to Rita immediately and tell her. Invite her to the wedding too! What a hoot! And if she pretends to have a heart attack at an invitation to a lesbian wedding, then I'll tell people about that fling she had with the window cleaner in the nineteen-seventies.' Grace tapped the side of her nose. 'I don't forget these things.'

'I don't want *anyone*,' said Ginger.

'We all want someone,' said Grace, suddenly sombre. 'Like I wanted Arthur and he wanted me. Nobody wants to be alone, darling, and Esmerelda, in her beautifully blunt way, is just saying that. She thinks that if you are thin, a man will appear out of nowhere. Nothing is that simple. You need to feel wonderful about yourself and then it doesn't matter what size, shape or sexuality you are. You'll find the love of your life. The only thing you have to lose is your emotional baggage. Deal with growing up without your mother and learn that you are not what you weigh, sweetheart.'

For a moment, Ginger couldn't speak.

Grace could always do this to her: say something so perfectly truthful and real that it reached right into her heart. But she was wrong, of course. If Ginger was thin, then maybe she might have a man. And she'd never known her mother in the first place.

'Enough of the philosophy,' Ginger said, composing herself and determined to change the subject. 'I just dropped in to see how you were and to discuss what we talked about last time, which is possibly getting rid of some of the stuff . . .?'

At this, Grace looked a little bit shifty. 'I'm not sure I want to get rid of things.'

'You won't be able to buy new things if you don't get rid of some of the old things,' wheedled Ginger. 'There's really no room for anything else . . .'

'There's room for jewellery.'

'Jewellery is interesting but comes in small boxes. The hall is full of big boxes.'

'Kitchen things,' said Grace happily.

She had a terrible weakness for cooking gadgets: slicers, dicers, things that could make soup, things that neatly went into the fridge and made the soup for you. She had them all.

'Esmerelda's just as bad as me,' Grace protested. 'You want to see her here in the evenings pointing at things on the television, saying, "we want that".'

'I know,' said Ginger, thinking the battle was almost won. 'Perhaps I could come around soon and look at all the boxes of things you haven't opened and perhaps consider selling them.'

She knew this was an enormous job. It would require a truck to get the older purchases to any charity shop decent enough to take them.

It was either that, or put half the house for sale on the internet, and Ginger quailed at the thought of photographing everything and trying to sell it online. But it had to be done.

'I might be out, you know.'

'No,' said Ginger, 'you can't be out. Besides, I'm going to bring somebody with me,' which was a total fib.

'Really?' said Grace, who loved a party. 'A pal? Lovely. A man? Or someone to replace that horrible Liza. I heard about it, you know, but we won't talk about it if it upsets you.'

Ginger shuddered at the memory. She should have known Grace would winkle the truth out of Mick and Zoe.

'Sorry, pet,' Grace said, reaching out to stroke Ginger's hand with her own one with its manicured nails and papery thin skin. 'Just be careful. You're such a soft-hearted person and the Lizas of this world take advantage of you.'

'Grace, you're just saying that to get me off the point. We need to do this or a TV crew will be arriving from America saying they're going to do an episode of *Hoarders*.'

'No,' said Grace. 'I don't want anyone tidying me up. I'm fine as I am.'

Ginger knew when Grace had put her foot down. She'd have to discuss the whole thing with her father and try to find a solution that way. 'Fine,' she said. 'For now. I suppose I should make us tea?'

'Ooh yes,' said Grace, finding her glasses and peering at the on-screen TV guide. 'They're doing cosmetics next. Some dragon fruit thingamabob that makes you look much younger. It was on earlier only we missed the best bits. Esmerelda has decided she wants it.'

'We must have it then,' sighed Ginger.

She made tea and then sat with the two ladies and the dogs and watched as a wildly made-up woman extolled the virtues of dragon fruit lotions and potions with the aid of before and after pictures that looked heavily doctored.

While Esmerelda and Grace discussed whether it would be worth it or not, Ginger ate some biscuits – Grace always had the best chocolate ones – and thought of Grace's comment about emotional baggage.

She had dealt with not having a mother. She'd dealt with it all her life, thank you very much. And as for saying she wasn't the sum of her weight . . . well, Grace hadn't been out in the world for a long time. The rules were different for bigger women: harder, more vicious, more cruel.

If Ginger could lose weight, she'd sort that out.

Guiltily, she put down the biscuit she'd just picked up. She had to start. Soon.

When she got home, her stomach was grumbling. A few chocolate biscuits did not a dinner make. She turned on the TV and went into the kitchen to pop a Lean Cuisine in the microwave. She was starting a diet, another one of the zillions she had secretly tried over the years, but this one was going to work because it was about time, she decided.

Time to change her life.

If her mother was alive, she'd have known how to diet and do stuff like that: the thought flew unbidden into her head. And just as quickly, she stamped it out.

No looking back and getting miserable. Not now, not ever. Her mother had been wonderful, or so Dad said, but she was in the past, killed in a horrific traffic accident when Ginger was a baby. Aunt Grace had been all for counselling when the three Reilly kids were in their teens.

'Do you good. You have to let go of grief. Some things, we have to let go in life,' she had said with the same imperiousness that would have made her a fabulous Roman empress.

'We're fine,' Ginger said hurriedly in later years when Grace came back to the subject. Keep moving on – nothing to see here.

Declan and Mick remembered their mother, but Ginger had been too small when she'd died. She only had the photos to remember her by and she had enough complexes without adding to them. No thank you, she was doing fine.

There was only one thing Ginger wanted to let go of: her extra weight. If she got thin, everything would be fine.

Callie

Callie was exhausted.

At five the previous morning, when the pre-dawn light was shimmering in the sky, she had woken, dressed, roused Poppy and together with Brenda, they'd slipped out the back of the house, through four other people's back gardens via side gates and into the lane where a friend of Brenda's named Tommy waited with a car. It was a beat-up old Renault, circa 1994. Callie had looked at the car, once a pale blue, now a combination of rust, dents and dirt, and thought of the glamorous Ferrari sitting in her garage at home. But it would get them where they needed to go.

'I know she looks a bit bashed-up, Mrs Reynolds, but my uncle has had her for years and she's a grand aul car. Lots of miles on the clock, but she won't let you down. I gave her a quick service and she's running fine. The tyres are good, the tank is full.'

Callie had felt like crying because he was being so kind, but no tears came: it was like they were all gone.

'I don't know how to thank you, Tommy,' she said, and she handed over the money for the car: five hundred euros, which seemed ridiculously low for a car and yet barely the price of a wheel on her Range Rover, she recalled.

Then she had turned and hugged Brenda tightly.

Poppy installed herself in the front seat with the distaste of someone sitting in the back of a bin lorry. She held her precious handbag up on her lap, not wanting to put it into the footwell which was definitely not valeted like the cars she was used to.

'Don't look at it like you're going to get a disease from it,' said Brenda, leaning in to give her a last embrace. 'It's a grand vehicle, it will get you to where you need to go.'

'And where's that?' said Poppy. 'Some shithole somewhere?'

Callie didn't even remonstrate with her, there was no point. Poppy had been in a foul mood all yesterday evening and it was as if the sweet teenager of the previous night, when Callie had removed her make-up, had gone.

'Thank you, Brenda,' Callie said. 'I'd have been lost without you.'

Brenda and Tommy had helped her sell her diamonds to a second-hand jeweller the previous afternoon to pay Fiona McParland's fee, and after that, she had 3,854 euros in cash in her wallet. The earrings alone were worth four times that much, but beggars could not be choosers. Apart from the rest of her haul – the watch, a few bits and bobs – it was all the money she had to her name.

'I'm your friend, you know that,' said Brenda, 'so keep in touch and tell me how you're getting on. I think what you are doing now is the right thing.'

Callie had needed just one more night before she left Dublin, just in case Jason tried to get in touch. So here they were, having spent the night in a cheap hotel on the outskirts of the city. Reporters had indeed got hold of her phone number and kept on calling, the *Sunday News* making her most upset as she could remember when she'd appeared in their fashion pages years ago, and later, in their society pages.

But Jason had changed all that.

She would have to take out the SIM card soon and replace it with the pay-as-you-go one that would ensure nobody could get hold of her.

She had hung up on every reporter and the one person she wanted to phone her, Jason, hadn't.

They were out of options.

I don't know how we're going to cope, she'd emailed to Mary Butler, who'd heard the news from Evelyn.

I will do anything, Cal, wrote Mary, in a heart-warming email where she promised that Poppy and Callie could come to Canada for a holiday and spend months there. *We've got the granny flat. You could have it, and you'd love it.*

I can't go anywhere until this is sorted out, Callie had written back sadly.

She was a prisoner in all but name. Not able to leave the country and not safe from the rampaging journalists keen to find some person connected with the story.

But soon, when it's over, Mary urged.

We'd love that, said Callie, thinking that it all felt as if it would never be over.

She and Poppy checked out of the hotel after much grumbling from Poppy about why she couldn't lie in bed seeing as she wasn't in school.

'Because we have to check out!' shrieked Callie, finally losing it. 'We are going to visit your grandmother.' She was putting on a bold front because her mother could turn them away from the door; she could have moved. They might be homeless in Ballyglen that night.

'She won't want us,' said Poppy furiously. 'I don't want to go there. Dad always said that it was a tip, that you guys came from nothing, from some crappy housing estate in the middle of nowhere.'

Callie bit her tongue. She would not respond, not say that it was a pity bloody Jason had forgotten his working-class background. He'd managed to make their daughter forget it too and if she ever got her hands on him . . .

Stop, she whispered to herself.

Somehow, they managed to get out of the hotel without killing each other and got back into the old car, which smelled even more than it had the previous day.

Pigs and sheep, Callie decided: the car had been used to transport them both. It was the only answer for that foul smell, and no tree-shaped air-freshener was going to fix it.

As she drove out of the hotel car park, Callie realised she was gripping the old steering wheel so tightly that she could see the veins in her hands. She breathed in and out deeply.

Breathe. She was going to be calm and get through the day.

'Did you find something on the radio?' she said to Poppy, attempting a normal voice.

'Find a radio station in this heap of shit?' said Poppy, glaring at her mother. 'I'm going to listen to my phone instead,' and she stuck her headphones into her ears.

Fine, thought Callie, deep breathing. A lot more deep breathing.

She found a classical station and let soothing ballet music drift all over her as they drove out of Dublin towards Ballyglen.

It was a long time since she had been on this road heading home. When she was younger, the big modern roads hadn't existed, and when she used to drive up and down to see her mam, she'd had her first car, an old Mini. Its suspension had been dreadful and she'd felt every bump in the road. She could recall getting stuck in a line of cars as everyone trundled along slowly behind some giant tractor dragging hay bales from one field to another. Yet the journeys had been hopeful. She'd loved going home then, loved seeing her family. Mam had never put a guilt trip on her, never said 'why don't you settle down around here, after all Jason is from here'.

No, there'd been none of that.

Mam had given her roots and wings, had let her fly, and what had she repaid her with? Callie thought bitterly. Ostracisation – just because Jason had fought with her mother and made Callie take sides.

Except, a little voice said in her head, *nobody made you take sides: you took his side, nobody can make us do what we don't want to do*.

Oh shut up, she said to the little voice and she turned the radio up louder to drown out her thoughts.

'It's too loud, I can't hear my music,' snapped Poppy.

Callie looked at her daughter, who was wearing expensive Beats headphones, and said: 'Turn the sound up, then.'

Poppy's eyes widened marginally. Normally, Callie talked about being careful of her hearing and not turning her headphones' volume too high.

But not today, Callie thought, and kept on driving.

Crone was in charge now.

She stopped when she came to a small petrol station with a tiny coffee shop.

'You're stopping here?' said Poppy in scandalised tones, as if *here* was a pigsty in the middle of nowhere.

'Yes, here,' said Callie, a hint of madness in her voice. Everyone had a limit, she thought, and she had just reached hers. Shattered mother had gone and Old Crone With No Filter was definitely in her place.

Let's hear it for Old Crone who is able to deal with irritating teenagers,' Crone whooped.

'Well, I'm not getting out.'

Poppy stared around her as if savages armed with spears and covered with cow shit were going to ram the car at any moment.

'Fine,' said Callie, just as decisively. 'You stay in the car. I'm going to have a pee, get a nice cup of coffee and maybe a bun. Buy sweets for the rest of the journey, but you're fine sitting in the car. You can mind it. Make sure nobody steals it.'

'As if anyone would want to steal this heap of junk,' snapped Poppy.

'Whatever.'

Two could play at that game.

Callie took the keys out of the ignition and climbed out, stretching to ease her aching bones.

After a moment, Poppy got out too. 'Thought I might visit the bathroom and I want a drink too,' she grumbled.

'Fine,' said Callie in a saccharine voice that sounded marginally better than the sarcastic one she really wanted to let out. She might get a job as a TV presenter yet: there was always time. Surely TV channels were always looking for the abandoned wives of fraudulent businessmen to front children's TV shows? On that basis, she'd get a job right away.

Callie's face had been on every daily paper in the country both in her glamorous incarnation and as she looked these days. Since being ambushed by the photographers, she'd worn her hair pulled back, had borrowed a pair of Brenda's old black-rimmed reading glasses and had a baseball hat on so that she looked different, hopefully unrecognisable from the woman with the long blonde hair who'd been caught with an anguished face going into Brenda's.

But all she needed was for someone to recognise them. Whatever get-up-and-go she had left would depart if she was confronted.

They needed petrol too so, after returning to the car, she drove over to the pumps, put some gas in the car, paid in the shop with her head down, and then came out.

She drove off the forecourt to an almost empty part of the parking area and stopped the car. Reaching over, she pulled the headphones from her daughter's head.

'Now listen,' Callie said firmly. 'Big talk time. We are in this together, Poppy. I don't like it any more than you like it. I know it's frightening, terrifying, horrible – our lives have been ripped apart and we don't know what's happening, but we have one thing.'

Poppy stared mutinously ahead.

'We have each other. So stop being a bitch to me. I'll try not to take my irritation out on you and we can get through this together.'

'But Mum, I don't want to go to my grandmother's house,' wailed Poppy. 'I don't want to go to Ballygobackwards, to somewhere I can't remember. I want to stay in our old house, I want Dad back.'

Callie closed her eyes for a minute.

What she wouldn't have given to get her hands on Jason at that moment and ask him what he was playing at. Jason, who she'd always thought had adored them both and would never have hurt Poppy for the world. For a while, she'd hoped there was some reason he'd gone and that he'd return, magically, to fix it all.

Now, she no longer believed this to be the case. Whatever had made him leave, it would never be excuse enough for the hurt he was putting them through now.

'You know what, honey,' she said softly, 'I want all those things too, but we can't have them. It's like a hurricane came and raced through our lives, whirling all the good stuff up and left us just about standing with the clothes on our backs and with each other. *That's* what we've got.'

A single tear slid down Poppy's face.

'So we've got to make the best of it,' Callie went on. 'It's a bit like one of your dystopian movies when people end up with nothing but they have to get on with it. We're stuck in a dystopian movie and we have to keep moving, sort this out.'

''Kay,' said Poppy, suspiciously snuffly but definitely brightening up.

Wow, thought Callie, thrilled. She should have used that dystopian movie metaphor before.

Poppy flipped down the visor to see the mirror, found that elderly cars often lost their passenger vanity mirrors, so instead adjusted the rear-view one to check her eyeliner hadn't run.

Callie managed to say nothing about how the rear-view mirror was for the driver and how with a car this old, it might just fall off altogether with any unexpected movement, but she waited until the primping was done, then calmly readjusted it.

Make-up checked, Poppy was satisfied.

'Let's do this,' she said, vigour in her voice.

Poppy was like her father, Callie decided as the *entente cordiale* continued for the rest of the journey. Once Jason made up his mind to do something, he did it with all his energy. Poppy was the same.

'Tell me about Ballyglen,' she said, giving her mother all her attention apart from a little bit of poking around with eyeshadow from one of her beautiful compacts. Callie eyed the compact and thought about how much it had cost in the first place.

Still, there was no point crying over money that was spent. Madness lay in that direction.

'Well . . . It's pretty different to Dublin.'

'You were, like, really poor, right?' Poppy said, as if such a concept was entirely unimaginable. 'I mean, Dad never talked much about it, but he said he and his brother used to steal coal. Imagine having to steal coal.'

Callie laughed. They had probably stolen a lot more than coal, and his older brother, who'd actually done time for hash growing, might well still be at it for all she knew.

Of course, Jason appeared to have no contact with his family, but maybe he did. She didn't know what to think anymore. Maybe he saw his mother, talked to her. Maybe it was just Callie who'd been forced to leave her family behind. Mam, Freddie, Auntie Phil . . .

She shook her head. The thought was disquieting, she wouldn't dwell on it.

'We didn't have much money,' Callie said, the way she always did, and then she thought she'd better elaborate a little more. If her mother was still living in Sugarloaf Terrace and would let them stay, then Poppy was going to see first-hand exactly how humble those beginnings had been: one small terraced house which had housed an entire family, with just one bathroom that had only been installed inside the house when she'd been ten. She laughed.

'What? So poor is funny, is it?' said Poppy, performing a volte-face with speed. 'They tell us in school that we shouldn't laugh at people because they have got no money. Ms Higgins tells us that the guy standing on the side of the road begging might have been just like you and me. He could have lost all his money or been on drugs or something, and then he ended up on the side of the road looking for help. We have to, you know, have sympathy and empathy and all that stuff.' Speech over, Poppy poked around a bit more in her MAC compact, adding another layer of eyeshadow. It was like watching a painter unable to put down the brush.

'I have sympathy and empathy for the homeless person and the person begging,' Callie said, not mentioning that she had not noticed such empathy in Poppy for a while. 'The thing is . . .' She paused. She really had to prepare Poppy for this. 'Your dad and I really did grow up poor. We weren't on the streets, but your father's dad died when he was a teenager so things were tough for his mum. It was a bit different in my house. Ma and Da both worked. My Auntie Phil lived with us – she's my mum's older sister and she worked in the bottle factory.'

'She worked in a factory?' Poppy said, horrified.

Callie almost laughed.

'Yes, a factory, the eight-to-four shift, a bit more if she got overtime. It was hard work, tiny pension, no prospects of improvement, but . . .'

'You're going to say, "but we were happy", aren't you?' said Poppy.

Callie laughed again.

'We were poor and we *were* happy,' she said. 'We lived in a real community. We knew there was more out there but we didn't have it. That didn't mean we were unhappy. I loved my family and I guess I had hopes and dreams.'

'Because you were beautiful and everything and you were going to be a model,' said Poppy as if her mother's career path had been written down in a great manuscript, something to be fulfilled no matter what.

'Mam helped me, she sent me to dance classes, ballet

classes,' Callie remembered and the flush of guilt washed over her again. They hadn't had much money but her mother had insisted that Callie have her ballet classes in Madame Celine's in the posher part of the town, so Callie could make something of herself.

'So why don't you see her anymore?' said Poppy, getting straight to the nub of it.

She had her father's ability to ignore things that didn't immediately interest her, Callie thought. *Now*, her mother's family was interesting, but not before.

'It was on my birthday many years ago. Ma came to the house and had a fight with Dad.'

'But she saw me, didn't she?' said Poppy.

'She saw you, she loved you, everyone loves you,' Callie said brightly, the guilt searing through her again.

'So the house, Granny's house – oh, what will I call her? Grandma?'

'You'll have to ask her.'

'What's the house like?'

'It's not what you're used to,' her mother explained. 'It's small and was always pretty, homey . . .'

That warmth was what Callie had tried to recreate in her own kitchen. The community feel of Ballyglen was something she'd never managed to find again in the upper echelons of Dublin society.

'Will I have my own bedroom?'

'I don't know if you'll have your own bedroom, lovie. You might be sharing with me.'

'Yuck,' said Poppy, horrified. 'That's sick. I can't share with you. Why can't we go back to Brenda's – at least there I had my own room.'

'We can't stay with Brenda, we have to get away somewhere nobody knows us until this all dies down and Dad sorts it all out.'

'He will sort it all out, won't he?' said Poppy in a small voice.

And for just a moment she didn't sound at all like the cool teenager who knew everything.

'Let's hope he sorts it out,' Callie said gently. She didn't think now that Jason was going to be sorting anything out anytime soon, but her daughter was still only fourteen, still a child. She couldn't let her know the truth just yet. She dare not think of social media and how girls from her school could have already told her. But if Callie kept up the facade, then surely Poppy would believe it.

Let them settle somewhere, hopefully in Ballyglen. Let them find some routine and normality to life and then, if Callie could get a job and had enough money to pay for counselling for Poppy, she'd tell her the unvarnished truth. Slowly, gently. Not all in one fell swoop. For a girl who idolised her father, it would be like hearing of his death.

Whatever had to be said had to be said gently. But social media was still the problem. Poppy was glued to her phone. Who knew what she'd see if she looked up her father's name.

As they drove, Callie could feel her nerves really straining now. Poppy had taken off her headphones and had the radio blasting loudly. She'd grumbled about not being able to get her favourite Dublin city station and about there not being a system where she could plug her phone into the car and let it pick up her music via Bluetooth.

'Useless car,' she'd muttered, before finding a cool local station she could turn up too loud, which was her preferred volume.

Callie said nothing but felt the coffee she'd had earlier churning in her stomach.

As they neared her home town, Callie could see the bottle factory that had given work to so much of Ballyglen was gone, but it was still a big farming town with fertile land to raise dairy cows. Just before the town, the road rose lazily into a gentle slope and then they were suddenly on a curve on the sweep of the hill, with the whole town laid out before them. Rich green fields filled with cattle and sheep straddled the roads.

Below lay Ballyglen, home to some twenty thousand souls, one large church, not to mention a large hotel and country club, with golf course and riding attached. A small river ran through the town and divided it perfectly.

From a distance, it looked like a town on a chocolate box: pretty stone walls around it, shops and houses painted soft colours as if a watercolour artist had had a hand in the whole thing. Old trees growing in the centre of the town and a bridge with elegant curved lamplights giving an air of timelessness to it all.

'It's pretty,' said Poppy in surprise.

'It is,' said her mother, smiling. 'What did you think? Something from a Tim Burton nightmare?'

'Well . . .' Poppy made the single syllable drag out. 'Dad said it was awful.'

'It's just a country town and we lived in the poorer bit. He never got over that,' Callie said, and then realised she'd been very honest with her daughter.

'Why didn't he get over it? You did.' Poppy was interested.

'Our area was once considered the bad area of the town and it's not nice growing up in a place where everyone thinks the worst of you because some of the neighbours aren't model citizens. My family, my whole road in fact, was lovely, but it wasn't all like that. Blackheights was the name of the place. Comes from the Irish – Aird Dubh. A history teacher once said it was probably a site of ancient Celtic ritual, but in Ballyglen when we grew up, it was where the poorer people lived, people who worked in the bottle factory when it was still open.'

They drove down the winding hill, passing the imposing entrance to the elegant golf resort hotel Callie had often longed to visit so she could see her mother. Had Jason stayed there to see his mother? Who knew? Anything was possible in this topsy-turvy world.

Finally, they were in the town itself and Poppy exclaimed once again at its prettiness, and then said she could see no nice clothes shops, which was bad.

Callie drove carefully, watching the streets as she got nearer to home, seeing the old bakery where she and her friends used to buy jam doughnuts. They drove past Cathedral Square and around the picturesque houses which Callie used to fantasise about the whole family living in as a child. Fat old trees sat outside the houses, apple trees with big trunks now and summer flowers in planters.

Then, they were driving higher up the hill on the other side where they arrived at the warren of streets that was Blackheights, a cluster of small terraced houses, built many years ago to house a workforce for whom there turned out to be no work.

There was the sliver of park that Callie could remember was where the rebel kids smoked when she'd been young. Smoked and drunk naggins of gin and vodka, whatever they could get. There had been drugs, but it hadn't been as all-pervasive as it was for Poppy's generation. Callie had tried hash when she'd been with Ricky but she'd hated it: it made her feel paranoid, out of place. Poor Ricky, he'd gone down that path for a long time. And Freddie – she stopped. It hurt to think of her brother.

She'd left Ricky then, long before he hooked up with the manager who finally helped him clean up his act and come off drugs. That was when Tanner had gone from being a hot band to being mega, worldwide superstars with Ricky as the rock god.

His parents still lived in Ballyglen, she thought, although she assumed his father and mother no longer worked in the local hospital – they must be retired now.

She flicked on the left indicator and drove down a road she'd walked down so many times on her way to school. Not long now till home.

Poppy turned the radio down.

'I didn't expect it would be like this,' she said quietly.

'Like what?'

'Er . . . you know . . . with these small houses? It's pretty and everything, but small.'

'Our house in Dublin isn't normal, Poppy,' said Callie. She corrected herself. '*Wasn't* normal. Most people don't have six bedrooms, giant reception rooms, a catering kitchen and a garage with a Ferrari in it.'

And neither did they – anymore.

'I know but . . .'

Callie kept her eyes straight ahead. The roads were narrow here with only room for one car because people didn't have driveways and parked on the road. Drivers had to zigzag from one side of the road to the other. Callie reached a T-junction and took a right. Now the houses were mainly grey or white. Small, terraced, well-painted because it was a long time since they'd belonged to the council and the owners had kept them beautifully.

Some had the frames around the windows painted bright colours; others had lovely trellises around the porches where flowers, roses or wisteria grew, giving the whole road a welcoming look that Callie couldn't remember from her youth. It was comforting, home.

For so long, listening to Jason's poison about their time growing up in Ballyglen, she'd remembered their home town only as a place she'd wanted to escape from. Now she could see the streets around Sugarloaf Terrace as they really were: a place where neighbours drove other neighbours to hospital appointments, where someone would walk your dog if you were sick, where people cared. A sense of community – that was it. Jason had never seen it and, to be honest, she wasn't sure she had either, until now, when it all came flooding back.

'So this is where you grew up?' said Poppy. 'I mean, the houses are small and all that, but it's OK.'

'This is it,' said Callie. 'I used to walk along this road in my horrible grey school uniform and meet up with my friend,

Bianca, just at the corner back there and we would cut through the lane and go to school.'

'Sort of hard to imagine you in a school uniform,' said Poppy, a smile in her voice.

'It was a horrible school uniform,' said her mother.

'But I bet you still looked amazing in it,' said Poppy, a hint of envy in her voice.

'You look wonderful in your school uniform, honey,' said Callie, the old familiar refrain. And then she stopped because Poppy wasn't going to that school anymore. In fact, she probably never would go back because St Tilda's was a private exclusive school and cost an absolute fortune. Unless Jason came back in a time machine and sorted everything out, Poppy wasn't going to school there ever again. The very thought made her want to vomit and she had to inhale deeply and force herself not to be sick. She would not pull over and throw up on the side of the road.

She would not think about possible futures or the past or things that had gone wrong, she would just concentrate on this moment, the way Brenda had told her.

'Just get through every day as it comes,' Brenda had said the morning they'd left, holding Callie by the shoulders.

'You sound like you're telling me to stay off the drink or something,' said Callie, trying to lighten the mood.

'It's a bit like that,' agreed Brenda, 'although even though you and I have got through a couple of bottles of wine, I don't think we qualify for rehab just yet. But what I mean is stop obsessing over the past and stop worrying about Jason. You have to take care of yourself and Poppy. If you think too far into the future, you'll crumble. Be strong and think about today.'

Be strong. Callie said the words silently in her head now. She had to be strong for Poppy because who knew what was awaiting her. Her mother might not forgive her. Her mother might send them packing and then . . . Callie wasn't really sure what the next option was.

She turned the last corner into a tiny cul-de-sac. Sugarloaf

Terrace. Ten houses, five on each side. This street had always been beautifully cared for even when she was growing up, even when many of the other houses in the area had been run-down because nobody had any money to paint them up. The council hadn't cared and the people living in them were too broke, too concerned with survival, to worry about whether the paint on their front doors flaked or not. But the Terrace had been different. Home to many strong women who wanted their homes to look as if they were surviving, because if you looked as though you were, you just might be.

'Here we are,' she said, trying to sound bright to hide her nerves.

'Here?' said Poppy anxiously.

'This is it.'

She parked the car in front of the house. It looked different now: her mum's garden had been transformed with lots of plants and containers and with paving stones so that a small car could be parked there, which was something nobody had ever done when Callie was growing up. The car which stood there now was a smart new little runaround. Silver-grey, one year old, and Callie wondered if her mother had moved. When she'd been young, her mother had never driven and where had she got the money for a car?

'Do you want to stay here for a minute while I go and just check if your grandmother is in?' she said to Poppy.

Poppy, looking strangely subdued, nodded. She pulled out a compact to examine her lipstick again. When Poppy was stressed, she went to her face, examining it and worrying over it as if lipstick application and perfect eyeshadow would make everything all right. Suddenly Callie saw all that primping for what it really was: anxiousness, worry. What would the long-term damage be to her daughter from all of this? She put her arm around Poppy's shoulder.

'It's going to be fine,' she said. 'We'll get through this, everything is going to be fine.'

She got out of the car, thinking that she'd lied again. She didn't know if it was going to be fine. That was motherhood for you: going from lying about the existence of Santa Claus to lying about how things would be 'fine'.

A curtain in the house next door twitched, but Callie pretended not to notice as she walked up the path.

Her mother's door was painted a lovely sky blue.

Callie knocked and could feel her heart beat a tattoo in her chest. Please let her mother still be living there, please let her mother allow her to apologise, explain and beg. She'd beg if she had to. She would go down on her knees, because she and Poppy needed somewhere to stay. Whatever about herself, she couldn't put Poppy through what they had been through in the last few days.

At that, the door swung open and her mother stood there, still small, her hair no longer platinum blonde but totally white and long, trailing back into a little plait. She'd aged. There were lines all over her face now, carved in by life, and she had, Callie realised, become an old woman. But her eyes were the same translucent blue as Callie's and they lit up when she realised who it was.

'Oh Claire, lovie: you've come home.'

Callie fell into her mother's arms and let the tears flow.

'I wasn't sure if I could come or if you'd see me or have us or anything, but I'm sorry, Mam,' she blurted out, 'I'm so so sorry. How can you forgive me . . .?'

'Shush, Claire, lovie, it's all right.' Her mother held her the way she used to years ago.

Callie had been taller than her mum since she had been about fourteen, but her mother appeared to have shrunk. Still, it felt so good being able to rest her head on her mother's shoulder, to smell that familiar smell of perfume. She didn't know what it was anymore, something with lilies, she thought. It was not one of the expensive perfumes of Callie's that Brenda had scooped up that dreadful night.

'I was hoping you'd come,' her mother said, 'really hoping, but I didn't know if you would. When I saw that that bastard had run away on you, I just hoped you'd come back to me.'

'He's not—' Callie began to say and then she stopped. She remembered the row all those years ago when her mother had called Jason a bastard and accused him of all sorts of stuff and Callie had stood up for him. And it seemed as if her mother had been right all along.

'Is that, is that Poppy in the car?'

Callie nodded. At this point, she could barely trust herself to speak.

'Oh the good Lord, get her in here.'

'Just don't say anything bad about her father to her – we haven't gone down that road yet.'

Her mother let go of her and flew down the path, wrenching open the door on the old Renault where Poppy sat, eyes wide open, watching this small vibrant little woman racing towards her.

'Poppy, love, will you get out of the car and into the house. Look at you! You're so grown-up, you're a young woman! I've waited for this for so long.'

Callie watched as Poppy was enveloped in the same tight grasp and Callie had to lean against the wallpapered wall in the hall, beside the holy Sacred Heart picture with the red light burning underneath, so she could breathe with relief.

Home. She was home. And welcomed.

It didn't take long to get all the suitcases and bags in. Poppy and Callie did it.

'No, Mam, you're not touching any of it,' said Callie.

Despite the speed with which her mother had run down the path to get Poppy out of the car, it was obvious that she was suffering now with severe arthritis: her movements were stiff, her hands misshapen, fingers covered with little arthritic nodules on the knuckles.

'I'm fine, sure, aren't I well able to carry a few things in,' said her mother.

'No,' said Callie. 'You make the tea, we'll drag it all in.'

Poppy looked like she might object, but Callie shot her a fierce glare.

'Where will I put it all, Granny?' said Poppy as she came in with the first load.

'We'll worry about that later,' said Callie, wondering who was still living in the house, what was going to happen. She thought of the phone calls she'd had from Freddie: furious, drug-induced, raging phone calls where he'd accused her of being a turncoat, of abandoning their family for that bastard Jason Reynolds. If Freddie was around, Callie wasn't sure they'd be allowed to stay. She'd given up on poor Freddie too.

'It's just me here now,' said her mother as if she could read Callie's mind. 'Your Uncle Freddie's in Kerry, doing well,' she said, with a nod to Callie. 'Very well. Very health-conscious, your Uncle Freddie.'

Callie let out a breath she didn't realise she'd been holding in.

Health-conscious – code for 'off the drugs'.

'Your Auntie Phil is still living in the big house near the golf club. Wait till you see it, Poppy. I'd never seen the like of it. Phil fell on her feet, ah but sure he was a good man, Seamus, a good man, a lot older than her now and I won't say she hasn't been through trouble with him through sickness, but they had such love.'

'Had?' said Callie anxiously. She'd loved Auntie Phil.

Auntie Phil was the glamorous one in the family, while Callie's mother, Pat, never went in much for any more than a slash of a bright lipstick, which was always flattened down to the tube end before she thought about replacing it.

'Lord almighty, Phil, you look fabulous. I wish I could do that,' Callie's mother would say as Phil emerged from the attic bedroom, face painted, platinum hair set and ready to go. 'New perfume?'

'It's Dinner in Paris,' Phil would explain. 'Or is it Lunch in Paris . . .?'

'Late Night Chipper in Paris?' Callie's mother would tease and the two sisters would bend over laughing, delighted with their humour.

They looked so similar, even with Phil all beautified: both a lot shorter than tall, lean Callie; both with hair dyed, home-dye jobs because who in Sugarloaf Terrace could afford the hairdresser. And both with the same hoarse laugh that sounded as if they'd spent years singing torch songs in night-clubs, although the hoarseness was part genetic, part too many cigarettes.

The teenage Callie had loved the sisters when they were like that: laughing and joking with each other, Phil all glittery and done up, with her nails – kept short for the factory – expertly painted bright red. Nobody made her mother laugh the way Phil did.

Pat Sheridan, manageress of the dry-cleaner's on Florence Road, could have a sharp tongue on her, but it was softer for her younger sister and softest of all for her beloved daughter, Claire.

She patted Callie's hand. 'Seamus isn't well, but I'll tell you all about it later, lovie. Phil will be dying to see you both.'

She led the way into the kitchen, which had changed totally. Extended and with lovely wooden cupboards, it was all amazingly different from the mad mustard units that had been there in Callie's time. The whole place had been extended till it was a lovely family room with a lantern ceiling window that allowed glorious light to shine in. The old kitchen table they'd all done their homework on was gone and in its place was a pale ash table that went with the wood of the floor. A soft couch and a TV in one corner filled it out.

'It's fantastic,' said Callie, looking around.

'Freddie's company did it, he's got a great business now in the building trade,' said her mother. 'Went into partnership with Seanie down the road. Managed through the crash and I tell everyone they're the finest builders in Ireland. Been in some of the magazines as well. They work a lot with this architect fella, decent lad. Younger brother of – ah, you wouldn't know him. They live and work in Kerry mainly. Freddie likes the quiet.'

Quick as a flash, Pat Sheridan changed the subject.

'He did this up for me, for my seventy-fifth.'

'You're seventy-five, Granny?' said Poppy, always fascinated with people's ages.

'Seventy-six now,' said her grandmother, 'and still no sense because I'm still going to the bingo. Not that I win very much. Your Aunt Phil's much better than me. Luckier. Your father always said she had the luck.'

'And Freddie?' said Callie. 'Did you tell him you thought I'd be coming?'

'I didn't share it with him but I'm sure he's thinking of it,' said her mother slowly. 'I mean, he rang me when he saw it in the papers. I don't know, Callie, don't know what to say to you, love. I'm not going to say anything now in front of the child.'

'I'm not a child,' said Poppy, outraged.

'As it happens, I'm not going to say anything in front of you anyway,' said her grandmother firmly. 'What's happened has happened but we have to move on and make a new life for yourselves . . .'

'We are not making a new life for ourselves,' said Poppy firmly. 'We're here for a visit. Dad's going to be back, everything is going to be fine, it's all a misunderstanding. We just needed somewhere because we were staying with Brenda and then, you know, the newspapers came and were taking pictures and we had to get out.'

Callie looked at her mother and saw the deep pity in her eyes.

'Quite right too,' said her mother cheerily. 'I'm glad you came here for a little break. I'll show you the room. Not that your mother needs any showing, she can bring you up. You can take the attic. You wouldn't want to be tall to be in it, so it was fine for your aunt because she was a bit of a short one like myself, and it will be grand for you. Not for your mother though. Not with those long legs. You could have Freddie's old room, Claire. It's all done up nice now, pinks and greys and Freddie kept saying they weren't the colours now, but you know I like them. And you could meet the dog. Ketchup. He's out the back doing his business. Let's get him in.'

Ketchup was a funny breed of dog.

'Ah sure he's a bit of everything,' Callie's mother said. 'Fifty-seven varieties and all that, that's why we called him Ketchup.'

'Brilliant,' said Poppy, who'd always wanted a dog. She sat on the floor and let herself be loved and adored by the off-white little creature with the tufty hair, the short tail, the brown eyes and a little face that said uncertain parentage was definitely part of the picture.

'We don't know how old he is,' Callie's mum said, as the two grown-ups watched Poppy turn into a kid with an animal. 'Some young lads had him one Halloween. Luckily, your brother Freddie got there in time and he said it would be good for me, you know, after the operation.'

'What operation?' said Callie, hating the feeling that here was yet another thing that she had missed.

'Ah, you know,' her mother began, then stopped, which was very unlike Pat Sheridan. 'Women's things. Ages ago, it doesn't matter.'

Poppy decided she didn't want to sleep alone and that since Ketchup had taken such a shine to her he would share her room.

'I'm just telling you he makes terrible wind in the middle of the night,' said her grandmother.

'That's fine, Nana,' said Poppy. 'I don't mind, I love dogs.' She was walking round holding Ketchup in her arms as if he was a pampered chihuahua or some other handbag dog instead of an adorably scruffy little mongrel with the most bewitching eyes that shone with happiness. Every few seconds, his pink tongue reached out to lick whatever bit of Poppy he could reach.

'She's a lovely child,' said Pat when Poppy went up to the attic with Ketchup to show him his new sleeping quarters before dinner.

They could hear her talking to him on the way up.

'Now you can have your bed on the floor, but if you really want, you can get into the bed with me and we can snuggle, but no smelly wind,' Poppy was saying. 'Although I don't mind, honestly, I still love you.'

'Yes, she's a great girl,' said Callie, sitting down on one ancient kitchen chair that had been there since she had been a kid. Even though the kitchen was changed, her mother had kept those parts along with some of the old family pictures still on the walls. There were lots of new pictures now, new pictures of a life of which Callie was no longer a part. How could she have been so stupid as to let Jason do that to her? Even thinking about the insults flung and how it had broken up the family made Callie want to cry.

'That's in the past, love,' said her mother, watching Callie's gaze on the photos that were stuck up haphazardly all over the walls. This was no beautifully created gallery wall – this was family life, the pictures stuck in every which way in all sorts of frames. 'No point looking back, got to keep looking forward.'

'Oh, Mam,' cried Callie. 'But I do keep looking back. I keep looking back wondering what's happening, what has he done? And now you're welcoming me in with a kindness I don't deserve. Why wasn't I here when you had that operation? Why did I abandon you? I'm sorry, I'm just so sorry. You must be thinking I'm getting my just deserts now.'

Her mother began stirring the soup she had made from scratch which was going to be their dinner, soup and home-made bread. It was so simple and yet it felt like such a long time since Callie had eaten a good, simple home-cooked meal.

'You're my child and I love the very bones of you, Claire Sheridan,' said her mother firmly. 'I love you and I have always prayed for this day. Jason had you under his thumb from the first moment he met you. We could all see it, your aunt and I, we used to talk about it. He was controlling, very controlling. But you couldn't see any bad in him.'

'There wasn't any bad in him,' Callie protested, and then stopped. He'd kept her from her family. He'd run off and left her with fraud hanging over her and no money. It was hardly a résumé a man would be proud of.

'He wanted to take you away from us and have nothing to do with us,' said her mother, the first time a hint of anger had shown in her voice since they had turned up on her doorstep earlier. 'That's badness: wanting to take you away from everything and everyone you love. That's a sign of control as much as if he was hitting you, Claire. I don't like that in a man and I never liked it in him. But I wouldn't say it. And I worried about how he made his money. I knew it couldn't be real, only gangsters make that sort of money. The time I did say that, well, he ran me out of the place, didn't he?'

'Brenda said a long time ago I should make it up with you, but I just . . .' Callie paused.

Telling the truth, she'd only recently admitted to herself, would hurt and yet she had to say it openly and honestly.

'I was always aware that if I tried to get in touch with you that Jason would disapprove and make me pick. He'd already made me pick and I picked him. I am so sorry, Mam.'

Saying the words out loud made her aware of how controlled she sounded, how stupid she'd been, not getting in contact with her family because her husband had stopped her. So what, there were plenty of things about Jason she didn't like, but she put up with them, because she loved him. And yet she'd let him walk all over her.

She'd lost ten whole years of her family's life for a man who had upped and left her and their daughter. What sort of a fool was she?

'What made you think he wanted to control me?' she asked her mother.

'Ah, just small things: the way he used to have a hand on top of you every time you were here. You *had* to sit beside him, he insisted. He'd have to have his hand on your knee or around your neck. Like he was showing off, that you were his.'

'It wasn't like that, Mam,' Callie said, shaken. 'That makes it sound weird.' Though she was starting to wonder whether there was something in what her mother was saying. Up to now, she'd been wondering how she hadn't seen what Jason and Rob's business really was. Now she began to wonder what else she'd blindly ignored because she was in love.

'Making your wife pick between you and her mother isn't what a good man would do, Claire.'

'Neither is leaving your wife and child to the mercy of the police and the media,' Callie said, and began to cry.

Her mam sighed. 'Lovie, you know I call a spade a spade. Too blunt, your Aunt Phil calls me. Whatever else he was, Jason was clever. If he knew the cops were after him, then he had a plan to get out and that plan didn't include you, Claire. So you have to think about that long and hard now. It's time to start making other plans, plans that don't include Jason Reynolds.'

Pat Sheridan gave the soup another stir. There was silence in the room and then they heard the footsteps of Poppy belting down the stairs with the little bouncing steps of Ketchup along beside her.

'Ketchup loves it upstairs,' she said delightedly. 'He didn't make any smells, Nana. Honestly.'

Pat and Callie both smiled tightly, smiles that said, let's pretend everything is absolutely fine even when it isn't.

Neither of them knew how to break all these revelations to poor fourteen-year-old Poppy.

Sam

Sam was filled with a sense of anxiety that meant that even when she was absolutely shattered with exhaustion and had a moment where she could possibly lie down and sleep, she couldn't relax. As soon as she'd put her head on the pillow with the baby monitor beside her, the fears would start. How could she protect India? What happened if someone broke in and tried to kidnap her? What would happen if Sam died? Who would look after India then? Yes, Ted would be there, but it wasn't the same. India needed her *mother*.

And Sam knew she was getting so much wrong. She could feed her daughter and change her and hold her tightly, but she was doing it all wrong – she *knew* she was because if she was doing it right, the feeds would be spaced out and India wouldn't be waking up all the time in the night. On the phone, Joanne had told her it was important to grab sleep any time she could: 'As soon as their heads hit the pillow, your head needs to hit the pillow,' she had said calmly as if it really was that simple.

But Sam wasn't finding it simple at all. When India cried in the night, she bottle-fed her the expressed milk.

Afterwards, Sam was never able to go back to sleep. She was on edge, waiting for something to go wrong, waiting for a disaster.

Her heartbeat raced, and she felt the adrenaline rush within her, the way people who'd taken amphetamines described it: one huge rush, one huge speeding sensation through her whole body. And yet if this was speed, why did anyone try it?

It was horrible, stressful and fearful. It made a sense of doom and fear envelop her.

'Are you OK?' Ted would murmur sleepily, turning in the bed.

'Yes,' she'd whisper, lying, wishing he'd know she was lying so she could sit up and tell him the truth.

That the fear was so huge. That her milk was drying up because she was so tired. She couldn't even do that properly. That when she slept, she had terrible dreams and in every dream, somebody was hurting India and Sam could never get to her baby in time to save her.

She often woke from these nightmares sobbing and it took ages for reality to kick in.

Worse, far worse, was the dark hole her mind went into: like an abyss she was standing on the edge of. Inside was darkness: no colour, just dark.

It was waiting for her, softly waiting.

Sam was afraid that if she fell in, she would never come out of the nothingness, never feel joy again.

When India slept, she sat in the chair in her baby's room and cried, with the abyss waiting for her.

When India was awake, she tried to banish it.

'I love you so much,' she crooned to her beloved baby. 'You are so loved.'

She knew India knew this, knew on a deep psychic level that her beautiful child could feel her mother's fierce love. Knew all the pain she'd gone through for India to be born. Her star, her shining child.

All those years of treatments.

Injections in the morning from tiny bottles kept in the fridge. Scans to see what was happening.

Great excitement at the harvesting of healthy follicles.

Huge hopes at the clinic implantation of tiny cells made up of her and Ted: him holding her hand tightly and music playing in the background, the nurse holding her other hand. Everyone wishing the best.

And then the disappointment.

The crushing, life-numbing pain.

The abyss had been there too, Sam realised: but merely on the edges, a faint glimmer that never managed to reach her properly.

Only now had it come to claim her, when she had this miracle baby she'd been given to cherish. Why now? Why?

'I love you, little India, with all my heart,' she said scores of times every day.

Yet still the darkness waited, and while she tried to keep it out until she was alone, it was creeping into her everyday life, making her eyes dull, her gaze full of pain.

Ted was concerned, she knew that.

He kissed her every morning but she couldn't respond.

'Are you sure you're feeling all right, Sam, love?' he'd said so often, his face creased with worry. 'You look so tired and worn out. Should you go to the doctor? Will I take more time off?'

'No, I'm fine,' she'd say.

Once, this man had been her world and now, she couldn't talk to him. The effort of explaining was simply too much.

Besides, he wouldn't understand. Who would?

He'd think she was going mad.

She couldn't even tell Joanne. Joanne had never felt like this. Sam was sure of that – she'd have told her if she had.

Sam had been in Joanne's house when Joanne's last baby, Posy, had been tiny and she'd watched, fascinated, as Joanne had wandered around the kitchen, Posy held against her expertly, and she'd done things: she'd taken phone calls, kissed Patrick, had entire conversations, all the while knowing that she was safely taking care of the baby.

'Make us a cup of tea, Patrick,' she'd call happily.

'Sugar?'

'Oh gosh, yes,' Joanne would say. 'I need the energy. And a bun, if you haven't snaffled them all.'

Patrick would laugh and say there was one left.

'For me!' Joanne would say triumphantly.

When the tea was made, Patrick would take the baby easily, and Joanne would sigh, grab her tea, rub her aching back at the same time, and sink into a chair, while Patrick, still holding Posy, would give her a plate with a bun on it.

It was like a seamless ballet of comfortableness, of people who knew what they were doing.

When Sam walked into her own kitchen, she was so full of fear something would happen: that she'd trip over one of the dogs, that they'd jump up and hurt India even though they were both knee-high to a midget and couldn't hurt anyone. But she was frightened she'd fall and bang India's tiny little head on a chair, on the kitchen table, on the floor. Babies were so fragile.

Looking at the delicate skin covering her daughter's beautiful little skull, Sam could see a filament of veins and she could feel the fontanelle. Under other circumstances she might have loved that word. It was otherworldly, but now it merely meant a tiny fragment of her precious child's skull where the bones were not fused and where injury could occur.

She was sitting on the floor in the nursery with India one day, holding her and trying not to cry, when the doorbell rang.

Let it ring, Sam thought. She could not move while India slept. But then she heard a key turn in the lock and knew it must be either her father or Joanne, both of whom had keys.

Joanne appeared at the nursery door quickly.

She slipped onto the floor beside her sister.

'You OK?' she said.

'Yes,' began Sam automatically.

'Ted phoned me. He said you won't talk to him and he's worried sick. What's up, lovie?'

Finally, the automatic pilot that had kept her pretending for so long went off the grid.

'Nooo,' Sam said in a noise that was half-moan, half-sob. 'I'm not OK. I don't know what's wrong.'

It disturbed India, who wriggled.

Expertly, Joanne took the baby and laid her in her crib.

'She never goes back to sleep when I do that,' said Sam.

'I am a baby whisperer or a baby witch,' said Joanne. 'One or the other.' She switched on India's crib mobile, little coloured butterflies that whirled slowly to gentle music. 'Come on.'

The sisters sat halfway down the stairs, the way they used to as children.

'Spill,' said Joanne, 'and don't give me any rubbish about how you're just tired. It's more than that.'

Sam spilled and as she did, she began to cry, relating the dreams and the fears and the terrible darkness that was waiting for her. Tears and snot mixed and eventually Joanne, who refused to move from her position holding her sister, handed over a scrunched-up tissue to dry the tears.

'You poor darling. It's going to be fine, I promise you. You're not going crazy, Sam, really. I'd say it's textbook post-natal depression,' said Joanne. 'Lots of women get it after pregnancy. You should have said something, lovie, but at least now that you have, it's going to be easier. We'll get you sorted. It's a chemical imbalance and antidepressant tablets will sort you out.'

'You never went through any of this with your babies,' said Sam miserably. 'I've failed India and Ted.'

She began to cry again at the thought of how she'd shut him out.

'For a start, all women are different,' pointed out Joanne. 'Plus, having a baby after a lot of infertility treatment can be difficult.' She looked carefully at her sister. 'I've read up on this and it's quite normal for people who have had a lot of treatments to get post-natal depression once they actually have a baby.'

'Really?' asked Sam, thinking of the social worker in the hospital and how she'd asked if Sam had ever had either depression or any previous pregnancy problems.

Joanne looked at her with wet eyes.

'Oh lovie, I should have said something, I should have said it to Ted. I just never thought . . . Yes, it's incredibly common. And you had to go through it all alone. I thought we were soul sisters forever and you were going to tell me everything, always.'

Sam managed a sort of laugh finally.

'It came on me and I got lost in it. I . . .' She searched for the right words. 'It came out of nowhere and was so frightening. Like I would never be happy again and the fear and pain of that – thinking that when I had India to take care of, when I'd longed for her for so many years.'

The sisters sat quietly.

Sam realised she was holding the little cuddly donkey Vera had bought for India. It was as soft as velvet and, as yet, India had no real interest in it, but it seemed so precious now.

She closed her eyes at the thought of her pregnancy and how she'd felt those moments of huge joy, and then those dark nights when she was too hot, her back hurt and her mind raced with all the fears she could never speak out loud. Not to Ted, not to Joanne, not to anyone.

At the time, she'd feared that she would never actually give birth, that something would go wrong, because she was not meant to be a mother.

Her genes were her mother's genes. Those genes were not meant to be passed on. Plus, she didn't know *how* to mother. She'd sit up those nights and remind herself tearfully that, yes, she could nurture and care. She had Ted, and her sister, her father, her darling nieces . . . so many people she loved and who loved her.

But the needling little voice went on.

'I thought I couldn't do it—' she began.

'Yes, you can,' said Joanne fiercely. 'You were scared. Scared of this older mother thing that you've glued onto yourself like a piece of gum stuck to your shoe.'

'Well I am an older mother,' said Sam, 'although that wasn't the thing that knocked me down into this hole.'

'It was part of it, and so was Mum.'

Sam's head shot up. 'What do you mean, Mum?'

'You're worried that you'd be the same sort of mother as her.'

Sam almost laughed. That fear was mixed in there for sure and yet it was only a part of the pain she felt right now.

'I was worried,' she admitted, 'but how did you know?'

'It wasn't hard. You are the career chick and that sort of defined you. When you weren't going to have a baby, it defined you even more. I don't think we needed a psychiatrist to figure that out,' Joanne said. 'You were scared you'd be her sort of mum.'

'Yes,' said Sam, exhaling on the word. 'It sounds stupid now, doesn't it?'

'Not stupid at all, but you're not our mum. You can be anything you want to be, you can be a different sort of mother. Am I like her? No. You can break the cycle. And – you're going to hate me saying this – but it's the way she's made. Not everyone should have kids, end of story.'

Sam nodded. 'Yeah,' she said fervently. 'I just want to feel better and to be a mother who isn't crying all the time.'

'Right, let's do something about this, then,' said Joanne. 'First, you need to go to the doctor about having post-natal depression. Let's phone now, and make an appointment. I'm coming too. It's medication time – pretty much the only answer here even if you feel you're almost allergic to meds after all the fertility drugs. Then, when the tablets begin to work, don't spend too much time looking at the books and trying to figure out what you should be doing exactly now,' she said, 'because that can be fatal. One book might say you should be feeding your baby this way or treating your baby that way, and when you are vulnerable that doesn't help. Just see if you can do it *your* way for a while.'

'My way?' said Sam doubtfully.

'Yes.' Joanne hugged her sister. 'Your wonderful way.'

Ginger

Ginger held tightly onto her takeaway coffee cup and went for nonchalant. It seemed to be the best attitude to strike as she and most of the paper's magazine team stood outside the glass conference room in the *Sunday News* office and watched the features editor, Carla Mattheson, flick back her chestnut hair, lick her already heavily glossed lips and swivel in her chair. She wore a short flirty skirt the wrong side of decent and with every move of those long, bare legs, it was sliding further and further up. This carry-on did not seem to bother either the editor or Zac, who both sat on the couch near Carla and appeared transfixed.

Up until her recent, thrilling and entirely out-of-the-blue appointment to the *Sunday News* a mere week ago, Ginger had never had much to do with Carla, but she was beginning to see why Paula hated her.

Paula called her a ho, and Ginger loathed name-calling and especially women slut-shaming other women. But after a week in the *Sunday News* on the magazine team, it was obvious that Carla used her sex appeal as just another bargaining tool in her climb to the top – plus, and this was the worst bit, she appeared to view fellow women reporters as competition to be trampled on.

If the teenage readers of Girlfriend wrote in and said: *my boss treats all women like crap and sucks up to the men*, Girlfriend would have some sage advice about how sisters needed to help each other, but that message would not cut it in this job.

Ginger now had to work with Carla and Carla had, in one short week, made it plain that nobody on her staff was her friend. They were all her competitors.

She never flirted with the guys on the features team because she didn't see them as a threat to her plan for world domination.

But for the women reporters, she made life hell. A subtle hell that would be damned difficult to explain out loud, but still hell.

'I don't understand her,' Ginger said to Paula after a couple of days, when they'd both managed to sneak off for a ten-minute sandwich. 'It's not as if any of us are any threat to her.'

'And still here we are, talking about how horrible she is,' said Paula, who'd been assigned to the paper's news department as part of Zac Tyson's reorganisation of the company. 'It's simple: you're women, so you could be. It's like that old *Highlander* series – *there can be only one*. If there's only one woman at the top in the *News*, it's going to be Mattheson, and the rest of you will have spiked heel marks all over your bodies from being trampled on.'

'What about feminism?' Ginger demanded.

'To her, that was a course in women's studies and politics in college,' Paula said. 'This is the real world, Ginger, where women like Carla don't burn bras but buy really good plunge ones when they want to go in and ask for a raise. This is sexual politics at the very dirty coalface. Instead of changing the game, Carla plays the old game.'

'Someone should complain,' Ginger said and earned herself a pitying look from Paula.

'Are you kidding? You see what happens when women in big London City jobs complain about bullying or sexism? Do they get a medal? No, they might get some payoff money but only after years of hell, two weeks of pain in court where they're pilloried and they will never work in the industry again. Complain at your peril.'

'How did I ever think being part of the *Sunday News* team would be a good career move?' said Ginger miserably.

'You're a dreamer,' Paula said. '*I'm* a dreamer. I keep giving Mr Zac Hotness the eye but he ignores me. Guess if Carla's heating his bed, his brain cells are too frazzled to notice anything. She probably uses handcuffs.'

They both laughed.

'Do you think she's the type to lock him up, leave him, then head off to the shops for an hour, just to show him who's boss?' Ginger asked.

'Totally.'

The conversation had made Ginger feel even more disillusioned with her own sex.

Between Liza, Charlene and now Carla Mattheson, it appeared as if sisterhood and feminism were just slogans for T-shirts and not for real life.

Finally, fifteen minutes after she'd summoned the team to the conference room, Carla stopped the flirt show and stood up: tall, sinuous, looking superbly good in her cobalt blue skirt, and a pale blue jersey blouse that had, yup, Paula was right, the definite outline of something that was undoubtedly called 'Ultra-Plunge – Defibrillator for stunned males costs extra'.

Ginger knew she would never have that aura of potent sexuality around her, but if she did, she hoped she'd use it for good instead of evil.

The editor came past the team and said hello to a few of them. Not to Ginger. She'd met him four times but he probably couldn't recognise her in a police line-up.

Good move, Ginger, she told herself sourly. *The 'all-black to hide your extra weight' look is really working out for you.*

Then came Zac, who said hello, by name, to everyone.

'Ginger, how are you doing?' he said.

'Great, Mr Tyson,' she said, channelling cool professionalism.

'It's Zac,' he said, smiling, and if her heart wasn't so bruised, it would have skipped a beat. Paula was right: he was sizzling hot.

But this was his patented charm offensive. Ginger had watched him use it on Carla moments before. And now Carla was watching her, with an arched eyebrow.

Ginger gave him a nod and turned to the front of the room as the meeting started.

It quickly turned into a bloodbath.

Nothing anyone had written was any good and all the ideas they'd come up with were hopeless – according to Carla.

A sick four-year-old with a temperature of 100 degrees had stopped one reporter from making a ten-minute interview slot with a singer who was in town promoting a forthcoming gig.

'Nobody else could go?' asked Carla in her silky-smooth voice, the voice of the class bully waiting to pounce.

Paula was right: it would be impossible to nail her for any sort of bullying as it was all so subtly done.

'It happened so quickly . . .' said the reporter, a harried mother-of-two.

'Your husband . . .?'

'Works too.'

'But *he* didn't give up a vital interview to get to the school and get your kid?'

Carla's tone made it clear that having children was for morons and that women with progeny either needed house husbands or to stay home and not interfere with her work.

Nobody in news had tracked down Callie Reynolds, who was hiding while her husband was on the run from the police for his part in the fraud of the century. Millions were gone, millions.

'Let's do a piece on women betrayed by men,' Carla said, eyes glittering. 'You.' She pointed at Fiona, recently transferred over from news, 'You do it. Do you think she was in on it?' Carla went on, daring them to answer back. 'She looked like a rich bitch.'

'She didn't when the photographers cornered her outside her friend's house,' said Ginger. She'd felt sorry for the woman – she'd looked haunted, betrayed. Ginger knew that look all too well.

Carla's eyes narrowed. *Trouble ahead for me*, Ginger thought.

The health and fitness writer was sick for the third week running.

'So much for the benefits of a vegan diet,' said Carla bitchily.

Worse, the health and fitness reporter's job included editing and correcting the many spelling mistakes in the weekly column of a well-known fitness guru.

It had gone into the paper unedited because the subeditors had been rushing and assumed it had been checked. Basic grammar, not to mention correct use of the possessive case, were not among the strong points of the fitness guru and the online teasing for the paper's errors had been severe.

Everyone looked down at the conference table. Co-ordinating this stuff was Carla's job or the deputy feature editor's job, but she didn't want a deputy features editor, in case anyone pulled an *Et tu, Brute* on her.

'You.' Carla pointed at Ginger. Trouble had arrived. 'You take over until our dear health and fitness reporter is back with the living. We've run out of articles. Cobble together some diet for next week – phone the publishers and find out what diet books they're trying to flog right now. I'll need it by tomorrow morning.'

Ginger's heart soared. An actual, proper feature! Never mind that this was hardly her expert area.

'And fitness. Get me something new.' Carla stared at her, beautifully made-up eyes almost evil. 'A new series, that's it! You try the regime out. Get photos. How to get fit – my journey, that type of thing. We're fine for next week, but starting the week after, I'm thinking of a four-week special. Anyone else want to join in? Shots of the entire team in bikinis – the bikini diet and regime: our team try them all out.'

Ginger shook. Getting to write a feature was amazing. A bikini shoot was utterly horrifying.

'I can't do that,' she blurted out.

'Oh come on,' said Carla slyly. 'It'll be fun. Some sessions with a personal trainer – you'll get the full treatment for free. Most people would kill for that. I'm thinking CrossFit for you. I know of a nice place – I'd like free membership there. This should nail it. I'll email you the number. The guy who owns it is very fit, he might train you himself.'

CrossFit! Personal training? Ginger was appalled. And her in a bikini?

But Carla outstared Ginger and Ginger, who knew that Carla

was too clever to be caught out with any sort of blatant discrimination, felt the flush of embarrassment flood her like fire.

Within minutes, the beauty reporter, a sweet brunette called Jodie Fawcett – who had neck and shoulder problems – was assigned to try a 10K with help from a running club.

Fiona, a reporter who'd done a lot of news work and had recently transferred into features, was sent to try Krav Maga, a form of self-defence used by the Israeli army.

'I know some already,' Fiona said flatly, the only person who dared to stand up to Carla. 'I did a week with the Army on manoeuvres on the Border.'

'You'll find it easy, then,' said Carla, who stared at Ginger speculatively. 'And don't forget the photo shoot for all of you – before and after. Punters love that.'

By Wednesday, male reporters and female non-journalistic staff were telling Ginger she was lucky to get such a plum assignment.

'A month of some guy helping you with CrossFit,' sighed Sinead, the deputy editor's assistant, who had a tiny under-desk fridge outside the deputy editor's office in which she kept cottage cheese, skimmed milk and her emergency dark chocolate rations. 'I'll bet you lose inches.'

Ginger, who was finding it very difficult to keep her tough and funny schtick going when she wanted to run home and hide under her bed, laughed.

'To paraphrase the great Joan Rivers – if God had planned for women to do any jumping jacks or squats with kettlebells, he'd have stuck diamonds on the floor.'

'Ginger, you are so funny,' said Sinead. 'I'll swap with you!'

'Oh everyone wants to swap, but hey, anything for a story,' said Ginger, wondering how she was going to do this.

Carla had picked her most vulnerable spot and stuck a poisoned dart into it. But why? Ginger was *no* threat to her. Ginger had only just started working for the *Sunday News*, had transferred from a free-sheet newspaper at that. She would hardly pose a threat to the powerful magazine editor in any way.

The only people not congratulating her were the features team who'd been in the conference room with her.

In the break room, Jodie, the young beauty columnist, who looked wan despite many columns on how to appear dewy and sun-kissed, sidled up to Ginger and muttered: 'Don't let Carla get to you. She hates competition. It's easier to just do what she says and take the heat. Then, she leaves you alone. If you fight her, she'll get you dumped from her team, and with all the redundancies, you'll be gone. You're on contract, right?'

'Yeah,' said Ginger, thinking of her mortgage, which had been a nightmare to organise given the fact that she was only on contract.

'Think of that and the fact that the features editorship won't hold her for long. Mattheson's got her heart set on being deputy editor, although the poor sucker currently in the job has no idea he's in such danger. She's probably grinding up glass to put in his morning coffee. Nobody would ever know.'

They laughed a little at that, then Jodie grew morose. 'I have whiplash, I take pain meds yet I have to try running even though my physio says the most I can do for the next while is light exercise. But I have to give it a go or I'm toast.'

Ginger grabbed the younger girl's arm and squeezed.

'Talk anytime,' she said. 'It's worse if you keep it all in.'

'Thanks, friend-slash-therapist!'

Ginger grinned. 'That's me.'

She phoned her sister-in-law, Zoe, that evening and blurted out the news.

'The photo's the afternoon after next – all of us in bikinis or sports clothes, revealing sports clothes. The before photos.'

Zoe almost growled down the phone. Ginger had explained that the chances of nailing her boss on any sort of harassment/bullying/discrimination charges would be impossible.

'And don't tell me to try. I want this job.'

'There are laws against this sort of thing, Ginger,' said Zoe, who worked in an ordinary office and couldn't quite imagine the subtlety of machismo and discrimination in some work arenas.

'Yes and they don't really work in my industry.'

'I don't believe that, Ginger. You have to stand up for yourself—' began Zoe.

'I will,' said Ginger calmly. Why did nobody think she couldn't stand up for herself? Probably because Liza had stomped on her for so long, nobody believed she had any backbone left.

'I'm going to do this,' she added. Despite the sheer fear in her belly. 'Your sister, Lulu, still works in styling, right? Do you think she could help . . .? Do something to fix me up in nice workout clothes or anything?'

'Yes!' shrieked Zoe. 'Brilliant idea. I'll phone her and she'll ring you in fifteen, promise. But why are you doing it, hon?'

Ginger laughed. 'I thought it was a good idea, time for me to lose a few pounds,' she said. This, suddenly, was a challenge that would push her to the limit.

Liza had said she whined about not losing weight. What if Liza was right? And what if she was OK really in her own skin but had never been brave enough to step outside in that skin? This was the time to test it all out.

Carla might think she'd handed Ginger a hand grenade but Ginger would lob it right back at her.

Lulu, gorgeous like Zoe but a total fashion-head who made her living styling weird shoots in forests where ethereal girls wore papier mâché antlers on their heads or tame foxes in their arms and drifted around in couture, was on the phone in ten minutes.

'Sounds like you've got a situation, Ginger.'

In those ten minutes, Ginger had completely changed her mind. She'd stared at herself in the mirror and had then misery-downed half a glass of wine and eaten half a packet of chocolate biscuits. She now no longer saw any way out but to give in her notice. She, size eighteen on a good day, eighteen-with-a-safety-pin on a bad one, could not pose in workout gear or swimwear in the magazine and ever hold up her head again. The humiliation would be too great. Who cared about actual working out. The photographs would be agony. The thought of people seeing it in the newspaper . . .

'Lulu, I'm size eighteen. I have never even owned a bikini. I must have been nuts to think you could help—'

'Stop right there, honey chile,' said Lulu, who apparently came over all Louisiana when she was in styling mode. 'If this was hopeless, we'd get an employment lawyer onto it. I know a really cute one.' She sighed. 'Didn't last. He was very strait-laced.'

She got back on topic. 'But as it's not hopeless, we have a canvas, but it needs work. Hair, make-up, a sculpting tan and gym clothes that make you look hot. I really need to see the brief your boss has given you so I know what we're aiming for.'

'No brief unless the photographer has it. The aim is ritual humiliation. Plus, I really hoped you'd mention some fat-sucking machine that will make me half the size,' said Ginger.

'The only machine we need is the one to suck your body anxiety out of your brain,' Lulu replied. 'Plus-sized models are the hottest thing ever now. But even the skinny models get as anxious as you. Womankind has been told that no matter what shape they are, it's the *wrong* shape. That's why beautiful seventeen-year-olds are in anorexia units thinking they're ugly. Until we take over the world, we have to get clever. Here's the plan.'

They met at lunchtime the next day. Lulu, whom Ginger had met at Mick and Zoe's wedding, was as tall as Ginger, raven-haired and dressed in something very cutting edge in shades of grey. She was also greyhound-thin.

Lulu brought Ginger into a small lingerie shop where she greeted the owner with a big hug.

'Ginger, this is Eugenia, and she can tell you your bra size from fifty paces.'

'Forty E,' said Eugenia, raising an eyebrow.

'Forty-two double E,' said Ginger, feeling embarrassed.

'Honey, you're wearing the wrong size,' Eugenia said.

'Did the stuff arrive?' Lulu asked.

'Two boxes. I called in the best from all over the place.'

Lulu rubbed her hands together. 'Let's get you into the cubicle. This is going to be fun.'

The last time Ginger had been in a clothes cubicle, it had been trying on bridesmaids' dresses like tents with Charlene and Liza giggling outside, admiring Charlene in a dress Ginger's leg wouldn't have fitted in. She still hadn't heard from Liza – not a single call or text. Her plan to do this to show Liza that she didn't whine felt like a very far-off plan indeed.

She stood inside for a moment, unwilling to strip off. Then she sat down on the small leather-look cream pouffe and started to cry.

In an instant, Lulu was in with her.

'I can't do this, Lulu,' Ginger said. 'I will feel so exposed. It will be just like the wedding all over again, but this time, in work. In photos. Photos everyone can see. I dress to hide myself, I can't do this.'

'You don't have to do it,' Lulu said, hugging her until the sobs subsided. 'Nobody says you can't file a discrimination complaint. The entire management can't think the sun shines out of that woman's butt.'

'They do,' said Ginger. 'I'm new to her team, still on contract, totally replaceable.'

'Yet she's threatened by you,' said Lulu, 'or else she wouldn't be trying to break everyone on her team. Ever wonder about that? You got more power than you think, girl: you need to find it. Honey, we've got the tools and under that tent of black, I think you've got the materials. Sexy comes in all sizes. I try not to call any fellow woman a bitch, but if the cap fits . . . so let's show the bitch that you're coming up fighting.'

'It's not easy for me,' Ginger said tearfully. 'I'm . . . I'm fat.

243

People aren't allowed to be fat. I hate it, but other people seem to hate it more.' The tears poured out of her and she blindly reached for tissues.

Lulu handed her one. 'Come on, girl. Let's try this and if you hate it all, then you walk. Deal?'

'But . . .' Ginger looked up at all the swimsuits Eugenia was hanging up on the rail. 'I thought we could try workout gear – like sweatpants with a long T-shirt or something . . .?'

'I got a brief from your photographic department. It's a swimsuit shoot. Swimwear only.' She patted Ginger comfortingly. 'I won't let you do it if you don't look amazing, I promise.'

The photography studio in the *Sunday News* was an airy, light-filled area with dressing rooms, a shower and proper hair and make-up stations. The photographer was surprised to see a team, led by Lulu, arriving with a hair and make-up person and an abashed Ginger bringing up the rear.

'Photos are not till half-two,' he said and looked at his watch. 'That's in over three hours.'

'Sweetie, we need time,' said Lulu, wearing something even more scarily high fashion today, dark hair dried poker-straight so her fringe sat Cleopatra-style over vivid green eyes outlined with don't-fuck-with-me eyeliner that matched her metallic charcoal eyeshadow. 'We've got hair, make-up and I'm styling. If a reporter has to be a model, we need the professionals,' she said, eyeballing him.

'Me, I love professionals,' he said, throwing a leather jacket on. 'Jack Hanratty. See you later. I'm off to lunch.'

Ginger had never had her auburn mane curled with rollers into a sexy tumble of curls. She liked make-up, but the things the make-up artist did with her skin and her eyes made her look exotic: huge eyes outlined into mysterious sexiness, and her face contoured properly so she really didn't recognise herself. Her lips were so glossed, she was sure they could be seen from space. Best of all was the tan – a rich bronze sprayed on by someone Lulu knew who'd spent forty-five minutes the night before contouring Ginger's body so that she would not have believed it was her in front of the mirror. It had been worth the forty-five minutes in the tanning booth, holding her boobs up, shivering as the cold spray hit her skin.

'No bikinis,' said Lulu and had found a sexy purple swimsuit with plenty of hold that came with a small sarong and, when worn with ludicrously high nude platform sandals, transformed Ginger into a 1950s pin-up with a beautiful waist, and long, long legs.

'Why are you covering these up?' said Lulu. 'You have the most amazing legs, and what a waist. Why do you tent yourself?'

'My waist is only there because this swimsuit has a tourniquet in the middle section made of industrial rubber,' bleated Ginger, 'and I'm not usually this colour.'

'Nobody is this colour,' Lulu said. 'Humans do not come in molten bronze with carefully applied highlighter. Well, except for Dwayne Johnson. A little old, obvs, but still, you would, right?

'Thing is, Ginger, if you can learn to love yourself with tan on, you might learn to love yourself without it.'

They practised posing with Lulu directing her, until Lulu made her face a full-length mirror and go through it all again.

'I can't look at me!' Ginger said in embarrassment.

'That's what the models do. Pose and learn. Figure out your angles. You have a great shape. Total hourglass. That's rare.'

Ginger had spent years avoiding herself in mirrors, but with Lulu barking directions, she had no option but to comply.

By two, the photographer was back, as were Jodie, the beauty editor, who had clearly had her make-up professionally done, and Fiona, the Krav Maga girl, who favoured purple lipstick and hair with blue tips, neither of which looked to have been touched up lately.

'You decent, Reilly?' asked Fiona as she barged into the

changing room where Ginger's crew were tidying up.

Ginger herself stood with her back to the mirror, breathing deeply with her eyes closed. She had to practise her stance a few more times, but she was getting so nervous . . .

'Fuck,' said Fiona. 'Ginger, you look freakin' amazing.'

Jodie, now clad in a bikini that showed off her slender porcelain-skinned body and long brunette hair, hurried in and stopped dead. Her mouth fell open and she didn't say anything for a beat. 'You're gorgeous, Ginger,' she said. 'Your hair, your make-up, your body . . .'

She went over to Ginger and began examining her with delight, testing the auburn curls styled into fat, glossy waves. 'Your make-up is incredible and this tan – the contouring. And the swimsuit . . . Why do you always wear trousers? Those legs!'

'Hidden masterpieces,' said Lulu. 'I'm Lulu, Ginger's friend. Swimsuit shots need work for non-professionals.'

'Screw that,' said Fiona, gesturing down at her outfit, an old and much-washed jungle camo T-shirt and leggings. 'This is my look. I'm not wearing a swimsuit for bloody Mattheson. You don't take down a guy twice your size using an Israeli martial art wearing a bikini, and if she doesn't like it, she can shove it.'

Jodie giggled.

'You ladies ready for this?' said a slightly bored voice outside.

Lulu went out and the women heard conversation.

Moments later, Lulu came in, grinning.

'Jack's ready to go. I've told him this will take time. We want nice lighting, mood music and another photographic assistant to hold up the gold reflectors.'

Fiona smiled. 'Nobody tells Jack what to do. He'll probably put the fish-eye lens on for a laugh.'

Lulu gave her a shimmering, dangerous smile: 'He'll do what I tell him and it won't be using fish-eye lenses.'

The women came out and Jack, clearly either primed or slightly pushed around by the force of Lulu's personality, was like a different man.

'OK, instead of doing this as a speedy shot, let's think *Vanity Fair*,' he said, spending more time than was entirely necessary staring at Ginger. 'Ginger, right? You look – different,' he said, eyeing her in a way that made Ginger feel weirdly aware of her own body.

'Yes,' said Lulu, 'my fault really. I advised her not to hit the newspaper staff with the full blast of her amazing sexuality when she started working there.'

Jack's mouth fell open as he considered this.

In the background, Fiona broke out laughing.

'I hear you,' she said, recovering. 'I mean, that's why I wear this sort of stuff. I don't want to let the full blast – were they the words you used, Lulu? – the full blast of my sexuality out in case anyone in the office couldn't cope with it. Us lesbians have to be careful with the full blast stuff.'

'Exactly,' agreed Lulu. 'I'd probably be too attracted to you if you wore a bikini.'

'Yeah,' nodded Fiona. 'Us girls, all we think about is sex, right?'

'Right,' Lulu agreed.

Jodie and Ginger bit their lips as they all watched Jack try to compute this.

'We ought to stop tormenting him,' Lulu whispered.

'Nah,' said Fiona. 'It's fun.'

'Let's get started,' said Jack, definitely confused. This was not the way he had figured that this photo shoot would go. Carla Mattheson had told him it was a quick shot for the magazine of three female staff members who were going to do various things for the bikini diet. He had not expected one of them to turn up in combat clothes.

Nor had he expected another one of them, the big red-headed one he thought it was going to be hardest to get a good picture of, to turn up looking like something out of a 1940s movie. She looked incredible, like some pin-up, but a modern pin-up, with those amazing long legs.

He had always known Ginger was tall but she just seemed sort of big because of all those great dark long jackets she wore. He'd got the impression she was a large girl underneath it all, but hey, there was a lot of action under all those clothes.

'Right,' he said, realising he had been staring at her a bit too long. 'Let's set this up.'

Lulu wasn't a stylist for nothing and before Jack knew it, she and his assistant were dragging out props from the cupboards, putting out a couple of cardboard palm trees, a few sun loungers, a little table and corny-looking plastic martini glasses that might make it look as though the girls were on holiday somewhere.

'You could always put in a cool background,' she said, looking at him.

'No budget,' he said. 'They won't do it. This is what we are stuck with.'

'OK then,' she said, 'you have to gold-light it up, it's the only way we're going to get that summer look for it.'

'Perhaps when we are doing the individual shots,' he said thoughtfully.

Lulu caught Ginger's eye, saw the anguish there. It was one thing to pose with the other girls but quite another to pose on her own.

'No,' she said, 'group shots: that's it. We are not doing this again, we are going to do some amazing group shots and we are going to look at them here and we are going to pick out a variety of ones which work.'

'Hey,' said Jack, 'that's not how I work. You can look at them on the computer but you don't get to pick them.'

'Sorry,' said Lulu, 'but I'm the stylist and I'm in charge of Ginger here. She no likee the picture, the picture no appearee in the paper.'

'Yeah and that goes for me too,' said Fiona. 'No picture that I don't like is going in, because I'm not letting Mattheson – or

248

whatever sub she currently has under her thumb – decide what shot of me to put in.'

'I agree completely,' said Jodie nervously.

'You can bully me all you want,' said Jack, 'but I just take the shots and I send up the ones that I think work.'

'Yes,' said Lulu, smiling, sort of an evil smile. 'We all like that idea – but they'll be the most amazing shots as chosen by us or no shoot.'

'I'm not someone you can boss around, 'said Jack. 'I'm a journalist, honey, I'm in a union.'

'Good for you, big boy,' smiled Lulu. 'We ready to rock and roll, or what?'

Ginger had never worked so hard in her life. It was exhausting: wearing the killer heels was exhausting, holding the poses that Lulu told her to hold was exhausting. She was in the middle for some reason. And beside her, Fiona couldn't help bitching about how boring it all was and how much work she had to do.

'But I guess I am getting to learn Krav Maga properly,' she added. 'I always wanted to do that. It's worth looking like a moron in this shoot. What's your thing, I forgot?' she asked Ginger.

'Personal trainer in CrossFit,' said Ginger, sucking her waist in and giving a sultry look straight down the lens at Jack as directed by Lulu. 'Haven't met him yet. Monday.' Ginger didn't add that she was mildly sick at the thought. What if he wanted to weigh her? He would want to. She knew it.

'Handy to get a few free personal workouts,' shrugged Fiona. 'That's the problem of working in an office – it's so sedentary. It's good to kick-start yourself with some exercise.'

Ginger waited for the moment when she'd feel humiliated by this remark, but it didn't come. Fiona didn't mean it in any rude way, not the way Liza had meant it that horrible night at the wedding. Liza had implied that Ginger was just too lazy to do any exercise. Fiona was saying, 'Yes, fitting in working out is hard but it's possible.'

'Do you work out much?' she asked.

'I used to do more,' said Fiona, 'but I moved in with my girlfriend and she's got a little boy. We spend all our time with him, it's fun.'

'Wonderful,' said Ginger. 'How old is he?'

'Three.' Fiona's eyes lit up. 'He's a beautiful little boy. I want to adopt him. That's why I don't let Carla Mattheson get to me,' she said, 'because I've got something else going on, another life. That's the trick,' she said, ignoring Jack yelling at them all to stop talking because he was going to start shooting again. 'Work is just work. My dad always said that when you die you'll never wish you had spent more time at the office.'

'Will you stop talking,' yelled Jack impatiently. 'I want to get some pictures here before the entire day is over. At least models don't talk.'

When the shoot was over, they all stood clustered around Jack's computer looking at the digital images. There were hundreds, literally hundreds. But even Ginger – who simply couldn't bear to look at herself at first – found that she looked great in the pictures. She wasn't thin, but she was curvy and . . . sexy? Yes, she definitely looked sexy and she'd never looked sexy in her life. Not once, not ever.

'You like?' said Jack, looking up at her, a little glint in his eye.

'Yes,' she said, utterly straightforward.

'You're a strange one,' he said. 'It's like you're surprised or something.'

'Just happy,' said Lulu, intervening. 'Ladies, why don't you all get changed and I will go through the photos with Jack here.' She put a firm hand on his shoulder. 'We'll nail it down to the ten that we like best.'

'Ten?' said Jack.

'Ten,' said Lulu.

'I've got your number, babe, just wish you'd let me give you mine,' muttered Jack.

'You old smooth-talker,' Lulu said, without an ounce of softness, 'but when we have a deal on the pictures, we'll discuss numbers. Until then, no dice.'

Between them, Lulu and Jack picked out ten pictures in which all three of the girls looked amazing.

'Carla won't like this – she was hoping for not-so-good shots to sell the "before" piece,' Jack said.

'But these look amazing and professional, which is what selling papers is all about,' Lulu countered. 'If she wants individual shots, you could crop them.'

'Wish I could hire you here,' said Jack. 'You're good at this.'

'Did it for a living for a long time with a lot of famous photographers,' said Lulu, 'but I don't have the time now.'

'What do you do?'

'Are we on a date?' said Lulu.

'Sorry, hands off, I know,' said Jack, putting up his hands in mock surrender.

Jodie, Fiona and Ginger laughed. Even the studio assistant, who had been laboriously putting away all the equipment and whose arms were worn out by holding up giant circular metallic gold highlighters, managed a laugh.

'I think our work here is done,' said Lulu. 'Get your stuff, ladies, we're out of here.'

Ginger watched Jack hand Lulu a bit of paper which had to be his phone number, which Lulu smoothly took up, folded and slipped into her jeans pocket.

'I'll call you after I see the magazine,' said Lulu. 'We might like a couple of those shots,' she added idly. 'Ginger would like a few nice ones of her.'

'No problem.'

Ginger managed to hold it together until they were out on the street and were separate from the other girls. Then she grabbed Lulu's arm and squealed.

'I never ever thought that could work! Lulu, you're a

magician! What you did was incredible. I have never liked a picture of me in my life.'

'You just never had anyone to tell you how to do this sort of stuff,' said Lulu simply. 'You didn't have a mum, and mums help with this sort of stuff. Or else friends do, and you had a crappy friend. I helped Zoe and she helped me, and our mum – who is fabulous and bonkers and loves fashion – helped both of us, but you didn't have that. Instead, by all accounts, you had a bitchy friend who made you feel like crap forever. You should be proud of how you look, Ginger. We're all shaped differently and the world makes it hard for anyone who isn't built for high fashion. For example, I have absolutely no tits whatsoever. I'm as flat as a pancake.'

'You don't look it,' said Ginger, surprised.

'Without the aid of major padding when required, I would be like a boy, but you've got to work with that. I wear things that show off the bone structure in my chest, and if I really want to make an impact in the boob way, I go for fakery. I've seen models who are so slim you can't see them when they turn sideways and *they* have bodies issues, so Ginger, you have got to learn to be comfortable with your body and look after it. It's the only one you've got.'

Ginger nodded fervently. Lulu was right.

They passed a shop with a plate-glass window and she caught sight of herself back in her street clothes. With the beautiful hair and make-up still on, she even felt as if she was walking differently, walking as if she finally believed she was a sexy woman.

She drew herself up and walked taller, not hunching, not trying to hide.

'Yes,' she said, more to herself than to Lulu. 'It's the only one I've got.'

Callie

Callie woke with Ketchup fast asleep beside her. It felt so strange being back in her childhood home, but feeling her mother accept her again had made her both so very grateful and so tired that she hadn't been able to do anything except relax into the feeling. After such stress, her body simply needed to let go of all anxiety.

They'd had a wonderful evening that first night, with her mother and Poppy talking non-stop to each other. Poppy even looked like her grandmother, Callie realised now.

Poppy had been so little when she'd last seen them together that she hadn't realised how alike they were in so many ways. They laughed and giggled, talked about the soaps they liked and discussed different people. It turned out that her mother watched *Keeping up with the Kardashians* and had her own ideas on which of the family was the more interesting.

It was early in the morning, just after seven, and Callie knew she ought to get up. From downstairs, she could hear her mother rattling around in the kitchen – comforting, familiar sounds. The dog had slept most of the night with Poppy but Callie had heard him come downstairs early on, probably because the attic was very hot at night. He'd panted loudly beside her in the heat until he'd finally fallen asleep.

'You're lovely but you are wriggly and noisy,' Callie had said to the little dog, as she picked him up, snuggled him and then carried him out onto the landing. There wasn't a sound from the attic so Poppy hadn't stirred. Sleeping the sleep of the exhausted and happy? At least, Callie hoped she was happy. Poppy had been through so much. From listening to her daughter and her mother, it turned out that lots of Poppy's friends had been in touch with her and most of them had been nice. A couple had apparently said bitchy things about her father, but her grandmother had airily said that it would all be sorted out soon, which was what she and Callie had agreed to say.

'I can't tell her everything yet,' Callie had said.

'No,' agreed Pat. 'She adores him, doesn't she? Poor child. Let's break it all to her gently. Softly-softly, I always say.'

The early-morning peacefulness in the house was shattered when she heard a car door slam. There were voices, one high-pitched, the voice of their neighbour who was always out doing her garden and therefore saw the goings-on of the road, and another lower voice that Callie would have recognised anywhere. Her brother Freddie.

She hurriedly pulled on some clothes and ran into the bathroom to scrub her face with a facecloth and brush her teeth. There was no time for primping or beautifying – not that she bothered with much of that these days. Her skin looked on the outside the same way she felt on the inside: dried up. She used a bit of her mother's deodorant and a quick squirt of a perfume she was sure her aunt had once had, and was therefore at least thirty years old, and went downstairs to meet her brother.

Who knew what he'd say when he saw her?

The tall man in the kitchen both looked like her younger brother and looked different: he'd filled out, grown older and had a beard that was greying. He was still good-looking, hair cut short, and there was the most wonderful sense of calm around him. His eyes, the same grey as her own, were warm as he saw his sister.

He smiled.

How could he look at her so warmly when she'd abandoned them all . . .?

But the thought stilled in her mind as Freddie crossed the kitchen to hold her in his arms.

Callie let the tears flow. 'I am so sorry. I thought you'd hate me, never want to see me again—'

'Cal, babes, I'm the one who was the heroin addict, I get to make amends and say sorry. Sorry for what I put you through. I'm clean for nine years now. And there's nothing to forgive. Drugs meant I wasn't there when you needed me. I hated Jason and he put you in a cage.'

'That's what I always said,' said Pat Sheridan, standing with a tea towel in her hand and watching her two children embracing. 'The heroin had a grip on you, Freddie, and Jason had a grip on you, Claire. It's like you were addicted to him or something. Now you're back.'

With that simple explanation of it all, she turned and went back to the stove where a panful of rashers and sausages were frying.

'Do you want eggs too, Freddie, love?' she said. 'I get the nice free-range ones.'

Freddie still held on to his sister, still hugging her as if trying to make up for the lost ten years.

'Eggs, lovely. Let's talk about all that another time,' he said. 'For now let's just sit down and try and visit. I want to hear all about my beautiful niece.'

Callie began to cry. She didn't deserve this but she wanted it so much. She held on to her brother, feeling the solidity of his chest as he embraced her. He was the same build as her father: tall, broad, with a barrel chest and solid arms.

'Hush,' he said now. 'You're back.'

They sat at the kitchen table as he ate his breakfast with relish and Callie drank coffee.

'Eat,' said her mother. 'You're too thin.'

'Ah, Ma, leave her alone,' said Freddie, and they both laughed.

It was like all those years ago, except Da would have been

pottering around and Aunt Phil would be belting in, fag in hand, lippie in the other, saying she was late for the bus and was going to get a ride on Larry from across the road's motorbike.

Someone would have made a remark about how a Honda 50 would only be marginally faster than walking to the factory but not much, and Phil would have roared laughing with that deep smoker's voice and slammed the door on the way out.

Aware of Poppy being asleep upstairs, Freddie kept his voice low as he told his sister about the years of addiction and where it had brought him.

'I owe you an apology, and Jason for paying for rehab when I ran off from it,' he said.

'You don't owe that piece of shit anything,' said Pat.

'No,' insisted Freddie. 'That's not how it works. I have to say sorry to the people I hurt and one day I'll say it to him. Well, maybe,' he amended, seeing the doubt on Callie's face. 'So I'll say it to you instead. I put Ma here through hell but she did her best to stay with me.'

Pat blushed with pleasure. 'It's what a mother does,' she said. 'If she can. I was nearly broken, Freddie, you know that.'

'I wasn't here to help,' Callie added guiltily.

'You had your own problems,' Freddie pointed out.

'How are you so calm?' cried Callie.

'I meditate and go to Narcotics Anonymous meetings. Kerry keeps me sane. Walking in the woods, feeling the air, the trees, nature all around me. I'm lucky: I got out and managed to stay out. Something like ninety per cent of heroin addicts don't. How could I say a word to you for your life choices, Cal? You didn't end up selling drugs on the street to keep your habit going, did you?'

Freddie, who used to smoke like a trooper, no longer smoked, so when Pat needed to light up one of her ten-a-day – 'I am going to give up!' was her constant refrain – Callie and Freddie sat outside in the garden and filled each other in on their lives.

'So you don't think he's coming back, then?' Freddie asked finally about Jason.

'I hoped he would. I hoped it was a bad dream, but it kept going on, and bad dreams stop. So no. He hasn't made contact with us. I was obviously imagining that he loved me, but Freddie, he adored Poppy. If he could leave her, just run off, then it must all be true: every word of it. He's gone and he's never coming home. He did all the things they said.'

When Poppy got up, she was at first shy with this new uncle, but soon the two of them were talking nineteen to the dozen, with Poppy asking endless questions about her mother as a child.

'She cut my hair once when I was asleep,' Freddie was saying. 'A weird fringe like a scarecrow – high up one side and longer the other. I was mutilated!'

'Don't listen to a word he says, Poppy,' laughed her mother. 'He's an awful liar.'

Poppy and Freddie took Ketchup out for a walk and Callie, worn out from the emotion of the morning, sat with her mother.

'I pray you never have to see Poppy go through addiction,' Pat Sheridan said fiercely. 'It was hell, pure hell. He started on the hash and then that wasn't enough, and he was on to everything he could get his hands on, and finally, because it was cheap, he moved on to the heroin. I kept thinking he'd overdose and he'd be gone. Now they have that drug, naloxone, and some families have it for their kids – it gets the lungs working if they overdose by mistake.'

Callie inhaled swiftly. This truth was so brutal, so real. Imagine a parent having to inject a drug into their child to overcome the effects of a heroin overdose. She'd been absent for it all, on the missing list when it came to helping her mother.

'Oh Ma, I know it was bad but I didn't see much of it,' she said, holding her mother's worn hands. 'I just took Jason's money and sent that. But you needed real help and I wasn't there. I'm so sorry. I can never pay you back for taking us in like this, after everything.'

'It's what mothers do,' said Pat again. 'You don't have to pay me back for anything. I got you and Poppy back. That's all I need.'

Freddie could only stay one day and when he left the next day, Callie felt unaccountably low.

Poppy and her mother had gone off to a garden centre – Poppy willingly going to a garden centre! – and Callie was alone with the dog.

Sitting there, hugging the small dog, she cried.

Alone at last, she let the pain and the betrayal emerge.

She hadn't known, hadn't seen, the real Jason. He had cut her off from her family, had conned her and abandoned their beloved daughter. How foolish had she been not to have seen any of this?

She cried till she didn't know if she could cry anymore.

What next for her and Poppy? How could there be any decent future for them? She had no qualifications to get a good job, and besides, she was forever marked by Jason's actions.

At that moment, she felt lower than she'd ever felt.

And then, even though Freddie had spent a day talking to her about his life, about the depths to which addiction had brought him, she thought of Xanax again, something to help her cope for a while.

It wasn't addiction: heck, no. It was just something to help her, to take the edge off, like the odd glass of wine. Plus, a doctor had originally prescribed them to her, so it was fine. Really.

Callie walked with a quick step the half a mile to the Russet Lounge.

The Russet was not the sort of classy establishment that Jason and his pals would have liked, as it did not feature any expensive Armagnacs or unusual craft beers handmade by an ancient order of monks.

No, the Russet Lounge catered for a wide variety of people, some of whom were unemployed and liked to watch sports on the television, some of whom had decent jobs and liked a few pints after work, and some of whom were less easily classified.

In Callie's day, her mother or her aunt would never have dreamed of going into the Russet Lounge on any but rare occasions where they'd partake of a small gin and tonic or a hot whiskey. But now there were plenty of women in there: women like Glory, who sat in the corner and played solitaire on her own on her phone.

Long before Freddie had turned up, Callie's mother had been filling her daughter in on the various local people and the troubles they'd had over the years. She mentioned Glory, an old friend's daughter, who was only in her early thirties but was known for selling drugs.

'Not the hard stuff, mind you,' her mother had said wearily, 'but enough to land her in court a couple of times. She can't stop, sells out of the Russet Lounge and they just leave her to it now. There's a market for it. She tells her mother she has the kids to look after and needs the money, but sure, her mother looks after those kids most of the time.

'Feeds them too,' Pat went on. 'Freddie says she's an addict but she's feeding other people's addiction too, which is part of the pattern. Sell to feed your own habit. I don't know whether to feel pity for her or to hate her.'

At the time, Callie's first thought had been that perhaps poor Glory had never had the chances in life to get clean the way Freddie had. And then that night in bed, her mind had begun clicking over.

Glory was somebody local and possibly, *possibly*, a safe person for Callie to ask about getting some Xanax. She'd had none left for ages now and she felt the loss keenly.

But she felt ashamed even thinking it after Freddie had talked to her about his time with heroin. The woman she'd been before would never have sunk to this level, but the woman she was now was desperate. She justified it to herself constantly: it was a drug she'd had before, just something to take the edge off. A few to tide her over. Just for a week, perhaps. Because she had to face her future and do something about getting a job. Buying prescription meds was not the same as being a proper addict, was it?

Walking into the pub, she spotted a woman sitting alone with a glass of something that looked like fizzy orange but might have been heavily spiked with alcohol, playing on her phone.

Glory had ombre hair – dark brown roots and blonde tips – but it wasn't the ombre of expensive salons. More the ombre of someone who didn't care what the world thought of her hairstyle or didn't have money to waste when she could use it on pharmaceuticals.

Nervously, Callie approached her.

'Glory?'

The woman looked up at her suspiciously. Then the suspicion went and she broke into a smile. Not a nice smile, either.

'You're that woman, aren't you? The one whose husband's done a runner with all the money.'

'Yes,' said Callie flatly, 'that's who I am. The woman whose husband has done a runner.' She sank into the seat opposite and kept her voice really low this time. 'I thought you might be able to help me with getting something I need.'

'Like what?' said Glory, raising her eyebrow.

'Xanax. I don't know any doctors around here and . . .'

Glory looked at her, then looked down to see Callie's hand shaking.

'I might know someone who could,' she said cautiously.

She watched Callie's shaking hand again for a moment. Assessing.

'An hour. Back of the pub. Have cash on you. Don't bring anyone with you. If you're messing with me, don't. I know you, know your ma's house.'

'OK,' said Callie, scared at the implied threat.

She got to her feet quickly and almost ran out of the pub. She must have been mad. How could she even think of doing this? Even if they were drugs that doctors prescribed, she was still buying them illegally. That was a criminal offence.

And it meant dealing with a woman who scared her.

But she couldn't cope on her own, couldn't afford to pay a doctor anymore and was out of options. Under her current financial and legal cloud, she would never qualify for the medical card that would entitle her to free medical care, so she would have to shell out cash for a local doctor. And with no income, that wasn't an option.

She spent the next half an hour going around in circles in her mind, torturing herself with the thought of what she was about to do. Then she went home, slipped in the back door and took forty of her precious euros from her stash. She hadn't asked how much the drugs would cost, but this was the most she could spend.

When the time was nearly up, Callie walked slowly towards the pub, hating herself. No. She was not going to do this. She would not sink this low. And then she thought about how she'd run out of tablets a few days ago, how it had stressed her, and how sometimes being able to take one was the only thing that got her through the day.

When the panic came, she felt the calmness as the drug hit her system and she could relax just that little bit. That's all she wanted – to be able to cope.

She met Glory at the back of the pub, her heart rate seriously elevated.

Glory was sitting on a wrecked old pub chair beside the bins and slowly smoking a rolled-up cigarette. Callie smelled hash, which she didn't think she'd smelled so close up since she'd gone out with Ricky all those years ago.

'Fifty quid for ten since you're a first-time customer,' said Glory, getting straight down to business.

'What?' said Callie, shocked. 'They're not that expensive.'

'Not if you are buying them in the pharmacy.' Glory's smile was cold. 'But you're buying them from Glory's Pharmacy, so the price is different.'

'I only have forty euros.'

'Fine. You can have eight.'

Callie handed over her valuable cash.

Glory, in a very skilled move, found her roll-ups pack and seemed to be messing with cigarette papers to the outside eye. But Callie could see her using a small razor blade to cut off part of a card of bubble-packaged tablets.

She then handed over the small package as smoothly as if shaking hands.

Getting to her feet, she took a deep drag on her cigarette.

'See ya around.' And she was gone.

Callie felt a rush of guilt and anxiety.

What was she doing? Who had she become?

She was going to use these Xanax to get her through and then after this no more. No more.

Sam

Sam sat on the floor in the nursery with India snuggled up against her. She felt calm even though she wasn't sure if the antidepressants could have kicked in so soon. It would surely take longer than ten days, but she felt better already. It was admitting that she was terrified of the darkness, terrified of falling into a hole of depression – that's what Joanne said.

Ted had taken that first week off and was there to take care of India so that Sam could sleep. Whenever he could, and when he thought Sam wasn't looking, he researched post-natal depression on the internet. She noticed it on his browsing history, and even though she could barely summon up the energy to shower each day, she wanted to dance with love for him.

'You need healthy foods, no junk,' he said gravely, coming home from the shops with what looked like the entire health food section in bags.

'You setting up a restaurant?' asked Joanne, who was there to babysit. Ted was keen that Sam had company in case she felt any sense of fear or loneliness returning. Sometimes it was Joanne, sometimes it was Liam, Sam's dad, who had been asked – by Sam – not to mention her current problems to her mother.

'It's nothing to do with you taking care of India,' Ted had said, holding on to her shoulders, determined to reassure her. 'You are the best mother in the world. India adores you and you are far better with her than I am. You are a natural mother.' He said those words a lot. 'But you need us around you, loving you.'

'A health food restaurant, yes,' Ted joked back. 'I'm going to whip up some nourishing chicken soup – it's not called Jewish Penicillin for nothing. My pal, Levi, swears by it. Cake. Yes, lemon and poppy seed cake. It's a Mary Berry recipe.'

Sam perked up. 'You've never baked before.'

Ted beamed at her. 'You always say that if you can read, you can cook, right? Well, I can read—'

Sam and Joanne laughed so hard at the notion of Ted baking that the dogs began barking and India woke up.

'I'll go,' said Joanne.

Sam laid a hand on her sister's arm. 'No, let me. I'm good. When I'm not so good, I'll say so, but I'm not an invalid. I want to take care of my baby.'

And she did.

Now, Sam looked down at India with absolute adoration.

'Mummy will mind you, take care of you and tickle you,' she said, doing more little tickles and India gurgled back. The sound filled Sam with love and, more than that, a feeling of trust.

As Joanne had advised, she'd abandoned all the baby books but one sensible one.

There were no insane routines, no hint in the writing that if the reader did not do everything *exactly* as it was written, they would fail. It was more of a: *babies are tougher than you think. You parents are brighter than you think. You will actually figure it out. But here are some tips.*

'It's a pity there aren't more funny guides to how to be a mummy, isn't it?' Sam said to India, who looked back at her mother with bright eyes.

The noise of the dogs made her realise Ted was home, but he was early, surely?

She looked at the clock on the baby monitor and saw that it was only just after two in the afternoon.

'Hello, my girls,' Ted said, beaming at them.

He bent his long body and sat down on the floor beside Sam, legs spread out much further than hers.

Leaning over, he gave her a long kiss. Then he gave India a tiny kiss on her forehead.

'Gimme.'

Sam passed over India.

'What are you doing home so early, you slacker?' she asked good-humouredly.

'It's an incredible day, the summer will be over before we know it and I thought: how about if we go for a drive and then a walk on the beach?'

Sam considered it. She'd gone with Ted, Joanne and her father individually for walks with India, but they'd been around the area, nowhere far.

Now Ted was suggesting going *out* out.

'Please?' he wheedled.

'OK.'

They drove to the nearest beach, parked the car and made their way down the path to the shore itself. It was a windy day and the waves whipped and whisked. Walkers belted along the shore, stepping to music or some invisible internal beat. Dogs frolicked in the waves, brave when the sea was out, running away excitedly when it was in and barking at it.

They gazed out at the sea, watching the white horses dancing on the waves.

'Imagine,' said Ted, holding India up carefully in his arms. 'Daddy's going to teach you to swim in the sea one day. We can splash in the sand, look for pretty stones, watch out for crabs.'

Sam felt her heart melt. He was so happy with his darling girl – with both his darling girls, she realised. She'd always known how much he loved her, but the way he'd taken care of her, the way he'd worried, showed how devoted he was.

She leaned against him, glorying in the strong feel of his body and the sun shining down on them.

'You never mentioned sandcastles, Daddy,' she said. 'Naughty Daddy!'

Ted laughed. 'With moats. I love moats.'

'Bet you I can build better sandcastles than Daddy,' teased Sam.

Ted turned towards her, eyes smiling. 'Bet you can, my love,' he said. 'You can do anything.'

Sam reached until she had her arms around him and India. '*We* can, together,' she said.

And they were silent then, staring out at the sea. Content.

Ginger

On the Sunday morning after the photo shoot, Ginger lay in bed and listened to the dawn chorus. She was never awake this early, but today her head was clear and she felt as awake as if someone had injected her with a triple espresso. Today was the day her picture *in a swimsuit* was going to appear in the paper's magazine supplement. In colour.

Showing off her legs.

More than her legs.

Her boobs . . .

The heat of pure mortification made her throw back the covers and get up.

She brought out some guinea-pig breakfast with her coffee, fed them, and then opened the window closest to the canal, where she could see the tree-lined path where early morning dog-walkers were already up. Church bells were sounding over in the big domed church in Rathmines. In the distance, the dome was peppermint green, while the sun shone on house tiles and made the soft red-brick houses shimmer in the early heat.

On a day this lovely, Ginger knew a sun-lover like Liza would have already organised herself in the garden, determined to get as many rays as she could. Liza went brown easily and never bothered with actual suncreams.

Jodie in work would not be impressed with her. Jodie believed in high sun factors the way ancient religions believed in flinging live sacrifices into volcanoes.

'Your face turns into an old leather handbag if you don't wear sunblock,' she said.

Yeah, Ginger thought. *You wait till your face is like an old handbag, Liza, and then come crawling back to me looking to be my friend.* And then she grinned. She'd thought about Liza without that painful ache inside her.

It still hurt – twenty-six years of friendship couldn't vanish that easily. But it hurt less. That was something.

The first text came at just after nine and was from Zoe:

You look incredible, Ginger. We are so proud of you! I hope you are too.

Shortly afterwards, Declan texted:

I'll have to take you into the office for show-and-tell now. All the lads will want to meet you. Fabulous. Love ya.

Ginger felt halfway between nauseated and excited as she clicked onto the *News* site. Carla had insisted that those pages were to be worked on by the subeditors away from the three participants and warned certain death if they defied her by trying to check them out in any way.

'No interference,' she'd snapped.

Nervously, Ginger waited for the page to load. Because she had automatic newspaper subscription, she got the whole paper online. There, on the front page, at the top, was a small pic of her and Jodie beaming, quite obviously in swimwear, with the tagline: 'Our Girls Get Fit! Full story, page 3'.

Her breasts . . . Ginger pulled the page-size up. Her breasts looked huge. Implant-huge. She cringed and sped through the paper till she reached the magazine where there, on the cover, she stood.

Not Jodie or Fiona – just her.

Jack or the subeditors had cut the others out of the photo till it was just her looking like a plus-sized chorus girl in her heels, hip out, smile in place and all she needed was a basket of fruit on her head to finish off the 1940s movie look. The shock of seeing herself in full colour made her look away, but then she forced herself to look back, to be dispassionate.

She didn't look hideous. The tan hid a multitude of sins and that swimsuit gave her curves like an hourglass. But still . . .

Shuddering, she looked inside where at least they showed a photo of the three of them together. But the headline with Ginger's piece, with yet another solo picture of herself, made her grit her teeth:

CURVY GINGER WANTS TO BE A SIZE TEN. WE FOLLOW HER PROGRESS OVER THE NEXT SIX WEEKS ON OUR BIKINI FITNESS PLAN!

If it hadn't cost hard-earned cash, Ginger would have flung her laptop across the room.

Curvy Ginger wants to be a size ten! She had never said that in her life. How dare Carla make that crap up!

Ginger Reilly felt the rage burning through her system: *Game on, Carla*, she thought. *Game on.*

Today was the day she'd picked to start tidying Grace's warehouse and when she rang the bell, Esmerelda opened the door slowly.

'My nails!' she shrieked as Ginger pushed in. 'Watch out! My nails! She is painted!'

'Oh, right.'

Ginger and Esmerelda negotiated round each other and the boxes, with Esmerelda holding her hands aloft, nails painted a coral unseen on any non-alien reef.

'The girl she here doing the nails,' Esmerelda went on.

'In here!' roared Grace, and Ginger made her way past the boxes into the living room where a young woman with café au lait skin was hard at work on Grace's cuticles.

'Louella, meet Ginger, my great-niece,' said Grace.

'Hello, Ginger,' said Louella, smiling. 'If Grace say you great, I think you great too.'

'Lovely to meet you, Louella,' said Ginger.

'Louella is from Guatemala,' said Aunt Grace. 'We have new nail stuff.' She picked up a bottle of lurid opalescent purple nail varnish. 'We got it—'

'Don't tell me: from the television?' said Ginger.

Louella giggled.

'Your aunt is very great also.'

Grace beamed.

'Yes, she is,' Ginger agreed. 'And kind. I thought we were going to do some tidying up today?' she added, trying to find somewhere to sit.

'This was the only day Louella could come,' Grace said gravely.

'OK, I'll start in the kitchen. By the way, the dogs are . . .?'

'In the groomer's. He picked them up in his van.'

'Just checking. I was afraid there was a mobile dog nail-painting business too.'

Ginger escaped to the kitchen where there was no Esmerelda, thankfully, to interfere with her plans, and unpacked the supplies in her small backpack. In the car, she had huge flat-packed boxes. She'd mentioned the plan to Declan, who said he'd drive over later with a friend's van to bring the first load to the online seller Ginger had found if – and it was a big if – she had made enough progress to fill a van.

She looked around the kitchen and tried to figure out where to start. It probably made sense to start with the bigger boxes first, because the little boxes would necessitate lots of opening to see what was in them, and she could be hours at that. At least with the big boxes, she'd be discovering big new things that could be sold on and she'd be making more space. She found a playlist she liked on her phone and set to work.

After about forty-five minutes, she found that she'd got sort of a rhythm going. So far she'd opened seven boxes and found a doughnut maker, an ice cream maker, an incredible machine that chopped, minced and sliced, and several other vitally important household goods. From the documentation that accompanied each box, it was clear these things had been bought a couple of years ago and had simply never been used. Or taken out of the box.

'Oh, Grace,' muttered Ginger to herself, as she photographed the last item and placed it in a big box.

Grace, she realised, was a totally addicted shopper. The only difference between Grace and the crazy TV shows was that Grace's stuff was pretty much new and unused, unlike some of the unfortunates on the television programmes who had piles of utterly ancient things that hid lots of mice droppings and generally dead mice too. At least, Ginger thought with a shiver, she hadn't come across any mice droppings so far.

Declan phoned by the time she was filling the second box.

'How's it going, sis?' he asked. 'Do you need me around with the van?'

'Actually, I think I do,' said Ginger. 'I've nearly filled the second big box and I've got quite a lot of stuff here. Judging by how much Grace paid for this stuff, she could make a tidy sum if she sold it all.'

'Yess,' said Declan, drawing out the word slowly. 'But you never make anything like the same money back on the resale, even if things are brand new and still in their boxes.'

'I know,' agreed Ginger. 'But it's the only way I could get her to agree to this. I told her that if we sold the stuff she hasn't used, she could buy lots of new stuff.'

'Isn't that enabling?' asked Declan.

Ginger agreed. 'But it's either that or have Grace and Esmerelda swallowed up by boxes of crazy kitchen implements and becoming mummified by dog hair.'

'What time will I come over with the van?'

'Can you give me another two hours and then come over?'

'No prob,' said Declan. 'Good luck, sis.'

Once she'd hung up, Ginger decided to go into the big sitting room to see how the beautification process was going on. As Esmerelda's toes were now done, she and Grace were sitting back watching the shopping channel with great interest while holding their nails aloft.

Grace turned to Louella. 'My great-niece is famous, you know,' she said in confidential tones. 'She had a beautiful spread in the newspaper today. Looks amazing, doesn't she, Esmerelda?'

'Very sexy,' agreed Esmerelda. 'You get a man no problem, or woman. I not forget, you might like woman.'

Ginger went puce. 'You mean you've seen my pictures in the paper?' she demanded.

'Of course,' said Grace. 'Esmerelda got it first thing. Do you think we'd miss that?'

'I wasn't sure if you knew about it,' said Ginger, feeling the embarrassment surge.

'We not forget about it,' said Esmerelda, walking on her heels over to a pile of newspapers and extracting the magazine with careful fingers. She showed Louella the front-page picture and Ginger cringed a little, the thought of this beautiful, lithe young girl looking at her with her boobs stuck out.

'You look beautiful,' said Louella.

'She does, doesn't she?' said Grace proudly. Then she turned to Esmerelda. 'Esmerelda, she doesn't want a woman. She told you that. It's a man she's after.'

'Beggars can't be choosers,' said Esmerelda loftily.

'Why didn't you mention it when I came in?' said Ginger.

'We didn't want you to go home because I thought you might be a bit embarrassed,' Grace said. 'My niece doesn't like pictures of herself, but this is fabulous. Get you all sorts of men.'

Her eyes glittered at Ginger.

'Aunt Grace, you're shameful,' said Ginger, but she was grinning too. 'I don't want all sorts of men.'

Grace cackled a little bit. 'Said no woman ever!'

For her first training session at the gym, Ginger bought a special pair of new trainers that had involved the mortification of going into a sports shop in the first place and being fitted for them.

'What you going to be doing?' asked the lithe girl assisting her.

'Er . . . CrossFit,' said Ginger, feeling the ludicrousness of the whole situation. This woman must be thinking: *you're fat! You can't cross-train. Go home and eat the contents of your fridge, babe.*

But she didn't seem to be. She treated the whole thing seriously, which was more than Ginger could do.

In a state of high anxiety, Ginger bought the first pair that fitted. Then she embarked on a two-hour excavation of her wardrobe to find something, *anything*, that would look reasonable in a gym.

So for her training session with a man called Will Stapleton, who owned the gym and looked disturbingly sexy on the website despite shaggy blond surfer hair, she was wearing an overlarge black T-shirt, an industrial-strength sports bra, a pair of loose black leggings and the new trainers.

In fear, she had weighed herself: something she almost never did.

She was nearly fourteen stone. Ginger winced. But at least she knew before the inevitability of the weigh-in. Better to know now, right?

The gym turned out to be a large, warehouse-style premises that was painted black and was pretty quiet at that point in the afternoon. Ginger made her way over to an inside reception desk where a friendly-looking young guy greeted her. He was about twenty and looked sweet, not at all threateningly fit and cool.

'Hi,' he said, 'can I help?'

Yes, thought Ginger, *you could magically explain all about CrossFit and let me leave here without having to do anything with some hot, muscly guy who'd look down at me for being a sloth.* But that was not the answer this guy needed.

'Er, yes . . . I'm here to see Will,' she said. 'I'm Ginger Reilly and—'

'Ginger! Will is looking forward to this,' interrupted the guy delightedly. 'Come on, I think he's in his office.'

'OK,' said Ginger. Her chance of running out of here was disappearing.

Courage, she told herself.

Getting to Will involved going through the centre of the gym, and even though it wasn't busy, there were plenty of people around working out, people who would look at Ginger and judge her. People who worked out always judged fat people.

But while she saw a lot of people lifting kettlebells and doing a confusing variety of lunges, nobody paid her the slightest bit of attention.

Neither were they all thin gym bunnies – they were normal-shaped people; some lean, some like herself, which astonished Ginger. They were all listening to various coaches or concentrating very hard on what they were doing.

All she needed was to talk to the Will person with the surfer hair, let him look her up and down and find her lacking, and then be sent off with the sweet young guy and let loose on a running machine or something. Even she couldn't mess that up.

Sweet young guy peered around, then stopped by a wall where a tall man with muscles on his muscles was coaxing a teenage girl into squats.

The man had his back to them but the girl was possibly eighteen and she made Ginger think of herself at that age: verging on the plump, with a lip bitten down from nibbling at it anxiously. Yet this girl didn't look as if she was uncomfortable: she looked determined. Her long dark hair was tied back in a ponytail and she held two small hand-weights.

'You can do this, Marina. We're going to do six sets, take a break, then six more. Sure, you're going to feel sore tomorrow, but that means you've worked your body. This is the last part of the workout.'

'OK,' said the girl, gritting her teeth. 'I can do this.'

'Yes,' said the guy, encouraging her, 'you can do this.'

Ginger and the sweet young guy watched Marina as she

squatted and as the big man counted down the squats, 'Six, five, four . . .'

Ginger could see how much effort it was taking out of the girl and it was obvious she had done a lot of exercise up to this point, because her simple T-shirt was wet with sweat. But the big man was gentle and encouraging, all the time.

'You can do this,' he said between counts.

When she'd finished one set of squats, he looked at his big manly diving watch and counted down. 'One minute break,' he said, 'but keep those feet moving.'

'OK,' said Marina, determination written all across her face.

Ginger wondered why they'd stopped here in their progress to get to Will, Surfer God's office, but she was enjoying this. This big guy was obviously one of the trainers and there was no sense that Marina was being humiliated in any way for being unfit. No, she was being encouraged every step of the way. Maybe the sweet young guy had stopped just to let Ginger see what it could be like.

After the second set, the girl's face lit up. She put the weights carefully away and then did a little jump in the air, a jump that completely surprised Ginger.

'Thank you, Will,' she said delightedly and hugged the big man. 'I couldn't have done it without you, I really couldn't.'

'Course you could,' he said, patting her on the back in an avuncular manner. 'You're well able to do it. You just need a little encouragement.'

This was Will? This man did not have blond surfer hair. While his hair was still naturally blond, it was cut short all over his head. The sweet young guy tapped him on the shoulder and Will turned around.

'Will, this is Ginger Reilly, the lady from the newspaper.'

Will Stapleton gave Ginger the full blast of what she had already defined as a very sexy smile. He looked as if he was delighted to see her, but then, she decided cynically, he was probably delighted to see anyone who was going to give publicity to his gym. He didn't know that Carla wanted free membership as part of the deal.

'Great to meet you, Ginger,' he said enthusiastically. 'I half expected you to come dressed up in that swimsuit,' he added as they reached the sanctuary of his office and he shut the door.

Ginger flushed the way only a redhead could flush and she wished she had one of her big black flowing coats to pull around herself as camouflage.

Words simply failed her, but then Will said: 'Sorry. I really didn't mean to embarrass you. It was meant to be funny. Me and my size thirteen feet. Let's start again.'

He held out one huge hand.

'I'm Will Stapleton. I'm thrilled you're here to write about our gym, I'm delighted to meet you and I apologise for putting both feet in my mouth.'

Ginger looked into his face and found him gazing down at her with absolute sincerity. So few men looked down at her. So few men made her feel small. But Will was genuinely huge. Tall, strong and looking every inch the man who owned a gym.

He was no longer the tanned surfer man from the photos and somehow, while he was still very gorgeous, he wasn't smug with it. He looked sorry. Understanding.

The man who understood that a teenage girl with weight issues needed to be treated with kindness as she worked out.

Instead of making some crack about how she only wore her swimsuit on her days off, the way she might have treated a smart comment at work, Ginger found herself being honest.

'I'm nervous as I'm not a gym person, and I've never worn anything like that before and certainly not for a photograph.' The words came tumbling out.

Will nodded slowly.

'Hopefully, I can make you a gym person,' he said. 'Some of us get frightened by the idea of exercise and feel that all our faults are going to be shown up, so we don't try.'

'We?' said Ginger doubtfully. 'You don't look like you understand that.'

'Oh, I do.'

Will pointed to a photo on the desk. It showed a tall, blond and undeniably chubby teenager hanging out with two skinny friends on either side of him.

'That's me in the middle. The larger kid. So yes, I understand. I hid from exercise and comfort-ate for all my teenage years.'

Ginger thought of herself and her Ben and Jerry's nights in front of the TV with only the guinea pigs for company.

'I went abroad for a gap year with this pair of nutters, we ended up surfing and I discovered exercise.'

'You certainly did,' agreed Ginger, no longer shy.

Will laughed. 'I love it. I love the endorphin buzz. So let's get you into it too. And if it's not embarrassing to say it, I did like those pictures. You should be proud of them.'

Ginger flushed again, but this time it was a flush of something Paula would have delightedly called excitement.

Maybe this workout thing mightn't be so bad after all.

Callie

In Ballyglen, Callie and Poppy's days had fallen into a relaxing routine, something that surprised Callie because she thought she'd have been so on edge all the time she was waiting for news of Jason. There was something about staying with her mum and remembering what it had been like to grow up in Sugarloaf Terrace that calmed her.

And the Xanax helped, no doubt about it. Callie, to her shame, had been back to Glory again and bargained. She'd sold more of her precious jewellery, but there would be no money unless she applied to the courts, Fiona McParland explained on the phone.

Callie couldn't face it – not yet, not when everyone believed she must have been in on Jason's scheme.

Meanwhile, she enjoyed the peace and watching Poppy blossom.

Her daughter had managed to decorate the attic like her old bedroom back home in Dublin, with fairy lights on the dressing table and make-up everywhere, and Freddie, her uncle, had dug up an old stereo system from somewhere that now had pride of place in the room.

'It's ancient but it really works, you know,' said Poppy delightedly as he plugged it in and fixed the speakers up. Freddie had laughed. It was apparent he was becoming very fond of this often truculent niece.

'This was high-tech back in my day,' he said.

And Callie had grinned at the sight of her daughter, who'd once only been impressed with the latest iPhone and sound-sharing systems, being thrilled with this elderly sound system that resembled four breeze blocks glued together.

'Can I decorate it, Uncle Freddie?' Poppy had asked.

'Do whatever you want to it,' Freddie had said good-naturedly. 'We don't need it anymore.'

'Thank you, you're the best uncle in the world,' Poppy had said and had thrown herself at him.

Watching this made Callie both very happy and slightly sad. Once upon a time, Poppy reserved those sorts of enormous hugs for her father. She still needed that male influence in her life and she'd turned to Freddie, little Freddie who'd turned his life around and now had a great building business, a lovely house and a smart new car. Poppy had started begging Freddie to teach her to drive when the time came.

Because Poppy adored her uncle – they were becoming real friends. He drove up from Kerry all the time and having him there was a joy.

Callie had spent time with her Aunt Phil in the big, glamorous house near the golf course. But Phil, sadly, lived there alone.

Her beloved Seamus was in a local nursing home with dementia.

'It's the best one there is. They really take care of people there. I couldn't have left him otherwise, although I'm in there every day,' said Phil, tears in her eyes.

'I'd love to visit him,' Callie said.

Phil just nodded and went to look for her tissues. She'd aged a lot. The glamorous auntie was gone. Callie felt sad to think that she had not been around to help dear Phil shoulder this massive burden.

Phil didn't reproach Callie either. Instead, she repeated what Pat had said, only with more anger: 'That man stole you from us. You were soft, Claire, love. Always soft. Ripe for someone like him. His own mother never saw him either. She moved away, you know, about nine years ago. Went to Somerset. Had family there. God love her.'

Callie was stunned.

Jason had once said his mother was too busy to bother visiting and Callie had thought he'd just palmed her off because her family weren't coming. But he'd merely meant he didn't want anything from the past to come into his new life.

The guilt gnawed at Callie. How'd she let Jason separate her from them for so long? She'd been so weak and stupid. It was, she saw now, part of Jason's attempts to isolate her from her family, to keep her for himself. Controlling, she realised now, seeing it through the prism of her mother's and Phil's eyes.

He'd liked to know what she was doing all the time. He liked to advise her on what clothes to wear to events. He'd warned her never to get her hair cut short, because he loved that long blonde skein of hair hanging over him when she was on top when they made love.

She felt so stupid thinking about it now. She'd thought she was smart but she was just another woman who'd believed everything a man said because she wanted to be with him. The argument alone shouldn't have been enough to drive a wedge between Callie and her family. All families had arguments and got over them. But this one had been like a scimitar dividing them all because Jason had wanted it that way. And what Jason wanted, Jason got.

Callie went to see Seamus in his lovely nursing home, Leap of Faith, where Phil went most days to help out.

Watching Phil in the company of the sweet man who barely recognised her, Callie wanted to sob. This was love, the way Phil fed him, talked to him and walked him gently round the garden.

It was a beautiful place, despite the pain that could have existed there, Callie realised.

The staff were a veritable hive of activity and yet an air of serenity reigned. There were fresh flowers from the garden on a table. Music played from the radio: old tunes that some of the patients were definitely enjoying.

'They love the music,' said Phil, watching her niece. 'Even Seamus loves it and he recognises nothing anymore, not even me.' Her eyes teared up.

'Oh but he does, Phil,' insisted a short blonde nurse, coming up and putting an arm around Phil. 'You know Marian who works nights? She has hair like yours, blonde and silvery, and your husband loves her the best. Do you know why? Because he thinks it's you, that's why. Don't write off that mind of his yet.'

'Really?' Phil could hardly believe this. 'I want to think he knows I'm here, that I come every day, that I would never leave him,' she said, tears coming properly. 'Because I love him and he's my husband.'

The nurse helped Phil to a seat, leaving Seamus to Callie, who instinctively linked her arm round his and began to walk the garden with him. She did what Phil had done and what other people were doing: just chatted about what was going on, talking gently and with dignity to this person whose mind was perhaps in another place altogether. And yet perhaps not totally gone there, not yet.

She told her uncle about his grand-niece, Poppy, and how she'd be in to see him.

'Poppy's fourteen now, going on for twenty-five, Seamus,' Callie said. 'She likes music, the way you love music. Remember how we used to talk about the old songs and you loved Glenn Miller music?'

Half an hour passed and she realised that Phil was sitting in a chair just watching. She was worn out with the daily visits and the stress. Having Callie there allowed her to feel Seamus was being loved by his family, and yet she could rest.

Callie vowed to come to see Seamus as often as she could. She liked this place too. Perhaps she could do some work for the nursing home. She loved the serenity of it and the kindness obvious everywhere.

Callie would do anything, she thought: mop out toilets, scrub floors, whatever. She had no misplaced pride left. She just wanted to help in this beautiful place where people were cared for with such gentleness and respect. Perhaps she could earn some money too.

'You ready for our walk, Mum?' said Poppy when she got home. Ready in her tracksuit bottoms and trainers, rattling the dog's lead. Every day, rain or shine, they did a three-mile walk. Ketchup sometimes looked as if he wasn't able to do that much of a walk, especially since he had very short legs, but he managed it valiantly.

'You are such a good puppy, aren't you?' Poppy said, getting down on her knees to croon at the dog. She adored him. He now slept on her bed all the time, and there were no complaints about smelly dog or fur all over her clothes. There was a lovely normality to it.

'You have totally spoiled that dog,' her granny said fondly, watching the two of them rolling on the floor together.

'But he loves it,' Poppy said.

Pat laughed. She loved spending time with her grand-daughter, making her take a trip on the bus one day into the town centre because 'you'll need to know the bus routes, love, for school'. And Poppy, who came from a group of girls who were driven everywhere, had been delighted with it. Pat said it would only be a few years till Poppy would need to drive, and it was very important that she learned how to drive a stick shift. Poppy, who used to have a retinue of friends and barely wanted to be at home in the glamorous Reynolds property, didn't appear to want to go anywhere else, although she had made a new friend – a fifteen-year-old girl from across the road, who had just done her first lot of state exams, and wanted someone to complain to about them. Poppy was engaging in a little bit of hero worship because the girl, Lauren, was tall, slim and stunning with long rippling pale brown hair. Lauren was beautiful without even trying and she was clearly very clever. She wanted to study medicine, and suddenly Poppy began to discuss what she might do when she was older instead of discussing where she wanted to live and what sort of cool apartment she might have.

Values, Callie thought: her daughter was learning values in the way that the posh house in Dublin with the underground carport hadn't taught her.

It was only at certain times, mainly at night, that Poppy's high spirits deserted her.

'Mum, what do you think is going to happen to us? Do you think Dad is going to come back?'

She had only asked this question a few times, but every time she did so, Callie felt her guts clench in such a way that if she'd had Jason there, she would have done him serious damage with her fists. How could he not try to contact them?

The police got onto her occasionally, checking to see if he'd been in touch, and Callie had been able to answer completely honestly with a firm 'no'.

'No, he hasn't been in touch,' she'd say, 'not a word.'

At least she had been officially eliminated from their investigation, which was great – but this information had not featured in any newspaper articles on rich people and their fall from grace.

But she couldn't say any of this to her daughter. Poppy was still fourteen years old, and when you were that age, you needed to idolise your dad, the way Callie had idolised hers.

'I don't know what's going to happen to us, darling,' she said most times, 'but you know, we'll manage.'

She was afraid to tell Poppy the truth because she was terrified of what it would do to her daughter. But in September, Poppy would have to start at the local school and she needed to know for sure before then.

'I think it might rain when you're walking the dog,' her mother said, looking out the back window.

'I've got my fleece and it has a hood,' said Poppy, the girl who once wouldn't dream of going out if there was any sign of rain in case it messed up her perfectly straightened hair.

'You're fine then,' said her grandmother, 'it will just be a little shower, and Ketchup loves the rain.'

Callie was just putting on an old rain jacket of her mother's when the doorbell rang. The doorbell rang a lot in Sugarloaf Terrace: there were always neighbours dropping in and out for a chat or to discuss the latest happenings of the day.

Callie found she really liked it. The house in Dublin had been quiet apart from Brenda. But this was different, this was homely, this reminded Callie of when she'd been growing up.

'It might be Lauren,' Poppy said, jumping to her feet. She opened the front door, but the person who barrelled into the kitchen wasn't Lauren, it was Nora, next-door neighbour and her mother's most stalwart friend for many years. In one hand she held a newspaper and the look on her face said the information in the newspaper was not good.

Callie, her mam and Nora exchanged glances.

'Do you know, we might have a cup of tea, Nora,' said Callie's mam. 'Poppy, love,' she continued, 'looking out, it's got darker. I think it's going to rain very heavily right now and you'll all get soaked. Why don't you go over to Lauren's and see if she's around. We'll wait until the threat of rain has passed.'

'Do you think it's going to rain heavily?' said Nora. 'Because I have my washing out.'

Callie watched her mother give Nora a subtle kick. Nora instantly sat down at the table, the way she'd been sitting in the Sheridans' kitchen for forty years. Message received.

'Of course, yes, forget about the washing. I'll run in if it rains. Desperate storms coming, Poppy,' Nora went on. 'I'm pretty sure Lauren is there. Her curtains only opened up a minute ago.'

'That,' laughed Callie's mam, 'is why we don't need Neighbourhood Watch stickers around here.'

Poppy headed off, and as soon as they heard the front door slam, Nora took the tabloid paper from under her arm and unfolded it on the kitchen table.

At least the story was on page three and not on the first page of the paper.

TAX FRAUD RUNNER LIVING HIGH LIFE IN MARBELLA, said the headline. In smaller capitals it said: JASON REYNOLDS AND HIS NEW GIRLFRIEND.

There was a grainy picture of Jason coming out of a shop, holding grocery bags, accompanied by a much younger woman. She looked, Callie thought in a distant way, rather like she had herself when she was younger.

The woman was slim and blonde, but she was wearing the sort of clothes that Callie would never have worn, even on a sun holiday: a halter-neck bikini top, enormous earrings and tiny little white shorts that barely covered her buttocks over long legs that ended with extremely high wedged sandals. She was looking up at Jason as though he had the power to grant her every wish under the sun.

Callie got her first look at her husband in nearly two months and what was shocking was that he looked exactly the same.

Not worried. Not anxious. Not vaguely haunted, not like she was.

He was wearing a shirt she'd bought him for a holiday in the Caribbean once: a beautiful pale blue linen shirt with the sleeves rolled up. Seeing it made her realise that he'd taken time to pack before he'd left. Somewhere along the line, her husband had known he needed to have a bag ready – but only for himself.

While he'd been telling her that this wonderful party was all for her, he'd been ready to run.

She wasn't sure what made her angrier: the sight of the other woman, or the fact that her husband looked happy.

He didn't even look like he'd lost weight.

Every morning when she looked in the mirror, she could see

285

her face growing more and more gaunt. She didn't bother with make-up much, and when she was on the phone to Brenda, Brenda always said: 'I hope you're using all those special lotions and creams. No need to let yourself go just because Moron Central has left the country.'

Moron had certainly left the country. He'd found himself another woman, a Callie lookalike, and he was having fun with her down in Marbella, while Callie and Poppy lived on almost no money with her mother in Ballyglen and Callie worried herself sick.

'It says here that the reporters tried to get a hold of him, but he ran and they sped off in a fancy car, a Jaguar with Spanish plates,' said her mother gently, holding the paper away from Callie. 'The police were notified but they weren't able to track him and the woman he was with. Sorry, lovie.' She put a hand on Callie's shoulder. 'I didn't mean to upset you by reading it out loud—'

'You didn't upset me, Mam,' Callie said brittlely. 'My husband upset me by running off. This is just proof he packed his clothes before he went.'

'What do you mean?' demanded Nora, who was trying to angle herself so she could get another look at the woman in the paper.

Callie jabbed the picture with her finger.

'I bought him that shirt,' she said, 'which means he left me and Poppy with no money, totally terrified, with me being questioned by the police, with our names mud, and yet he still had time to pack and get out of there. No note, no explanation, no phone call to tell me he was really sorry. Nothing but a carefully organised suitcase.'

She sank down heavily onto a hard kitchen chair.

'Fellows like that are all the same,' said Nora. 'Full of themselves, always after the next big thing, leaving a trail of destruction behind. Listen, Callie, there are women on this road who could tell you stories that would make your hair curl.

God help them, but some of them married men who were a waste of space. Plenty of the sons aren't much better – except for your brother, Freddie, now that he's off the drugs, and your dear father, God rest him, and my Johnny. The most decent boy who ever lived. Have I told you he's a priest?'

Callie surprised herself by laughing out loud. Nora had offered to introduce her to her priest son many times in case he could offer her wise counsel. And Callie, who could remember Johnny from when he was a spotty teenager and dallying with bottles of cider in order to gain the kudos to hang out with the cool kids, could not get her head around the idea that Father Johnny would be able to offer her wise anything. To her, he would always be a spotty teenager and she had had enough advice to last her a lifetime.

'Thanks, Nora,' she said, 'but I have to deal with this on my own.'

'What are you going to tell Poppy?' asked her mother.

'I don't know,' said Callie. 'I don't want to break her heart.'

'You haven't broken her heart,' said her mother. 'Jason has. You're going to be the one delivering the news. The only plus is that if people see where he is and that he's with another woman, nobody is going to be thinking you had a hand to play in any of this fraud business.'

Callie laughed again, but this time with no warmth: 'Yes, there's always a bright side to finding out your husband has another woman,' she said.

The theoretical bright side was a final slicing of the marital link. If Jason had wanted to divorce her with an assassin's blade, he couldn't have done it more successfully.

It still hurt. Before, she'd assumed the worst. Now, it had been confirmed. Jason had simply packed and left, thinking nothing of her or their child. They were clearly nothing to him.

With instructions to her mother to hide the newspaper, Callie left Nora and her mother sitting at home, grabbed her coat and went out. She didn't take the dog and her mother didn't ask her to. There was one thing the picture of Jason and his new woman had done to her — it had made her realise that she needed more Xanax. She was down to two and she wanted to take them now.

She couldn't cope with this on her own. The pain of being lied to; the pain of thinking Jason loved Poppy, loved her, and then finding out it was all fake; she simply couldn't deal with that. She needed to take the edge off.

If he'd wanted a divorce, she'd have been utterly heartbroken but she'd have given it to him. But Jason had told her he loved her all the time. Told *everyone* he loved her. Told everyone he was the happiest man on the planet with her and Poppy and now she, and everyone else, knew it had all been a lie.

She dry-swallowed the remaining tablets as she walked down the road, desperate for some relief.

In the pub, she had two vodkas straight up, which she'd have never done before, and ordered a third, with some tonic, before finding Glory sitting inevitably in her spot.

'Xanax. I need some. Now. Stronger dosage,' she rapped out.

'Keep your voice down,' said Glory. 'I'm tolerated here, not a paid-up member of staff.'

'Meet you out back in an hour,' said Callie.

'Fine. You're a right narky bitch,' muttered Glory. She got to her feet. 'You staying?'

Callie picked up her glass and took a deep draught. 'Oh yes,' she said.

She'd had enough, absolutely enough, and this evening, she wanted to be totally and utterly numb. Whatever it took.

Sam

Sam took India into the office for everyone to admire and even Andrew, who clearly looked terrified of babies, said she was adorable.

'Little pet,' said Rosalind, tickling India's cheek.

Gareth, who talked nineteen to the dozen to Sam about the big data research he was doing on key words linked to dementia, wanted to pick India up and snuggle her.

'Three older sisters, and therefore plenty of nieces and nephews,' he said, holding India expertly and nuzzling her joyfully.

She cooed back at him.

'Aren't you the little darling?'

While Gareth talked to India, Sam talked to Dave, her stand-in, and they discussed the Ballyglen crisis.

'Nothing in the media yet. Andrew's paid the debt out of his own money—'

'Wow,' said Sam. 'That's incredible.'

'I know. It could have ruined us – still could have a terrible effect, but so far, so good. The only hangover from it all currently is a nursing home in the area, Leap of Faith. It's a charitable trust nursing home and they got a lot of funds from us. We can't simply cut them off because one of their prime supporters was siphoning off cash for gambling. I've got letters here from their director wondering if the funding cuts are going to keep continuing.'

They both winced.

'We need to visit them,' said Sam.

Dave nodded. 'It sounds like a great place. They say they

know the focus of our charity has changed, but if only someone could come down and see them, then we would reconsider.'

'I'll go,' said Sam, feeling a frisson of excitement at the thought of taking on a little bit of work. It was as if a part of her was coming back. 'We can't leave them in the lurch. It'll be good to ease myself back into work slowly. Don't worry, Dave, your contract is safe. I'm not coming back early.'

'How could you, with that little pet?' he asked, grinning. 'I've got three kids and leaving them each morning is hell. Kids change everything – total world shift on the axis sort of thing.'

Sam nodded, smiling at the tableau where Gareth was instructing a nervous Rosalind in how to hold a baby.

'Yup: it's a total world shift. You said it. My sister used to laugh when I said I thought life would be the same but just with a baby. I get it now.'

And she did. Even if she was offered the world's best job, it would still come second to India.

She was still smiling at that thought when she got home and began to put a nearly asleep India, tired from her morning out, down into the cot.

The doorbell rang and the dogs started their normal manic barking.

'Oops, someone coming to see us,' she said, mentally planning to figure out how to make the dogs bark less noisily and the doorbell ring less loudly. But India was awake now. Sam picked her up again. When she'd dispatched the visitor, she'd do the sleeping routine once more. Outside the nursery, the dogs were dancing with excitement.

'Hush,' she said, as they kept dancing when she opened the door.

There, looking as dressed up as ever but not quite as calm as she normally looked, was her mother.

'Why are you here, is it Dad? Is he OK?' said Sam, taking a step backwards.

'Yes,' said her mother, 'your father is absolutely fine. I just wanted to come and see you.'

'Why?' Sam's shock couldn't have been more evident and her mother looked uncomfortable.

'I don't need an excuse to come and see my daughter,' she said and some of the recently subsided anger burned up again inside Sam.

'Mother, you're the woman who sent me emails to find out how I was during pregnancy,' she said wryly. 'You almost never visit, so yes, I'm shocked.'

'Can I come in?'

'Sure,' said Sam in crisp tones.

She didn't feel like pretending. Her mother had interrupted her lovely day.

Sam talked to her father most days, twice some days, and he made every excuse to come over and see India, bringing her books and adorable toys so that the nursery was already overstocked. Ted was worse. Every day, he came home with something new.

'You're a shopaholic,' Sam teased him.

'I'm a family-aholic,' Ted would say, holding India in his arms and leaning against his wife, sighing.

Her mother only came on official visits with her husband.

'Sit?' said Sam to her mother, gesturing to a chair.

She thought if she kept this in the one-syllable department she might just be able to cope. A few minutes ago she'd been feeling better, but there was a limit to what antidepressants could do. The doctor had said no stress, after all. Perhaps stress ruined the positive effects of the drugs?

'I came to see how you were doing since you haven't been well,' her mother said.

Sam felt her annoyance rise. Taking antidepressants would no doubt be a sign of weakness of character to her mother.

'I'm fine,' she said, which was true, now.

'Your father told me you were suffering from post-natal depression,' her mother said.

And even hearing the words come out of her mother's mouth heightened Sam's irritation.

She didn't hide it when she spoke:

'Failed again, have I? Are you worried that this might slow my return to my career? Because career comes first, after all. Don't worry. I'll drop the baby off with a baby minder as soon as I possibly can, or better still, I'll get Ted to give up his job and he can mind her. Because that's what men are for – to mind the babies while the women go out and rule the universe. Have I got that right?'

She glared at her mother, no longer caring that the full blast of the rage was uncoiling within her. In her arms, India fretted and began to cry.

Sam knew India was sensitive to everything that went on around her and she cradled the baby close to her chest, holding that soft little head against her, nuzzling into the beautiful downy hair. 'Sorry, honey,' she whispered softly.

'What do you really want, Mother?' she asked in louder tones.

'I wanted to see if you were all right, but if my being here upsets you, I'll go. I'd just like to hold her perhaps . . . I haven't held her often,' Jean said awkwardly.

Sam stared. Jean was in full control of every situation.

Except this one, it seemed.

'That's because you didn't appear to want to,' Sam said, truthfully. 'You look uncomfortable when you're holding India, as if you can't wait for it to be over.'

Her mother licked dry lips. 'It's true I'm nervous, but I want to get to know my granddaughter.'

'Why?'

'Because I just do, please.'

It was the please that did it. Her mother never said please for anything – not in that way. Oh yes, she had perfect table manners and said please and thank you when they were at the dinner table, but *please* in that longing way . . .? Never.

'You can sit beside me on the couch and you can hold India

on your lap for a moment,' said Sam, not sure why she was doing this.

It would be the quickest baby-holding ever, she decided.

Jean moved so she was sitting beside her daughter.

'Take off those necklaces,' Sam said irritably. 'They'll just get tangled up and hurt her.'

'Oh, right,' said her mother anxiously, messing up her hair in the process of removing the necklaces. Then she held out her arms as if she was about to accept a present.

'Not like that,' Sam said, 'like this.'

'OK.'

Sam was still not sure if this was the right thing to do or not, but she passed India over to her mother. 'You've got to support her head.'

'I know that,' said her mother gently, and she held the baby tentatively, awkwardly. 'I read every baby book there was, learned all the facts. But I still wasn't very good at it.'

Sam paused. She didn't think she'd ever heard her mother say those words before.

'I wasn't a good mother,' said Jean quietly, head bent over India. 'I'm really sorry that I wasn't because I'm not the motherly type and you were afraid, weren't you, you were afraid you were going to be like that? I know, I could see it in you because I was the same.'

'Mother, spare me the psychobabble,' said Sam, but she said it half-heartedly.

'No, I came here to say this and I'm going to say it,' her mother said with the air of someone who had never backed down from a challenge in her life. 'I thought I was a failure.'

'*You* thought you were a failure?' said Sam. She reached in and adjusted India so the baby was nestling more comfortably against her mother's bony frame.

'This feels nice,' said Jean. She leaned in and smelled India's soft curls. 'I was bad at it,' she went on, 'bad at all of it. My maternity leave was hell, I couldn't do all the things the other women did, I felt a failure, not maternal. But you, you got to choose.' She looked at Sam over India's head. 'Your generation gets to choose. You don't have to have children, you have choices.'

'Are you saying you didn't want to have kids?'

'No, no,' said her mother, sounding slightly panicked so that India, picking up on the tension, began to fret.

'Give her to me.'

Sam shushed the baby and took her back, feeling a sense of relief as India's tiny body was nestled against her. She *was* good at this, she thought. There were so many things she could do with her baby. If the tablets meant the anxiety was kept at bay and the joy of motherhood could flood in, then she would take them as long as she needed them.

'Your generation can decide not to have kids. Or you can simply say you're not the stay-at-home type, go out to work and people think you are amazing. In my day, that didn't happen,' went on her mother, as if this was a speech she'd rehearsed. 'It was different then. Being a mother was your job and if you messed up that job, it didn't matter how good you were at anything else.'

'So why did you have children?' Sam didn't know where the words came from but it felt good to get them out. 'What was the point of giving birth to children if you had no interest in them? Because you didn't, you left all that to Dad. He was the one who took care of us, who brought us for ice creams and for walks in the park. You wouldn't even let us get a dog. No dog, you said, because a dog might require looking after or walking or cleaning up of dog shit, and yes, I know you told us all often enough, was there anything worse than baby poo.'

She had put on her mother's elegant voice for these words and Jean winced slightly.

'You can't know this, Sam, but in Ireland when you were born things were very different. Do you have any idea what it was like to be a working mother in this country and in those days? Now, we live in a world where you can arrange to work from home. Nobody looks at you like there's something wrong with you if you get someone in to mind your kids because you're out at work. But when I was working, it was totally different.

'Did you know that when I started out in teaching, women had to leave their jobs once they got married. The marriage bar, they called it,' she said mirthlessly. 'No matter what the feminist movement did, that bar was there and, oh yes, it was a bar, like a damned big iron bar to stop women progressing because God forbid a married woman took a job away from a man. And even with that gone, it was still difficult. We weren't getting even half the amount of money as men. I couldn't take a day off if you or Joanne were sick.'

'Don't be ridiculous,' snapped Sam, 'you were working in a school.'

'Working in a school! Do you think that made the slightest bit of difference? Do you think the board of governors would have cared that we were an educational establishment and I was taking time off to look after my kids? No they wouldn't. And do you know something really important?' Her mother stared at Sam fiercely. 'I wanted to work, Sam. Most mothers looked at women like me and thought we were unnatural.' Jean's tone was bitter.

'Feminism wasn't just the fight on the streets then, it was in the offices, in the classrooms, and that's where I fought, so women like you could go out to work. Now you look at me and think I was a useless mother. Fine,' Jean snapped. 'I wasn't maternal, but that's what women my age did: we got married, we had kids and then we had to figure out where to go next.

'I'm sorry I'm not what you wanted. I love India, you, Joanne and her children. I love all of you. I'm just not very good at showing it. I wish it was different but that's not the way I'm made. All I'm asking is that you try to understand that.'

With that, Jean picked up her coat, her keys, her handbag and left, swishing past the dogs, who'd snuffled around her heels. Neither of the dogs were terribly fond of her because Jean was not a doggy person any more than she was a baby person. Sam sat down on the couch, breathing in heavily, holding India to her closely.

That was one hornets' nest she had stirred up. She wished her mother had talked to her like that before. Sam had never even considered what it had been like for her mother to be at work in an era where working women were not the norm, certainly not working women in positions of power.

Still hugging India to her, she picked up her mobile phone and texted her sister:

Had the most amazing conversation with Mother. We need to talk.

'Wow, can't believe she said all that,' said Joanne on the phone later. It was too late in the afternoon to drop round: she was busy feeding her three girls after playdates, extra art and Irish dancing.

Isabelle loved Irish dancing, which seemed to involve a lot of hopping energetically to Sam's eyes.

'I'm still reeling,' said Sam, talking quietly because she'd finally got India to sleep. 'I feel—' She searched for the word.

'Guilty,' supplied Joanne. 'Me too. I never thought of it that way. I just thought she was remote.'

'Dads were supposed to be remote and mums were supposed to be warm and cuddly,' Sam said, thinking of how they'd viewed the world from their childish imaginations.

'No reason it couldn't be the other way round,' Joanne said. 'Poor old Mother. What are you going to do?'

Sam sat down on the couch and both dogs instantly leapt up beside her, delighted with the attention. 'Learn to forgive her, I guess. It's not her fault I developed post-natal depression.'

'You really can't lay that one on her,' Joanne agreed.

Roars broke out from Joanne's end of the line.

'War,' said Joanne. 'Gotta go and negotiate a peace deal.'

Sam laughed. 'Me too,' she said.

Ginger

Ginger leaned against the wall of the gym and pleaded with Will to stop.

'No more,' she said. 'I have nothing more to give, please . . .'

The sweat was dripping down her back and into the crevice between her breasts. Any deodorant she'd put on that morning had long since sweated off.

'You're torturing the poor girl, Will,' said Simon, who was walking by, holding a couple of the heaviest kettlebells as if they were bags of sugar.

'He is,' agreed Ginger. 'We've been at it an hour and I only came in to say I could do twenty minutes because I was so tired and it was late.' She looked at the gym clock. 'It's five to ten!' she said. 'I am shattered, you tyrant.'

Will laughed, reached out and pulled her back into a standing position.

'You stay out of this, Simon. My girl needs her training and I have vowed to be the man to train her, whether she likes it or not.'

Ginger's heart skipped a beat. *My girl?* But she didn't falter. Will was kind to everyone. So, they'd had coffee a few times and he'd bought her an after-training sandwich in the deli bar across the road, but that was just friendly, wasn't it?

'Whether she likes it or not?' she added, in pretend outrage.

'Oh, a conjugal. I'm off,' said Simon. 'Not getting involved in that row. You can lock up, Tyrant. I need to eat and watch crap on the box. See you, Ginger.'

Will began tidying up. The gym was emptying out. They closed late on Thursdays but it was amazing how many people liked to get in a late workout.

'Conjugal row, ha. Simon says the oddest things.'

Ginger felt her heart leap a little. Simon could see what Will couldn't: that she'd fallen for him. Not for how gorgeous he looked, although that didn't hurt, but for his kindness.

He'd come one day with a giant SUV and helped her haul off some more of Aunt Grace's endless boxes after she had confided in him about Grace's problem and her mission to clear the house. When Jack, the photographer, had arrived to take the after-the-workout photos for the paper in the gym, Will had been there with Lulu and her hair and make-up team, encouraging Ginger every step of the way.

He'd admired the photos when they'd gone in, but he'd never said anything specific, nothing like 'I really like you'.

'Mr Hunk really likes you,' Lulu had said on the day of the shoot.

'Shush!' Ginger had hissed. 'He'll hear.'

'I hope he does,' added Lulu irrepressibly. 'Say something to him – he's as shy as you are.'

But Ginger's fear of rejection kept her from saying anything and she treated him the way she treated her brothers, and nothing else.

'I was thinking,' Will said, when Ginger had finished her workout that evening and felt as if she'd been in a Turkish bath for a month, 'er ... would you like a drink after we hit the showers? Or a coffee? You know, something casual. We could grab a bite to eat ...?'

Ginger stared up at him in utter astonishment and the words that came out of her mouth just flew out: 'Like a date, you mean.' She blushed. 'Sorry! I know you didn't mean that. Forget I said it. I get dizzy when I'm tired and—'

'Yeah,' he interrupted her. 'Like a date.'

A little buzz of sheer excitement began to thrum through her.

'Yes,' she squeaked.

They sat in a small Italian restaurant round the corner and Ginger wished she had stuffed something better in her gym bag than a comfy khaki sweatshirt with a picture of a cat on it, and her equally comfy harem pants which were miles looser on the waist than they used to be. She was never going to be skinny – she didn't want to be, she'd decided. But she was more toned, felt healthy and working out had given her an appreciation for her body.

Will was in an equally comfortable T-shirt over which he wore one of those red flannel shirts, open so that Ginger could – if she allowed herself to – look at his beautiful chest defined by the T-shirt.

'Hey, Will, nice to see you,' said a guy coming over to him in chef's whites.

'Ginger, meet Mario, owner of this den of iniquity,' said Will. 'Mario, this is Ginger.'

'Gina Lollobrigida,' said Mario.

'No, Ginger,' said Ginger, confused.

'My da's Sicilian and he loves the old movie stars. Saw you in the paper last week – liked the bikini, by the way – and said you were a dead ringer for Gina, fifties movie star. If I phone and tell him you're in, he'll be round in a flash. He'll have you sitting on his knee, telling you the dreams he had about her in his youth.'

'I love your father, but don't phone,' begged Will. 'We want a quiet night.'

Mario raised an eyebrow. 'You two . . .?' he asked Will. 'Because if this is friends, I might ask Ms Gina if she would care to go out with me—'

'Hands off,' said Will evenly. 'Not friends.'

Ginger perked up.

Will reached across the table and grabbed her hand. 'We're

299

on a date, Mario. Skedaddle. Or I'll load up the weight bar next time you're in and see how you cope.'

'Gotcha.' Mario shot a finger at Will, blew a kiss at Ginger and went back into the kitchen.

'Half-Sicilian, half-Belfast, fiery combination,' said Will, still holding her hand. His large fingers began to stroke the underside of her palm and Ginger found it to be the most erotic thing anyone had ever done to her – and that included her encounter with her fake wedding-date.

'*Is* this a date?' she asked, wanting to know before she said the wrong thing. Because it couldn't be . . .

'Do you want it to be a date?' Will kept holding on to her hand.

Ginger nodded.

'You're like a wild deer in the forest, Ginger Reilly,' he said, looking into her amber eyes. 'You look sassy and tough, but you're shy, vulnerable. Like you've been hurt. I wanted to take it slow but I couldn't. Now that the article has been done, and the final shoot is over, you keep coming back and I'm afraid that one day, you won't show up anymore.'

Ginger could say nothing. She could only breathe. For the first time in her life, she felt *seen*. Utterly understood by a man who was not a relative.

'I want it to be a date,' she said, in a breathy tone that was not like her and not fake. It just came out like that. 'But—'

'But you have no confidence and you aren't sure?'

Ginger looked at him across the table.

'How do you know?' she asked, all artifice gone. No longer sassy office Ginger. Not don't-look-at-me Ginger. But just pure Ginger, all her heart and soul spiralling into that one simple question.

'I can see it in you.'

There was silence. He still held her hand.

Will sat up a bit straighter. 'OK, this is my story. I haven't dated in a while,' he said. 'Got my heart broken a few years back, takes a while to get over that, and then I saw a few people. Nothing felt right. I wanted—'

'—a connection?'

'Yes.' His warm eyes roved over her face, not her body, just her face. Seeing her, drinking her in. 'Exactly. I'm thirty-four and my mother worries herself sick I'll never find the right person. She's an artist: thinks the women who fancy me are all gym bunnies who care about the superficial and she hates that. She and my dad have something special: something deep. I want that.'

'It's what I want too, but I've never had it,' said Ginger. She'd never been this honest before. Not ever, really. Girlfriend would approve. *Be honest. If he can't accept you as you are, but only as the version of you he likes, then he is not the right man. YOU are good enough.*

She kept going. 'My heart's been broken but only by – by me, I guess. By me pretending to be people I wasn't, trying to fit in. By someone I considered a best friend who humiliated me.'

'Who? Tell me?' he demanded.

Ginger shook her head. 'Not now.' She smiled. 'Another time.'

There would be another time.

'That first day in your office, after you'd been working with that girl, I could see the decency in you. You understood her and her fears. And then you showed me the picture of you when you were . . .' She didn't want to use the word fat anymore. It was a horrible word. A word to put people down. She would never use it again. 'Like me,' she said instead. 'A bigger person in this thinner person's world.'

'I understood that. I try to change that in my gym. It's part of our ethos: we make the real you stronger.'

A waiter arrived, apologising for the delay, blaming a sick member of staff, an eclipse, something. They both grinned at him, not listening.

They let go of each other's hand just to take the menus.

Ginger had often wondered what she'd eat if she ever was in a restaurant with a man. How crazy was that? Imagining what to order so as not to look like a crazed foodaholic.

The gym had great leaflets on good foods. There were no bad foods, just moderation. Exercise. Moving more, being happy.

'Pizza, Hawaiian,' she said firmly.

'I love Hawaiian,' said Will delightedly.

'And sweet potato fries.' Healthier than fries, she knew, and she loved them. 'Sparkling water.'

'Same,' he said to the waiter, his eyes on Ginger.

They ate, and talked as if they'd both been in a desert for years, starved of human company.

They talked about his family, hers. He loved Aunt Grace, whom he'd met when he'd helped with the endless unopened boxes.

'Should have her own TV show,' he said.

'Yes, with Esmerelda in it too: they could sell jewellery and add hints on life.' Ginger giggled. 'Esmerelda is worried I won't ever find a man, so she is suggesting women lately. Once I get the ring on my finger, that's all that matters. Esmerelda has a very clear-cut view on life.'

'She and Grace both look like women who have lived good lives, enjoyed the heck out of it,' Will said.

'Yeah.' Ginger looked up to find Will watching her wiping her mouth with her napkin. His eyes were a little glazed as he watched and Ginger realised she was turning him on.

Right there in the restaurant, she felt herself heat up to about one thousand degrees.

'Let's go,' he said.

In the gym car park, they looked at their two cars. 'I don't want this evening to end,' Will said. 'Would you like to sit in mine and talk before you go home?'

'You mean we're not going to spend all night together?' teased Ginger, astonished at her own daring.

Will groaned. 'Please, don't tease me. Let's do it slowly, go slowly. I would sell my soul to go to yours right now and rip that cat sweatshirt off and hold you, but . . .' He took a deep breath, steadied himself by leaning both hands against his car. 'But slow. Right. I've tried the fast thing and it doesn't work.'

Ginger nodded as if she knew this too, when she really had no idea. She felt jealous of him going fast with anyone.

They sat in his car, some jeep type thing that was high up.

'Right now I'm sorry I don't have one of those classic old American cars with the bench front seat,' he said, turning to face Ginger, and she grinned. She knew exactly what he meant.

It was slow. Will leaned forward and took Ginger's face in his two hands, cradling her, and then his mouth was on hers, moving softly. And suddenly, it wasn't slow at all. He kissed her with intensity and this time, Ginger didn't even have to think about where to put her hands. She felt safe and sexy, wanted to be holding him, to be held by him. Their tongues melded, her hands strayed to his T-shirt, pulled it up to rub her flat palms over the sculpted beauty of his chest.

'Don't,' he moaned.

'I want to touch you.'

'I want to touch you too, but not here, not in my car in the car park.'

'Five more minutes,' Ginger said, and pulled him back to her.

This time, his hands slid under her sweatshirt.

Both their breathing caught as his hands reached her full breasts, his large hands roaming, making Ginger moan at the exquisite sensitivity of it.

'Oh Ginger, not here.'

Will sat back in his chair, looking seriously rattled, his eyes dark with desire.

'We are doing this properly, in a bed.'

Sanity reasserted itself. 'Right. In a bed,' Ginger agreed. 'Whose bed and when?'

Will laughed. 'Very soon,' he said. 'Or I might just explode.'

The next day, Jodie was stinking out one end of the giant newsroom, the features end, testing nail varnishes.

'Can you not do that somewhere else?' groaned Fiona.

'How am I supposed to test these damn things otherwise?' said Jodie.

She held up one hand with each finger painted a slightly different colour. In front of her on the desk were a gaggle of beautiful little nail varnish pots in various shades.

'I sort of like this one,' she said, wiggling her index finger in Fiona and Ginger's directions. 'What do you think?'

'I think they all look exactly the same to me,' said Fiona, 'and they stink. I'm sure it's a health hazard.'

'That one's the cutest,' said Ginger, pointing to a pearly pink on Jodie's ring finger.

'Bit of a classic,' said Jodie, going into beauty-speak.

From her corner, Fiona grinned. 'We are not the readers. We know this stuff because we have been sitting beside you for ages.'

Ginger smiled. It was funny how the three of them had bonded over the fitness articles, even though Ginger felt you couldn't get three more different women if you tried.

She and Jodie had gone out to dinner one evening and then Ginger had brought Jodie back to her place for tea where Jodie had gone into blissful admiration over the adorableness of Ginger's house and been thrilled to meet the guinea pigs. Jodie lived in a tiny rented flat and said she'd have killed to live in a beautiful little house like Ginger.

Now that she knew Jodie, she could see that the other girl was a lovely twenty-six-year-old woman who'd just started dating a decent guy called Peter. She wasn't into the club scene like Liza or her friends and she didn't seem to think there was anything wrong with Ginger because she wasn't interested in those things either. It was comforting being with Jodie, having a friend.

Ginger went back to working on her article and was in the writing zone when her desk phone rang. It was the managing editor's personal assistant.

'Mr Leon would like to see you at half four, if that is convenient?' said the assistant in a voice that implied that unless Ginger was having something amputated at that precise time, it had better be convenient.

'Yes, yes, of course,' said Ginger anxiously.

'Shit,' she said, turning to her colleagues.

'What now?' said Fiona. 'I have got to have this filed in ten more minutes.'

'I'm being summoned to see Mr Leon in forty-five minutes,' said Ginger. 'What do you think I've done?'

'Written some bloody good articles, that's what you have done,' said Fiona. 'Sorry, can't talk, gotta type.' She swivelled her head back to her computer.

'It's got to be good,' said Jodie, pulling her wheelie chair over closer to Ginger's. 'Our fitness series has had a huge number of hits on the site and your piece is the most popular, so could he want to see you about that?'

'Dunno,' said Ginger. 'A couple of months ago I was writing advertorials about peanuts and industrial estates and now this . . .' She shivered. 'What if I'm getting the sack?'

'He's not going to fire you,' interrupted Fiona. 'He doesn't do the firing. Someone from human resources delivers the news and you get a box to clear out your desk. So either he wants hints on working out, or he has some brilliant new thing he wants you to do. Now shut up, you pair. I am going to need earplugs to work soon.'

Ginger bounced back to her desk an hour later.

'What is it?' said Jodie. 'Is everything OK?'

'Course it's OK,' said Fiona, grinning. 'Tell us, then!'

Ginger could barely hold it in. 'The editor says I've been writing such brilliant pieces that he wants me to take over a lot more major feature writing. I'm getting a two-year contract and more dosh! Isn't that amazing?'

'Oh, Ginger,' sighed Jodie and hugged her friend. 'I am so pleased for you. You deserve this. You're a brilliant writer and . . .'

'. . . And that will be one in the eye for Carla Mattheson,' finished Fiona with glee. 'That will shut the old cow up.'

'That's not the point, obviously,' said Ginger quickly, 'but . . .' she paused, '. . . it would be nice to have it recognised that I'm not just something to be kicked around.' And the three of them laughed uproariously.

They were still chattering and discussing exactly what Ginger's new role would be when a sharp cough made them all look up. Carla Mattheson stood close by, elegant and perfect as ever. Long legs encased in a skintight but somehow elegant skirt, and a little swishy top that managed to conceal and not conceal at the same time. She looked amazing, Ginger thought with a hint of irritation. And then felt guilty. Carla Mattheson did bring out the worst in her.

'Ginger,' said Carla, in a sort of husky, come-hither voice she normally reserved for the men she wanted to impress around the building. 'Can I talk to you for a moment in my office?'

'Sure,' said Ginger, about to grab her pens, notebook and tablet.

'You won't need any of that,' said Carla.

Ginger followed Carla's gently swaying hips. How did a person do that? she wondered. Some sort of motorised hip movement that just made everything sway. No wonder all the men were crazy about her.

In her office, Carla shut the door, that friendly smile still on her face. It was the smile that was making Ginger really nervous. It was the sort of smile that a woman-eating snake gave before she swallowed a person whole, reticulated jaw opening up to gulp them right down.

'So.' Carla sat elegantly behind her desk and motioned with one perfectly manicured hand for Ginger to sit too. 'I hear you've been promoted. Won't be working on our little magazine anymore.'

'Yes,' said Ginger, not even slightly surprised. The editor hadn't said that he'd told everyone else, but then of course Carla was on the management team and she'd know all about it . . .

'I was all for it,' Carla said gravely. 'I really believe in women getting ahead.'

It was all Ginger could do not to laugh out loud, but as it was she managed to hold it in somehow. She and her friends helped each other. Carla never helped anyone but herself. But if Carla wanted to think denial was a river in Africa, that was fine by Ginger.

'You did a really good job on those gym pieces. Funny and real. The readers really liked them. Great ratings and a lot of readers on the internet version of the paper.'

'Yes,' said Ginger carefully. She wasn't sure where this was going, but there was a hint of danger. As if Carla was already working up her jaw for the whole body-swallowing thing.

'That guy Will Stapleton who runs the gym,' went on Carla. 'What a charmer he is. I knew you'd like him. Everyone does, totally gorgeous and sexy, isn't he?' She smiled then at Ginger, a smile that said so many things. 'I put him onto you because I knew he'd take care of you. He's great with people who need . . .' Her eyes scanned Ginger's body. 'With people who need extra help. And he's kind, you know. Kind to everyone. Of course, women are always falling in love with him . . .'

Ginger could only stare at her. All the joy of the previous night vanished.

'He is kind of charming, isn't he?' she said, doing her level best to smile. She would not break down in front of this bitch.

'Yes, very charming, and as I told him when I set up that initial meeting with you, it would be so good for his gym to be featured in the paper. After all, people would kill for that sort of PR. Two months of articles in the *Sunday News*. Who wouldn't do *anything* for that?'

Ginger had no more fight left. She just stared at Carla.

'I rang the gym earlier to check on my free membership and guess what, some guy on the desk said you and Will had been on a date last night? Sweet,' Carla went on. 'I'm sure you had a great time with him, but I have my eye on him. So hands off. He's out of your league. I asked him if he'd come with me to the newspaper awards and, naturally, he said yes. He knows it would be fabulous publicity and think of all the contacts he'd meet. I hear on the grapevine you might be up for one . . .'

'Really? I've never been, and no, I hadn't heard that rumour,' said Ginger. Somehow, she rose gracefully, smiled, and said, 'Lots of work to do, Carla. Bye.'

'What's wrong?' asked Jodie when Ginger raced over to their corner and frantically grabbed her handbag and her phone off the desk.

'Nothing,' said Ginger. But she knew she was going red, knew she'd cry any minute now and she had to get out of the office before that happened, before anyone else witnessed her pain. Even Jodie and Fiona, her dear friends. She couldn't let them see how hurt she was. Because Will had used her. Will and Carla had used her. First Liza, and now them.

Will answered on the first ring.

'Hey, gorgeous,' he said in a warm tone.

Ginger felt like a volcano that had been building up pressure for thirty years and today it was going to blow.

'You never told me you knew my boss, Carla. And how could you agree to go to the press awards with her? Why did you agree?'

'Ginger,' he protested, 'she phoned this morning. She's sort of pushy. I knew she wanted a free membership when she suggested us for the magazine feature, and the gym needs more publicity, but it's just work, Ginger.'

'Just work. Which part? Her or me? At least I know now, Will.'

'It's not like that,' he protested. 'Damn it, Ginger, after everything we shared last night—'

'Exactly. You didn't share one vital thing. All the old girlfriends, yes. The fact that you know my bitch of a boss, and were capable of going to an event with another woman when you're allegedly going out with me, no. You never told me any of that. So case closed. Goodbye, Will. It was, briefly, nice knowing you. Until you showed me your true colours.'

And she slammed down the phone.

He kept phoning and phoning, but she blocked his number and deleted it. He could try to wriggle his way out of this one, but it was no good.

Ginger knew that Carla had simply seized upon the opportunity presented to her because she was angry that Ginger was being promoted. But why did Will have to go along with it? There were ways to get publicity without going on a date with another woman. He could have said: 'Sorry, I'm dating Ginger Reilly.' But he hadn't. He'd been ready to jettison Ginger for publicity, and who knew if the 'date' with Ginger had just been publicity too . . .? She might never know. But she no longer cared. Ginger had had it with men.

Will sent flowers to the office, a giant bouquet of pink flowers that made the delivery person almost stagger in carrying them.

There was also a note.

Please answer my calls. I am so sorry. I'll get out of it. She is work – you were never work, Ginger, never. I'll wait and hope you phone. I won't give up.

Will.

She crumpled the note into the bin and sent a simple text: *Go with Carla. Publicity comes first. Stay away from me. It's over.*

Who needed a man, anyway?

The Caraval table was by far the noisiest at the Press Awards. The media group had taken out four wildly expensive tables and the staff were making full use of the free bar.

Ginger was excited despite the pain in her heart. Her friends were thrilled that she was nominated for best feature writer of the year. She'd never expected to be up for an award, had thought that Carla had just been taunting her, but it turned out to be true. Totally unexpected as far as she was concerned, but true.

She didn't have a hope in hell of winning, particularly when someone as experienced as Carla Mattheson was up for it as well. When she thought nobody was looking, she ran her finger over the names of the people who'd been nominated. She never let her finger touch Carla's name, as if mere contact with that name would contaminate her. Carla contaminated everything.

'I hope that ho Mattheson doesn't win,' said Paula, settling herself down beside Ginger, when the MC had finally insisted for the fourth time that people had to come in from the bar and sit down because the awards were going to begin, and that the bar would close if they didn't all shift it.

'You know she will,' said Ginger glumly, not bothering to correct Paula for her use of the word 'ho'. She'd spotted Carla clinging on to Will and her heart had felt like the proverbial stone. If he looked good in gym gear, he looked utterly delicious in an evening jacket.

And not hers, she reminded herself. Stupid Ginger – again pining for someone who would never be hers. It astonished her how much it still hurt. Nothing had ever hurt so much.

They'd become friends all that time in the gym, she realised. They'd laughed and joked as he trained her. He'd been a part of her life as a friend and she'd fallen in love with him. Deeply, heart-wrenchingly. How was it that her heart ached in a way that no squat could ever make her thighs ache?

'You should win,' said Paula.

'Oh come on, this is my first time being nominated, nobody wins on their first time,' Ginger said, and then followed it up with the lie she'd been telling herself all evening: 'This is fun, I'm having fun.'

'Me too,' said Paula, casting dark glances over at a guy from the sports department who was gorgeous, and clearly fancied her right back. In honour of this event, Paula was dressed in a knock-off version of a Hervé Léger bandage dress which was moulded to her body like a second skin. She had bought an incredible Victoria's Secret push-up bra to help with the cleavage department.

Ginger knew *she* didn't need any help in the cleavage department, but she was still pretty pleased with her appearance. Thanks to the personal training, she looked different, incredibly different. Nobody was ever going to call her skinny, but she was standing up for bigger, curvier girls in the best way possible. Her sister-in-law, Zoe, had helped her pick out the dress and she wore the amethyst silky sheath with pride. It was strapless, therefore wildly dangerous.

'Try this,' Zoe had said in the shop, when Ginger was in the changing room flinging evening dresses on and off with great abandon.

'Are you nuts?' said Ginger, looking at the sheath dress. 'I have boobs, Zoe, big boobs. When you have anything in that department, you cannot go strapless, because this dress would be down around my ankles in about four minutes, and this is not the sort of event where I can let that happen. I am up for an award.' She did not mention that the man she'd once been crazy about was going to be there with a woman she hated.

'I promise you that will not happen,' said Zoe. 'You just need the right strapless bra.'

'You're crazy; I can't wear this. Look at it, it's a sixteen and I can't fit into a sixteen.'

'Try it, it's got an inner control panel.'

'Designed by NASA?'

Only because she wanted to please Zoe and because she thought it might be interesting to see if she could actually fit into the dress, Ginger had squeezed into it. 'I can't do the zip up the whole way,' she said.

Zoe popped her head into the changing room. 'Ginger, you look incredible!'

'I look like I'm about to go out on the game,' said Ginger, grinning. Before she'd toned up, she could not have fitted into this. She liked feeling fit, and Will – oh, Will – had been right about fitness making a person feel strong and healthy. She had to join another gym. She obviously hadn't been back to his.

'You look extremely sexy and *soignée*,' said Zoe.

'I can't quite close the zip,' said Ginger, 'and I don't know what sort of bra is going to hold my breasts up in this, but it better be industrial grade.'

'Don't worry, leave it with me. Lulu insists that undergarments are the key to all. There will be no wardrobe malfunctions.'

Thanks to a really amazing strapless bra that *must* have been designed by NASA because it cost so much, Ginger fitted into the dress. She wore her beautiful hair up, her skin was porcelain pale and Jodie had done her eye make-up for her. She looked the best she had ever looked in her life and that included the original photo shoot for the fitness article. She hadn't been toned then. Toning was the key, it was nothing to do with being fat or not being fat, as Will had said to her on many occasions.

'It's to do with fitness levels,' he used to say. 'There are many incredibly thin, skinny people and they're totally unfit, Ginger. Being fit – that's what matters. Fit, toned and strong. Gives you strength and confidence on the inside too.'

Her heart certainly didn't feel strong these days, but she'd recover, Ginger thought miserably, extending an arm and admiring the emergence of biceps as she did so. She might have biceps but Carla had Will.

Still, she'd get over him if it killed her. She'd become aware of a few of the guys from work watching her, and she'd even caught Zac looking her way in admiration once or twice this evening. But maybe she was imagining it. Zoe had told her she looked amazing: 'You look fabulous, Ginger. I wish you'd believe it too.'

The room was reasonably quiet as the MC made a few jokes and then started the countdown to the various awards. It really was a lovely night, thought Ginger, her mind going off into the ether. She wished she'd been able to bring someone from home: Mick and Zoe or Dad or Declan and Margaret. They'd have enjoyed it, enjoyed seeing her name written on the list of people who were nominated for the best feature writer.

Even though there was just no way in hell she was going to win it, it was something to be nominated. It was like this big start to her career, saying she'd arrived. Therefore, in expectation of not winning, she wasn't in the slightest bit nervous as the presenter read out the list of people nominated for her award. Carla sat at one of the top tables wearing a short metallic dress that had probably cost thousands – or would have if she'd actually paid for it. Paula said Carla was notorious around town for getting discounts out of designers and designer shops. Plus, if she wore something that was photographed, it was good publicity for the designer and tonight she looked quite amazing with that sleek bob and her usual push-up bra. Beside her sat Will, looking so familiar and so handsome, Ginger's heart ached.

She was so busy in her contemplation of Will, Carla and her glossy beauty that she wasn't listening and suddenly Paula was poking her painfully in her side with her elbow.

'Get up,' said Paula.

'What,' said Ginger. 'What is it?'

'You've won.'

'Won what?'

'You've won the award.'

'You've won best feature writer, Ginger!' said Brian, who was sitting at their table, smiling at her.

Suddenly all eyes were on Ginger. Was this a joke? Was this like Liza's wedding, everyone ganging up on her to make her look stupid? And then she saw the huge screen and saw her name on it. *Ginger Reilly, Sunday News, Feature Writer of the Year.* Her stomach swooped.

'Really?' she said.

'Really,' hissed Paula. 'Now get up there and say thank you to everyone. Remember to say thank you to the important people at the top, too, or you will never work in this town again. Don't fall over anyone on the way up. I give you free leave to bring a glass of wine and throw it into Carla Mattheson's face en route, if you want,' added Paula, but a startled Ginger was gone, pushed happily along by other people.

'I don't believe this,' she said and people smiled as she passed, because it was quite clear that this tall, statuesque girl, with her fabulous piled-up hair and her beautiful warm face, genuinely hadn't expected to win.

She managed to get up on the stage without tripping even though her shoes were incredibly high. Because she was tall, she towered over the presenter.

'Oh my,' she said, looking around her. 'I don't know what to say.'

She took a deep breath. She would not make a fool out of herself. A man she was trying desperately to get over was down there looking up at her and he didn't want her. He'd chosen someone else.

But she was a warrior woman: she would not let his presence upset her. She had a career to think of.

'This is my first time here and I do not have a handy speech tucked into this dress. Nothing else will fit.'

Everyone laughed.

'I wasn't really a proper feature writer until a few months ago. Up until then, I was writing advertorials where, for the uninitiated, you have to write about peanuts and garages and make it all sound terribly thrilling but keep it under a thousand words.'

Everyone laughed some more.

'And suddenly I'm here, nominated for an award and I win. I wasn't thinking about that. I was looking around the room and thinking how wonderful everyone looked and wondering how soon I could take my shoes off because they are so tight.' She poked a shoe out from under the dress, a dress with a side split that showed off those amazing legs.

Whoops accompanied the laughs this time.

She went on to make a list of thank yous, carefully mentioning all the people she worked with, including her pals Paula, Fiona and Jodie, right down to the girls who cleaned up in the evening, whose life stories she knew.

People were clapping, for her!

'Finally, I'd like to thank my dad, my two brothers, Michael and Declan, my two sisters-in-law, Zoe and Margaret, and my Great-Aunt Grace for always being there, because they believed in me when nobody else did.'

And then Ginger made her way down the steps holding her glass award.

People tried to grab her and congratulate her.

'You must come and work for us, you know,' said one guy in a dark suit.

'No, we saw her first,' said his pal.

'She could turn our magazine around,' said a woman in fuchsia.

'I'm happy where I am, but thank you, thank you,' said Ginger, smiling at everyone with that great warm smile that captivated people.

'You and I need to talk,' said Alice Jeter, grabbing her. 'I have a wonderful idea if you want to go along with it. I know your writing as Girlfriend is very personal—'

Ginger blinked. 'You knew that?'

''Course I knew. It was written from the heart, all really moving, full of empathy. You can't fake that. That's why I didn't think you'd want to be outed, so to speak. But you're too good, Ginger, to hide behind a pseudonym. What do you think?'

Ginger breathed in carefully. Too much breathing in and she might pop out of her dress. She'd been sure the Girlfriend thing was something Alice had constructed to hide Ginger behind. Not this – she had never foreseen this.

'I'd love that,' she said on the exhale. 'Scary, but I'd love it.'

Alice smiled. 'See you Monday morning,' she said.

Beaming, Ginger finally made it down to their table, where Zac had suddenly materialised along with several bottles of champagne

'Got to toast the winning writer,' he said, a dangerous glitter to his eyes.

In her heels, he was the only man apart from Will who was taller than her and he was a full two inches taller. In her bare feet, he'd be six inches taller and that dinner jacket was made for him. Some men wore suits as if they'd been forced into them at knifepoint, but Zac wore his as if he was born into it. He filled a glass and handed it to her, standing really close to her. He then picked up another glass.

'For a proper toast,' he murmured, 'the tradition is that we wrap our hands around each other, to get closer.'

'Oh,' said Ginger. Out of the corner of her eye, she could see Paula making big thumbs up signs in the background, nearly bouncing out of her bandage dress.

'Like this,' he said.

'OK,' said Ginger, on a buzz after both her win and her conversation with Alice.

Zac moved closer and she was overwhelmed with the scent of

his cologne. It was something woody and expensive, like him. His hair was short and slicked back, and oh, those eyes could almost see into her soul. He linked her wrist with his and then he said, 'drink', and she did, the whole glass, straight down.

Ginger was not a big drinker and because she had had very little to eat beforehand, it went straight to her head.

'Congratulations,' Zac said and he leaned forward and kissed her on the cheek. 'Do you know how sexy you are?' he said, following it up with: 'Would you like to celebrate later? With me. Alone?'

Out of the corner of her eye, she could see Will staring over at her, eyes boring into her. *Blast you, Will*, she thought.

'I'd love that,' Ginger said defiantly. Why not?

It was time to go. Ginger had partied, been congratulated and had far too much champagne. She was making one last dash for the loo when suddenly Will stood in front of her, handsome in his evening jacket.

'Congratulations,' he said, eyes roaming over her hopelessly overexcited face.

Ginger longed to throw herself into his arms, but she knew, just knew, that somewhere in the background, Carla was there, watching.

'Thank you,' she said, summoning up good cheer from somewhere. 'Hope you're having fun.'

'No,' he said. 'I keep watching you—'

'Baby.' Zac's arm slid around her waist. He was quite drunk, she realised. 'I've got your things: bag and award. Now let's really party.'

He shot Will a look of triumph.

Will stepped back.

'Is this wise?' he asked Ginger, and she felt herself grow furiously angry.

'That ceased to be any of your business some time ago,' she said, steering Zac away from him. 'Bye.'

Ginger ordered a cab and when it arrived, she and the driver manhandled Zac in. He was definitely drunker than she'd thought. He must have thrown back some more champagne in the past few minutes. The gorgeous dark eyes were crossed now, but he was gazing at her breasts like it was Christmas and she had a stocking full of presents hidden in the front of her dress.

'It'll cost extra if he gets sick in the back of the cab,' the driver warned.

'I know,' said Ginger.

Slowly, she extracted Zac's address from him. He kept trying to kiss her, but she held him off and gave him her award to hold.

'His place first,' she said, leaning forward to talk quietly to the driver. 'Then can you wait till I get him into his place, and I'll come out and go home.'

'Fine. On your credit card, love, we can drive all night.'

It took a while to get Zac into his rented apartment, which was a total man cave with lots of boy toys and a TV the size of a cinema screen. Zac had by now moved from happy drunk into sleepy drunk. Somehow, she got him onto his bed, loosened his bow tie, put a glass of water by the bed and left to get the taxi the rest of the way home.

'Look what I won!' she said to Squelch and Miss Nibbles, and then she sat down on her couch, still in her gorgeous dress, and started to cry. She'd won an award, everyone loved her and she was back in her apartment with her guinea pigs. Where were Will and Carla going? she wondered miserably.

Was this her life for evermore? Always the one home alone, thinking about other people having fun.

PART FOUR

Three Months Later

Callie

Freddie was being shifty. 'It's a surprise,' he said, 'a weekend away.'

'Why?' asked Callie suspiciously. She'd gone right off surprises.

'What's the big deal?' Freddie demanded. 'Can't I treat my mother, my sister and my niece to a nice weekend away?'

The mention of Poppy did it. Callie somehow relaxed.

Over the past few months, Poppy had decided exactly what she wanted to do with the rest of her life. She loved art and she loved make-up.

'I'm going to be a make-up artist,' she told her astonished mother. 'It makes total sense. I'm really good at it and I have loads of brushes and stuff, things that other girls in school wouldn't have.'

Her new school was nothing like the school she'd been in originally, but she'd made lots of friends. Poppy still talked to some of her old friends on the phone, and she'd been invited to Dublin for weekends, but Callie was putting that off for the moment.

'I think it's too soon,' she said to Mary Butler on Skype. 'What do you think?'

'I agree. Give it time,' said Mary, her lovely face filling the screen of the tablet Callie had bought for Poppy. 'Imagine if she heard something horrible about her father . . .'

'Yes,' winced Callie.

She'd spoken to her daughter about Jason and discovered that Poppy knew a lot more than Callie had thought.

'Me and Lauren looked him up on Lauren's phone in her house,' Poppy revealed. 'I've seen all the stories, Mum.'

She looked guilty but Callie felt like the guilty one.

'Honey, I never wanted you to find it all out like that,' she said.

'Yeah, you can't get away from news with Wi-Fi,' Poppy said, shrugging. 'Although from BuzzFeed, I do know what Disney princess I am.' She managed a laugh. 'I know what Dad is supposed to have done.'

Callie nodded slowly. She had to let Poppy tell her this, even if she wanted to find Jason and stick pins in his eyes.

'I know he must have done it because he ran away and left us, but I know it probably wasn't his fault. I hate Rob. Bet he did it all. But Dad ran away too and he hasn't talked to us, so . . .'

Poppy began to cry, silent tears rushing down her face.

'I hate that he did that, Mum.'

Callie pulled her daughter close and they cried together.

'I hate that he did that too, lovie,' Callie wept. 'Not for me but for you.'

Incredibly, Poppy seemed to have come out of it all better than Callie could have hoped.

The resilience of youth? she wondered. Or just that Poppy was growing up, becoming interested in different things.

She'd been to a youth club disco with some of her friends from school and even though Callie had been on tenterhooks all evening, when she'd picked them up, all giggling and teasing each other about boys, Poppy had been euphoric. Driving them all home had been like driving a car full of girls fizzed up with firecrackers inside them, and Callie had felt so relieved. At least Jason hadn't taken all vestiges of a normal childhood away from Poppy.

There was hope they'd both come out of this.

'So where were you thinking of going, exactly, for this lovely weekend away?' Callie asked her brother now.

'Kenmare,' said Freddie, his eyes lighting up. 'I did some work there once. The Park Hotel. Beautiful place, old-world elegance, charm and style. The owners, the Brennans, are wonderful hosts. Nobody will recognise you, and even if they did, no one would breathe a word. It's a safe place, I promise you,' he added. 'You'd be amazed how many famous people live around there and nobody knows.'

The Park Hotel in Kenmare was indeed beautiful, and as they drove up to the lovely front of the old castle-style hotel, Callie couldn't help but think of the last time she and Poppy had stayed in a hotel. Sitting in the back seat with her, Poppy turned and said:

'Do you remember the last—'

'Oh gosh yes,' said Callie fervently, thinking of the hotel on the outskirts of Dublin where they'd done nothing but fight and where the future had seemed so bleak. 'Where everything was brown . . .'

'. . . And it smelled all smoky,' Poppy said. Suddenly they were both laughing.

This glorious hotel was everything Freddie had said it would be: welcoming and friendly. There were books in Callie's room, huge windows where you could look out to the bay and an amazing four-poster bed. Sitting on top of the bed was a fluffy white toy sheep. She picked it up and hugged it tightly.

'I think I love this place,' she said.

It was the sort of hotel that Jason would never have gone to. Jason liked modern, starkly modern, and if he'd seen a fluffy sheep toy anywhere in a room, he'd have been out the door so fast he'd have got a nosebleed. But this little oasis of comfortable luxury was just what Callie needed.

The four of them ate dinner that night and laughed and joked, watching the driving rain outside and feeling snug inside. And then later, Callie slept better than she'd slept in a very long time.

Kenmare was settled on the edge of the coast, perched on a rocky finger of land that stretched towards the Atlantic Ocean, and in the hotel, there was a sense that time stood still. Callie imagined she could be dressed like a Victorian lady going down to breakfast and it would be perfectly apt.

At breakfast, she ate everything in sight.

'Mum, I haven't seen you eat like that for ages,' said Poppy, laughing at her mother.

'Must be the sea air,' said Callie. 'I suppose I better walk it off. What are you going to do today, Poppy?'

'I'm going into the town with Gran, then I might go to the hotel spa and I don't know, just chillax.'

'After that,' said Pat, 'I just want to do nothing, read the paper, look out the window and have tea brought to me where I don't have to wash up the cups myself.'

'That sounds nice,' said Freddie, busying himself with his phone. 'There's a great walk down there past the garden where you can go right out to a little headland. There's a bat sanctuary, although I don't know if there are many bats in it, but it's beautiful and wild. Spiritual.'

It was indeed beautiful, Callie thought, half an hour later as she walked in the fresh December air, enjoying the sense of peace and calm. A lady with a small dog waved a hand of hello, and Callie waved back, for once not scared she'd be recognised. As she kept walking, she warmed up and she felt the beauty of crunching along through the big stones with the water lapping to one side and the trees on the other. Bathing in the forest, the Japanese called the experience, and it made sense. Bathing in nature was a wonderful way of relaxing.

Here, nothing could touch her. Here, she was just herself: not trying to be the perfect mother in the midst of all her traumas and not trying to run from anyone. There was peace in this beautiful place.

In the distance, she saw someone coming towards her, a

man. And on some deep level, he seemed familiar to her. She couldn't figure out why and then she kept her head down in case it was someone from the past, and goodness, she didn't want to see anyone from their past life now, she wanted to get away from that. Quickly she moved on towards the wood, but the man called out, 'Callie,' and then she stopped dead. She waited until he was closer.

'Ricky,' she said, looking up at him in utter astonishment. He was no longer the lean boy he had been, but a man now, filled out, with a man's face and those amazing eyes that she could remember being haunted by many years ago, during the drug years. Yet he looked at peace with himself now.

She stared at him.

'Why do I feel as if I was set up?' she said. This was too much of a coincidence to be a random meeting.

'Busted! Freddie and I set it up,' said Ricky.

'Freddie?' said Callie. 'Why?'

'He wanted to talk to you but he didn't know how to do it himself, so I'm here. I've known you nearly as long as he has, well, apart from all those missing middle years.'

'What does he want to talk to me about?' asked Callie, feeling panicky because she was terrified of what he was going to say. He couldn't know . . . Freddie couldn't know. 'I don't need your help, Ricky, thank you but I'll get out of this on my own, and I know you're rich and everything and it's lovely of you to be here, but—'

He held a hand up.

'It's not that,' he said. 'I would love to help you financially and I am here anytime to help you get back on your feet. But you might need my help in another way. Freddie says you do. Come on, sit down.'

They found a few rocks to perch on, Ricky stretching his legs out and turning until he was half facing her.

'I met up with Freddie lots of times when he was on heroin. I was clean and sober then, so I tried to help for old times' sake, but he didn't want to be helped. He needed to be ready himself,' said Ricky. 'But I suppose you understand that? If you give up for real, there's no place to hide anymore. There's no going back.'

Callie flushed.

'What are you talking about?'

'Freddie knows you're taking something and he wanted me to talk to you. He couldn't trust himself to do it, because he's too close. Is it benzos?'

'What?' Callie cried in shock.

'Cal, they've all noticed. Your mother, your Aunt Phil, and obviously Freddie. After what they've been through with Freddie, they know what an addict looks like, whether it's heroin or benzos. One minute you were tense, and the next you were Mrs Happy. Only one thing does that. Freddie did say you were drinking a fair bit, but it's not that. And I understand you've been through a lot, but—'

'Xanax,' Callie blurted out, feeling shamed. But she had to say it: this was her chance to come clean and get rid of her dirty little secret.

'Yeah,' Ricky said, 'Freddie figured as much, said you were buying them from Glory in the Russet Lounge.'

Callie looked down at the pebbles on the beach.

'Is that really the way you want to go, Callie? It's just you now, you and Poppy. The whole family and me, if you want me, we're all there for you. You're Poppy's mother and you can't let her down as well as Jason. Consider this an intervention.'

Callie could say nothing, she just sat there feeling the shame and embarrassment rise up through her. As if he noticed nothing, Ricky looked out and pointed off into the distance.

'I've a house over there; myself and Valerie, my wife, live there. We've a little girl, beautiful little thing, Fleur. She's ten. Smart as paint. She doesn't know about me and the drugs, although one day I'll tell her, because it's in the genes. Might be in your genes, too, and maybe Poppy's. But you need to deal with it, Callie. Now.'

Finally Callie managed to speak.

'How do you deal with it?' she said. 'I don't have the money to go in somewhere and get rehabbed. I don't know what to do.'

'You could go to Narcotics Anonymous like your brother and I do, and try and stay off whatever it is you're addicted to one day at a time. That's how it works. It's that simple, that complicated. You may not need NA but you need to be aware that you can't touch drugs like that, not ever again. First you've got to admit you've got a problem.'

'I know I've got a problem,' she said quietly. 'I've known for a long time, but I just haven't been able to stop.'

'None of us can stop on our own,' Ricky said ruefully. 'We need the support of other addicts. Freddie and I can help you with that, if you want?'

'But I never took anything before, I was never a drinker before, I don't understand how it happened,' cried Callie.

Ricky touched her for the first time and he held her hand in the same sort of brotherly way Freddie would hold it.

'How about you don't try to understand for the moment,' he said, 'but just stay with the fact that you're an addict. Take it slowly.'

'I hate myself for taking them, for relying on them,' said Callie, beginning to cry. 'I drink, too. Drink and the Xanax. I'm narky without it, desperate if I think I'm low on stocks, and I can't afford it really and I hate myself! Sometimes I curse Jason for bringing me to this and then I think, he didn't make me buy the bloody drugs.'

'One day, you'll look back and you won't hate yourself,' Ricky said, putting an arm round her.

'I can't imagine that,' she said bitterly.

'You will, I promise. Stopping is the first step. Admitting you've a problem and stopping takes some people years. But think of what you have to lose: Poppy. Plenty of people lose their kids because they're addicts. Don't be one of them.'

Callie was crying silent tears of pure pain. Ricky was right, Freddie was right. She was an addict and she was risking so much by continuing to see Glory, by taking the drugs, by drinking too much. She'd come to rely on those relaxants so much, but at what cost? If they meant losing Poppy, then she needed to stop.

Ricky let her cry and he held her as she sobbed till her face was raw.

'Thank you,' she muttered earnestly. 'I didn't want to hear that but I needed it.'

'Nobody wants to hear it,' he said. 'There's a meeting tonight we could go to in Tralee. Will you come with us?'

Callie nodded. She would do anything.

They walked back to the hotel the way Callie had come.

'I feel like such a failure,' she said.

'There are lots of us failures out there living great lives,' Ricky said. 'Me, Freddie, and it could be you too.'

Callie hugged him goodbye, whispered 'thank you' into his shoulder, and went into the hotel. In her beautiful, elegant room, she looked at her stash of tablets with disgust, then made herself flush them all down the toilet. It took all her strength not to take one more, just one – but she had a child to take care of. She had to start again, in every sense. No more self-pity, no more blaming anyone, just starting again. Being true to herself and her darling Poppy.

Sam

Sam felt relaxed as she drove away from her home on her first official back-to-work trip, which was to the nursing home in Ballyglen. Vera was over minding India, and there was no doubt about it, Vera took care of India as if she was the Christ Child himself. In fact, Ted and Sam joked among themselves that if Vera was still minding India when she was much older, India would probably think that she was a combination of the Dalai Lama and some sort of fabulous princess into the bargain. Vera laughed when they said this.

'Ah, go away out of that,' she'd say, flushing with pleasure. 'She's my granddaughter. I just love her.'

'And probably spoil her a tiny bit,' Ted teased.

'You can't spoil a small baby,' Vera insisted.

'She's right there,' agreed Sam. 'And we are not spoiling our little princess anyway. She's just being treated the way she deserves to be treated.'

'Exactly,' said Vera.

Sam's mother had said she could babysit if they were stuck, but she'd added that she knew she wasn't good at it, and would need her husband too.

'You two can do your bit, don't worry,' Sam had said. And she'd meant it. But for a long trip, Vera was a better option.

She still hadn't really talked in depth with her mother after their conversation, but now Jean came round more often, always with her husband, but she was doing her best. For two women who so rarely shared their feelings, it was enough.

'What can I do to help?' Jean would ask formally.

'Fold those baby clothes for me, if you wouldn't mind,' Sam would say, just as formally.

Even though neither of them was able to discuss their confrontation, this new plan was somehow working. Jean was seeing her granddaughter and Sam was slowly learning to come to terms with the fact that motherhood did not come automatically with a complete set of maternal feelings.

She thought of the quote Joanne had found for her and had had laminated: 'You can't change other people: you can only change how you react to them.'

'Who said this?' she asked, staring at it.

'Dunno,' said Joanne, 'but it's good. Sums it all up. Read and repeat every morning, big sis.'

In the meantime, Vera was their go-to help. If there were any problems, Vera could always call on Cynthia next door, who was only mad to get in and have a go at India herself. Cynthia was the backup babysitter and was getting into training, as she explained, because Shazz was pregnant.

'I don't know how this has happened,' Shazz had said, the day she'd imparted the news to Ted and Sam in the driveway. Shazz was still tall and beautiful and there was a hint of a tanned bump spreading out from underneath her crop-top. Her belly button was an outie and it had already popped out a little bit.

'No idea how it could have happened?' said Ted, deadpan.

'I don't know, I mean it's . . . confusing,' Shazz said, as if she'd never had a single sex education lesson in her life.

Cynthia was more prosaic about the impending birth of her first grandchild.

'Shazz never did pay much attention in school and I think she thought that pregnancy happened to other girls. It's not that she doesn't know how it happened, it's just that she has absolutely no idea how it happened to her. Because Shazz is one of those people who coasted through life with good things happening to her.'

Shazz certainly seemed to be enjoying pregnancy and delighted in going around with her tiny bronzed beach-ball belly on show for all to see.

'Mum says it's winter and I should be wearing more clothes, but you know, I'm hot,' she said.

Sam giggled. Even in previous winters, Shazz had worn skimpy little clothes all the time and being pregnant wasn't really changing that, except for the fact that her pink hair was now blonde and tipped with a fabulous feathery purple.

'Have you got names for the baby?' Ted asked. Ted loved Shazz and her dizzy madness. He looked at her as if she was a sort of slightly daft alien from the planet Moon-Dust, a planet where normal rules did not apply and where the inhabitants lived in a lovely hazy world of rainbows and moonbeams.

'Yeah,' said Shazz dreamily. 'I just can't get my head around the right sort of names. Petal and Flower, I love all those names, but Unicorn – that's so pretty and I have a unicorn tattoo on my lower back. Have I ever showed it to you?'

'Yes,' fibbed Sam.

'Yes,' agreed Ted hurriedly, 'we're fine, we don't need to see the tattoo. Today. Again, I mean.'

Sam grinned. While Ted loved Shazz, he was also a bit scared of her.

'I was going to get it coloured in, but I've been told that you shouldn't have any tattoos done when you're pregnant, so I'm going to be careful because I'm going to be a good mum, like you, Sam. You can explain to me how to be a good mum.'

'Your mother could explain how to be a good mum because she's amazing,' Sam had said.

'I know,' said Shazz, 'but she's, you know, old. I mean you're old too, but you're different old, you're young old, you know.'

Sam grinned at the memory as she drove off down the road. With Cynthia and Shazz living next door it was always lively. Vera and Cynthia had struck up a surprising friendship and spent much time talking to one another about baby India's routine. All in all, thought Sam as she headed towards Bally-glen, she was incredibly lucky.

She'd downloaded a book onto her phone, stuck the jack into her car dashboard and prepared to listen to Jane Austen all the way there. All was right with her world.

Ginger

December had arrived with a ferocious blast in Dublin. An unexpected flurry of snow overnight had turned mainly to slush and as Ginger looked out of her bedroom window onto the street below, she could see nothing but a mild dusting of early snow on the car roofs. She could still feel the chill in the air, even though her heating had come on. No matter what the weather was though, she walked, although today it would have to be a speedy one – today she had a horrible job to do in Ballyglen and a photographer was picking her up in an hour.

Carla must have mentioned that no newspaper had still got the exclusive on Jason Reynolds' abandoned wife – now apparently exonerated by the police – and thought it would be wonderful to 'have someone with Ginger's empathy talk to her'. Yeah, right.

She pulled on her dressing gown, went down to the living room, switching on lights, and greeted her beloved guinea pigs.

'Good morning, darlings,' she said, reaching into their luxury guinea pigs' duplex. There was no sign of either of them: burrowing in their soft nests against the early cold, she figured.

Her walk had become an integral part of her day. It was her meditation. How had nobody told her that when you walked and breathed in the fresh air, and looked at the trees growing around you and the canal floating beside you with its birds and wildlife, your mind could be freed to rest. It wasn't the hardcore workout sessions she'd done with Will, but in some ways it was better.

She tried not to think about Will so much anymore. It was easier that way. Love hurt.

That was another thing she thought a lot about on her morning walks, that love hurt so much. She must have been crazy to have dreamed of love and men and finding that perfect person to spend her life with. What if you found the perfect person and they still hurt you? What happened then? She had meant to throw out all the novels she'd loved for years, where heroic men won the hearts of women who had been through so much, but she couldn't bear to do it and now she allowed herself to read them, for comfort.

Sometimes you need to comfort yourself because nobody else is going to do it. You need to be kind to yourself. Remember that, girls: you have to take care of you and find the simple things that make you happy. For me, it can be books, but for you it might be chocolate, or a run, or talking with your friends or talking to your mother or hugging your pet.

Ginger had given that advice in a Girlfriend column just the other week and she hadn't flinched when she'd written about her mother. She'd been so lucky with her family, even if her mother hadn't been there. But her mother had left her so many wonderful things, like her father and her two brothers and Aunt Grace, and then Esmerelda had come along, as had Zoe, Margaret, Jodie, Paula, Lulu and Fiona. There were so many wonderful people in Ginger's life.

Besides, she'd changed so much in the last six months, it was incredible to think of herself now and compare herself with the Ginger who'd been so heartbroken on her birthday. Oh, she was still the same girl but stronger and wiser and more confident.

She and Alice were discussing her coming out from behind the Girlfriend pseudonym.

Ginger had asked for a bit of time to get ready for it.

'I've had a slight setback,' she confided to Alice, no longer astonished that she was having a meaningful conversation with this woman who'd once intimidated her so much.

'OK,' said Alice. 'But I have so many plans for you, Ginger – you can be the face of bigger, beautiful women, like that fabulous model, Ashley Graham.'

'I'm not exactly beautiful,' Ginger had said, laughing.

'Course you are,' stated Alice, almost crossly. 'How can we stop women being blackmailed by "thin is best" messages if the advice giver lets herself be blackmailed too?'

But she'd grudgingly agreed to give Ginger some time.

'OK, go off and sob about your long-lost love, honey, but think of your career too.'

It was freezing when Ginger stepped outside the apartment and started off at a brisk pace towards the canal. She liked to use this time to think about the advice she was dispensing through her column to her online readers. It was one of the online magazine's most popular pages. She had learned so much in the past six months and that wisdom was springing out of her and she wanted to help other women with it. Thanks to her new and stronger advice, and the honesty and candour with which she gave it, Girlfriend was growing a huge audience. Ginger was making more from that than from her job on the newspaper. Alice was right – it was time. Then she wouldn't have to schlep down to doorstep a poor woman who'd been abandoned to the wolves by her own husband and who was probably in so much pain, she didn't know which way was up.

'I'll send a good photographer with you,' the features editor said. 'He can do the actual doorstepping. You just need to get her into your confidence.'

Ginger was sick, thinking of that.

Sometimes she hated this job.

Callie

Callie had begun working on the reading for the care assistant and psychology night courses. She wouldn't be able to enrol until the following September, but when she'd mentioned it to Rona, the director of nursing at Leap of Faith, Rona had been thrilled and had produced massive textbooks the next day.

'I think it's a wonderful idea,' she had said, 'and here are some books to get you started.'

The books had given Callie a new impetus and she was consumed by them, reading when Poppy was doing homework, sitting up late in bed at night, working and making notes while Ketchup roamed between their rooms. She loved the nursing home and today, when a petite and attractive dark-haired woman arrived and began walking through the locked ward where Callie worked most, she assumed this was a person with a relative who was ill.

Callie found that they generally needed as much help as their ill family members.

'I feel so guilty – we should be taking care of my mother, but I can't, not anymore. She needs twenty-four-hour care,' the person would sob and Callie instinctively knew to take them into a quiet room and explain that there came a time when the most loving and dedicated families couldn't possibly provide the round-the-clock care that a person with dementia required.

So when Rona asked her to go upstairs to talk to the lady who was checking out the home, Callie felt confident.

'It's not a relative,' Rona said. 'Sam wants to talk about a charity who are going to help us with funding again. They stopped for a while, but it would be amazing if they helped us out. They used to be called Cineáltas, but they've rebranded as Kindness, which is lovely. Their sole function is dementia. She was watching you downstairs and she thought you were the perfect person to talk to. One of the girls told her that you helped your uncle and it led on from there.'

Callie felt a frisson of anxiety.

'Rona, you know I have to be careful who I talk to.'

Rona knew the whole story and now she stared at the quiet, gentle woman who'd made such a difference to everyone on the locked ward. Quietly and unobtrusively, Callie Reynolds' lovely presence had enhanced the lives of the patients and the staff alike.

'It's totally informal. Would you like me to sit in with you?'

'Yes,' said Callie eagerly.

At her afternoon break, Callie did her normal things: phoning Poppy to see if she was out of school and how she'd got on that day and checking that Ma was there for her at home. If Callie herself had changed over the past months, Poppy had changed just as much. She was a different girl from the one who had gone on the road trip with her mother six months before. Jason might have wrecked the family but perhaps, Callie thought, it had been the making of them.

Ginger

Ginger took her own car and wasn't surprised when the photographer, Johnny, who was young, eager and drove far too fast, made it down to Ballyglen by three.

'Told you I'd do it in an hour and a half,' he said.

'If you get any more points on your licence, you'll be off the road,' Ginger told him severely. 'I'll be there in another fifteen. Find somewhere to stop for coffee and directions, and I'll meet you there then.'

A retired *Sunday News* guy who now lived in Wexford had told them the rumour that Callie Reynolds and her daughter were back living in Ballyglen, but another far bigger financial crisis had knocked the Reynolds affair off the general news radar, so nobody had bothered with it. However, word had it that Jason Reynolds' girlfriend's mother was dying and he might come back if she did.

'A cop contact told us that,' the news editor told an increasingly edgy Ginger that morning. 'If you do your magic, we could be in before anyone else. Bet the wife will want to kill him.'

'Thought she knew nothing about it all, has no money?' said Ginger.

'Exactly. The story "woman he fooled and left" makes for lots of newspaper sales.'

The thought of writing that story made Ginger sick.

In the coffee shop, Johnny had already asked for directions to the nursing home. Ballyglen was a close-knit town, the Wexford ex-reporter said. 'She and Reynolds both came from a tough area. If they're on her side, you won't find out anything in there. Try the nursing home.'

Ginger hated this. It was not the sort of thing she'd signed up to do. She'd followed the case, sure, but her sympathies had been with Mrs Reynolds and the poor kid. And now she had to go and try to extract Callie Reynolds' pain from her like a dentist removing a tooth.

Sam

'Music,' Dr Arnold, the director of the nursing home, had told Sam when she first arrived, 'is often one of the last links to our world that people with dementia have. See how everyone's eyes light up when they hear music? Or even if their eyes don't light up, they automatically move, remembering. The mind is the last great undiscovered field, but we are beginning to learn a little more about it. But here at Leap of Faith, we are not keen on researching our patients, we want to make them happy.'

Sam had been touring the nursing home for over two hours and it was thrilling, glorious, to see how people with dementia could be taken care of and stimulated.

'We can do both,' she said, writing in her notebook: 'make them happy and do a little research, that's part of what Kindness wants to do. Our aim is to help organisations like yourself and help to fund research into areas of dementia that may not have been covered before. If only we could get some researchers in here to investigate what sort of music works best, just to give people peace and happiness.'

Dr Arnold, an older man who walked with a stick, looked thoughtful.

'I don't see what harm it would do,' he said, 'but the researchers have to be mindful about the people we work with. They are the most important people in this place.'

Sam smiled at him. 'That's why I'm here,' she said, 'because of that ethos.'

'Walk around, make yourself at home,' said Dr Arnold, 'I'll

have one of the team come out later to show you around the whole facility. I'm afraid I've a meeting right now. Your boss is pretty persuasive though.'

'He is,' agreed Sam, thinking of how long it had taken her to persuade Andrew to change the charity's name to Kindness instead of the beautiful Irish name that nobody outside Ireland could pronounce.

As she walked around the nursing home, she became aware of a sense of lightness and happiness that she hadn't felt in any of the other care homes she'd been in. The music was a huge part of it.

Each area in the home had speakers and music played from them. Upstairs, there was classical in one room and gentle Big Band stuff from the forties and fifties in a sitting room.

The ward for the people with the most serious level of dementia was locked.

'People move from upstairs to down here eventually,' said the director of nursing, letting her in. 'That said, we do our best to make this a very special place.'

Wards and rooms surrounded a large airy room that led into a beautifully maintained garden. There were flowers on the windowsills, Glenn Miller was playing in the background, and feet were tapping.

A very slim blonde woman was gently feeding the tiny, frail old lady who was seated on a chair covered with a beautiful piece of sheepskin to protect her delicate bones. There was something vaguely familiar about the woman carer, although Sam couldn't quite say what it was. Yet there was just something . . . The woman was tall, older than Sam for sure, and had blonde hair tied back in a very severe ponytail. She was murmuring gently to the little old lady as she fed her.

'Come on, Mildred. Just a tiny bit more and we can stop. You've got to keep your strength up. How are you going to go dancing with Stanley later this afternoon if you haven't had any lunch at all?'

Again, Sam marvelled at the gentleness of the carers who worked with these people. It wasn't always easy, she knew. She watched the woman for a little while, watched Mildred holding her tiny head up to be fed, like a beautiful little bird.

When lunch was over, the woman very gently cleaned Mildred's face with a soft cloth and then laid a gentle hand on her cheek.

'Now, my darling,' she said, 'you're beautiful again. You're always beautiful, but even more so. Shall we get your lipstick and your powder?'

Mildred nodded, the first sign Sam had seen that she understood anything.

'I'll be back in a jiffy,' said the woman, smiling.

As she walked towards the corridor, Sam noticed that the woman had a word for everyone, a smile, a touch on a shoulder, a gentle 'How are we doing today?' One of the nurses whirled past and Sam interrupted her.

'That carer, she's very good, isn't she?' Sam said.

'Cal?' said the nurse. 'Brilliant. She came in initially to help out with her uncle-in-law, Seamus over there. But she stayed. Don't know what we did without her to be honest. For some people it's a job, but for her, it's a vocation.'

That woman, Sam decided, that woman would be perfect to talk about what caring for someone with dementia meant. She was connected to the nursing home by family and yet she had that rare and precious gift of being able to take care of people.

Rona, Callie and Sam sat in a small sitting room and shared a pot of tea.

'I'm trying to get a vision of what it takes to be a carer,' Sam explained to the woman who'd been introduced to her as Cal, who looked a little uneasy. 'Rona tells me you started coming as a volunteer to help with your uncle and it turned into a job?'

Callie nodded mutely.

'Are you feeling all right?' asked Sam. Her instincts were

pricking like crazy – there was something wrong. This poor woman was very stressed.

'No – I, I think I'm going to be sick.'

Callie bolted from the room.

'Callie,' said Rona, standing up.

'I'm fine,' Callie said as the door slammed.

The name made all the puzzle pieces fall into place.

'Callie Reynolds,' Sam said suddenly. 'Oh gosh, no wonder she was so stressed. Poor woman. I am so sorry – I never meant—'

'It's my fault,' said Rona shamefacedly. 'I was so desperate for money and Callie is so brilliant with patients, and she could tell you so much and . . . Please don't tell anyone she's here.'

'Of course I won't,' said Sam, horrified. 'I read the papers too. I think she's suffered enough.'

Ginger

Johnny got them into the nursing home and Ginger went into the loos to try to collect herself before they started this horrible job. She couldn't do it. Couldn't ruin someone's life. This wasn't why she had come into journalism. Girlfriend was. That was her calling: helping people.

A very thin blonde woman came out of one of the cubicles, crying.

Their eyes met in the mirror.

It was her, Callie Reynolds. The blonde hair was still blonde, but the face, the amazing face that had graced so many newspapers, looked tireder.

She looked like a hunted animal, huge grey eyes dark with fear.

This woman had been let down, hurt. She had a daughter to protect, and people wanted to hound her. At that moment, Ginger knew what she had to do.

She was Girlfriend helping women, a woman who would not let another woman down.

Taking a deep breath, she said: 'You don't know me, but I am here to help you. There is a photographer looking for you. I'm the reporter.'

Callie recoiled.

Ginger shook her head. 'No. Actually, you know what: I quit. Right now. I am not making a living hounding people.' She reached forward and grabbed a startled Callie's hands. 'Please believe me.'

Callie, her heart pounding, nodded.

'We need to keep you out of sight because he will know what you look like,' said Ginger, desperate to make this woman believe her. 'I need to find someone to say you never worked here, right? Where can we go?'

Callie, although she had no reason to do so, somehow trusted this young woman. It was her face: wide, open and honest. Callie was, she realised, trusting her gut, something she should have done a long time ago with her husband.

But people let you down . . . That doubt was written across her face.

Ginger thought frantically about what she could say that would make this woman understand: confession, she realised. That would do it. 'My name is Ginger Reilly, I write an online column called Girlfriend—'

'My daughter reads that,' said Callie suddenly, surprised.

'How lovely. Well, that's what I want to do, but I do it under a pseudonym and I am too scared to come out from behind that because I thought I wasn't "aspirational".' She made air quotes with her hands. 'But then it turned out my editor didn't think that at all. Only I haven't done it yet because I'm trying to get over this guy—'

She stopped. 'I'm sorry – I'm telling you my life story. I don't do that. People tell stuff to me.'

'Well, they do if you're a reporter,' Callie said.

'No, really, people open up to me and I just did it to you. Weird.'

'It's Ballyglen and this place,' Callie said. 'It's peaceful, makes you think of what's important. I never knew that before. I guess you need to lose everything to see what's important.'

Ginger stared at her silently.

Lose everything.

That was strangely what she felt she'd lost. She'd got her family, her new friends, work success, and yet losing Will had somehow wiped out all these triumphs.

Will had helped her to love herself in a way she'd never

experienced before. She'd been a butterfly locked in a rock-solid cocoon and his friendship – and love? – had cracked it open. And all the pain of the past had been able to tumble out.

Ginger burst into tears.

'I tried so hard not to mind,' she said brokenly. 'I tried to pretend I didn't care about having a mother, but I did. Like I care about losing Will. How can you have your heart broken so easily?'

'Hearts are fragile things,' said Callie truthfully. 'But they're strong, too.'

Ginger nodded and Callie put her arms around the younger woman.

'Your mother died?' she asked.

Ginger nodded again. 'She's buried in Ballyglen and I haven't been to her grave since I was a child and my father brought me. "It doesn't matter", I said, but it does.'

'You poor pet,' said Callie. 'Pain has to be gone through. You can't ignore it or put it on the backburner. You have to make your way through. I have a lot of experience of that lately, but it's possible to do it.'

'Thank you,' sobbed Ginger.

And somehow that was how Sam found them, hugging in the nursing home bathroom, with Ginger sobbing and Callie saying that it was all right, that even though Ginger's heart was breaking now, she would recover.

'There's a newspaper photographer outside,' said Sam urgently.

'And a reporter here,' said Callie with great calmness as she held the sobbing Ginger in her arms.

Sam stepped back. 'What?'

'It's OK. Gut instinct. She doesn't want to do this.'

'It could be a ploy,' said Sam, and then she looked at the lurid red of Ginger's face as she sobbed and decided that even though her mother had never brought her up on the concept of gut instinct, it still made sense.

'Ginger's mother is buried here and you . . . you never knew her?' Callie asked gently.

'No,' wailed Ginger. 'I've missed her every day of my life. Now I miss Will too and he's gone. I wonder, did I push him away, because I might have . . .'

Over Ginger's fabulous hair, Sam and Callie's eyes met.

'First things first: we need a plan to get rid of the photographer,' said Sam.

They hustled Ginger out of the bathroom and into the music room where, for once, Miss Betty was not playing the piano to a crowd of enthusiastic listeners.

'Can you lie?' Sam asked Ginger.

Ginger thought of all the years she'd pretended to be two people – sassy Ginger at work and normal Ginger at home. She nodded.

'But I've been crying—'

'Somebody's bound to have a make-up bag,' said Sam in a businesslike manner. 'We'll fix you up. But here's the plan.'

Plan explained, Sam raced back to the room where Rona sat and quickly filled her in.

'We need to lie,' she said.

'But lying—'

'Is sometimes necessary for the greater good,' Sam pointed out. 'Get me a white coat.'

Johnny had gotten bored and had taken some outside shots and when Sam emerged ten minutes later, he was back in the hallway, waiting.

Sam had put on a white coat and stuck a pen in the top pocket. She'd borrowed somebody's spectacles so she'd look a little different. She didn't want to be implicated as a charity boss lying to a newspaper, but, and it was a very important but, neither would she sit by and let the woman she'd seen caring for the very ill be hounded. Nobody who had read the story of Jason Reynolds and his abandoning of his wife and child

347

could imagine that they were tied up in it. Callie Reynolds had certainly suffered enough.

Ginger, poor thing, was being filled up with sweet tea to help her recover. Anything less like a cut-throat reporter was hard to imagine.

Rona accompanied Sam to the lobby.

'Your reporter found me,' Sam said to Johnny in a pleasant, nothing-to-see-here voice, 'and we did have a relative of that woman's here but he was transferred into hospital. Very sad.'

Rona nodded.

'All our visitors are logged in and the only person who visited the relative was his wife and, naturally, we cannot give you her details. Now, we do have a problem: your reporter tripped and hurt herself in the music room – snooping, I might add – and she's very upset. She's lying down, but I think we'll need to wait until the doctor comes to look at her leg. Painful bruise, I think she might need a crutch.'

Johnny looked aghast – and relieved that Ginger had not travelled down here with him.

'Do you want to see her?'

'Er, sure.'

Ginger was laid out on a couch in the music room with one of the home's carers with her. Callie was nowhere to be seen.

'I'm sorry, Johnny,' she sobbed. 'Piano stool. My leg – but they never saw Mrs Reynolds here. Damn it. A wasted trip and I have to hang on till a doctor comes.'

'I think it's only a sprain,' Sam said, sounding as medically minded as she could.

'Do you want me to stay?' asked Johnny without eagerness.

Ginger shook her head.

'No, you go.'

Gratefully, Johnny patted her shoulder, said he'd tell the boss, and was out the door.

'Some men do hate illness,' said Sam cheerfully.

Ginger's phone pinged.

That was a waste of a day, and get well soon, texted Johnny.

This was too good not to share, so she showed it to Sam, who grinned.

'I think we need strong coffee and nice chocolate biscuits to get us over this. Let's get Callie too.'

Callie and Rona arrived, and Callie didn't look remotely like someone who'd just dodged a photographer's bullet.

'I'm sure I'll have to talk to someone from a newspaper one day,' she said ruefully.

'I promise he's gone,' said Sam.

'And I promise you I am not writing about this, any of this. On . . .' Ginger cast about for something suitable. 'On my mother's grave,' she said slowly.

Sam and Callie exchanged glances.

'I believe you,' said Callie cheerfully. 'As the older woman here and the one who has gone through hell these last few months, ladies, I'd say you need to see that grave.'

Sam nodded. 'Not today, maybe, but one day?'

Ginger nodded back. 'I think you're right.'

'If I've learned anything this year, because I've a baby daughter, India' – Sam's face glowed with pride – 'it's that you have to confront the past to move on.'

'Snap,' said Callie wryly. 'Or if the past bites you, you have to learn how to let go and live with yourself.'

'Or forget about all the people who hurt you because there's nothing to be gained from thinking about them,' interrupted Ginger. 'You have to move on.'

'Moving on,' they all agreed.

'But first,' Callie went to the door. 'Biscuits.'

Ginger

Ginger pulled herself up to her full height. She wore high heels a lot now. Funny that she never wore them before, but wearing flat boots had somehow fitted in with the type of person who didn't want to be seen as feminine. Didn't want to be girly. Because trying to be girly would admit that she wasn't girly – that she was tall and big and that no man would ever want her. After her heartbreak with Will, she wasn't sure if she wanted a man anymore. She'd enough self-respect to live with that. To deal with that.

So what if Zac kept eyeing her up and had once, in deep embarrassment, muttered that he couldn't remember much of their night.

'Maybe some other time, Zac,' said Ginger, 'but you know, I worry that other people might not like us dating. It might appear unethical.'

Unethical was a magical word when it came to office politics, and Zac had nodded.

'Yeah,' he said, adjusting his collar automatically.

Ginger had to stop herself grinning every time she saw him. And as for Will – Will was in the past. Another lesson. Was there a set limit to the number of lessons a person had to learn before the lessons stopped? She really hoped there was.

Going live with her Girlfriend column, saying who she really was, coming out from behind the screen – that was what she was meant to do and, finally, she was ready for it, so ready for it.

The morning after Ballyglen, she'd walked into Alice Jeter's office and said she wanted to stop hiding behind the Girlfriend pseudonym.

'I want to run a platform where people can be who and what they want.'

Alice's eyes had lit up.

'Finally!'

Alice had made an offer that would change Ginger's life. It had taken the trip to Ballyglen for her to see it: she had let the past hurt her and she had things in her past she'd never dealt with. It was time for a change, many changes.

With two columns on two e-sites, and a series of TV and YouTube ads Alice was planning, there was a campaign being set up for her to be a figurehead for helping people. And Ginger didn't feel scared; she felt invigorated and happy. She knew her family were thrilled for her. She hoped her two new friends, Callie and Sam, were thrilled for her too.

Now, Ginger didn't knock, but just walked into Carla's office.

'Yes,' snapped Carla, looking up, surprised.

If Ginger didn't know any better, she would have sworn that Carla was playing Candy Crush on her phone. That was a waste of company time.

'I wanted to talk to you before you heard it from someone else,' Ginger said in the silky tones she'd sometimes heard her Aunt Grace use. Grace was pretty good with people when it came down to it. Probably why she still had loads of boxes in her house despite Ginger's best attempts to shift them. She was not a woman to be trifled with.

And neither was Ginger Reilly. Not anymore.

'Heard what?' said Carla, eyes narrowing. 'Sit?'

'No, I'll stand,' said Ginger. 'I've got another job, so I'll be leaving.'

'What sort of job?' said Carla.

'It involves the internet edition and Alice's plans to have much more e-copy than previously. You know about the moves we're making in that direction?'

Carla stiffened. 'Naturally,' she snapped.

'I'll be working on that,' said Ginger still in the same silky tones.

'Doing what?' demanded Carla.

'I'm going to be a senior editor for all the women's e-titles,' Ginger said. 'We're aiming at a . . . younger audience than here.'

She stared pointedly at Carla as she said this.

She might not be as thin or as beautiful or as sexy as bloody Carla Mattheson, but she was younger. In the art of war, you had to use any weapons you had.

'You?' said Carla, nonplussed.

'It's the Girlfriend column,' said Ginger.

'What do you know about the Girlfriend column?' Carla was scathing now.

Just a few more words and she'd leave.

'I write it,' Ginger said calmly. 'I've been writing it all along, and the features that go with it. It's worth far more to me financially than this.' She gestured around the office and the newsroom with one hand. 'So rather than let me go, they're paying me a lot more money and giving me a great new job. Isn't that fabulous?' And then she left.

Bye–bye old world, and hello new one.

Callie

The call came early in the morning. Callie was used to waking very early now. The curtains in her mum's front room were not the blackout blinds she'd had in the Dublin house and she woke when the sun did.

She had stopped flicking through her phone for a story written by Ginger Reilly. Instead, there had been much social media activity about how the Girlfriend writer had turned out to be a tall, curvy, plus-sized woman who said she wanted her column to be a platform for all girls – and boys – who felt they had to be the same to fit in. She'd got a big new job and was going to be running her own YouTube channel.

Ginger Reilly was some girl, Callie thought fondly. She owed her a call and a big thank you. Before Ginger had left Ballyglen, the three of them had exchanged numbers and promised to meet up.

'I'm not in Dublin often and I'll probably be wearing a dark wig if I do come,' Callie said jokily, 'but I'd love to meet you both – and baby India.'

'You have to meet Aunt Grace too,' Ginger said. 'You would adore her. And you never have to talk about what happened with your husband. Nobody can force you to. If he goes to trial, the world will know you weren't involved.'

'If . . .' said Callie.

But when the phone rang this morning, and she saw Detective Superintendent John Hughes' number on the line, she felt sick to her stomach. This couldn't be good news, she thought. Early morning phone calls rarely were.

'Yes, Detective Superintendent,' she said.

'We've got your husband,' he said bluntly.

'Oh.' It sounded totally not the right thing to say after so many months of waiting, and yet, what else did you say?

'How did you get him?' she asked, as if she was enquiring about a distant acquaintance.

'He came home for his girlfriend's mother's funeral. I'm sorry, Mrs Reynolds,' said the detective superintendent. 'I know that's not the news you wanted to hear.'

Callie got out of bed and pulled the curtains back. On the street below she could see people getting up, going to work. Going to jobs where they'd earn in a week about as much as she might have spent on a dress. It was a world away from the one she used to inhabit. A world she'd never inhabit again, and yet, what difference did it make? That world had been false.

'Perhaps they are the words I needed to hear, Detective Superintendent,' she said. 'I gave up hoping for the fairy-tale ending a long time ago. You told me he was guilty and it was obvious he was. And he betrayed my daughter.'

'He betrayed you too,' said the policeman bluntly.

'I think he betrayed me a long time ago, Detective Superintendent,' she replied. 'I was just too blind to see it.' She let out a deep breath. 'Now, what happens next?'

'We've arrested him . . .'

'Will he get bail?' she asked.

On the other end of the phone, the detective superintendent snorted.

'I sincerely hope not, given that he is a flight risk. You'll be able to see him if you want.'

Callie rolled that thought around in her brain. Finally, she could ask Jason all the hard questions.

'Yes,' she said firmly, 'I'd like that very much. There are a lot of things I want to ask my former husband.'

'Former?'

'Obviously it's going to take a little while for the divorce to go through, but as far as I'm concerned,' Callie said, 'he's my former husband.'

They discussed the logistics and then hung up. Callie sat down on her bed. It was six-twenty in the morning and she didn't have to be up for another half an hour, but she wouldn't be able to lie in bed and read, and she certainly wouldn't sleep. Her heart was racing. Damn Jason. Damn him for creating this havoc in her head again. Once, she would have reached under her bed and found her stack of tablets, but not anymore. Beating her Xanax habit had been hard, no doubt about it, but Freddie had made her see exactly what she'd have lost if she lost herself to addiction.

'It's never just the one spliff or the one drink when you're an addict,' he'd said. 'It's so many that you're numb. You can't do that to Poppy.'

Every day she dealt with beautiful people who had had their cognisance taken away from them. Addiction meant she'd unwittingly thrown her own away too. She had lots of people in her life who truly cared for her. But first and foremost she had Poppy, and she had to be there for her daughter. Jason was going to go away for a very long time and Poppy would need her mother to be strong.

She'd gone to a couple of NA meetings with Freddie and Ricky, but she wasn't sure if it was for her. So far, she was coping on her own and she knew now that someone with her genetic history was better off without any sort of drug. Herbal tea and early morning walks with the dog, before anyone else was up: that was working pretty well so far. But Callie knew the serious help was there for her if she needed it.

The gates of Mountjoy Prison loomed large and slightly threatening to Callie when the taxi dropped her off. To the left was the red-brick building she knew housed the Dóchas Centre, which was the women's prison.

She'd had so many chances growing up, despite there never

being a spare ha'penny in the Sheridan household. She'd been loved, fed and educated. Her mother had paid for those dance classes. She'd had every opportunity and she'd squandered a large part of it on a stupid man called Jason.

The men's prison was old and she felt scared as she entered. Scared because she felt as if she might never get out of it once she got in. She still had that fear that she had been complicit in all of Jason's terrible actions because she'd spent the money. She'd never asked where it came from. She'd bought his story, hook, line and sinker. She'd been part of the public face of Jason and Rob and people had looked at her and believed everything. When had she become so stupidly trusting?

Finally, she was in the visiting room. Prisoners were walking in to see their visitors and then, there he was: Jason.

He looked diminished somehow. Not the suave and un-concerned Jason of those photographs from the newspaper all those months ago, when he'd been wearing the beautiful linen shirt she'd bought him. No. Now he was wearing a tracksuit and runners with no laces. He hadn't shaved either. No wonderful electric razor in here, she thought. He sat down in front of her and reached forward to grab her hands eagerly, as if he'd just come out of the desert and she were a long, cool draught of water. But Callie pulled her hands away and put them on her lap. Startled, Jason looked at her.

'I just—' he began.

'Don't touch me,' Callie stated in the cool, clear voice she'd promised herself she would use. 'I came to see you to ask you questions. That's it.'

'But, Callie – I love you. You're my wife. I have to explain . . .'

Callie stared at him in astonishment.

Over six months of nothing, six months when she and Poppy had been through hell, and he still thought of her in terms of being his wife?

'Jason,' she said, unable to stop the anger from rising, despite all her best efforts to prevent it. 'We're over. We were over the moment you planned your escape and left us behind.'

He buried his face in his hands and his voice was muffled as he spoke.

'I know I should have brought you with me, I'm so sorry, I just panicked and then . . .'

Callie looked at the man she'd loved for so long and it would have been so easy to reach out and touch his hair. It was the same dark hair with perhaps a hint of grey at the temples. She could feel the charisma coming off him in waves, and yet, it wasn't charisma today, she realised: it was something else.

Desperation.

He needed *her*, wanted her for something. A complete reversal of fortune. For all of their lives together, Jason had been the one with all the power. She'd had none, Callie realised. Her mother, her aunt – they were all right in that regard.

Startled by this internal revelation, she stared at him now, feeling nothing but the cool well of anger. Whatever he needed now, he would have to find it without her. Without Poppy.

'What about Poppy?' she said.

His head shot up.

'Is she here? I'd love to see her.'

Instinctively, Callie shoved her chair backwards.

'Are you crazy? Do you think I'd bring her to see you purely because you happen to have been caught in this country with your girlfriend? You didn't come back for us. That will hurt her more than you can imagine, Jason. I won't stop you having a relationship with your daughter, because that would be wrong, but . . .' She paused. She almost couldn't think of a way to put it that would imprint the message upon Jason's brain.

'What we went through was appalling. You abandoned us, to the police, the press, while Rob went off with Anka and the baby and you left us two to suffer. Do you have any idea what it was like for us? We had no money, nothing, nowhere to go: Poppy and I, the two people you say you love. If that's your version of love, you can keep it.'

This time, Jason lowered his eyes first.

Callie felt the fire in her, the same fire she'd felt when she was fleeing Dublin with her daughter, fleeing from the press. That lioness would not let this man destroy her or her daughter.

'You have every right to see your daughter, and even though we will be getting a divorce, I will make sure you see her because it will be important for her development, but she's got other role models in her life now. She's got my brother Freddie and . . .' She paused again.

Callie was not a vindictive woman and she knew this would wound him. Still, he needed to know who the male presences were in his daughter's life.

'She has Ricky,' she said without relish and Jason's head snapped up.

'That bastard,' he said. 'As soon as I'm gone, he's sniffing around you—'

'No,' said Callie fiercely, 'it's not like that. I don't want or need a man in my life. I have had you in my life for what, twenty-five years, and look what you did to me. Men are way off my menu. Plus, Ricky has a lovely wife and child, on whom he is not cheating.'

She let that one sink in.

'My biggest relationship is with my daughter, then with my family, and then with the friends who've supported us through this time. Brenda, Evelyn, Mary Butler. They've kept in touch, talked to me, helped me.'

She thought of the Skype calls and the emails from Mary.

'Ricky is my friend, but that's all he is. He cares, like my family, the family you tried to separate me from. I came here for five minutes to find out why you left us.' She looked at her watch. 'You've three minutes left. Start talking.'

'I don't know,' Jason said, his voice low. 'I was scared and I didn't want you to see it and then we were gone and I couldn't get you.'

'That's it?' she said in disbelief. 'That's the best story you can come up with?'

Jason squirmed.

'You didn't try to contact me. Why not?' said Callie.

'Because . . . because I knew they'd be watching you and waiting and . . .'

'And they might catch you, which was not part of the plan,' she snapped. 'What about the woman in Marbella? She was just to keep you amused?' she asked, and found that she didn't mind really. Not anymore. 'You've no idea the trouble I've had trying to keep that picture from your daughter, who was wondering where you were and why you hadn't talked to us.'

'That – that . . .' Jason stopped.

He couldn't explain his way out of that one.

'Poppy's having counselling, by the way. Just a few sessions to help her understand things. I need her to feel good about herself. Not everyone says nice things to a kid whose father has defrauded so many people. I tried to keep the worst of it from her, but she knows most of it. I tell her people sometimes do stupid things but life goes on and she is loved.'

'Don't, Callie.' Jason buried his face in his hands.

'Don't what? Tell you the truth? You've been a stranger to the truth, Jason, but your running off meant that I got very well acquainted with it. The truth of having no money, the truth of not knowing what to tell my broken-hearted daughter who had to leave her school and her home and her friends. The truth of being a pariah. Was it nice in Spain, by the way? And what's her name, your woman? The one you came home with?'

He looked up finally. 'When did you get this hard?' he said.

Callie laughed. 'I'm not hard, Jason. I'm simply telling you the truth. You didn't get caught coming to see us, you got caught coming home with another woman to go to her mother's funeral. You can see why I might have a problem with that.'

'I know I made mistakes, but I left you something, just one account,' said Jason, desperately.

Callie pushed away from the table in disgust. 'I don't want to touch your dirty money,' she said. 'I don't care how poor we are, we'll manage.'

'No,' he said, 'it's clean, it really is clean. I set it up a long time ago for Poppy and you. That detective superintendent guy, he can talk to my accountant, it's clean money. It's for you two.'

Callie got up from the table. 'Yeah, right,' she said. 'Clean money and Jason Reynolds aren't two phrases that go well together. And the cheque's in the post too, right? Bye, Jason,' she said. 'I'm sure I'll see you at the trial. I imagine I'll have to be there.' And she turned and walked away without looking back.

At the gate, Brenda was waiting for her.

'I wish you'd let me come,' she said.

Callie fell into her friend's arms and let the tears flow, finally. 'I needed to toughen myself up before I saw him.'

'Coffee or tea, or wine?'

Callie laughed. 'Tea, I think.'

They drove out towards Brenda's and stopped at a small coffee shop.

'I thought my house may be a bit dodgy because the press might think you'd be there in order to see Jason.'

'I got an offer of another place to stay,' remarked Callie. 'Sam, that charity boss woman who sprang into action when the *Sunday News* came to Ballyglen, she offered. She's been texting. She's a lovely woman. Actually,' she paused because she still couldn't believe it herself, 'her baby was born on her fortieth birthday, which was the same day as my fiftieth.'

'Wow. Big night.'

'I know. And Ginger, the reporter, she was thirty that same day. How's that for coincidences?'

'No such thing as coincidences,' said Brenda sagely. 'In some weird way, it all links up. I almost can't believe that the reporter girl decided not to reveal you were there,' she went on. 'As my mother used to say: *what's rare is wonderful*. So, you going to stay with Sam?'

'Not tonight, I'm going home.'

Brenda's eyes filled with tears then. Callie wasn't sure if she'd ever seen Brenda cry.

'I'm so glad you're calling it home,' she said, finding a paper napkin and wiping her eyes lest anyone spot the tears. 'I miss you, though.'

'You could come for a visit.'

Brenda nodded. 'Definitely. Now, tell me about Poppy and all the goings-on, and really, you and Ricky are just friends . . .?'

Callie laughed. 'Just friends.'

On the train home, Callie rang Poppy to tell her it was all OK and she'd be home soon. Then she took advantage of the time to text everyone else. Finally, she did something she'd been meaning to do for ages: she texted Ginger Reilly, as well as Sam.

I was in Dublin today, girls, but I couldn't meet up. But next time, OK? We're the three amigos – three women with the same birthday. It must mean something, right? xxx Callie

Sam

India looked beautiful in her christening robes and she loved having her photo taken.

'Little poppet,' said Sam's father, as he took what felt like the millionth shot of his fourth granddaughter who was being held by her granny Vera with adoration.

'Why is she wearing that dress. That is my dress!' said Posy crossly.

The whole family had decamped to a big hotel for the day after the ceremony as Sam and Ted's house was too small for the party, and Sam didn't want it at her parents'.

Posy had taken umbrage at the sight of the baby wearing the christening gown that all three of Joanne's children had worn.

'You wouldn't fit into it,' explained her father equably.

'I would.'

'No, you wouldn't,' said Pixie, grabbing one of Posy's little fat arms with their adorable elastic band lines where her hand and forearm met.

Posy gave her father and uncle her fiercest look.

'Get it off her. I will try it on.'

'No,' said Joanne.

Posy tried some foot stomping and then, because that wasn't working, she lay on the floor on her stomach and did a full-body tantrum.

Sam, in a flowing Ghost dress in dark crimson, laughed so much it hurt, and then lay down on the carpet beside her niece and began to bang the floor too. 'Waaaaaa,' she wailed.

Instantly, Posy stopped.

'What you doing?' she demanded. This was her tantrum. Guests were not invited.

'I thought it was a game,' said Sam, straight-faced. 'There's going to be chocolate cake soon. Do you want some?'

Posy got to her feet at speed, while Sam picked herself up with more decorum.

'Old people are very slow,' Posy remarked.

Sam nodded gravely. 'Chocolate cake?' she asked.

Posy put a small hand in her aunt's. 'Yeah. I want a big piece, the biggest, biggerest.'

Joanne grinned at her sister. 'Looks like you've got this mother thing cracked,' she said.

It was a glorious day. Tribal, almost, Sam thought as the whole family sat around a huge table, raising glasses to little India, who slept blissfully through most of it.

'I hope she won't be up the whole night, now,' said Ted.

'We'll manage,' said Sam with confidence, and she meant it.

It was nearly time for her to come off her antidepressant drugs and she wasn't in the least worried. She felt like a different person now. The woman who'd had post-natal depression was gone. So too was the woman scared of doing everything wrong.

There was, as she had discovered, no one right way to do anything. All babies were different.

Work was going wonderfully. Kindness would have its big relaunch soon and Sam felt she had a great team around her. They could make a difference in people's lives, she felt, and that was incredibly rewarding.

By the time the meal was over, India had woken up, been smiley and delighted, and then finally fractious and tired again.

'Lots of people tire babies out,' said Sam, taking her darling baba back and holding her expertly. They were staying the night in the hotel and Cynthia was taking care of the dogs

– and Shazz. 'I think I'll put her up for a little snooze in our room.'

Vera leapt up. 'I'll stay with her and you can come back down.'

Sam could see that her mother had half risen in her seat but had settled herself again, assuming that her help would not be needed.

'Vera, I might get my mother up,' she said, and Vera, who knew it all, nodded wisely.

'Me?' Her mother looked shocked at this offer.

'Yes, Mother, come on.'

It was time to let the past be in the past, Sam had decided. If Callie Reynolds could move on from what had happened to her, then she could move on too.

In the bedroom, Jean said: 'Are you sure?'

Sam had never heard her mother so tentative.

'We'll feed her, change her and then lay her down for a nap. Once she goes to sleep, I'll leave you for an hour, and if she wakes up and you can't settle her, call me.'

It was, Sam thought, something she would never have been able to do even a few months ago. The very idea of leaving her mother alone with India was unthinkable then. But Jean had changed. The admission of her failures had oddly strengthened her relationship with Sam.

Sam was different too.

'Mother is just Mother,' she said to Joanne one day. 'We can't change her any more than she can change us. We just have to figure out how to live with her.'

'I thought I was supposed to be the younger one who knew nothing,' teased Joanne, then hugged her sister.

'If India wakes and cries when she sees me, what then?' said Jean, still clearly very anxious.

Sam patted her mother's back gently.

'Babies are a steep learning curve. Just soothe her, sing her a little song, hold her close. Stay calm.'

'I can do calm,' agreed Jean. 'But singing?'

'You were in a choir for years. Murmur something gently. A lullaby.'

'OK, a lullaby.'

Half an hour later, when India was settled in her cot, the lights were low and Jean was settled in a chair with a magazine, Sam let herself out.

She stood outside the door, thinking that she'd never imagined this day would come. But it had. Another steep learning curve. But then, love and learning – that seemed to be what life was all about.

Ginger

The trees were sprouting the first buds in Grace's garden as Ginger parked outside Grace and Esmerelda's.

'Dogs rolled in mud. Pooey,' announced Esmerelda, opening the door and almost running away. 'Me busy. We going to your father's to spend night. No time to clean stinky dogs.'

Ginger was wearing her walking gear because she planned to go walking in the countryside later and she backed off as the two dogs leapt delightedly at her.

'Down,' she yelled at Cloud and Pepperpot, who looked more like chimney sweeps than cockapoos. The stink was incredible.

'Blasted dog walker,' said Aunt Grace, standing in the hallway with a barrage of boxes in front of her to keep her safe. 'I don't suppose you could wash them? They'll stink out the car . . .'

'Can you fire that dog walker and hire one who stops them rolling in crap?' said Ginger, groaning.

'He's cute and I think you might like him,' said Grace irrepressibly.

'I already hate him,' said Ginger.

Trying to keep the dogs at bay, she got dog treats from the kitchen, then coaxed the animals upstairs and locked them in the bathroom. The special doggy shampoo sat where it was last time she'd had to do this.

She stripped off her sweatshirt and her T-shirt until she was down to her sports bra, then hoisted Cloud into the bath.

'You are not a cloud, you are putting on weight,' she

murmured to the dog, feeding treats and talking doggy non-sense so Cloud would not be scared as the water started.

Twenty minutes later, Cloud and Pepperpot were clean, about six dirty towels destined for the boil wash were on the floor and everything she was wearing was wet.

Since there was nothing of either Grace's or Esmerelda's she could wear, she was going to be wearing this outfit for the evening.

Grace was at the door when Ginger unlocked it.

'Esmerelda, let them out!'

The dogs whizzed past Grace and down the stairs, a blur of wet fur.

'Now, I have two things to show you,' said Grace, leading the way to her bedroom.

On a desk sat a computer where Grace liked to order things from the internet, but tonight it was set up to a social media site.

'Look,' said Grace.

'I didn't know you were into social media,' said Ginger, peering.

'I don't do that Instamatic thing or the Twitters but I like this one. I have some old friends on it and I like looking at the rubbish people put up. A lot of people lie, you know.'

'So I've heard,' said Ginger.

It was Facebook and she realised the page was Liza's.

Moving swiftly back, she said: 'I don't want to look at this.'

'No, do,' insisted Grace.

Unwillingly, Ginger looked at where Grace was pointing a spindly but manicured finger.

'See: single. They've split up. Her and that big idiot. Pair of idiots, really.'

Grace was Facebook-stalking her former best friend.

'I should never have told you,' she said, half laughing. 'Stalker.'

'I thought I might keep an eye out. She has no privacy

settings, but then she never did have an ounce of sense. Silly girl. Well?'

Still wet, Ginger sat down on the bed. 'Well what?'

'How does it make you feel?'

Ginger considered it. The previous June, knowing that Liza and James had split up would have seemed like divine intervention, but now she merely felt sad for her former friend. Now that she had real friends, good friends, she understood that Liza had never been one.

'I feel sorry for them both,' she said.

Grace beamed at her.

'You are a wonderful girl, Ginger Reilly. Just wonderful. You deserve all happiness in life.'

'Yes, and wet dogs in my car,' laughed Ginger.

'They can come in my jeep,' said a deep voice.

'You haven't met my new dog walker,' said Grace, her grin truly devilish. 'Should I fire him? You decide.'

Ginger turned and saw Will standing at the door of Grace's bedroom.

With surprising speed for a woman of her age, Grace slipped past Will and could be heard beetling down the stairs.

'What are you doing here?' said Ginger, no longer able to summon up any hostility. It had been months, after all. Although why Will was walking her great-aunt's dogs made no sense to her.

'Looking for you. Trying to make it up to you.'

'Why? You were never interested in me,' she said flatly.

'Who told you that?' said Will and he moved so that he was sitting on the bed beside her.

'Carla—'

'Very reliable woman, Carla,' said Will. 'Great liar. I knew that by the time I'd agreed to go to the ceremony with her, but I couldn't back out. And then . . .' his eyes, those amazing brown eyes that looked so stunning with his blond hair, darkened, 'when you left with that smug git, I knew there was no point.'

368

Ginger bit her lip.

'Except I couldn't live without you.'

'You appeared to manage,' Ginger said tartly.

'I had to when you blocked my number and ignored my note. I also thought you were seeing Tyson,' he replied. 'And then Grace got in touch.'

'*Grace got in touch?* Is she secretly CIA?' Ginger asked.

'Let's just say I think she has a good grasp of Facebook and she knows all your secrets.'

'I have to stop telling her things,' Ginger said, beginning to grin.

'So, do you think you would give me the pleasure of taking one of the most beautiful, strong, clever women I've ever known out for dinner?'

Smelling of wet dog, Ginger did something she'd never done in her life: she sat on a man's lap and didn't think for even one second that she might be heavy, that she might crush the life out of him. Will Stapleton wanted her and she wanted him. Had wanted him since that night in his jeep.

'I might,' she said and then his hands cupped her face and he was kissing her.

This was how it was supposed to feel, she realised, as she felt him holding her like she was something precious.

This was worth waiting for.

And a week later, in her pretty bedroom in her tiny house, Ginger found that kisses were not the only thing worth waiting for.

'I understand all those romantic novels now,' she said, as they lay together, panting, smiling, bodies touching because they couldn't bear to be apart.

'You'll understand it more the second time,' said Will. 'I love you, Ginger Reilly. Every glorious inch of you.'

PART FIVE

The Next Birthday

Callie

Callie's car had finally given up the ghost.

'Goodbye sweet car,' said Poppy, patting it affectionately as it was towed away. 'You have been a good and faithful servant.'

Callie laughed out loud.

'Once, you barely wanted to sit in it,' she said fondly, putting an arm around her daughter.

'Yeah,' said Poppy, 'I wasn't an enlightened being then. And do not say I was a spoiled brat, Granny,' she warned her grandmother, who'd come out to witness the farewell.

'Nothing spoiled about you, Poppy pet,' said her grandmother. 'You didn't know any better. When you know better, it's different. What's the plan now, Cal?' She'd come around to calling her daughter Cal instead of Claire and it helped Callie. Claire was someone she'd left behind and the real Callie, the one who was bringing up her daughter and surviving, was someone she was growing nicely into.

'The money from work is not really enough for a replacement,' Callie said ruefully.

'Time you sorted out that account that Jason says is clean,' said her mother.

'No,' said Callie. 'I'm not touching a penny of that money, even if none of it came from any fraud. There are people who need their money back and I feel a responsibility for them. If there's any left over at the end when everyone's paid back, well – fine.'

They'd gone over the argument many times before.

'Yes, Gran, we have to pay Dad's debts,' Poppy said earnestly.

'Nita across the road has the same thing. Her dad owes the moneylenders and even the money she earns in the hairdresser's at the weekend goes into the pot.'

Callie felt her heart swell with pride. It wasn't a traditional Hallmark moment, but it said how far they'd come. That Poppy, who once would have sold her soul for a new designer handbag, cared about paying back people her father had defrauded was heartbreaking. They'd never pay it all back, of course, but the police had recovered plenty of it. Callie was thinking of petitioning the courts for money for herself and Poppy to live on.

'Honey, I promise that if you need it for anything serious, I will find money,' Callie said fiercely. 'You come first. I won't raid that bank account for me, but for you, yes. So you are not to limit yourself in your dreams. But I can figure out how to buy a new old banger. And wait till I've got my new qualifications in health care – we'll really be in the money!' she joked.

The three of them walked inside with Poppy eagerly chatting about a make-up artist she was following online and who had the most incredible YouTube tutorials.

Callie actually knew exactly how to get a new car but she didn't want to say yes to it: Ricky had offered her one of his.

'It's ancient,' he'd said on the phone. 'You'd be doing me a favour in getting it off the forecourt.'

'Freddie wasn't supposed to tell you. He's like a parrot,' chided Callie. 'Ricky, I can't take your car.'

'Why not?' he'd asked.

Because, Callie thought, it would mean relying on someone. She had come to rely on herself. That felt powerful.

'If I'm stuck, I'll get back to you, but give me a chance. I still have a few tricks up my sleeve.'

Sam

Sam was woken on her birthday this year by another phone call, but not quite as early. She was awake anyway – India's time-keeping still meant there were no lie-ins in their household.

'Mother!' she said as her mother came on first.

'Just wanted to wish you happy birthday, darling,' Jean said.

This was new – the 'darling'. Sam liked it.

'I have a small gift for you, and your father and I will drive over before you go down the country, if that's all right.'

Once, Jean would have dropped something at the door and gone on her way.

Progress had definitely been made.

'Thanks, Mother,' said Sam.

'You'll love the pressie,' said her father irrepressibly in the background.

When she got off the phone, Ted had prepared breakfast in bed for his wife.

From the kitchen, India could be heard roaring for her own breakfast.

'Happy birthday, my darling,' he said, kissing her. 'Nothing can compare to last year's gift but here are . . . more earrings!'

He laughed as he handed her a beautifully wrapped box.

'The gold is not supposed to come off these.'

Sam grabbed her husband and pulled him down onto the bed.

'Do we have time?' she said, biting his earlobe.

Another roar came from the kitchen.

'Tonight?' said Ted hopefully.

'It's a date.'

They drove to Ballyglen in a leisurely way. They'd booked a tiny separate house on the estate because it might be noisy at the birthday party. Joanne and Patrick had been invited but Pixie had a bug.

'You go and have fun with your new friends. How often do you get to have a birthday party with two friends whose birthdays are on the same day,' said Joanne. 'I'll stay here and mop up sick.'

'You poor love,' said Sam. 'I hate you missing it. Ginger's brothers and their wives are going, and her dad, plus Callie's daughter, her aunt and mother.'

'I can meet them another time. Go and have birthday fun and when we are non-toxic here, we can meet them.'

In her baby seat, India cooed at her mother.

Sam grabbed her phone and took another photo.

Ted, eyes on the road, laughed. 'I think we'll need more iCloud storage,' he said.

Sam grinned at him. 'Definitely,' she said. 'I think we should try for another baby. We are so blessed to have India, but wouldn't it be amazing if she had a sister? Look how Joanne and I are so close. I mean, now I've done it once—'

'Try for more?' said Ted. 'I am so definitely up for that.'

Ginger

Ginger was looking at her belongings stacked in the tiny hallway of her house and wondering if she'd overpacked, as usual. The guinea pigs were thrilled to be going on an adventure and were squeakily squabbling over who got to use their wheel.

'You'd swear you pair never got to go anywhere,' Ginger laughed, peering in at them affectionately. 'If we get to go on our next big adventure after this birthday party, I'm buying you a second wheel and a bigger luxury duplex.'

And keeping it high up, she added mentally.

The next big adventure was that she and Will had decided to move in together to a fixer-upper house they'd discovered half an hour from the gym. Because Ginger would work from home a lot more, and because Will's hours were flexible, they'd decided to get two dogs.

'Rescue ones,' said Will decisively.

'Yes,' said Ginger fervently, thinking of the stories she'd written about sad-eyed abandoned animals in shelters, staring up at her and waiting for a forever home that didn't always come.

Dogs would love the guinea pigs: in a sandwich, out of a sandwich, whatever. She could not put her two beloved guinea pigs through that. So careful plans to keep the guineas safe would have to be made. Her dad would be delighted to help. He could build some yoke of a bookcase that was dog-proof and high enough for the dogs not to notice. Well, she hoped so.

Her dad loved Will, almost as much as Declan and Mick

377

did, who – after an initial period of assessment while they grimly decided if he was good enough for their little sister – had adopted him as practically another brother.

Her phone pinged with a text:

Sorry, Ginger, just leaving. Got delayed. Love you.

Her heart did that little skip that Zoe, her sister-in-law, said was not atrial defibrillation but a woman in love.

Will always said he loved her in texts. He'd practically moved in already, and might be the worst in the world at cleaning up the bathroom and used the washing machine on 60 degrees every time, so he shrunk sweaters, but he knew Ginger needed reassurance. He understood her. That was worth more than ruined sweaters any day.

When the doorbell rang a moment later, Ginger was still in that loved-up place, and, without thinking that Will had his own key, would hardly be using the doorbell and must have travelled via *Star Trek* technology to get there at this speed, she opened it, beaming.

Except the visitor was not her tall, handsome, beloved man. It was Liza.

A Liza who was still thin, no longer tanned, possibly Botoxed, Ginger thought in some alarm, and sobbing her eyes out.

'James has left me,' wailed Liza and, for a millisecond, Ginger's brain went into a slight confusion.

James . . .? And then she remembered. James, the love of Liza's life. Groom at the wedding from hell. Amazingly, she felt nothing – not a quiver, nothing.

'I know he left you,' Ginger said bluntly. 'It was on Facebook, ages ago.'

Liza burst into fresh sobs.

Even though she was small, she had a lifetime of pushing Ginger around and, somehow, she made her way into the apartment, where she immediately sat down on the most comfortable armchair. Arranging her feet up under her, she began to cry again. She was clearly there for the long haul.

'Do you have anything to drink? A white wine spritzer, perhaps?' said Liza, between sobs.

The new, improved Ginger reasserted herself.

'No,' she said. 'It's morning, for a start. This isn't a bar. And you can't stay, Liza. I'm going away for a few days.'

'But I need you,' wailed Liza. 'I have to get him back!'

Ginger thought of the talks she now did in schools and colleges about women empowering themselves and not allowing themselves to be defined by either society or one person.

She had never used the precise example of her friendship with Liza to illustrate this fact: that would be cruel to Liza. But she explained how she had allowed her feelings of not fitting in due to her weight to allow herself to be walked on, made to feel less than.

'Sometimes you simply have to learn the lesson and sometimes you have to confront someone,' she said in her talks.

Now was her chance.

'Why did you come here for help?'

Liza employed her tried-and-tested wobbling bottom lip technique: 'You're my best friend after all, Ginger, and I need you.'

The sheer gall of that answer spurred Ginger on.

'If I am your "best friend",' she began, 'where have you been this past year?'

Liza still did not look remotely ashamed.

Time for the big guns.

'Why did you dress me up like some seventeenth-century bar wench in that bloody awful dress and let James tell your cousin that I was in possession of virginity that needed to be got rid of like a bad case of lice? Why would you do something like that, if I was your friend? Or was I someone to use?'

All of this had occurred to Ginger recently. The prism of time allowed her to see their friendship for what it was: and it had been more equal than she'd remembered. She had been the clever one, the one who'd corrected Liza's homework, the one who made sure Liza scraped through school. Yes, Liza had given Ginger a protection of sorts, but perhaps, without Liza's bitchy influence, Ginger might have made other friends, the people like herself who were clever and definitely not a part of the fabulously beautiful gang. Without Liza scaring those clever but shy girls off, Ginger could have built up real friends during her years in school. That way, she might not have felt like the cuckoo in the nest of Liza's glittering entourage.

'You used me, Liza, and I couldn't see it because I trusted you.'

'Look where trusting James has got me,' sniffed Liza, self-pity evident in every word.

Ginger's mind flew through the months when Liza had pursued James. How she'd gone out of her way to capture him, weaving a web until he was caught. Their relationship had suited them both. Liza had a handsome, wealthy boyfriend and James had a beautiful, party-going girlfriend who always had the right clothes, the perfect hair and make-up. It was hardly a firm basis for a strong marriage.

'You chose James because of what he was on the surface,' Ginger said, not wishing to be cruel but dropping all attempts to be conciliatory. 'He chose you for the same reasons. How did you think it would end?'

Liza's face crumpled. 'We had a fairy-tale wedding,' she cried.

Did fairy-tales allow for random cruelty in the middle of them? Ginger wondered. Of course they did. That was how the lessons of the past were passed down. The wolf ate Grandma, after all.

'That day wasn't a fairy-tale for me,' she said simply. 'It was devastating.'

'Then you know how I feel now,' wailed Liza. 'Devastated.'

Ginger looked at Liza, still beautiful even though her face was streaked with tears and her long blonde hair could have done with a wash. The shine had gone from her, as if the fairy godmother who'd promised her beauty had taken the gifts away.

Even now, when Ginger had asked why Liza had hurt her so much, Liza couldn't answer. Either she had no answer or, simply, Ginger was not important enough for her to think one up.

'Why did you let your mother talk you into making me chief bridesmaid?' she asked, the journalist in her coming to the fore.

'She nagged me,' said Liza absently.

'You could have said no.'

'She and Dad were paying for the wedding,' snapped Liza, as if this explained everything.

'And you were going to dump me as a friend afterwards?' The questions that had once haunted her no longer hurt as much as Ginger thought they would.

'People move on. You're in your fancy job now, mixing with all the celebs.' There was no disguising the jealousy in Liza's voice. 'Let's forget and be friends again.'

Ginger shook her head. 'No, I can't forget it. I don't do friendship edits,' she said. 'But you and I haven't been proper friends for a long time. I didn't realise that, I used to be a bit blinkered. I have friends in my life now that I can rely on. Let's go our separate ways.'

'No!' For the first time, Liza sounded anxious. 'We've known each other since we were four, Ginger, we've history together. You can help me go to cool events like the things you go to now. James will see me in the papers and magazines and get jealous.'

Even by Liza's standards, it was a breathtakingly callous plan.

It deserved Liza being thrown out on the street and screamed at. It deserved well-aimed insults . . .

But Will would be there soon. And if Ginger had learned anything in this past year, it was that, sometimes, you had to let things go and take the wiser path.

'I deserve a friend who really is a friend, Liza,' she said softly. 'You're not. I have good friends now who don't want to use me. I'm sorry about James.'

She meant it. She hated anybody to suffer, but Liza needed to learn her own truths.

Liza stood up, shaking back her hair defiantly. 'So you won't help me?' she demanded.

Ginger opened the front door.

'Take care,' she said. 'I mean that, Liza. Have a good life. Take care of your friends.'

Liza's face was screwed up with fury as she tried to think of something to say.

'Hey, Ginger, darling,' said a voice and Will stood in the doorway.

Automatically, he reached in to grab Ginger and pull her into a hug. He'd changed out of his gym clothes into jeans and a T-shirt and with his hair wet from the shower, he looked like a magazine advert come to life. 'Who's this?' he murmured into Ginger's ear.

'Liza. Someone I went to school with.'

Liza was gazing at Will as if he was the answer to all her prayers.

'Liza?' he said to Ginger. 'The bride . . .?'

'Yup.'

Liza was clearly about to launch into full-on flirt mode with Will. Ginger had seen it before. But not this time.

Will reopened the front door. 'Thanks for calling, but good-bye, Liza.'

Ginger was stunned.

Liza was stunned.

'I just—'

'You should go.' Will smiled a polite, businesslike smile and opened the door wider.

'He's right,' agreed Ginger. 'We're not friends anymore and

we have nothing to say to each other. Goodbye.'

Slowly, Liza walked outside but turned quickly. 'I never meant—'

'That's the past, Liza.' Ginger put an arm around Will. 'Goodbye.'

And Will shut the door.

'Right,' he said, picking her up, 'I think you need a serious kiss after that.'

'So do I,' said Ginger.

Epilogue

The big living room in the biggest house you could rent on the posh golfing estate in Ballyglen had been transformed with fairy lights and flowers into a birthday bower.

The dining table was immaculately made up with the finest napkins, candles, glasses, silver and plates, all from Grace's home. Piles of wrapped boxes sat on one side, ready to be opened.

Grace Devaney looked around the house with pride. She and Esmerelda had worked hard – well, instructed hard – to get the place into shape. This was going to be a very special birthday party, a party where the three birthday women had been through the fire and had come out the other side. Grace had it planned perfectly.

The rental agent hadn't batted an eyelid at the list of instructions.

'I can get people to do all this,' she'd said, calmly, studying the list typed up on Grace's state-of-the-art computer. 'You're supplying the extra furniture, I see, and the movers will put it into place. But a butler with his shirt off . . .? We'd all love one of those, Mrs Devaney, but Ballyglen is a bit short on help of that sort or . . .' The rental agent threw her head back and laughed so much that her cat's eye glasses fell back off her face and into the nest of her purple rinse. 'I'd have hired him myself. Personally, you'd do better with a few of the agricultural college students helping around the place. They're all gorgeous.'

'On the scale of, what is it – one to ten?' demanded Esmerelda, who had very specific views on men and their beauty. She liked these Irish men more now that the country contained so many nationalities and a lusty woman could find a man with skin of any colour and a voice like honey. Variety was the spice of life, as her grandmother, God bless her in heaven, used to say.

'Esmerelda,' chided Grace. 'It's so hard to grade men.'

'Not impossible,' said the rental lady, fanning herself now with her clipboard. 'These boys are all handsome and polite. But I don't think we can ask them to serve the party with their shirts off. It would be sexist.'

She caught Grace's eye and they grinned evilly.

'But such fun,' said Grace. 'Fine. Dinner jackets for them all. Add the rental to the price.'

Since everyone had arrived, Grace had been enjoying herself thoroughly as hostess, greeting everyone, making sure all of them were happy with their bedrooms, hugging randomly, telling Ginger she was beautiful and looked so on the television.

Ginger had blushed.

'Redheads are so darling when they blush,' Grace said to Will, and then she chucked him under the chin. 'He already thinks so, Ginger,' she called out. 'He's besotted.'

Pat, Phil and Grace had had a marvellous time with Esmerelda recounting tales of their youth, and Poppy had listened in, fascinated.

Callie went over to Sam and Ted's cottage and gave them a hand with India while they dressed.

'Babies smell so delicious,' she said, inhaling the scent of India's little dark head.

'We're thinking that we might try for a second baby,' Sam said. 'Is that madness at my age?'

Callie smiled. 'What's mad about loving another child? Why not?'

At seven on the dot, everyone had to assemble and toast the birthday girls: Ginger, Callie and Sam.

Grace had made up a glorious elderflower cocktail for the non-drinkers and had champagne for anyone else.

'Who would have thought that three such incredible women would have significant birthdays on the same day,' Grace said, her voice clear as a bell. 'And you have all had, let me say, interesting years.'

Everyone laughed, the three women most of all.

'Time does not go backwards for any of us so we are not celebrating thirty, forty or fifty, but the joy of thirty-one, forty-one and fifty-one and surviving with grace and courage. That is the true mark of a strong woman.' She raised her glass. 'To Ginger, Sam and Callie.'

'To Ginger, Sam and Callie.' Everyone drank, the waiters watched and lovely dance music from Grace's favourite era, the 1940s, came on in the background.

'The staff,' said Grace wickedly. 'They follow my every silent command. Now, you must all sit.'

Everyone sat, with Grace at the head of the grouping, standing with her stick in one hand.

'I believe they call them DLEs,' said Grace proudly, with her bifocals on and looking deliciously eccentric with her fluffy hair and her new – shopping channel – pink lace dress dolled up with plenty of new jewellery – off the internet – accessorised with the old porridge cardigan she was devoted to.

'DLEs?' asked Phil. 'I never know any of these new words.'

'Damned Learning Experiences,' finished Grace, like the opera singer delivering the final, triumphant note. 'It means you have all gone through a year of learning and really, darlings, haven't we all learned enough?'

Everybody laughed. Even the handsome agricultural students in the kitchen could be heard giggling.

'I am a big fan of the old ceremonies . . .'

'The old whatsits?' said Ginger's father, who was definitely going a bit deaf. *That darned bandsaw*, Ginger thought, whispering 'old ceremonies' to him loudly enough so he could hear.

'When we get back, I am taking you to get your ears sorted,' said Grace. 'Men always go deaf first when, in fairness, it should be us women so we no longer hear when we get roared at about when dinner is ready.'

Declan and Mick laughed out loud. Grace had never tolerated anyone shouting at her about their dinner.

'Anyway, as I was saying, we need a ceremony to say goodbye to this learning year so we can usher in the new one.'

'Is this from some new book you and Esmerelda got off the internet, Grace?' demanded Ginger.

'No look at me for this madness!' said Esmerelda. 'I do the praying like all my family.'

'Only when you want something,' said Grace testily. 'I don't believe in all that praying. I like my smudge stick—'

'The thing that smells like the drugs the people smoke in the wacky cigarettes,' stage-whispered Esmerelda.

'It's dried herbs, not that cannabis muck,' said Grace. 'It has cleansing properties. Tonight—' She raised her arms like a pink-lace-and-porridge-clad goddess and gently shooed the dogs away, who had decided it was a game and wanted to join in. 'Tonight, we all need to think of all the pain we went through, write it down on these pieces of paper in the centre of the room and burn them in the fire, then I will smudge the room, we will wish for better things. And tra la la! The old year will be gone, and the new one will come.'

'Sounds great,' said Poppy enthusiastically. 'Do we wear special make-up?'

'If you want, sweetie,' said Grace, who had taken a real shine to Poppy from the first time she met her when Poppy, Callie and Sam had come to visit her and Esmerelda in Dublin. 'Something ancient . . .?'

'Egyptian,' decided Poppy and ran upstairs to get her make-up kit. She loved the Egyptian look.

'What's the aim of it all?' asked Callie with interest. Nothing surprised her anymore and she loved Ginger's crazy old great-aunt. Grace had such spirit. Nobody would cheat on her or run a fraudulent business under her nose.

'Ah, Callie,' said Grace softly, 'it helps you move on, forgive yourself and stop thinking that only you were stupid.'

Callie felt suddenly that Grace must be a witch because she had seen so clearly into her soul. She teared up at the idea of her soul being so open.

'You have a beautiful face and those eyes tell everything,' said Grace gently. 'Why is that a bad thing? It's not. It's only bad if the person with the eyes has not learned to protect themselves and if a bad person takes advantage of them.'

Callie could only nod. Grace had pretty much laid out her whole year in that statement.

Sam reached over and touched Callie's fingers with her own.

'Courage,' she whispered.

'I keep thinking that you could go back to modelling, Cal,' said Phil, wiping away a tear.

'Older models are in,' said Ginger, not adding that bigger, sexy ones were too. Her billboards for the sportswear were up all over the country and if there were negative comments, Will was hiding them from her.

'I don't know,' said Callie. 'I was so young and I felt like a non-person. It's different for you, Ginger, because you are in a position of power.'

Ginger felt her heart swell with happiness at the compliment.

'You're going to be helping me with my study on the effect of music on people with dementia,' said Sam. 'I need you. And you'll definitely have to travel – so no time to model.'

'Write down the pain,' said Grace loudly. 'Because I'm starving.'

Dutifully everyone wrote.

Normally, Ginger wrote so fast but she couldn't just now.

Liza betraying her? Working with Carla who'd done her best to humiliate her? Feeling betrayed by Will for that horrible period? And yet, Liza had done her a favour. So had Carla

– without her, she'd never have met Will, and he'd always been true. It had all been terrible at the time, and yet she had risen from it all like a phoenix. Tomorrow, she was going alone to visit her mother's grave and she was determined to face up to the past and deal with the long-buried ache of not having a mother as she was growing up. She closed her eyes and wished that the love and friendship she had in her life would continue. She wished for strength and courage, always. Then she threw her empty piece of paper into the fire.

Callie stared at her paper blankly. 'Jason,' she wrote. His fraud, his life, his abandoning them, his other woman . . . the lack of money. She still worried about money, always would. The damn Xanax. That had been terrible but she hadn't touched one since and never would again, if she could possibly help it. Then she thought of what she had now: Poppy; her family; herself. Perhaps Jason had done her a favour. She scrunched up her paper and threw it into the fire. *To appreciating all that I have and to being me, always*, she said silently.

Sam looked at India asleep in Ted's arms. Joanne was right: the more noise a baby got used to, the more she could sleep when you were out or hoovering. She thought of the darkness of the post-natal depression. It had been terrifying, devastating, and yet she had come out of its black embrace. She had India and Ted, her darling sister and her family, her father and, yes, her mother too, who was trying very hard to change.

'Pain' was the one word she wrote on her paper; she threw it into the fire and wished for her happiness to continue. *And please, please, another baby*.

'Smudging,' announced Grace.

Ted brought India outside in case it was bad for her baby lungs.

It took a few goes for Grace to light the fat bundle of what looked like dried twigs and herbs and then the scent hit the room. It was a combination of sage and lavender and thyme and after that, nobody was sure what it was. But it had a smoky herbal scent as well as a hint of singed twigs

'Let us let go of all the dark and sad moments of the past year and welcome in a new one,' Grace said, entirely delighted with herself in her new Celtic priestess incarnation. She waved the smudging stick around. 'Let us open our hearts to new happiness.'

After a bit more smudging, she put the collections of twigs and herbs down in a bowl and let it go out.

'Now,' she said, 'how about we celebrate with a fabulous dinner. Boys!' she called into the kitchen. 'Bring on the birthday feast!'

Acknowledgements

I always say that writing the acknowledgements is a nightmare for a person who is terrified of upsetting any of my dear friends, hence, this takes nearly as long as the book itself. But with fewer plot issues. But I *love* other people's acknowledgements – don't you? So ignore the higgledy-piggledy way this is done and let's begin.

Firstly, thanks to my beloved readers, without whom I would undoubtedly not be writing acknowledgements on this, my nineteenth book. Nineteenth! Obviously, I started writing when I was twelve . . . Please keep talking to me: I love your emails and messages.

Thanks to my darling agent, Jonathan Lloyd, one of the kindest men I know. Thanks, too, to dear Lucia Walker, brilliant author Melissa Pimentel, Emma Bailey and all at Curtis Brown, who are a joy to work with. Thanks to my wonderful new family at Orion who are stars, all of them: huge thanks to David Shelley, Katie Espiner, Harriet Bourton, Clare Hey, Bethan Jones, Richard Kitson and Sarah Gravestock. Thanks to Elaine Egan for her hard work (I will bring an extra lamp to Liverpool next time!). In the spectacular marketing department, huge thanks to Sarah Benton, Lynsey Sutherland, Jen Breslin and Brittany Sankey.

No book would hit any shop without the sterling work of sales, so thank you so much to Andrew Taylor, Jo Carpenter, Mark Stay, Hannah Methuen, Lucy Tucker, Sneha Wharton, Viki Cheung, Sharon Willis and Jen Wilson. For always-exquisite art, thank you to Rabab Adams, Debbie Holmes,

Nick May, Joanna Ridley and Lucie Stericker. In audio, huge thanks to Paul Stark and Amber Bates. I always feel I am the bane of the lives of all in production and design, so sorry! And thank you to Helen Ewing, Ruth Sharvell and Charlie Panayiotou.

In Ireland, enormous thank yous to the Orion team of Breda Purdue, Jim Binchy, Ruth Shern, Siobhan Tierney, Joanna Smyth and Bernard Hoban. Finally, I would have fallen into a puddle of high anxiety long ago were it not for the calm professionalism of my Irish publicist, Aileen Gaskin, and the wisdom of Terry Prone, both of The Communications Clinic. Huge thanks to Gillian Glynn O'Sullivan without whose expertise and friendship this book would not have been finished.

Thanks to the wonderful publishers around the world who publish my books so beautifully, and make me so proud when I put them on the shelves in my study where I feel truly international, even if my languages extend to English, Irish, profane and schoolgirl French, but spoken with the accent of a would-be actress. Thank you, too, to the marvellous foreign language readers who write to me in my language and tell me such wonderful stories.

Thanks to all my dear friends at UNICEF Ireland who allow me to help in some way with the incredible work UNICEF does around the world, helping people in countries torn apart by war and famine, and who let me do a tiny bit to help mothers like myself who have to watch their beloved children die from illnesses like measles, malaria and tetanus, diseases which rarely kill in the western world.

Thank you to the generosity of Lorraine Butler and dear Xanah who donated generously to the Martin Fund so that Mary Butler could have a character named after her in this book. I hope she likes her go-getting and clever dermatologist! The Martin Fund was set up to help fund treatment for little Cathal and Ciaran Martin, small boys both diagnosed with a rare genetic disorder, MLD (metachromatic leukodystrophy). I wish them well with all of my heart.

Thanks, too, to Fiona McParland as both she and her husband donated generously to the Jack and Jill Foundation so that her name could be used in this book. Hope you like your straight-talking lawyer, Fiona. Finally, thanks to Jodie Nicholls and her husband Peter, who donated to UNICEF Australia so that Jodie's name could be used in this book for her thirtieth birthday! I even got Peter in there too, darlings!

For research in this book, a huge thank you to the Garda Bureau of Fraud Investigation and my amazingly brilliant advisor therein who asked not to be named, but who came up with a lovely plot twist! Thanks also to Nigel Swann, husband of about-to-be-mentioned Helen, who gave me a brilliant plot device. All mistakes (and I bent things to make the story work) are my own. I mean, all the mistakes . . .

I am lucky to have so many friends – real friends. I am blessed. Emma, you are my rock, too. The strongest, most courageous woman I know. Gai, we will go into practice together! Wise Women Inc.? Lyn, you are my star, too, unicorns of fire. Nothing can stop us. Patricia, you are there for all the great moments with a candle, like darling Aidan Storey, who is indeed angelic. LisaMarie and Shona, you are like part of our family. Kelly, you are my darling twinnie. Kindest, most generous woman on the planet. Marian, you are always there when I need you, strong, wise and a dear soul sister. Judy, you have a light shining around you. Helen, you are a star and a dear, always-there friend. Kate, the country is not the same with you in Perth! Thanks to gorgeous Andréa, who is so kind and such an exquisite craftswoman. Thanks also to Brenda, darling beauty with whom I share so much, and Marguerite, who is so wise. In fact, without my amazing team of women friends, including Libby, Caroline, Alice, Deirdre, Rita, Emer, Elaine, Santina, Annie, Catherine, Stephanie, Clodagh, I would be lost. Same goes for beautiful Alyson Stanley; my dear Eva

Berg, an angel; Helen – we are the school play make-up queens but you are a professional, so a genius – Cindy and Teresa.

I have so many writer friends; some of them are already mentioned, but special thanks must go to the ones with whom I can giggle on email: Sheila O'Flanagan, Sinead Moriarty, Jennifer Ryan in Washington, Eleanor Brown, Stephanie Preissner, Claire Hennessey, Fanny Blake and Felicity Hayes-McCoy. I know I must be leaving people out as I'm a sieve-head of the highest order, but please forgive me.

Thanks to my beloved family, as always: Francis for always being a tower of strength, wisdom and humour. Thanks, big bro. Thanks to Lucy for being kind and loving, and for being a sister of the soul as well as of the flesh. Thanks to Dave and Anne, who are always there being wonderful, strong and loving. Thanks to my darling nieces, of whom I am *so* proud: Laura, Naomi and Emer; thanks to Robert and Katie for being darlings and doing the London Marathon with Lucy and Dave; thanks to Matt, my godfather and a person of such wisdom and kindness that you helped me be the person I am today.

There is not enough I can say when it comes to thanks and love to John, Dylan and Murray: you three are my beating heart. And as for the Puplets – Dinky, Licky and Scamp – they are joy in small furry bundles of pure love, who have never been fed enough. Honestly.

Finally, this book is dedicated to my mother, Gay, who never stops encouraging me, who should have written her own books, who makes me laugh so. Thanks for everything and huge love, Mum.